Praise for the Alice Quentin series

'An original and exciting story made all the more disturbing by the fact that the underlying premise is based on real events. An excellent read.' Rachel Abbott, author of *The Back Road*, on *Blood Symmetry*

'Excellent . . . based on a true, fascinating and shocking story.' *Literary Review* on *Blood Symmetry*

'A pacy yet emotionally involving thriller, with an authentic and nuanced heroine in psychologist Alice Quentin: Kate Rhodes' latest is a terrific read.' Anya Lipska, author of the Kiszka & Kershaw series, on *Blood Symmetry*

'Like Nicci French, Kate Rhodes excels at character, pace and sense of place.' Erin Kelly

'Quentin is one of a cast of really believable and entertaining characters and both the plot and the writing keep one thoroughly engaged throughout.' *Daily Mail*

'A fast-moving, entertaining mix of sex, suspense and serial killings.' *Washington Post*

'Rhodes is a poet whose linguistic precision is very much in evidence throughout the novel and Alice is a vividly realised protagonist whose complex and harrowing history rivals the central crime storyline.' Sophie Hannah, *Sunday Express*

'A pacy psychological thriller that makes good use of its London setting.' Laura Wilson, *Guardian*

The Alice Quentin series

Crossbones Yard
A Killing of Angels
The Winter Foundlings
River of Souls

Kate Rhodes

Kate Rhodes was born in London. She worked as an English teacher and university lecturer before becoming a crime writer. She writes full-time now, and lives in Cambridge with her husband, an author and film maker.

Kate is the author of two prize-winning collections of poetry, *Reversal* and *The Alice Trap*. There are four previous novels in the Alice Quentin series, *Crossbones Yard*, *A Killing of Angels*, *The Winter Foundlings* and *River of Souls*. *Crossbones Yard* was selected by Val McDermid for the Harrogate Crime Festival's New Blood panel championing new crime writers, and in 2014 Kate Rhodes won the Ruth Rendell Short Story Award, sponsored by the charity InterAct.

Visit Kate's website at katerhodes.org or follow her on Twitter @K_RhodesWriter.

Blood Symmetry

KATE RHODES

MULHOLLAND
BOOKS
HODDER

First published in Great Britain in 2016 by Mulholland Books
An imprint of Hodder & Stoughton
An Hachette UK company

This paperback edition first published in 2017

1

A CIP catalogue record for this title is available from the British Library

Paperback ISBN 978 1 444 78563 0
eBook ISBN 978 1 444 78562 3

Typeset by Hewer Text UK Ltd, Edinburgh
Printed and bound by Clays Ltd, St Ives plc

Hodder & Stoughton policy is to use papers that are natural, renewable
and recyclable products and made from wood grown in sustainable
forests. The logging and manufacturing processes are expected to
conform to the environmental regulations of the country of origin.

Hodder & Stoughton Ltd
Carmelite House
50 Victoria Embankment
London EC4Y 0DZ

www.hodder.co.uk

For those killed by tainted blood, and for those that survived

I

The trees on Clapham Common are aflame with autumn colour. A couple are holding hands on a park bench, watching the leaves turn from red to gold in the early sunlight. They're sitting in a deserted copse, the path ahead shrouded by thickets of hazel.

'Maybe they won't come,' the man says, the chill already sapping his strength.

'Give them time. Not panicking, are you?'

'Of course not. It was my idea, remember?'

She leans over to kiss him, face shadowed by the collar of her black woollen coat, but the moment of intimacy soon passes. The man strains forward as he hears footsteps crunching on gravel – someone racing towards them through the trees.

'Now,' he whispers. 'Let's put it right.'

The first jogger is a slim brunette in a blue tracksuit. A young boy drifts in her wake, his smile wide and unquestioning, frame so slight that his sweatshirt flails in the breeze. The man steps out from the shadows and grabs the jogger from behind; she fights hard, a look of stunned recognition on her face. Her elbows gouge his ribs as she yells at the boy to run, but the woman has already caught him. The child goes down fighting, thin form collapsing as he inhales the anaesthetic, a blindfold covering his eyes. A chloroform pad is pressed to his mother's mouth, before she's dragged into the bracken.

I

The couple lift the victims' inert bodies on to the back seat, their car camouflaged by thick foliage. The man's hands fumble as he covers them with blankets, morning traffic thickening as the woman slips into the driver's seat. The most dangerous stage is over; all they have to do now is deliver mother and son to the laboratory. When the man peers under the blanket, Clare Riordan's face is pale as candle wax, the child's body curled behind the driving seat. His gaze shifts to the road ahead.

'Not far now, almost there.' He repeats the words like a mantra.

Close to their destination they pause on a side street, a delivery van blocking their way. But when he looks back there's a flicker of movement. Through the rear window he sees the boy sprinting across the tarmac.

'Jesus,' the woman hisses. 'I thought the doors were locked.'

The man's heart thuds as he spills out on to the road, his skin feverish. The boy has vanished. His gaze skims over houses and empty front gardens. At the junction he comes to a halt, heaving for breath, frustration flooding his system. Thank God the child didn't see their faces. The mother will be killed once she provides the information they need, but her son is beyond their reach.

2

The city smelled of bonfires and decaying leaves. At eight a.m., the mid-October chill was fierce enough to turn my breath to smoke as I walked down Carlton Street, pedestrians marching to keep warm. The prospect of running my first team meeting at the Forensic Psychology Unit was making my stomach queasy. Public speaking always brought panic as well as excitement. Despite years of training as a psychologist, I still expected the walls of my professional life to tumble whenever I faced a crowd.

My outfit had been selected with abnormal care: a charcoal grey dress from Jigsaw, no-nonsense boots with three-inch heels, hair pinned into a business-like French pleat. The ensemble was on the severe side of smart, softened by an outrageously expensive Hermès scarf. Power-dressing was a trick I'd used for years. At five foot nothing, blonde and weighing seven stone, I was easy to ignore. Strangers often treated me like a child, even though I was thirty-four years old.

I pulled my iPod from my bag, Scott Matthews' mellow voice soothing me as I reached Dacre Street. The tall brownstone which housed the Forensic Psychology Unit of the Met was discreet to the point of invisibility. It looked like any other genteel home in St James's Park, with nothing to indicate that two dozen psychologists were hidden inside, solving the nation's worst cases of murder, rape and organised crime.

The receptionist offered me a sympathetic smile. It was no secret that some of the senior consultants had opposed my appointment. For decades the FPU's management had gone unchanged, with Christine Jenkins at the helm. It had gained a world-class reputation but followed its own mysterious rules. In such a closed environment, any newcomer was bound to threaten the status quo.

The building's odd smell hit me as I climbed the stairs: furniture polish, dust and secrets. The corridors were lined with worn carpet and photos of pioneers from the halcyon days of psychoanalysis: Carl Jung, Freud, Melanie Klein. Given half a chance I'd have gutted the place and enlarged every window to admit more light. My office was a small ante-room beside the consultants' open-plan workspace, but it was a thrill to see my new title, 'Deputy Director', on the door plaque. Most shrinks saw the FPU as the Holy Grail. The unit worked at the cutting edge of criminal psychology using the Home Office's latest software.

I was running through my agenda a final time when someone rapped on the door. My boss walked in without waiting for a reply. Christine looked thinner than before, as if she'd been making too many trips to the gym. Her bobbed grey hair hung in a precise line, matching the stark elegance of her clothes: black trousers, a white silk shirt, discreet pearl earrings.

'Ready to wow them, Alice?'

'More or less.'

'Let's have coffee at Enzo's later, to celebrate your new role. There's something we need to discuss.'

The announcement was typical of her cryptic style, every statement a double-edged sword. A year of acquaintance had convinced me that she'd missed her vocation – her air of mystery would have made her the perfect spy.

4

Twenty consultants had gathered round the long table in the meeting room. My tongue sealed itself to the roof of my mouth; most of the psychologists had international reputations, their average age fifteen years older than mine. The only person to grin at me was Mike Donnelly, whose white hair, overgrown beard and stout build made him a dead ringer for Santa Claus. Apart from Christine, the irrepressible Irishman had been the only colleague to congratulate me on my promotion. There was silence as I introduced the first agenda item, but most people contributed to the discussion, despite the stiff atmosphere. During the meeting I kept the atmosphere light, attempting a joke about the vagaries of psychology. Most of my colleagues looked relieved by the end, more smiles than I'd expected as they filed from the room. Only one consultant stayed behind. Joy Anderson had scarcely spoken to me since my appointment; she wore a fussy high-necked blouse, her expression combining gloom with hostility, long grey hair scraped back from her face.

'I was away when you were appointed, Dr Quentin. I hope you'll enjoy working with us. I'm afraid I don't know anything about your professional background.'

'Thanks for the welcome,' I said, smiling. 'My last consultancy was at Guy's. I've been researching violent personality disorders and childhood psychopathology.'

'And you've consulted on some high-profile cases?'

'Four successful murder investigations. Why don't you come by my office one afternoon for a chat? I'd like to hear about your research.'

Dr Anderson held my gaze. 'Forgive me for saying this, but you seem inexperienced to run such a complex organisation.'

'Christine's still in charge. As her deputy I'll be allocating cases and resources. Now, I should let you get back to your work. Feel free to set up a longer meeting when you have time.'

She gave an abrupt nod before walking away. The consultants were still standing in the corridor, chatting in cliques. They gave the impression of a group that had melded into a single unit over time. It could take months to tunnel under their defences. I retreated to my office, but no one knocked on my door while I grappled with my new computer.

Enzo's was deserted when I arrived at eleven. From a distance, Christine's tension showed in the set of her shoulders as she pored over a report. She shut the folder abruptly when I approached, her smile on the cool side of professional. I still couldn't tell if a personality existed under all that sang-froid.

'Dr Anderson's not my biggest fan, is she?'

'Joy's not keen on change, that's all. She'll come round.'

'This century, I hope. You never take breaks, Christine, this must be important.'

'We can talk here without being interrupted. Let's order, then I'll explain.'

Informal chat clearly unsettled her. Our conversations never strayed beyond professional matters, and I had no idea whether she lived with a partner or alone. The silence was thick enough to slice by the time our drinks arrived. She took a sip of her espresso as I waited for her to announce that she'd been offered an OBE or promoted to the Home Office. Instead she slid a manila file across the table.

'I want you on this case, Alice.'

I scanned the first page. 'This story's national news. The woman went running with her son at the weekend and never came home.'

'Whoever abducted her left a sample of her blood outside an office block. It was in a hospital plasma bag, labelled with her name.'

'Where's the boy?'

'A psychiatric nurse is caring for him in a safe house. I want you to consult on the case and supervise his care. Since the police picked him up two days ago, he hasn't said a word.'

'That's not surprising. Seeing your mum abducted would silence most kids.' I turned to face her. 'Do I get a choice about this?'

Her eyebrows rose. 'Another therapist has seen him already, but the kid attacked him.'

'Badly?'

'Just a few bruises. The boy hit out, probably to show he wasn't ready to talk.'

'Mike Donnelly's got more experience with disturbed kids. Why not use him?'

'The therapist needs to be female; the boy's close to his mother. He's got no male relatives, and you've worked with traumatised children. We need the facts before he forgets them. You could live in the safe house until he opens up.'

'The maximum intervention would be alternate days – more often could be damaging. Even then it might take weeks to win his trust.'

She gave a forceful smile. 'You can start this afternoon, Alice.'

I leafed through the pictures in the crime file. The boy's mother was an attractive brunette of around forty-five, hair tied in a sleek ponytail. Something shifted in my chest when I studied the photo of her eleven-year-old son. My brother had worn the same vulnerable look as a child: thin-faced with ethereal blue eyes, dark hair crying out for a trim.

'Why's he in a safe house?'

'The police think the abductor tried to take him too. He's got no family apart from an aunt who doesn't see him regularly; Riordan took out an injunction against her for harassment.'

'Where's the father?'

'He died in a road accident when Mikey was five. The boy took it badly, by all accounts. His school says he was mute for six months afterwards. He's bright for his age, sporty and artistic, but finds it hard to integrate.' She put down her cup. 'There's one more thing you should know – Don Burns is the SIO. Scotland Yard wanted a safe pair of hands.'

'I thought there was an embargo on couples working together.' Very few people knew about my relationship with Burns; I'd only told Christine in case it led to a conflict of interests.

'Head office has made an exception.'

'Who told them about our relationship?'

She gave me an old-fashioned look. 'Word travels, Alice.'

'The timing's wrong. I'd rather focus on my job and allocate another consultant.'

'No one else would be as effective. This case will be big news; you and Burns both know how to handle the press.'

I knew from experience that journalists would be desperate for information, the story producing millions of clicks on websites by triggering every parent's worst fears. Christine's stare continued longer than felt comfortable. I had no choice but to accept a case which might result in a vulnerable boy learning that his mother had been murdered. The prospect was so sobering that I didn't reply. It looked like my boss was feeling the pressure too. When she stood up to leave I noticed again how thin she'd become; in the two months since my job interview, she'd dropped a dress size. She insisted on paying the bill, then left me to choke down the last of my cappuccino.

I was still preoccupied on my return to the FPU. Even though my hand had been forced, the case already had me hooked. By the time my cab arrived, Clare Riordan's polished smile was imprinted on my mind. I tried to put myself in her son's shoes as the taxi cut south through Holborn, heading for the river. My eyes drifted across the suits milling on the pavement, clutching coffee cups large enough to drown in. The child had rejected all help so far, attacking the trauma therapist then curling into a ball. Despite Christine's good faith, there was every chance he'd treat me the same. I pulled my phone from my bag to send Burns a text, but got no reply. Now that he was DCI for the whole of King's Cross, he was responsible for hundreds of staff. It took a small miracle to reach him during work hours.

The safe house was on a cul-de-sac in Bermondsey, the copper beeches beside it blackening in the fading light. A squad car was parked outside, but neither of the two uniforms batted an eyelid when I approached; clearly small blondes didn't feature on their list of potential threats, even though I could have been armed to the teeth. The semi-detached house had little kerb appeal. Built from crude yellow bricks, its ground-floor windows were obscured by a high fence, the front garden a tangle of overgrown lavender.

When I rang the bell an Indian man of around my age answered so rapidly that he must have been waiting on the other side of the door. Gurpreet Singh had a gentle expression; he was medium height with a lean build, black hair in a short ponytail. He gave a tentative smile as I shook his hand.

'Good to meet you, Alice.' He led me down the hallway. 'Mikey's watching TV. I've been letting him do pretty much what he likes, provided he follows my routine for meals and bedtime.'

'Sounds like a wise strategy. Has he been speaking?'

'Just a few words. I haven't seen him cry or smile yet, but it's only been forty-eight hours. The other therapist pushed too hard. He used dolls to make him re-enact as soon as he arrived.'

'I'll try to be more subtle.'

'A word of warning: don't get too close. He'll lash out again if he feels cornered.'

The skin on the backs of my hands prickled as Gurpreet led me into the lounge. There was something disturbing about the room, the air sticky and overheated; drab olive-green walls, the furniture threadbare. Mikey Riordan was huddled on the settee. He looked too small for an eleven year old, wispy dark hair framing his face. The boy kept his gaze fixed rigidly on the TV. A line of bruises trailed from his temple to his jaw, eye socket turning every shade of the rainbow. He seemed so frail that I had to stifle a wave of anger; too much empathy would only cloud my judgement.

'This is Alice, Mikey. Are you okay seeing her by yourself, or do you want me to stay?' Gurpreet stood there for a full minute, the boy's unblinking stare fixed to the screen. 'Okay, I'll be in the kitchen if you need me.'

The child was watching a cowboy film with the sound muted, a dozen men on horseback were firing silent bullets at a runaway train. I made a deliberate effort not to stare as I sat on a floor cushion, remembering the guidance about body positioning: traumatised children only relax if they feel physically in control. I kept my eyes on the TV as I spoke.

'I like westerns too. All those horses make me wish I could ride.' His likeness to my brother at that age was even clearer now. Twenty years ago, Will had worn the same lost expression, fidgeting in the same restless way.

'I'll be here for an hour, Mikey. There's no pressure to talk, but if you feel like chatting, that's great. I'm helping the police look for your mum, so you can ask me about what's happening.'

He still didn't meet my eye, but his shoulders relaxed. Knowing that my visit would be short seemed to ease his mind, and my calm tone of voice probably helped too. Gurpreet reappeared with a tea tray. He placed a glass of milk in front of Mikey and handed me a cup of tea, hovering in the doorway for a few minutes before disappearing again. We sat in silence until the film ended, then I took a pack of coloured pencils and two small sketchpads from my bag, placing one on the sofa, close enough for him to reach.

'I hear you like drawing, Mikey. I do too, but I'm not much good.'

His lack of response filled me with concern. So far there had been no sign of non-verbal communication; he'd ducked behind a barrier of silence too thick to penetrate. Even my distraction activity was failing to drag him from his shell. I cast my eyes around the featureless room; it looked like the last occupants had stripped the place in a hurry. The only adornment was a vase of red chrysanthemums wilting on the mantelpiece.

'I'll try those flowers. Draw anything you want, if you fancy joining me.'

When I glanced at him again, his knees were folded against his chest. He hadn't touched the pad, but he was watching my efforts. I spoke to him as my pencil skimmed the paper, explaining that I'd worked with other children who'd been through hard experiences. I knew how scared he must be, but he was in a safe place, and I hoped he'd let me help. His silence expanded like a gas cloud as I finished the drawing. When the visit was due to end, I held up my pad to show him my sketch.

'Not great, is it? But it was fun trying.'

His expression remained solemn, pale gaze flickering across the page. Sometimes when you work with kids there are moments when it's hard to maintain an appropriate distance, and this was one of them. He looked so fragile that I wanted to touch his hand. But he was holding himself together so tightly that any direct contact could blow his coping mechanisms apart.

'The pad and pencils are for you.' I put my card on the coffee table. 'You can text or call me, any time. Would you like me to come back tomorrow?'

His eyes stayed fixed on the floor, but his lips moved for the first time, producing a dry whisper. 'Almost there. Not far now.'

'That sounds like a yes. I'll be here by five thirty, with pizza.'

I hoped he'd speak again but no more words arrived. Gurpreet was waiting for me in the hallway. I got the sense that he'd been primed for me to bolt, just like the others. He offered a wide smile, as if I deserved a medal for lasting the hour.

'Shall we chat in the kitchen?' I asked.

I regretted the choice immediately. The room's shoebox dimensions coupled with mustard-yellow paint triggered my claustrophobia, but I ignored it as we sat down to discuss care strategies. The boy was displaying classic signs of hyper-reactivity: anxiety, sleep and appetite disturbance, as well as elective muteness. Loud noises and sudden movements terrified him, and there were signs of infantile regression. He went on the attack when agitated and had wet the bed both nights he'd been at the safe house, even though he was eleven years old. I made notes as Gurpreet described the child's symptoms.

'Has there been any re-enactment?' I asked.

'So far it's just avoidance. He daydreams and fixates on the TV, but he's getting more responsive. He seems tuned out, but I think he's listening.'

'How does he react to his mum's name?'

12

'Complete withdrawal. I've been reassuring him that the police are doing all they can.'

'Does he accept hand-holding or a pat on the shoulder?'

'Not yet. He bites or hits out if I go anywhere near.' He held up his wrist to show a deep red scratch on his hand.

I gave him a look of sympathy. 'He's bound to be terrified. Once he accepts me I can spend alternate nights here.'

'That's good news. My own kids'll forget me if I don't go home soon.'

'He said a few words just now: "almost there, not far now." '

Gurpreet nodded. 'It's his catchphrase, but there's no real communication.'

'It must mean something, if it's the only thing he's saying. Can you keep a log of any conversation? It could help us guess the context.'

I thought about Mikey Riordan's symptoms as I walked home. It didn't surprise me that he was unable to sleep. He'd already experienced far too much pain, losing his father at the age of five. Even if that memory was buried, it must surface often in his nightmares, and now the trauma was happening again. The secret to his mother's disappearance could be locked inside his head. My only chance of piercing his shield of silence would be to stay close, trapped in the airless living room of the safe house.

Burns welcomed me to his flat on Southwark Bridge Road that evening with his phone wedged between jaw and shoulder. He dropped a distracted kiss on the crown of my head before waving me through to the lounge. A towel hung round his neck, wet hair almost black, his expression distracted. I still found myself staring at him in amazement sometimes. He was the opposite of the men I normally fancied: tall and solid as a heavyweight boxer. All of his features were exaggerated, from his raw cheekbones to his broken nose and dark eyes with their take-no-prisoners stare.

He towered over me as he slung his phone down on the coffee table. 'How did the team meeting go?'

'The consultants aren't thrilled by my arrival.'

'They're just scared you'll outsmart them.'

'Maybe I will. This job'll make me an expert on every homicidal psychopath in the land.'

'Is that your biggest ambition?' He reached down to brush his hand through my hair, fingers skimming my collarbone. 'When did you get it cut?'

'Saturday.'

'Stop there, can you? I prefer it long.'

'God, you're a cliché. I only came by to check on the Riordan case.'

'Liar, you're expecting food.'

'How did you guess?'

His arm stayed round my shoulder until we reached the kitchen. I leaned on the breakfast bar to observe his version of cooking. His meals always involved meat seared at nuclear temperatures. He dropped steaks on to a griddle then upended a bag of salad into a bowl. A tug of attraction pulled at me as I watched him lope around the kitchen.

'Did you tell head office about us, Burns?'

'Stop using my surname, for God's sake.'

'Yes or no?'

He gave a casual nod. 'I sent a disclosure notice last week.'

'Without my permission?'

'You'd have said it was too early.'

'Damn right I would.'

'Tongues are wagging, Alice. This way we control the information.'

Even though it was true, I still felt irritated that he'd revealed personal details without consulting me first. He made up for it by producing a meal that was basic but enjoyable: good-quality rib-eye, a hunk of French bread, chicory salad and red wine sharp with tannin. I savoured a mouthful then relaxed in my chair.

'The boys made me take them paintballing yesterday.' He gave an exaggerated shudder.

'And you loved it?'

'It was a living hell; they drenched me in bright red slime. I had to take them home when the Riordan case hit my desk.' He frowned as he put down his glass. 'I'm not thrilled that you're my consultant.'

'Charming.'

'You're the best in your field, but we agreed not to work together.' He studied me again. 'It'll be the biggest news story this year: a pretty woman gets taken, and only her cute blue-eyed kid saw the baddies. They're already howling for pictures.'

'Keep them away; he's hanging on by a thread. What have you got so far?'

'A neighbour saw them on Clapham Common, Saturday, seven a.m. It was their pattern; a long run as soon as they woke up, followed by a big breakfast. A witness saw them go into a wooded area, then a few minutes later a car pulled away.'

'An abduction?'

'Looks like it. The kid was found in Walworth hours later; we don't know how he got there. Someone left a pint of Riordan's blood on a doorstep in Bishopsgate late that night. She was a senior consultant in blood disorders at the Royal Free Hospital.'

'That's an interesting connection.'

'She worked in haematology her whole career.'

'You're using the past tense because you think she's dead?'

'Abducted females are normally raped then killed fast. You know the pattern.'

'But this is atypical. It could be someone she knows, with access to her schedule. How was the blood delivered?'

'In a plastic pack, by hand. The building's out of shot of the nearest CCTV. He probably walked up a side road, then sauntered away.'

'Taking that much risk makes the location important.'

'Or convenient.'

'It's got to be symbolic.'

The message was obvious: Riordan had already lost a pint of blood. She had limited time to survive. 'This is too measured to be sexually motivated. Are there any links to past crimes?'

'Not yet, but let's put it on ice till tomorrow. We're meant to be off duty.' His mobile rang again as we finished eating, making him curse loudly. 'The sodding thing gets switched off after this.'

He stomped into the hall but I knew there was no chance of his phone being silenced until Clare Riordan was found. I couldn't resist delving into the folder he'd left on the kitchen table, pulling out a picture of the site where the doctor had last been seen. It showed a glade of trees casting dense shadows over a winding path. A sign had been tacked to a tree, too distant to see clearly. It seemed to hold two vertical stripes – one white, one black – printed on a grey background. It caught my attention, but could have been pinned there days before Clare went missing. Nothing else struck me as unusual, so I returned the photo before Burns could protest, then curled up on his outsized sofa.

Burns had lived in the rented flat for four months since separating from his wife, and the pile of cardboard boxes in the hallway was gradually dwindling. Two landscape paintings filled the living room's longest wall. They were beautiful but stark, winter sunlight falling on a charcoal sea, birds spiralling above an island of rough-hewn granite. I could hear him arguing as I studied the rest of the room. It bore no resemblance to my flat's bare walls and minimal furniture. Every aspect of his life was on display. Photos of his two sons were clustered on a huge pin board, gym bag left on the floor, newspapers and sketchbooks scattered across the furniture. The neat freak in me longed to dump everything in a cupboard and hide it from view.

A muscle was ticking in Burns's cheek when he returned. I'd seen that expression dozens of times over the years and recognised the trait in myself; neither of us rested easily while there were problems to solve. He switched off his phone, then sprawled on the sofa beside me, his hand settling on my thigh.

'Did you paint those?' I asked, pointing at the landscapes. His year at Edinburgh Art School was a secret few of his police colleagues knew.

He nodded. 'I went to my parents' caravan in Oban one January. You can see Mull across the bay. The light's amazing.' A few degrees of tension slipped from his face.

'Can I buy them off you? They'd bring some class to my living room.'

'God, no. I need to see the Hebrides when I get in from work.'

'You'd like to go back?'

'I'll take you some day. But how would you cope with me in a caravan when it's blowing a gale?'

'I'd survive.'

'How, exactly?'

'Card games, Monopoly, cups of tea.'

'That's your idea of entertainment?' He looked amused.

I couldn't resist leaning over to kiss him, my palm flat

against his chest, his fingers snagging in my hair. It was his smell that undid me: plain soap, musk and fresh air. I'd been kidding myself that I could leave straight after dinner, but the desire on his face was hard to ignore. I concentrated on the weight of his hands, needy and insistent, grappling with the zip of my dress. The sex was quick but satisfying, my shoulder blades pressed against the settee, his arm pinning me in place like he expected me to try and escape. Afterwards my skin glowed from all that passionate touch, but my first reaction was laughter. He was still wearing most of his clothes, while mine were strewn across the floor.

'What's funny?'

'You were in a rush, that's all.'

'Your fault, not mine.' His grip tightened round my wrist.

'I should get moving. Tomorrow's an early start.'

'Can't you stay for once?'

'Not tonight.'

'But soon?'

'When I figure out what's stopping me.'

He gave an exasperated sigh. 'I thought shrinks knew how to control their fears.'

'Other people's, not our own.' I gave him a farewell kiss then rose to my feet.

The sound he made was somewhere between a groan and a laugh. 'What made you pick me, anyway?'

'Lust, mainly.' I could have said honesty or integrity, but it was easier to lie.

'Is that all?' His thumb skimmed my cheek. 'My boys think you're imaginary. They keep asking to meet you.'

'It's too soon. You and Julie have only just separated.'

'They know we got together afterwards. It's not a secret.'

'Don't you ever give up?'

'Not till you agree.'

I slipped back into my dress to end the conversation. It was only when I retrieved my coat from the hall that panic washed over me again. Something shiny glistened between the jackets and scarves: a leather strap, glossy with use, a black-handled gun tucked inside the holster. I stared at it in amazement. I'd known Burns four years without realising he carried a weapon. I was still rooted to the spot when he strolled out of the living room, shoes dangling from his hand.

'That's a surprise.'

'It's not loaded. I should have locked it away.'

'I didn't know you were licensed.'

He gave a slow shrug. 'Every station needs firearms officers. It makes sense that I'm one of them.'

'You carry it all the time?'

'Only at work. It doesn't get much use.'

I wanted to ask how it felt to wear a piece of lethal hardware beside his heart, but his blank expression showed he had nothing more to say. Despite the awkwardness, he insisted on walking me home. All the bars had closed, the river sliding through the city unnoticed, a scatter of stars over Canary Wharf. We strolled in silence at first, then he talked about the case. I asked him about the sign that had been left at the scene, with its mysterious black and white marks, but he couldn't explain its meaning. He was more interested in discussing Clare Riordan. She had been a diligent single mother and a long-serving NHS consultant until her abduction – not the type to harbour dark secrets. I remembered her son's face, pale as milk that afternoon. My feelings for Burns kept bubbling to the surface as I listened; the fact that he carried a gun was a reminder of the dangers he faced. Part of me felt ashamed. I was a professional psychologist, licensed to delve into other people's minds, yet our relationship had me frozen in the headlights. Maybe it was because it was uncharted territory. Until then I'd stuck to short flings and one-night stands, but Burns was a different matter. He was the most dogged man I'd ever encountered. If I tried to run, it would only be a question of time before he tracked me down.

3

The woman casts her gaze around the laboratory and finds it clean as an operating theatre. Walls, ceiling and floor are bleached white, the cold air reeking of iodine and fresh paint. There's little furniture except a cabinet and metal table. A strip-light fills the space with its harsh glare. She spent days here helping the man install soundproofing, pulleys and black-out blinds. Her gaze shifts back to Riordan's face; eyes swollen shut, a raw wound marking the side of her neck, dark hair losing its lustre. The doctor is still unconscious, her body strapped to a leather dentist's chair. The woman tests the ropes attached to the ceiling. Once she's satisfied the restraints will hold, she turns to the man.

'Ready?'

He nods in reply. 'Go easy on her. We just need the information.' Beads of sweat stand out on his forehead. She can tell he's weaker today, more afraid than before, although he'd never admit it.

'I still want the boy brought here.'

'What good will it do?'

Her eyes glitter. 'She'll crack faster when she sees him.'

'It won't be easy to find him.' The man's arms fold tightly across his body.

'Why are you worried? The others didn't bother you.'

'They gave names straight away. She's fighting us.'

'Not for long. Help me turn her over.'

She watches him struggle, suddenly aware how much his illness has weakened him. The exertion of lifting the victim on to her side leaves him breathless as he secures the leather cuffs. She concentrates on her task, yanking a lever until Riordan's arms straighten. Now her body hangs suspended from the ceiling by her wrists, feet dangling above the ground, so heavily sedated that she only surfaces when the extraction needle plunges into her back. A dull scream echoes from the walls as blood gushes into the plasma bag. Once it's full, a last spurt flows on to the tiles. The thin red line is destined to be wasted. It follows the path of least resistance, snaking across the floor.

'That'll loosen her tongue.' The woman extracts the needle slowly.

'How do you know she'll talk?'

'She'll have to eventually. The pain will be unbearable.' She leans down until her eyes meet Riordan's, hissing into her face. 'You'll blab like a child, Clare. All of you are going to suffer before we tell the press you're guilty.'

When she looks at the man again, something behind his eyes has flicked shut like a door slamming. Riordan's head lolls on her chest, but he keeps his face averted.

'After everything they did, you still hate seeing them die.'

'I can handle it,' he says quietly.

'You don't have the stomach to hunt for the boy, do you?'

He shakes his head. 'Of course I do. A child's life is nothing compared to everything I've lost.'

The woman is unconvinced, even though his voice sounds forceful. He plans the attacks and organises every detail, yet he's too squeamish to hurt the victims. Torn between anger and a desire to comfort him, she drops the needle into a jar of sterilising fluid, as Riordan's whimper rises to a scream.

4

The FPU was empty when I arrived at eight a.m. the next day. I'd slept badly, fretting about Mikey Riordan, restlessness driving me from my flat too early. I dumped my newspaper on the desk and studied the picture on the front page. His mother gazed back at me with a wide-eyed smile, as if she'd never performed a single bad deed. I sat at my desk and tried to focus. My head felt muzzy, but time alone in a calm environment was my best chance of forming an image of her abductor. I logged on to the Police National Computer, then typed key features into HOLMES 2, aware that there would be a long wait before it spat out facts. The Home Office's major incident software was in dire need of an overhaul. It held details of every recorded crime for decades, but moved at a snail's pace. The search category I chose was for similar fact evidence. The overarching theme was blood; a haematologist had been targeted, her own blood left as a calling card. My computer buzzed loudly as it sifted through past cases.

I stood by the window gazing towards St James's Park. Scarlet leaves on a distant copse of trees danced above the rooftops, a trick of the eye making it look like the entire terrace was on fire. So far my morning hadn't been a great success. Two consultants were holding a heated debate in the office next door, their outbursts filtering through the wall. I thought about Mikey Riordan, pining in a house without comforts. My determination to find his mother was rising steadily.

The printout spewed from my computer an hour later. One case was so grisly it would have been better to read about it on an empty stomach. Five years ago a man had killed a rent boy in Paddington, drinking some of his blood before sending samples to the victim's relatives. The senior investigating officer had been so traumatised by the murder scene that he'd had a breakdown. I rubbed my eyes, unwilling to burden my brain with more horror. Several other cases held similarities, although the perpetrators were already behind bars. I laid the report on my desk and compared details from previous attacks with Clare Riordan's abduction, but soon had to admit defeat. In the past twenty years there had been no direct parallels. Riordan's abductor had struck an original note by using her blood as his calling card, which made me wonder if he was motivated by posterity – maybe he didn't just enjoy hurting his victim, he wanted a place in the annals of true crime.

When I looked up again Christine was at my door. Her off-white dress gave her a ghostly appearance; even her smile was insubstantial.

'How's the Riordan boy?' she asked.

'Still in the first stage of trauma: speechless with shock, prone to violent outbursts and panic attacks.'

'You've done great work with child victims on previous cases.'

'Mikey's under more pressure; everything hinges on what he saw. There's no family supporting him.'

Christine gave a slow smile. 'He's in safe hands, Alice.'

She vanished without another word. Her communication style was so cryptic that even her encouragement sounded threatening.

I sifted through the interview transcripts with Clare Riordan's friends and colleagues, but they yielded frustratingly little. Her CV showed a woman who had worked tirelessly, becoming a consultant at thirty, serving on a dozen ethics panels and the drug advisory board. It intrigued me that there seemed to be no flaw in her glossy professional record. Her only known conflict had been with her younger sister, Eleanor. They had been locked in a legal battle for two years, cause unspecified. The blank space surrounding Clare Riordan's life needed to be filled before I could find the reason for her disappearance.

It was a relief to escape from the office at one thirty. I had arranged to visit the victim's house in Clapham, hoping the place would reveal details of her personality. I drove south through light midday traffic, my car slipping past Mayfair's upmarket shops and the mansions of Chelsea. The tone changed when I crossed the river to Battersea. Elegant Georgian squares were replaced by an ocean of glass, high-rise apartment blocks sprawling as far west as the eye could see, testament to the developers' belief that a river view was worth a king's ransom.

Stormont Road was a genteel row of Victorian semis, the green expanse of Clapham Common unfurling in the distance. A police cordon surrounded Clare Riordan's house and the road was a hive of activity, uniformed officers standing on doorsteps, still conducting house-to-house interviews. I wondered whether Mikey would ever return to the home his mother had maintained so carefully. Limestone steps climbed to a wrought-iron porch, the front door an elegant pale blue, sash windows gleaming. I was opening the gate when a woman of around sixty appeared at my side. She had a hard-eyed stare, the skin around her mouth deeply furrowed, suggesting that her first action each morning was to light a cigarette.

'Are you with the police?' she asked.

'My name's Alice Quentin, I'm an advisor on the investigation. Do you need to see a detective?'

'One came by yesterday; I didn't like his attitude. Disrespectful, I'd say.' Her small eyes blinked rapidly. 'Can you spare a minute?'

She led me into the house next door to Riordan's. Her lounge was overfilled with furniture, the air too sweet, as if someone had spilled a bottle of cheap scent.

'I didn't catch your name,' I said.

'Pauline Rowe. I've lived here forty years.'

'And you've got some information, Pauline?'

'It could be nothing.'

'Don't worry – small things are often helpful.'

Her gaze drifted to the floor. 'It said on the news that Clare was single, but she was seeing someone. I heard them in the garden.'

'They were talking?'

'It was more like a full-blown row.' Her breath rattled as she inhaled.

'Did you hear what it was about?'

'Clare was sobbing her heart out. She kept saying "it has to end," but the bloke was having none of it.'

'Was this recent?'

'Two or three weeks ago.'

'Did you see the man?'

She shook her head. 'It had to be her boyfriend. Arguments like that only happen when you've got strong feelings.'

'Do many other people visit her house?'

'Not really. I saw this couple on her steps a few times. The bloke was smartly dressed, but they could have been Jehovah's witnesses.' She paused to light a cigarette.

'No one else she rowed with?'

'Just her sister, but she hasn't been round in a while. That girl's a headcase.'

'How do you mean?'

'Forever causing trouble, yelling, then slamming out the front door. Mental problems, if you ask me.'

'Is there anything else I should know?'

'Mikey worships his mum. They're always together, except when she's at work.'

'They sound very close.'

'He's a sweet kid.' Her gaze locked on to mine. 'Is there any news?'

'The police are making good progress. Thanks for the information, Mrs Rowe.'

Pauline seemed reluctant to say goodbye, chattering as she walked me back to the front door, wafting cigarette smoke. I wondered about her lifestyle as I approached Clare Riordan's house: maybe retirement hadn't turned out like she'd hoped, boredom sending her outside to eavesdrop on her neighbour.

The first person I saw at Riordan's house was Pete Hancock, Burns's chief scenes of crime officer. My heart sank. He stood in the hallway scribbling on a clipboard as I donned my sterile suit, his expression unreadable.

'This is the worst time to visit.' His words were delivered in a monotone.

'You always say that, Pete. I know we're looking for different things, but it would help to compare notes. When's your next break?'

'I'm not taking one.'

'Give me half an hour, I'll buy you a cappuccino.'

'I don't drink coffee.'

'Tea then.' I checked my watch. 'At three o'clock.'

Hancock looked stunned, but didn't refuse. For the first time in years he forgot to bark at me as I toured his crime scene. I took care to stay on the plastic sheeting, avoiding rooms that were still cordoned. My concern rose as I explored the ground floor. Everything about the decor spoke of an exclusive mother-son relationship. A row of black and white portrait photos in the hallway had been taken at yearly intervals, starting when Mikey was an infant, cradled in his mother's arms. The boy grew taller in each image but the intimacy never weakened; in the final picture they stood arm in arm, beaming at the camera with identical smiles. Every room in the house confirmed my sense that few people had encroached on them. Maybe losing her husband had bonded Clare to her son so closely that no one else mattered.

The living room was an example of tasteful neutrality. Items stacked on the coffee table reflected both their interests: her interior design magazines and copies of *The Lancet*; his games console and dog-eared comics. Mikey's room seemed typical of an eleven-year-old boy: football trophies above his bed, a signed poster from the Chelsea squad. It was only on closer inspection that I realised soccer wasn't his only passion. Several large drawings had been tacked to the wall – exuberant landscapes, with an outsized sun almost filling the sky, breakers lapping a white line of cliffs, full of light and energy. Framed certificates showed that Mikey had won his school's art competition two years running. The space was unusually tidy for such a young boy; the air smelled of soap and fresh linen. His mother's room was orderly too. The contents of her wardrobe appealed to me: suits from Ghost and Karen Millen, jeans and silk shirts for the weekend. But her taste was wilder than mine. Tucked at the back were outfits only a femme fatale would choose: skimpy cocktail dresses, a leather skirt, agonisingly high stilettos. The clothes hinted at a woman with two lives. She was a hard-working professional, but confident enough to parade her attractiveness when the chance arose.

My frustration mounted as I reached the hallway. Sometimes a victim's home speaks volumes about the habits that made them vulnerable but, apart from Clare's choice of clothing, her domestic life seemed easy to interpret. It revealed good taste, middle-class comfort, and a high degree of trust between parent and child. That intimacy made me even more concerned about how Mikey would fare if his mother never came home.

When I reached the porch, Hancock was standing there. He gave me a baleful stare as I peeled out of my Tyvek suit.

'There's a café close by,' I said.

'Okay, if you're buying.'

He said little during the short stroll to Lavender Hill, giving me the chance to observe him from the corner of my eye. His combination of white hair and lowering black eyebrows made him look like a younger, more hostile version of Alistair Darling. My request for a double espresso clearly disgusted him.

'That stuff'll give you a stomach ulcer.'

'It's a gamble I'm willing to take. Where are you from, Pete?'

'Tyneside, originally.'

'I recognised the lilt. So, do you dislike all shrinks, or is it just me?'

His frown deepened. 'I spend my days on my knees, scooping up fag ends and bodily fluids, so people like you can pontificate about modus operandi. You even get paid more.'

'And that annoys you?'

'I solve the cases for you, but most shrinks show me zero respect.' He took a gulp of mineral water.

'Then they're missing a trick. Seeing what the killer touched or the shoes a victim wore tells me more than any photograph. I can't do that without your help.'

'You want me to stop moaning when you drop by?'

'Is that possible?'

He cast me a shrewd glance. 'Burns says you're good at your job.'

'I hear the same about you.'

'Why aren't you in some swanky private hospital charging two hundred quid an hour?'

'I could be crazy, but forensic work trumps a big salary for me.'

The answer seemed to satisfy him. When we got back to Riordan's house, it was clear Pete's team had been working hard in his absence. Two white-suited SOCOs squeezed past us on the steps, carrying plastic evidence boxes bound for the lab. But my hour with Pete hadn't been wasted; for the price of a bottle of mineral water, I'd reversed some of his prejudices. He'd confided that he was a lapsed Catholic, married with two kids in their twenties, a passionate Newcastle supporter with a penchant for jazz. In exchange I'd revealed my desire for a motorbike and confirmed that I was in a relationship with his DCI.

'That's old news, Pete. Didn't you hear?'

'I'm not one for gossip.' He was already slipping his feet back into plastic overshoes.

'Have you found much in there?'

'The IT boys are checking her computers, but there's something you should see.'

I donned my sterile suit again reluctantly. I'd always hated the synthetic smell and feel of them, fabric crackling as we walked down the hall.

Hancock came to a halt in the kitchen. 'Notice anything?'

'A lot of expensive kit.' I scanned the bespoke units, granite work surface and black and white floor tiles. It looked typical of a family with money: there was even a top-of-the-range juicer and Gaggia coffee machine sitting on the counter.

'Look again.' He shone a blue light on the floor and a shadow emerged, just over a foot wide. 'Someone's tried to scrub it away, but we sprayed the floor with Luminol. The UV light's picking up blood molecules.'

'It may not be hers.'

'Whoever it came from, it would have been one hell of a wound. You'd need half a pint to spread that far.'

'Can the lab tell if it's hers?'

He nodded. 'We'll take a scraping from the floor. They'll cross-match it with her son's DNA, but they won't be able to date it.'

'Why not?'

'Bleach in cleaning fluid destroys everything except the genetic profile.'

When I left at two o'clock, Hancock accompanied me to the door, spectral in his white suit as I looked back at the house. Uniformed police were still guarding the copse where Clare Riordan and her son had last been seen. The consultant appeared in my mind again on the drive to King's Cross. She might still be alive, her blood being harvested for reasons unknown. But why would her abductor take her home, then scour the place before removing her body? I gazed through the windscreen. Fallen leaves lay piled on the road; thick daubs of red, staining the tarmac like clots of blood.

5

The police station on St Pancras Way was thronging with uniforms and detectives when I arrived, the air buzzing with energy. Violence had quickened everyone's pulse. For months the humdrum work of crime prevention ticked along, then once or twice a year an abduction or murder case fractured the routine. I could sense the anticipation as the team prepared to raise their game.

Burns was too busy to notice me. He stood by the bank of windows in the incident room, favouring everyone with the same intent stare, his hulking stature giving him a natural advantage. Stress made me fidget, but he grew impassive as a statue, his physical energy locked away. His face had a battered intensity, more like a football manager's before a big match than a detective's. Despite his role as SIO in charge of a huge team, there seemed to be an understanding that anyone could ask a valid question. Officers circled him, all waiting their turn. I made myself look away and focus on the job in hand.

Around thirty detectives and SOCOs had arrived for the overview. Two poster-sized photos of Clare Riordan were tacked to the evidence board. One showed a slender, well-preserved brunette, giving the camera a professional smile. The other image was much more candid. She sat on a sunlit beach in shorts and a sun top looking preoccupied, as if she was fretting about something outside her control. Mikey was sharing her beach towel, beaming at the camera. The boy looked nothing like the hollow-eyed waif trapped in the safe house, too burdened by terror to make a sound.

Burns called the meeting to order simply by raising his hand. 'The Riordan case has been allocated to us because we've got the city's best murder conviction rate. We'll be working with officers from Clapham, but it's too soon to forecast whether Clare Riordan's dead or alive. She's an NHS consultant, at the top of her professional game. Her superiors say she's an outstanding department leader, with an impeccable record. What happened the morning she went missing is harder to pin down. A reliable witness saw her and her son run into a copse three days ago on Clapham Common. The same man saw a blue hatchback car pull out of the copse minutes later, around seven fifteen a.m.; it looked like a parks vehicle, with flashing across the bonnet. We think Clare was abducted by the driver of that car. Mikey Riordan was found wandering down Walworth Road that afternoon in a confused state. His mother may be being held hostage, the kidnappers waiting to make contact. So far the only signs that she's been treated violently are a large bloodstain on her kitchen floor, and her blood being left outside an office block on Bishopsgate. I'll hand over to DI Tania Goddard now – she'll be running the operational work, with help from DS Angie Wilcox.'

I studied Tania's appearance when she rose to her feet. Burns's deputy was showing no sign of the physical injuries she'd suffered three months before, after almost drowning in the Thames. Despite a week in hospital, her glamour had survived intact. Her short black hair fell in glossy waves across her forehead, French navy dress accentuating hourglass curves. To the untrained eye she looked invincible, but I wondered how she was faring mentally. She prided herself on being a tough East Ender, but another murder investigation must feel challenging so soon after her own ordeal.

'The pint of blood was left in a hospital-issue transfusion pack. They're not hard to find: wholesalers sell them to care homes, health centres and hospitals. This one carried a printed label with her name on it. It was wrapped in brown paper, no fingerprints.' She pointed at an enlarged photo on the evidence board. It showed a transparent bag filled with dark red liquid. 'Whoever we're looking for knows how to extract blood, so we could be looking for someone with a medical background, but it's not hard to learn. There are plenty of training clips on the Internet that show health staff how to tie tourniquets and hit the right vein. You don't need to be a trained nurse to take a sample.'

I thought about my first attempts with a phlebotomy needle at medical school. Calming the patient had required far more concentration than inserting the needle, but whoever had taken Clare Riordan wouldn't care about bedside manner.

She switched off the projector. 'Riordan's life seems to focus on her son. We need to identify every call made to her mobile and landline. Investigation teams will carry on interviewing neighbours, friends, colleagues and patients. She's widowed, with few close relatives. Her mother died last year and she's fighting a lawsuit against her sister over property. We need to find everyone who's crossed her path.' Tania's cool gaze skimmed the room as she passed the meeting back to Burns.

'Make sure every public statement goes through me, or the tabloids'll be running vampire stories for months.' His low voice boomed from the walls. 'Right now, Clare's son is our only witness. Dr Alice Quentin from the FPU will be profiling the abductor for us, and working with the child.' He gestured for me to stand.

Some old-timers smirked when I rose to my feet, as if my opinions were bound to be hokum, but the tide was turning. In the tribal world of the Met I'd won major points that summer by helping to catch a serial killer on the banks of the Thames and bringing one of their team home alive. 'Mikey Riordan turned eleven last month. He's small for his age, vulnerable and close to his mother. The boy lost his dad when he was five, and he's suffering from a condition called elective muteness, brought on by trauma. He can't speak, and any more stress could damage him permanently. I'll be helping him find the confidence to tell us what he saw. It's too early to profile the killer, but right now his personality seems to be divided. He's cool enough to plan a complex abduction and leave coded messages, yet he's also a violent risk-taker, prepared to walk through city streets carrying a pack full of his victim's blood.'

When he took over again, it struck me that Burns could act any part he chose. At work his behaviour was macho, the heft of his shoulders making his toughest colleagues believe he was unassailable. But at home chaos reigned; he could sit for hours scribbling in his sketchbook, his voice a quiet Scottish burr.

I waited for a flurry of people to finish bombarding him with questions, then joined him in his office. Once I was inside he pressed his back against the door, as though someone might try to batter it down.

'The case is the top story on News Unlimited; they're gagging for information,' he said.

'Riordan may not be as perfect as they think. Her neighbour reckons she was in a bad relationship; she heard her rowing with a man in the back garden.'

His expression brightened. 'That's interesting. She was single by all accounts; I'll get it checked out.'

'How's it going here?'

'Too slowly. We're doing house-to-house all over the neighbourhood. There's no evidence she was being watched, and no reports of anyone hanging around her house or car.'

'Hancock hasn't found much apart from the bloodstain.'

His jaw dropped. 'Pete spoke to you?'

'Miracles do happen. I'd better go, I'm having pizza with Mikey Riordan.'

'That'll work. Small boys love bribes.'

'Just like big ones,' I said, nodding. 'When can I meet Riordan's sister?'

'Why? Her alibi's solid.'

'She can tell me about Mikey. Any insight could help me unlock what he knows.'

'I'll set up a meeting.' He frowned as I backed towards the door. 'Are you coming round later?'

'I'm seeing Lola. Better leave it till the weekend.'

'That's a long wait.'

I said goodbye before he could argue. My only hope of keeping my head above water was to separate personal and professional feelings until the case was closed.

I exchanged a box containing two family-sized pizzas for a grateful smile from Gurpreet when I reached the safe house.

'This should cheer Mikey up. It took forever to get him out of his room this morning,' he said.

'He's bound to be scared at first.'

'He's been drawing on that pad you gave him.'

'Much eye contact?'

'Just a few scowls. I don't want to push him too hard.'

'That's good, if we rush him, he'll panic.'

Mikey was curled on the sofa, birdlike hands clutching his knees, watching a rerun of *The Tomorrow People*. He made a show of ignoring me. I smiled at him then sat on the floor in the same position as before.

'Do you feel like talking today?' He hunched his shoulders more tightly round his ears. 'That's okay, but I'd love to hear your voice. I hope you're hungry. I got a veggie pizza and a meat one too, just in case.'

His gaze met mine without changing expression; the effect was unnerving, as if he was looking straight through me. After a few seconds he rose to his feet and wandered to the French windows. When I stood beside him his frustration was obvious, his hands were flattened against the glass. The look on his face was pure aggression, jaw set, David ready for Goliath. Scared as he was, his face made me certain he'd find his voice eventually, if only to scream his story to the rafters.

'Almost there,' he muttered. 'Not far now.'

'Almost where, Mikey?'

He didn't reply; too busy staring ahead, as if his worst enemy was waiting in the shadows. But his fighting spirit had faded by the time we reached the kitchen. He only managed a tiny amount of food, chewing each mouthful repeatedly like he was struggling to swallow. The bruises on his face were fading, but his eyes were still jacked open a little too wide.

'I'd like to stay over soon. Is that okay?' His slice of pizza hovered in the air, eyes fixed on the kitchen wall. 'Maybe we can cook together.'

He ignored my comment and slipped from the room.

'This could take for ever,' I muttered.

Gurpreet nodded. 'I'm worried about him. He calls out in his sleep but by morning he's mute again.'

'That often happens. It's a dress rehearsal for normal speech.'

'His catchphrase is all he says. What do you think it means?'

'The fact that he's repeating it makes me wonder if it's something the abductors said to him. Hopefully it'll come out as he gains confidence.' I studied him again. 'You'll be able to take a break soon, Gurpreet. He's nearly ready for me to stay over.'

37

'I want to stay with him till he's calmer,' he replied. 'His sketchbook's on the counter. Do you think he wants us to look?'

'I'd say it's an open invitation.'

Mikey's talent was evident in every drawing. The first one showed cars, buses and trains cruising through open countryside. He'd sketched the flowers in the living room with better results than mine, scarlet blooms spilling across the page. It was the last picture that bothered me. The trees on Clapham Common were a jumble of russet colours, the domed bandstand resting on a vivid field of grass. But the scene had been depopulated. The location where his mother had gone missing was stripped of human activity: no cars, dog walkers or cyclists. The scene had been returned to its pristine condition, as though he'd wiped the attack from his mind.

'He hardly ate a bite,' Gurpreet commented, loading a slice of pizza on to a plate. 'I'll give him this.'

I tagged along to say goodbye, but when I stood by the open door of the living room, Mikey jumped to his feet. Something must have upset him – the constant fussing, or his nurse invading his space. He flew at Gurpreet, small arms flailing. I kept my back pressed to the wall, knowing his panic would increase if we both tried to calm him. The nurse held the boy gently by his shoulders while he kicked and threw punches, his voice a quiet murmur. After a minute the tantrum subsided. Mikey's face held a mixture of fury and anguish as he ran upstairs to his room.

'Are you okay?' I asked.

'I'll live.' Gurpreet's expression was sober as he studied a new scratch on his arm, a single drop of blood oozing down his wrist.

★   ★   ★

I was still processing Mikey's reaction when I reached Morocco Street that evening, aware that soon it would be me facing all that pent-up rage. Lola's cat-like smile was frazzled when she greeted me, auburn curls cascading over her shoulders. Her flat was full of shabby-chic furniture, swathes of velvet festooning the windows in dramatic folds, a look that only a pair of flamboyant actors could pull off.

'Don't make a sound,' she whispered. 'The monster's asleep.'

'Can I see her?'

'If you wake her, I'll have to kill you.'

My three-month-old goddaughter Neve lay in her Moses basket, arms raised as if she'd just fought fifteen rounds. She was a miniaturised version of her mother, with the same delicate jaw, a lick of coppery hair trailing across her forehead. I quelled my urge to pick her up and joined Lola instead. She was draped across her chaise longue, giving me an exhausted grin.

'She's beyond gorgeous.'

Lola looked intrigued. 'Getting broody, Al?'

'God, no. I haven't got a maternal bone in my body.'

'That's rubbish. You're great with her.'

I shrugged. 'Maybe I'll steal her.'

'Feel free. The little beast kept me up all night.'

'Didn't Neal help?'

'We took it in turns.' She studied me thoughtfully. 'Are you okay? You seem distracted.' Lola had been reading my mind ever since secondary school.

'I'm working on a nasty abduction case.'

'There's something else, isn't there? How's Burns?'

'Same as ever. Still a macho controlling workaholic.'

Her face broke into a grin. 'He's perfect for you.'

'You think so?'

'Last time we had dinner you couldn't keep your hands off each other. How long have you been together now?'

'A few months.'

'So it's serious?'

'Jesus, you're nosey.'

She gaped at me. 'You're not getting cold feet, are you?'

'How is that any of your business?'

'He's six foot four, built like a brick wall, and he's crazy about you. What's the problem?'

'There isn't one.' I stared at my hands. 'I don't want to screw it up, that's all.'

'Why would you?'

'Think about it, Lo. How would you describe my boyfriends so far?'

Her smile returned. 'Mad, bad, or dangerous to know.'

'Exactly.'

'Burns is different. You'll both survive if you fall for him.'

'It's moving too fast. He wants me to meet his kids, for God's sake.'

'Because he's super keen,' she said, squeezing my hand.

As if on cue, Neve gave a heart-rending scream, freeing me from Lola's cross-examination. The next hour was spent cooing over her. She was growing more alert every day, green eyes watchful as she wriggled in the crook of my arm. Her smell was a heady blend of milk, talcum powder and ripe peaches. But the thing that amazed me was Lola's transformation from gin-swilling party girl to doting mother. She breezed around the flat with Neve balanced on her hip, taking it all in her stride. Her high spirits were still there, but until now her gentleness had been concealed. It was dark outside by the time I kissed them both goodbye.

'When are you seeing Burns again?' Lola asked.

'Saturday, probably.'

'Want my advice?'

'No thanks.'

'Tell him your deepest, darkest fears, then move on.'

'I'm the shrink, Lo, remember? I can handle my own love life.'

I was still envying the simplicity of her world-view when I got home. Too edgy to sleep, I switched on the TV. After flicking through a dozen satellite channels I came eye to eye with Burns. He was standing outside the station on St Pancras Way, asking the public for information about Clare Riordan. He looked nothing like the man who'd spent the last few months scaring and delighting me by equal measure. He addressed the camera with a hard-edged stare, as though he'd never experienced a moment's self-doubt in his life. I turned off the TV and made an effort to focus my mind. The blood theme was inescapable; Clare Riordan's abductors had extracted a full pint from their victim. Not only was the doctor a haematologist by profession, Pete Hancock had discovered traces of the substance on her kitchen floor that couldn't be bleached away.

I stood by the living-room window, searching the city's floodlit skyline. All I could hope was that Mikey Riordan's mother was out there somewhere, being kept alive.

6

The woman is alone in the laboratory, the man's illness keeping him at home. Even though she misses him, her work is easier without his interference. She's spent the past hour tending to Riordan: giving her a hunk of bread, forcing her to swallow enough water to keep her alive, then piss in the bucket by the door. It's taking a long time to gain her secrets, but the outcome will be worth the effort.

She pulls on surgical gloves before lifting the plastic bag from the fridge and holding it to the light. The liquid is cool in her hands, the truest shade of crimson. Blood still fascinates her, despite the damage it's caused. It's as individual as a signature, revealing every human trait. Thirty years ago, no one fought hard enough to keep it pure, her family torn apart. Now it's her responsibility to right the wrongs. A dozen more transfusion packs lie in a cardboard box in the corner, waiting to be filled. She crosses the room to gaze at Riordan, suspended upside down like a chrysalis, arms jerking at her sides, too exhausted to scream.

'Ready to give me a name, Clare?'

No sound emerges from her mouth, apart from another ragged breath. When the rope unwinds, her body thumps back on to the chair. The woman leans closer until their faces are inches apart.

'Tell me, then I'll let you rest. I want you to betray each other, just like you betrayed us.'

'Let me go, you mad bitch,' Riordan hisses.

'You're not helping yourself.'

The woman feels a rush of anger. This is nothing like the other victims, who each yielded a name quickly before they were sacrificed. Silence will worsen Riordan's punishments. She pulls the lever, until the doctor's body is suspended once more from the ceiling, blood dripping from an incision on her throat. She would prefer to use a scalpel and despatch her fast, but her information is essential; Riordan may have to spend months in this room, atoning for her crime. Her hair has worked loose from its ponytail, long tresses splayed across the ground. The woman grabs a pair of scissors and makes the first cut, hacking close to her scalp. Riordan's crowning glory falls at her feet in handfuls, filthy and matted with blood.

7

Wednesday 15 October

I went for a jog the next morning to clear my mind. The city was stirring into motion as I cut through Shad Thames, passing factories and warehouses tall enough to block out the light, the names of Victorian tea importers ghosted on their walls. My mood lifted when I found my stride as I ran east along the river from Cherry Garden Pier. Trees glowed on Shadwell bank, red dots of brightness punctuating the grey.

The rush of endorphins was still boosting me when I switched on the TV after my shower. Clare Riordan's disappearance remained the top news story, the picture a reminder that we had plenty of interests in common. It showed her completing the Race for Life, tanned and long legged as she crossed the finishing line; like her, too, I had served as a hospital consultant. She looked resilient enough to deal with the toughest challenges. In the next image her arm was wrapped tightly around her son's shoulders, his face blurred into anonymity. She was being depicted as a beauty with a heart of gold, but soon the age-old pattern would re-establish itself: journalists might already be hunting for secrets to deliver the knockout blow and topple her from her pedestal.

It was just before nine when my taxi pulled up outside the Royal Free Hospital. I had asked to meet some of Riordan's colleagues, to gain insights into why she and Mikey had been targeted. I still had a sense that Clare might be being held hostage by someone she knew intimately, who understood her habits. The hospital campus was a wedge of grey concrete slapped down beside Belsize Park, impregnable as a fortress, so vast and featureless the entrance was hard to locate. Angie was sheltering by a turbine of rotating doors. The DS was only a few inches taller than me, several years younger, dark red hair cut short to frame her elfin face. She talked nineteen to the dozen, filling me in on progress as we followed signs for the haematology department.

'We've searched the common again.' She blew out a long breath. 'I spent most of yesterday waist-deep in brambles, but there's nothing definite.'

'Any news on her phone records?'

'Not yet. We spoke to her neighbour again about that row she overheard, but we've got no evidence Riordan was in a relationship, apart from a number on her mobile we still need to trace. Someone called dozens of times from a pay-as-you-go phone.'

'Married, probably, covering his back.'

'More than likely. Have you got time to visit a friend of Riordan's after this? She was too shocked to make sense when I saw her on Monday.'

'Of course, it'll help me find out more about Mikey.'

Angie came to a halt when we reached haematology. 'We're meeting her deputy, Dr Pietersen, and a junior consultant called Dr Novak. Pietersen's been seen already, but he was frosty as hell. I need to know why.'

'You ask the questions, I'll observe him.'

The universal smell of hospitals in winter hit me as we entered the department: wet overcoats, antiseptic and recycled air. The receptionist greeted us warmly. She was a large middle-aged woman who clearly took pride in her appearance, fingernails painted the same deep magenta as her hair. I glanced at her name badge and saw that she was called Brenda

45

Madison. She gave Angie and me a professional smile as we signed the visitors' book.

'Step this way, ladies. Anything you need, just ask.'

She led us down the corridor at a smart pace. Ten metres away a young male patient was dragging an IV trolley towards a treatment room. Through an open doorway a woman was flicking through a magazine while medication dripped from a plastic bag into her bloodstream. Brenda rapped on Dr Pietersen's office door then left us to wait. A tall, bald-headed man of indeterminate age stood on the threshold. His face was so gaunt that I wondered if he was ill. He considered us through muddy green eyes then stepped back into his consulting room, where classical music was playing at low volume.

'Debussy,' Angie said. ' "Clair de Lune".'

'You're a classical fan?' The doctor's expression brightened. 'I often listen to Radio Three between appointments. It's a great stress-buster.'

She returned his smile. 'I had that piece at my wedding.'

I stood back to admire her technique. Angie had mellowed in the last year, no longer blundering ahead for a quick result. Judging by Pietersen's reaction, she had relaxed him enough to lower his guard.

'It's hard to imagine something like this happening,' he said quietly. 'Clare's incredibly hard working.'

'Could you tell us a little about her job here?'

'Most of our patients are seriously ill. They have blood-borne viruses, like HIV or hepatitis, or illnesses like leukaemia. The majority respond well to treatment, but Clare's role as head of department leaves her with difficult choices. Funding decisions are her responsibility.'

'Did she get any complaints?'

'Not as far as I know. But some patients don't receive the treatments they want, due to budget cuts.'

'That must be frustrating for you all.'

'It's the worst aspect of the job.'

'Do you and Dr Riordan see eye to eye, on a personal level?'

He shuffled papers across his desk. 'We've had conflicts, but it's never affected our work.'

'Professional differences?' Angie asked.

'We both applied for the top job in April. I've had more training, served more years, and my record's flawless. I complained about her appointment to the trustees.'

'Did that make things awkward?'

His frown deepened. 'I'd never let personal matters affect my patients. Once the issue was resolved she got my full support.'

'Do you know if Clare had fallen out with anyone?'

'I don't keep track of my colleagues' disagreements.'

'Can you tell us how you spent the morning of Saturday the eleventh of October?'

Pietersen's sluggish eyes widened into a stare. 'Are you suggesting I caused her disappearance?'

'Everyone will be asked the same question.'

'I was on weekend duty here, dealing with emergency referrals. The receptionists will confirm I arrived before nine a.m. If you ask around, you'll learn that Clare and I have a sound professional relationship.' His charm had switched off as abruptly as a water supply.

'Dr Riordan was taken much earlier, at around seven fifteen a.m.'

'Speak to my wife, if you doubt my word. I was at home until eight, then drove straight here.'

'That's helpful, thanks.'

'You'll have to excuse me, I need to prepare for my patients.' He began leafing through his in-tray, as though we'd already vacated his consulting room.

The second doctor was a junior consultant called Adele Novak. Her office stood directly opposite Pietersen's; through the open doorway, I saw a slim woman of around my own age with cropped dark brown hair leaning over her desk, absorbed in a report. When Angie tapped on the door she gave us a calm smile. Novak was attractive and fine boned, pale skin dusted with freckles. Her consulting room was more welcoming than Dr Pietersen's: greeting cards and photos tacked to a pin board, a jug of yellow carnations on her coffee table.

'Thanks for making time to see us,' Angie said.

'I'm glad to help.' Her gaze shifted between us.

'Do you know Clare well?' I asked.

'Not socially, but I've got her to thank for appointing me. She's been my clinical supervisor since I arrived in January.' Her words were delivered slowly, as if she was considering each statement.

'How would you describe her?'

'Professional and committed, but she doesn't suffer fools.'

'In what way?'

'She makes quick judgements about people.'

'Would you say she's well liked?'

'I enjoy working with her, but I can only speak for myself. Most colleagues respect her, certainly.' She hesitated. 'Clare tends to see things in black and white.'

'How do you mean?'

'She made six people redundant last year. Apparently she didn't lose any sleep over it.'

'Could you tell us their names?'

'It was before I arrived. HR will have a list.'

'Do you know if Clare's close to anyone in the department?'

'That's not her style. A few of us go for a drink sometimes after work, but she never comes along. She goes home to her

48

son as soon as her shift finishes.' Novak stopped talking abruptly, as if she had decided not to expose a secret.

'Anything you share could help us find her, Dr Novak,' I said.

'Call me Adele, please. Look, I won't beat around the bush. I admire Clare, but she's a strong personality. She's close to the trustees, so her opinion carries a lot of weight. That puts people on edge.' Novak's voice petered out, as if she could be demoted for speaking out of turn.

'Thanks for being so open.'

She studied me more closely. 'Is Clare's son okay?'

'He's shaken, but getting good care.'

'It's awful for him.' Her eyes abruptly filled with tears. 'The poor kid must be terrified.'

I let Angie question her after that, measuring the doctor's reactions. Her distress was obvious, even though she had hinted that Riordan was a difficult boss. When Angie gave her a card she examined it carefully before slipping it into the pocket of her white coat. She came over as a woman who left nothing to chance, a little too sensitive for such a challenging role.

Angie turned to me when we got back to the hospital's crowded foyer. 'That was an eye-opener. Pietersen's bedside manner stinks, and she made Riordan sound like a toxic force.'

'That's survivor guilt for you.'

'How do you mean?'

'Pietersen resented Clare getting the director's job. On a subconscious level he probably feels bad for ill-wishing her, and Novak's scared of her boss. Maybe the whole department feels that way. It's worth finding the people Clare sacked and checking their alibis.'

She nodded. 'I'll get a background check on Pietersen too, and have his room searched. He had no need to be so defensive.'

49

I'd seen that glint in Angie's eye before; the senior doctor's brusque manner had raised her antennae. The Debussy refrain stayed with me as she drove south. It seemed odd that Pietersen had described music as a stress-buster, even though his temper was so ill-controlled. Gradually the city's noise replaced the melody. All I could hear were taxis revving, pedestrians' voices, and the drone from Angie's police radio. For once her chatter fell silent. Maybe she was obsessing about Riordan's disappearance too. The doctor seemed to have vanished into thin air, leaving only a raft of unanswered questions and a distraught child.

We arrived at Denise Thorpe's house in Wandsworth by half past ten. A plain three-storey box dating from the 1970s, its most striking feature was its proximity to St Mary's Cemetery. Gravestones and weathered statues were visible through the railings ten metres away, sycamore trees guarding the entrance like sentinels. Their scarlet leaves were still so glossy it seemed unthinkable that soon they'd be littering the streets, brittle as cigarette papers.

The woman who opened the door had a dreamy air, as if she'd just risen from a nap. Her frizz of mousy hair flew in all directions, oval face free of makeup. She was dressed in a black turtleneck and shapeless grey skirt, deliberately hiding her attractiveness. Angie and I waited in silence while she prepared tea in the kitchen. Her living room was the opposite of Clare Riordan's stylish lounge. The shelves were full of holiday mementos; two long-haired cats curled on an armchair, beside a basket full of yarns and knitting needles. The place felt like the home of an elderly spinster, even though Denise was married and under forty-five. A packet of co-codamol tablets lay on the table: the strongest pain relief available over the counter. If she was taking them for a chronic illness, that might explain her distracted manner. Denise soon reappeared, carrying a tray loaded with bone china and packets of biscuits.

'I wasn't sure which you'd like,' she said, 'so I brought them all.'

'That's kind of you.' I smiled at her then pointed at a photo on her mantelpiece. 'Is this your daughter?'

Her face relaxed. 'Emma's studying law at York Uni. I'm glad she's not here to face all this.'

'It must be hard for you too,' Angie commented.

'I can't seem to concentrate. It hasn't sunk in yet.'

My sympathy increased. If Lola had been taken, I'd be in pieces too. 'How long have you and Clare been friends?'

'Since school. Everyone said we were chalk and cheese, but we shared a flat right through university. She even introduced me to my husband.'

'They worked together?'

She nodded. 'At the same hospital, years ago. Simon's a psychotherapist. I'm afraid he's upstairs with a client today.'

'That's not a problem. Did you train for medicine like Clare?'

She gave a vague smile. 'I only practised for a year. I write exam papers for science students now. Clare's always been the fearless one.'

'Does she confide in you?'

She looked flustered, cheeks colouring. 'We know each other's secrets. Or I thought we did.'

'And you meet regularly?'

'Her house is ten minutes away. I drop by most weekends, or she brings Mikey here.' Her eyes were welling. 'Simon and I are the closest thing he has to a family. We offered to look after him, but they wouldn't let us.'

'Mikey's safest where he is for now. It's possible the abductors targeted him too,' I said quietly. 'Can you think of anything he'd find comforting right now?'

'He loves helping Clare in the kitchen. It's his favourite place.'

'Thanks, I'll keep that in mind.' I put down my cup and saucer. 'We think Clare was having a relationship with someone. It's important we rule the man out. Do you know his name?'

Her gaze slipped out of focus. 'She told me not to speak about that.'

'It might help us find her.'

'Simon doesn't even know.'

'But things are different now, aren't they?'

Her fingers gripped the handle of her teacup. 'When she comes home, you mustn't say I told you. She'd be so angry.'

'We won't, I promise.'

'I've never met him, but his name's Sam Travers. He lives in Islington.' She looked regretful about her disclosure as Angie scribbled the name down, as if she'd betrayed her friend.

'You've done the right thing, Denise.' I touched the back of her hand.

Her eyes latched on to mine again, full of anxiety. 'When can I see Mikey?'

'I promise to let you know.'

We were about to leave when the living-room door swung open. Simon Thorpe was a very different physical specimen to his wife: medium height, thin, with black hair and penetrating blue eyes. Everything about him was hard-edged and definite, the opposite of her dreamy softness. His pallor and the shadows under his eyes suggested that he spent most of his days indoors. It was only when his smile animated his features like a light bulb that I realised why his wife had been drawn to him.

'Sorry, I've been with a client. Did you want to see me too?' He had a soft West Coast American accent.

'Your wife's helped us already. She's answered all our questions.'

'Nothing I can do?'

'Not today, but thanks for the offer. We'll come back if we need more information.'

'To be honest, we were upset about Mikey not staying here. He needs to feel safe until Clare's found.' His face tensed with concern.

'We can't allow that yet, I'm afraid,' Angie said.

'We want the best for him.' His gaze intensified. 'Please keep us informed. He should be with people he loves.'

'Of course, but I promise he's getting excellent care,' I replied.

The couple looked anxious as we prepared to leave. Denise's fingers clutched mine tightly as we shook hands goodbye, her husband's expression sober. It interested me that the couple hadn't made eye contact once during the exchange, and I guessed that their relationship was being tested by Clare's disappearance. It made sense that they would be frantic about the disappearance of such a longstanding friend, and anxious about the welfare of her child. The abduction was having a ripple effect; the people closest to Riordan touched in different ways by her absence.

Angie called in the news about Sam Travers immediately, as if he was bound to be the culprit. She talked nonstop on the drive back, updating me on her private life. She was waiting for the results of her detective inspector exams, her husband's construction business was booming, and they were planning a holiday to Mauritius. I was an expert on Angie's home life by the time she dropped me at London Bridge, but why Clare Riordan had been taken remained a mystery.

8

Burns was hunched over his desk when I found him that afternoon. His tie was slung over the back of his chair, dark hair in need of a comb, his jaw rimed with stubble. I did my best to ignore the jolt of attraction that arrived out of nowhere.

'I hope you called me here for something urgent, Don.'

He rose to his feet. 'You wanted to see Clare Riordan's sister. She's not best pleased about being brought in again.'

'Has anything else happened?'

'We've had three more sightings of a couple by the copse where Riordan went missing.'

'Reliable witnesses?'

'A teacher, a nurse and a fitness trainer, all out walking their dogs or jogging. They were too far off to give much detail; but we know a man and woman in dark clothing were hanging round the spot when Clare was taken. They were seen inside the copse, sitting on a bench.'

'Life just got more difficult then. Couples are harder to spot; they can pass as normal so easily. You heard the news about Riordan seeing someone called Sam Travers?'

'Tania's chasing it.'

'Have you got anything on her sister?'

He glanced at a computer printout. 'Clare took an injunction out against her this summer for harassment.'

'Never a great sign of affection.'

Burns updated me as we walked to the interview room. Tania's team had been busy checking the records of Clare Riordan's patients to see if any had complained about malpractice, but nothing had emerged yet. The IT boys were still checking her phone and email records, and Angie had been sifting her professional and social contacts for likely suspects. She had also tracked down the six staff Clare had sacked at the Royal Free, but they had scattered across the country looking for work. All except one had firm alibis. Angie had made an appointment for us to interview the only one still living in London at the end of the week.

I shifted my attention back to Eleanor Riordan's fact sheet while I waited in the corridor. She was thirty-nine, a freelance sales consultant living in south London, a stone's throw from where I'd grown up; she owned a flat in the Paragon, an elegant sweep of Georgian houses on the edge of Blackheath. The file shed little light on her conflict with Clare, sparking my curiosity when the door finally opened.

Eleanor Riordan looked so eerily like her sister that I did a double take. She had the same sleek brown hair drawn into a ponytail, oval bone structure, and amber eyes that reflected the light. It looked as if she'd been at a business meeting; a well-tailored suit hung from her slim frame. Despite their difficulties, Clare's abduction seemed to have ruined her peace of mind. Everything about her looked brittle, facial muscles stretched tight over high cheekbones.

'Thanks for coming, Ms Riordan.'

'I don't know why I'm here.' She shot me a hard stare. 'They've questioned me already. I've got nothing more to say.'

'Mikey's very upset at the moment; I'm keen to talk to people close to him. Perhaps you could tell me about his relationship with Clare?'

'How would I know? She stopped me seeing him last year.'

'Can you explain why?'

'She told the police I was bothering her, but I just wanted a rational conversation.' Her arms folded tight across her chest. 'After our mother died, Clare took over her house – lock, stock and barrel. She said it had been promised to her.' The anger in her voice rose with each statement. 'That's an outright lie. I think she destroyed Mum's will.'

'But you own a flat in Blackheath now, don't you?'

'That's irrelevant.'

'The case has been running for two years?'

'I don't even know if Michael got my birthday cards. My boyfriend thinks I should let it go, but blood's thicker than water, isn't it?'

Her reference to blood pulled me up short. So far Burns had kept the abductor's grisly calling card out of the news, by issuing the finders with a gagging order. 'Can you explain why the property means so much to you, Ms Riordan?'

She stared back at me. 'My sister was always my parents' blue-eyed girl – smarter and more confident. But I loved it there, playing on Clapham Common with friends after school, even though Clare acted like I didn't exist. She did everything in her power to prove she was better than me.' Riordan's nonverbal communication continued in the silence that followed. Her jaw had locked so tight it looked as though she might never speak again.

'Did things improve as you got older?'

'Mikey brought us together for a while. I loved babysitting for him, but Clare was already angling for the house, putting pressure on Mum.'

'That sounds painful.' Her face was tense with anger. 'Could you tell me about your job, Eleanor?'

'I advise international pharmaceutical companies on sales strategies.'

'I bet that keeps you busy.'

'It does.' She almost managed a smile. 'My job involves quite a lot of travelling.'

'Do you still hope to see your nephew?'

'Of course, but I'd prefer my sister's blessing.' She crumpled forwards in her seat. 'I'm not stupid, I realise she may not be found. But I won't accept it till there's concrete proof.'

'That makes sense,' I said, nodding. 'Is your boyfriend in sales too?'

'God, no, he'd be hopeless. He's a novelist.'

'Would I know him?'

'His name's Luke Mann. He hasn't had the success he deserves.' Eleanor's tone gentled when she spoke of her partner, some of her tension slipping away.

'Can you give me any more details about Mikey, to help me support him?'

'He never forgets anything you say, and he's got a mind of his own. Ever since he was small he's wanted to do things for himself.'

'You've been very helpful. Feel free to contact me if you want to discuss the case. I'm afraid we may need to talk again.' I handed her my card.

'I don't mind.' Her eyes glistened as she fastened her coat. 'I want her found as much as anyone.'

'Thanks again for coming in.'

When I pressed a button on the wall, a fresh-faced uniform arrived to escort Riordan to the exit.

Burns's hands folded across the back of his neck once we were alone. 'She's more uptight each time I see her.'

'She knows her sister might not come home.'

'Why would she care? They hate each other's guts.'

'Blood's thicker than water, like she said, and unfinished business is hard to bear. Are you sure her alibi's sound?'

He looked sceptical. 'You think she'd abduct her own sister?'

'Family members are always top of my list, but I'd like to know more about Sam Travers and the Thorpes. Even if her lover and close friends turn out to be innocent, they can give us insights into her life. But right now Eleanor's our best fit; she seems to be at cracking point. Anxiety about the court case and all that wasted money could have sent her over the edge, or maybe losing access to Mikey made her lash out.'

'She'd have struggled to hide her sister somewhere, dump the car, then get back to Blackheath for ten a.m. Her neighbours saw her on the forecourt then, briefcase in hand.'

I shook my head. 'If it's a couple that abducted Clare, her accomplice could have done the dirty work. Does she live with the boyfriend?'

'He's got a place in Camberwell. But we can't be one hundred per cent sure a couple took her, just because a man and woman were seen nearby. So far we've got no concrete proof.'

'Eleanor seems obsessive enough to plan a campaign, if she had someone helping. Whoever took Clare knew her routine well enough to forecast exactly when she'd leave the house, and her running route.'

'You think she hates her sister enough to hurt her?'

'She's got a high sense of childhood grievance.' I scanned the notes I'd scribbled on my EF1 form. 'She sees her sister as the aggressor, but she's volatile and caught up in family power issues. Clare's neighbour says Eleanor couldn't control her temper. Maybe something finally snapped her control.'

'We'll keep tabs on her. She doesn't strike me as strong enough to harm anyone, but with the press crawling everywhere, I can't miss a trick.'

'Clare seems like a complex character. She didn't socialise at work; her colleagues think she put ambition above personal loyalty.'

His gaze settled on my face. 'Not like you.'

The abrupt shift of topic pulled me up short. 'How do you mean?'

'You work hard, but you make time for Lola, your brother, friends.'

'But not for you?'

'You read my mind.' He shot me a grin. 'Cook for me tonight and all is forgiven.'

'I'm at the safe house.'

'Pity.' Burns scanned the wall to check that the door was shut, then his hand closed over my wrist. 'You'll need this, sooner or later.' He placed a key on my palm.

'You're giving me an office here?'

He shook his head. 'It's for my flat.'

I passed it back to him. 'There's no need.'

'Take it anyway.'

He dropped it into my pocket, then picked up the phone that was jangling on his desk. I wanted to argue, but the station was the wrong place to debate territory. A queue had formed outside while we'd been interviewing Riordan, and I felt a pang of sympathy. Half a dozen members of his team were waiting to offload their worries.

The police presence had lightened when I reached the safe house; just one officer in the squad car outside, immersed in a newspaper. So many uniforms were doing house-to-house in Clapham that every spare human was needed on the streets. The tense expression on Gurpreet's face told me that he was in need of a break. The house's dark walls seemed to have squeezed the last breath of oxygen from the air.

'He had a rough night,' the nurse said. 'Bed-wetting and standing by the window for hours. The kid's so tired he can hardly keep his eyes open.'

'I'll do my first night shift tomorrow.'

'If you think he's ready. You still want social contact kept to a minimum?'

I nodded. 'Any demands will put him under more pressure.'

Mikey was hunched in a chair in the lounge, keeping the world at bay; the TV was switched off, no external stimulus to lighten his state of mind. We would need to move to the next level fast, even though he was so vulnerable; if his feelings stayed locked inside, they would fester until his nightmares grew toxic. I knelt on the floor before making direct eye contact.

'I'd like to stay here tomorrow night, Mikey. If you write down a list of foods you like, we can cook together.' I drew a notepad from my pocket, and a set of playing cards.

The child ignored me, his body folding in on itself.

'Want to play Solitaire?'

It felt like a minor victory when he gave a minute nod of agreement. I dealt the cards myself the first time, to show him the rules. It seemed as though he'd ignored me, but he laid new cards on the floor with a shaky hand.

'Good going,' I commented. 'You're quicker than me.'

I waited until he was absorbed in sequencing the cards before speaking again.

'It must be hard keeping your feelings to yourself. If you write some of them in the notebook, you'll feel better. I won't make you talk till you're ready. But lots of people would love to visit you: mates from school, your aunt, Denise and Simon.'

His body language changed when he heard the names, shoulders stiffening, the cards spilling from his hand.

'It's okay. You don't have to see anyone yet.'

'Not far now,' he whispered.

'Not far from where, Mikey? Try and tell me what you mean.'

His eyes glazed as he stared at the wall, making me wonder if the names I'd mentioned had triggered his fear. I carried on talking in a soothing voice, but it had no effect; by the time I left he was hunched in his chair once more, like my visit had never happened. I cursed silently as I got into my car, wishing I could pinpoint what had caused such a strong reaction. His traumatised state had me convinced that he'd witnessed something that might lead the investigation directly to his mother.

I walked to St Katharine Docks that evening to clear my head. It was after seven when I arrived, the sight of the marina lifting my spirits. There was something heartening about the garish houseboats, side by side in their moorings, tightly packed as pencils in a box. The boat my brother Will and his girlfriend Nina shared had seen better days. The *Bonne Chance* was a Dutch barge in need of TLC, moored at the end of a jetty. When the galley door opened, Nina gave me a tentative smile. We'd seen plenty of each other in the last few months, but she still seemed gripped by shyness. Her knitted dress emphasised her slim build, cropped black hair revealing lines of tattooed script tracing the contours of her neck. She stepped back to admit me to the narrow galley. The space had an overcrowded charm, bright enamelware filling every nook and cranny, simple wooden furniture painted in primary colours.

'Will was just talking about you,' she said.

'Nothing scandalous, I hope?'

'He was speculating about your love life.'

My brother kissed my cheek. 'You're cold, Al. You'd better sit here.'

Will made room for me by the log burner. He looked in good shape. The shadows under his eyes had disappeared, and so had the ragged beard he'd worn for years. He was almost as clean cut and handsome as he'd been a decade ago, before his bipolar disorder took hold.

'Tell us about your new man,' he said.

'Not till I've had a glass of wine. How's work going?'

'Pretty good. I can make smoothies and clean toilets with the best of them.'

'You still like the people?'

He nodded. 'The juice bar's like the United Nations. I can say hello, goodbye and thank you in Russian, Arabic and Swahili.'

'That's three more languages than I've got.'

It still seemed odd that someone with a first-class Cambridge degree in economics had ended up in a café in Covent Garden, but any job was better than none. When his illness was at its height, it had seemed like he might never work again.

'How's the FPU?'

Telling the truth was off limits. If he knew I was working on a brutal abduction case, it would trigger an all-out panic. 'It's full of boffins with no social skills.'

'You'll fit right in.'

'Charmer.' His upbeat mood made me chance a risky question. 'Have you seen Mum lately?'

His smile faded. 'We went on Saturday.'

'God, you're good. It's my turn this Saturday. How was she?'

'Bitchy as hell, but I managed not to hurl anything at her.'

'Admirable self-control.'

Tension eased from his face. 'Have dinner with us. Nina's made chicken casserole.'

'You don't have to ask twice. It smells heavenly.'

The evening turned out to be a pleasure. Will's first relationship for a decade fitted him like a glove, his connection with Nina stronger than ever. They even linked hands under the table as we drank coffee. It was only at the end of the evening that she volunteered the news that she had enrolled at London University to do a PhD on Romantic Poetry.

'That's wonderful,' I said. 'Can you stay on the boat?'

'We've got it for another year. My friend's contract in New York's been extended.'

Will's gaze had slipped out of focus, his arm settled round Nina's shoulders. Witnessing their happiness made me want to shut my eyes, in case I tempted fate.

'Lola says your new boyfriend's a cop,' he said.

'She's such a gossip. You met him years ago. It's Don Burns.'

'I don't remember him. Is it serious?'

'How would I know? The idea terrifies me.'

Nina leant forwards, revealing a tattoo below her jaw, a line of blue-black words too small to read. 'You deserve some happiness, Alice. Maybe it's time for a leap of faith.' Her soft French accent almost had me convinced.

I walked home across Tower Bridge reflecting on her advice. Until now I'd kept my feet firmly on the ground, and that could have been my mistake. I made up my mind to call Burns when I got home. If Will could form a relationship after watching our parents' marriage implode, it must be possible, even if it would be an uphill journey. I walked faster as I passed a pub on Tower Bridge Road, two drunks catcalling from across the street, begging me to take them home. Taking men home had never been my problem; it was letting them stay that provided the challenge – unlike for Burns, whose marriage had lasted fifteen years. By the time I reached Providence Square, the brisk stroll had blunted my fear. I listened to his Scottish burr on his answering service but hung up without leaving a message. Telling him how I felt would need to be done face to face. My thoughts switched back to work as I prepared for bed, turning Mikey's words over in my mind: 'almost there, not far now.' The phrase seemed hopelessly over-optimistic while no sign of his mother had been found.

9

The man drives through the city's empty streets, peering into the darkness. The woman sits beside him, a package balanced on her lap.

'Are you okay, sweetheart?' she asks, her tone irritating him.

'Better than yesterday.'

'Less pain?'

'For God's sake, stop nursing me. It's not your job.'

He rarely complains when his symptoms are bad; there would be no point. Most days it feels like ice water's coursing through his veins. The side effects are growing harder to ignore, weight falling from him, his skin paler than before.

'What are we going to do about the boy?' he asks.

'Leave him for now. It won't be hard to track him down; the child protection service is pretty lax. I phoned to ask where toys for Mikey Riordan should be sent, pretending to be a delivery company. They told me to ring the psychiatric care team in Southwark.'

'That's a start.'

'The borough's got forty community psychiatric nurses. Any of them could be looking after him.'

He studies her while they wait at a red light, feeling a mixture of love and fear. Her excitement fills the car like cigarette smoke, their mission keeping her rage in check.

'Park here,' she says. 'If I'm not back in ten minutes, don't wait.'

'Let me do it. I've got nothing to lose.'

The man lifts the package from her hands, kissing her to silence any protest. He drops the car keys in her lap then sets off down Newcomen Street, raising the hood of his coat. It doesn't take long to cross the hospital's quadrangle. He stands in the shadows to open the plasma bag, splashing its contents across a locked door. Blood spatters the paintwork, releasing its sour metallic smell – a reminder of the thousands of human guinea pigs killed by medical ignorance. He drops the empty pack on the step outside the pathology department: an appropriate tribute for the experts in white coats who care nothing for their patients. The dark history of the place crowds him as he hurries back to the car. His only comfort is that the murders begun here will soon be wiped clean.

10

Thursday 16 October

The consultants' conversations drifted through my office wall at 8.30 a.m. on Thursday. I made a point of greeting the early arrivals, connecting faces to names. Their replies were pleasant but wary, as if they had made a group decision to withhold judgement. It was a relief to bump into Mike Donnelly in the corridor.

'How are you settling in among us freaks and psychos?' he asked, winking at me.

'I'm finding my feet slowly.'

'Anything I can do?'

'Keep smiling, it helps no end. Can I run some ideas by you in the fullness of time?'

'My expertise is yours. All you have to do is buy me lunch.'

The grin buried inside his white beard stretched wider as I said goodbye. Once I got back to my office I studied the new printouts from HOLMES 2; the Clapham team had completed hundreds of house visits and interviews. More eyewitnesses had confirmed seeing a couple in dark winter clothes sitting on a bench in the stand of trees on the morning Clare was taken. The idea worried me; two perpetrators were always more dangerous than one. Partnerships caused rapid escalation, inciting the most extreme violence. I felt sure the computer system must be able to offer more insights, so I typed the word 'haematology' into the search engine, knowing the results could take hours to arrive.

I scanned the forensic team's report on Clare Riordan's home in the meantime. If her abductor had taken her there he must have used a key; there was no sign of a struggle, no bodily fluids or smears on the walls. The only unexplained factor was the pool of oxidised blood on her kitchen floor. Who would target a hard-working medic? No professional grievances had been raised against Clare. If one of her patients had harboured a homicidal grudge, it seemed odd that I could find no formal complaints on record. Angie had checked out the staff she'd made redundant, and all except a nurse we had yet to interview had cast-iron alibis. So far the only credible suspect was her sister, but Eleanor's volatility made her seem brittle, not strong. She gave the impression of someone who could fly apart at any moment. There was nothing in her background to explain why she would have a blood obsession, or the ability to use an extraction needle; I could imagine her lashing out in a moment of anger, but not planning a campaign of violence. If my theories were correct, she would have to be acting in partnership with someone far more cool-headed and strategic.

My concentration was broken by my printer whirring into action, the HOLMES system yielding results with unexpected speed. It had produced two outcomes, but neither looked promising at first sight. The earliest was a medical researcher called John Mendez, killed on his own doorstep in January, in what the police had recorded as a mugging gone wrong. When I studied the facts again, an odd feeling tingled across the back of my neck; his research specialism had been blood diseases. The next was a missing person's case: a doctor called Lisa Stuart had left work one night in April, never returning home. She had been working as a doctor on the haematology ward at Bart's Hospital. I called Burns immediately and asked him to run searches on both crimes. He sounded polite but sceptical, as if the idea of someone targeting blood specialists was too far-fetched, but the link felt too strong to ignore. There was no way of proving it yet, but if Riordan's abductors had taken her as part of a series, we had an even bigger job on our hands. There was a low drone of traffic behind Burns's voice when he spoke again.

'Another blood pack's been found at Guy's Hospital. This time they emptied it outside the path lab. A nurse found it a few hours ago; apparently it was spattered everywhere.'

'How much was in it?'

'A pint, like last time; Riordan's name was on the label. Are you coming to the station?'

'Not yet. I'm seeing Clare Riordan's mystery man with Tania.'

I puzzled over the information as the taxi trailed east towards Islington. Events seemed to be gathering pace. Leaving the blood of an NHS consultant inside a hospital campus had to be symbolic, as if her sins were coming home to roost. Her abductors were taunting us with cryptic clues about their obsession with blood, but the locations must mean something. So far Riordan's career history showed a clean slate, apart from a turf war with her deputy. It seemed more important than ever to find out exactly why the two other blood specialists had come to harm, to see if they were connected, professionally or personally.

The cab slowed as we passed the Union Chapel on Upper Street. The air in the café opposite smelled of melted chocolate and fresh baked bread as I reached Tania's table by the window. Her glamour always made me wonder why Burns had chosen me instead of her, especially since they'd been friends for two decades. She wore a dark green dress, cashmere or merino wool, the thin fabric hugging her curves. Her chic haircut helped her blend in with the hipsters who had turned the district into an intellectual ghetto, her face glossy with makeup and poise.

'Coffee?' she asked.

'I'll have camomile tea, I'm on overload.'

'Very disciplined.' She surveyed me again, her eyes one shade cooler than turquoise. 'Do you want an update?'

'Please.'

'We got Travers in for an interview the day we heard he'd been seeing Clare. He admitted to the affair, but there's no evidence he was near Clapham Common the morning she was taken. We took his prints at the station; the team have just found one of his thumbprints on a kitchen cupboard. I want you to assess him in his home environment, see if there's cause for concern.'

'Do you know any more about the bloodstain?'

She gave a distracted nod. 'They think Clare could have been marched to her kitchen, stabbed, then carried outside, but that normally leaves a trail. Hancock says the place is clean as a whistle apart from that one stain.'

'What about the abduction itself?'

'We still think Clare and Mikey were attacked in the copse, by The Avenue. It's a local pick-up spot. The SOCOs found needles and condoms galore on their fingertip search.'

'Pete gets all the fun, doesn't he?'

She managed a smile. 'We've tracked the getaway car at last, based on the first witness's ID. It had fake plates, caught by a road camera driving south through Wandsworth, two people in the front seat, but the image is too blurred to make out their faces. It's a standard blue Nissan hatchback, with stripes on the bonnet to make it look official. It hasn't been picked up by any other cameras, so they must have changed the plates and removed the stripes soon after that last shot.'

'At least it clears up that we're looking for two attackers. But they haven't given us much to go on. How are you bearing up anyway?'

She grimaced. 'Not bad, except Siobhan's a royal pain in the arse.'

'That's her job. She's thirteen, isn't she?' Tania only ever shared personal details about her independent-minded teenage daughter.

'She's on a curfew. If that fails I'll need a cattle prod.'

'I thought she seemed pretty mature.'

'That's her act for strangers.' She pulled a notebook from her bag. 'Here's the lowdown on Sam Travers: he's forty-two, a freelance film-maker. He met Clare in the first week of January when he was making a documentary about the health service. He's been married eight years to a German woman, Isabel, who runs a media agency nearby, no kids.'

'What do you make of him?'

'I won't prejudice you.' A look of distaste crossed her face. 'He says he was working at home when Clare was taken. His wife's confirmed it, but they could be protecting each other.'

The entrance to Sam Travers's house was between a bookshop and a vintage clothes store. When I pressed the buzzer the lock clicked loudly and a male voice summoned us to the first floor. Travers met us on the landing, but his home made a bigger impression than its owner. He looked like a typical media executive, blond with a neat beard, dressed in tight jeans, brogues, and a tailored shirt. He seemed to be aiming for an intellectual look, wearing heavy-framed glasses and an aloof expression. His living room had pale blue walls, so much light flooding the space it felt as if autumn had been replaced by summer; every piece of furniture was positioned to best effect, an abstract glass sculpture glowing on the mantelpiece. The computer screen on his table showed a man sprinting

71

down an alleyway, buildings behind him exploding in flames. The sequence kept repeating in the corner of my eye as I perched on the edge of a sofa. Sam Travers looked irritated, as if we'd interrupted a productive morning's work.

'I can only spare half an hour, I'm afraid. There's a meeting I have to attend.'

'We won't take long,' I replied. 'Would you mind talking me through your relationship with Clare Riordan?'

'I interviewed her for one of my films. We had lunch, or met at her house sometimes. It was casual. She only came here once, to dinner with friends. Isabel didn't need to know about it.'

'How do you mean?'

He rolled his shoulders. 'Even open marriages have rules; it's disrespectful to rub your partner's face in it. Isabel probably protects me the same way.'

'But your wife knows about the affair now?'

'How could I hide it? The police called here to take me to the station.'

'Is your wife at work today?'

He nodded. 'Her office is round the corner on Liverpool Road.'

'And she was out the morning Clare was abducted?'

'Isabel was staying with friends. She got back around ten a.m.'

'Forgive me for saying this, Mr Travers, but you don't seem very concerned about Clare's situation. Why didn't you report your relationship as soon as she went missing?'

'Of course I'm concerned.' His expression hardened. 'But we haven't seen much of each other lately. She was a vulnerable person. If I'd known that, I'd never have got involved.'

'How do you mean?'

'Clare's sister bullied her, and she had trouble at work. She seemed terrified of losing her job.'

'Did she say why?'

'To be honest, I didn't ask.'

When I looked up from my notes, Sam Travers's attention had been diverted. He might have been talking about Clare Riordan, but his gaze lingered on Tania's hourglass figure. His distraction allowed me to glance around his living room. A large black and white photo showed a stunning platinum blonde with a beaming smile twined around him in a flutter of confetti. Travers's expression was neutral, as if his wedding day was no reason to lose his cool. After a few more questions, we took our leave and returned to Tania's car.

'Either he's suppressing his feelings or he's genuinely cold,' I said. 'Open marriages only suit people who can compartmentalise their emotions. His body language was tense, though. He's definitely hiding something and, like you said, his wife could be covering for him.'

Tania gave a loud sigh. 'She doesn't seem the type to lie. Isabel wept buckets when she found out he had a mistress; it's bollocks about their marriage being open.'

'It's interesting that he said Riordan was having work problems. We know she was unpopular with a few colleagues. Maybe a case of medical negligence came back to haunt her.'

'Her record's clean, but I'll check her employment history again.'

'HOLMES 2 brought up a murder and a missing person case earlier this year, both blood specialists. I gave Don the names.'

Her eyes widened. 'You think it's a series?'

'It's possible. With the blood link it'd be a big coincidence if there was no connection at all, wouldn't it?'

Tania offered her usual crisp nod when I said goodbye. It would be easy to imagine her with someone like Travers, elegant and polished, unwilling to let emotions break the surface. But I felt certain Tania was grappling with her passions, while his were neatly locked away.

I spent the rest of the day at the FPU writing up assessments, scheduling meetings and working on my profile report. Eleanor Riordan and Sam Travers made very different case studies; Clare Riordan's estranged sister demonstrated a high degree of agitation, while her lover seemed unnaturally calm. They were both smart enough to conduct a well-organised abduction with its grim calling card. It was too early to rule either of them out of the investigation, although her sister seemed the best fit, given their antagonism ever since childhood. If Travers had been honest about the affair being casual, only Eleanor had a powerful enough motive to trigger an attack. But Riordan's abduction could be the latest in a series, so I needed to discover why either of them would want to hurt other blood specialists.

I drove to the safe house slowly, making an effort to clear my head. It was important to seem relaxed for Mikey's sake. His trauma was deep enough without absorbing anyone else's concerns. It was six p.m. when I finally relieved Gurpreet, the concern on his face increasing my liking for him.

'Call me later,' he said. 'I'll come back if you need me.'

'You deserve a night off, Gurpreet. We'll be fine.'

It was obvious that he'd grown close to Mikey, despite the child's outbursts. He'd done well on a professional level too, emailing me daily case notes. The boy's hyper-arousal was still intense: loud noises, sudden movement and changes to his routine induced a state of panic. But there were small signs of improvement. His attention span had lengthened, nonverbal communication increasing. He was starting to respond to questions by nodding or shaking his head. But the future could still go either way: he might slip into a silence which lasted months, or recover fully from the tsunami of shock that had crashed over him. I took a deep breath before tapping on the living-room door. Mikey lay on the floor watching the third *Spider-Man* movie.

'Feel like cooking?' I asked. 'I'll be in the kitchen.'

He stole into the room too quietly for me to hear. His jeans and T-shirt looked as if they'd been borrowed from an older boy, swamping his thin frame. When I smiled at him the corners of his mouth quirked upwards for the first time, so I took a chance.

'If you ever want a hug, that would be fine. Even adults need them sometimes.' He stayed rooted to the spot. 'But right now, I could use a kitchen helper. Can you find a pan for the spaghetti?'

It was clear Denise Thorpe had been right about Mikey enjoying time in the kitchen with his mum. He chopped tomatoes and lettuce for salad and stirred the ragù sauce until it came to the boil. I kept up a steady flow of talk, telling him about where I'd grown up and places I'd gone on holiday, familiarity helping him relax. When we sat down to eat he managed a bigger meal than last time, but still looked haunted, his eyes never focusing on anything for long. It was difficult to judge how much of my monologue he'd heard.

Clare Riordan had trained her son so well that even on autopilot he remembered kitchen etiquette. He piled his plate and cutlery into the dishwasher, eyes still glassy. We spent the evening playing card games. A couple of times his lips formed shapes, but no words emerged. I made sure that he followed Gurpreet's routine, sending him off for a bath at nine o'clock. When I checked on him again he was in his room, the single bed swamping him, nightlight burning at his side.

'Sleepy?' I asked.

'Not far now,' he murmured.

His thin arms lay on top of the duvet and I let my hand settle on his wrist, but his expression was unchanged. I wanted to ask what he meant, but there was no point. He was trapped in a daydream too absorbing to penetrate.

The living room felt even more smothering when I got back downstairs. I twisted the key to open the French window and stepped outside. The garden was in darkness, apart from a glow of streetlight above the fence. The space felt almost as claustrophobic as the house, with tree ferns and cordylines crowding the lawn, the air filled with the odour of rotting leaves. If the place were mine, I'd have uprooted most of the undergrowth to give myself breathing space. The only sounds I could hear were the city's murmur of traffic, someone laughing in the distance, and branches shifting in the breeze. I can't explain why the garden spooked me, apart from its dense shadows; the stress of the case was making my nerves jangle. I checked every door and window was locked when I got back inside, but the sight of the squad car parked by the porch restored my calm. A middle-aged uniform with a morose expression sat inside the vehicle; no one could approach the building without him raising the alarm.

It was eleven thirty when I put my head round Mikey's door again. I switched off his bedside light, reassured by the slow regularity of his breathing. Knowing that he was fast asleep helped me relax when I finally lay down, even though the midnight-blue walls of the bedroom made me homesick for the pale decor of my flat.

A loud noise woke me just after two a.m. I flung on my bathrobe and raced across the landing towards the penetrating scream that came from Mikey's room. He was sitting up in bed, releasing a wail of protest, eyes staring. I sat on the bed to hold him. At first he tried to pull away, then stopped fighting, his thin arms locking round my waist.

'You're safe, sweetheart.' When I stroked his forehead, panic had plastered his hair to his skin. 'What did you dream?'

His face pressed against my shoulder, jaw clicking like a rusted hinge. 'I left her there,' he whispered.

'You had no choice, Mikey. Can you say what happened next?'

I carried on holding him, fighting my urge to bombard him with questions. He had already slipped behind his wall of silence and any attempt to probe could make him retreat permanently; after a while his arms slackened and I smoothed his covers again, leaving the light burning. The long embrace might have calmed him, but it had the opposite effect on me. I lay in the dark, fretting about what would happen if his mother was never found.

II

Friday 17 October

I was washing strawberries for breakfast when Mikey appeared in the kitchen at eight a.m., still in his pyjamas. I put my arm round his shoulder to give him a gentle squeeze.

'Morning, sweetheart. Do you want cereal with these?'

He nestled closer. Clearly it was physical reassurance he'd wanted, not food. He burrowed against me as I switched off the tap with my free hand and pulled him closer for a hug. It made sense that he would connect with a female carer more easily than a man, just as Christine had predicted; he'd lived alone with his mother since he was five, his father's presence a distant memory. It took a conscious effort to retain my professionalism. My work as a psychologist had taught me that compassion was necessary but empathy was pointless. Letting your heart bleed resulted in poor judgements, yet I couldn't suppress my desire to spring Mikey from the confines of the safe house and care for him in my flat.

The boy's face blanched as I prepared to leave when Gurpreet arrived. Maybe he expected me to vanish permanently, like his parents, one by one. He retreated to his usual position in the living room, and I saw that he was clutching the London *A–Z* that had been lying on the hall table. I crouched in front of him but he wouldn't meet my eye.

'I'll be back tomorrow, I promise.'

He dropped his gaze to the book, keeping his face averted. After my handover meeting with Gurpreet, I escaped into the street, thoughts churning. I gazed back at the safe house. While Clare Riordan's son was walled inside its airless rooms, someone was holding her captive, harvesting blood at regular intervals. And that was the best-case scenario. She might already be dead. Although I sensed that her abductor was enjoying the chase too much to finish it soon. What had Riordan done to warrant that kind of punishment? The act seemed loaded with symbolism, too organised for a random act of sadism, and although the MO altered with each attack, the abduction could be part of a campaign. But the attack on Riordan differed from the quick slaughter of John Mendez. Her suffering was so protracted, it still made me believe that she was connected to her abductors in some way, the vengeance far more personal.

Angie was waiting for me at Belsize Park Tube at ten thirty, her pixie-like face avid as she checked messages on her phone. During the years we'd worked together, I'd never seen her do anything by half measures. I'd asked to meet the only member of staff Riordan had sacked from her department at the Royal Free, who lacked a convincing alibi: her name was Moira Fitzgerald, single, thirty years old. My heart sank when I saw the skyscraper that housed her apartment. It was a featureless concrete rectangle, without balconies or gardens to soften its hard edges. Living there would have forced me to pack my bags and leave London. The lifts were out of order, forcing us to walk to the eighth floor.

'I should renew my gym membership,' Angie panted.

The woman who answered the door seemed to be bouncing with more physical energy than she could contain, like a gymnast or ballet dancer. Moira Fitzgerald was medium height, slender, shifting from foot to foot as she welcomed us with an overstretched smile. She was pretty, with sable-coloured hair that fell past her shoulders, straight as rain. Her

Irish accent gave her statements a gentle lilt as she led us inside. Her bedsit was so minute that her desk pressed against her narrow single bed, which seemed to double as a settee; a TV balanced precariously on top of a bookshelf. The three of us were almost touching elbows as we squeezed round the table in her kitchenette.

'Is this about Clare?' Her smile dimmed for the first time.

I nodded. 'You'll have heard that she's missing. We're tracing people who know her to see if they can shed light on her disappearance.'

'I haven't seen her all year. To be honest, I haven't got much to say.'

Angie sat forwards in her seat. 'How do you mean?'

Moira's blue eyes hardened. 'I gave up my job at Bart's to be senior nurse clinician in her department. It was the job I'd always wanted. After six months she gave me a great appraisal, all smiles and congratulations, then weeks later she fired me.'

'Did she explain why?'

'Budget cuts, of course, but it was the way she did it. I was out of her office in five minutes flat, no apologies.' Her cheeks reddened as she spoke.

'That sounds tough,' Angie commented.

'I complained but the HR guys took her side. I've been doing agency work ever since; the hours are crap and there's no security. Senior nursing vacancies are like needles in a haystack.' Fitzgerald's voice had lost its softness, tone sour enough to curdle milk.

'Can you think of a reason why Clare would be taken?' I asked.

'She treats people like dirt. Maybe that pissed someone off.' Her eyes fizzed with anger, but I could see she was holding her feelings in check. 'Of course I'm sorry about what's happened, but she got a kick out of hurting me, I could tell.'

I gave a slow nod, then glanced around the small room. 'Have you always lived here alone, Moira?'

She released a huff of laughter. 'Where would I put a flatmate? That's another story. I was so down about losing my job, my boyfriend chucked me.'

The air in the small room resonated with ill feeling. For once Angie fell silent, clearly more interested in observing the nurse's reactions than asking questions. Fitzgerald seemed so upset by her redundancy that the events might have happened yesterday, rather than a year before. When I quizzed her about her alibi, the nurse claimed that she had been filling out a job application at home at the time of Riordan's abduction.

Angie reserved her comments until we reached the landing. 'Not Clare's number one fan, is she?'

'She took away her dream job. Moira seems to blame Riordan for her relationship failing too.' When I gazed down from the landing, a bird's-eye view of the compound of the Royal Free was visible two blocks away. Confronting her former workplace every time she stepped outside must be keeping the nurse's anger alive.

'Do you think she's upset enough to hurt someone?' Angie asked as we trotted back down the stairs.

'It's possible, but this could be part of a series. If it is, we need to know if she'd met Lisa Stuart and John Mendez.'

'I'll do some digging.'

Angie said a quick goodbye before racing back to her car. I set off for the FPU at a slower pace, mulling over Fitzgerald's comments. Despite her bitterness it seemed unlikely that a nurse would have her former boss abducted simply because she'd been sacked, but it threw a new light on Riordan's behaviour. It sounded as if she could be tyrannical, making enemies among those she ruled, yet able to impress her seniors.

*   *   *

Burns was waiting for me at Butler's Wharf at nine that evening, sitting outside the Brewhouse, gazing vacantly ahead, as though he lacked the strength to stand.

'Feed me,' he said. 'Then get me drunk and seduce me in the back of a cab.'

'All that in one evening?'

We ended up in a Turkish restaurant on Borough High Street, eating grilled halloumi, followed by marinaded lamb, with a bottle of house red. I sat beside him in the narrow booth, a candle guttering on the table.

'Tell me what's happened.'

He took a slug of wine. 'My lot have been chasing those names you found, but it's not conclusive. Mendez's attack looks like an opportunistic mugging – knife wound to the heart, phone and laptop stolen. Lisa Stuart was last seen cycling home from work, around ten p.m. None of her credit cards have been used since. She's probably dead but hasn't been found.'

'There must be a link, Don.'

'The three of them trained at different hospitals. Mendez and Stuart both worked at Bart's, but not at the same time. They didn't attend the same conferences or training courses. We're looking at their social lives: hobbies, sports clubs, holidays. So far, nothing matches.'

'Three blood doctors being attacked in one city in a ten-month period can't be a coincidence.'

'Thousands of violent assaults happen here every year.' Burns shrugged. 'What did you think of the nurse Riordan sacked?'

'Angry as hell, but that's not enough to make her a credible suspect. She seems too isolated to be able to convince anyone to help her drag Clare into the getaway car.'

'She was at Bart's the same time as Lisa Stuart. Angie's looking into it.'

'I need to see the primary evidence in Mendez's and Stuart's crime files.'

'The archive's delivering it bright and early Sunday morning.' His frown deepened. 'Denise Thorpe pitched up at the station today, wanting access to the Riordan boy. The woman's relentless.'

I thought of Clare's friend's odd house with its view across the cemetery. 'That's understandable. If Lola went missing, I'd want Neve with me. She's under a lot of stress.'

'She gives me the creeps, but her alibi checks out and so does her husband's. They were at her mum's care home early on the morning of the abduction. Their names are in the visitors' book, and a nurse saw them arrive.'

'I'm more concerned about Sam Travers.'

'Pete's team are doing an extended search at his house. He was lying about not seeing much of Clare; one of her neighbours says his car was outside her house several times a week. His documentary on the health service put him in contact with loads of medics. He was tracking staff at five different hospitals.'

'So he could have met Mendez and Stuart?'

'If he did, there's no record.'

'Let me interview him again,' I said. 'If Clare rejected him, he's got the biggest motive.'

'I'll set it up.' Burns rubbed his hand across his jaw. 'So far our earliest sighting of the kid is from a CCTV camera on Walworth Road at midday, staggering like he was drunk.'

'Or drugged?'

'Whatever they gave him had cleared his system by the time he was examined.' He pushed his plate away. 'Can we take a break, just for half an hour?'

'You want to make small talk with all this going on?'

'Work doesn't stop when we down tools,' he said firmly. 'My team are going flat out.'

'Have you always been so rational?'

'I'm a dour Scot, remember? Tell me your secrets, Alice.'

'You know them all.'

'I don't have a clue about your relationships before me.'

'And that bothers you?' I took a sip of wine. 'You want details.'

'I'm trying to understand you.'

'Why don't you go first?'

His smile reappeared. 'Lorraine Salmond asked me out in year seven, then broke my heart a month later. I dated a girl at sixth-form college, but that ended in tears when I left for art school. After a few years of short flings Julie came along, when I was a newly qualified cop.'

'She's the first girl you fell for?'

'I met her at a party, she had the loudest laugh in the room.' He stared down at his empty plate. 'Twelve good years, then it fell apart.'

'Did Lorraine Salmond leave a mark?'

'God, yeah. The little cow dumped me on my twelfth birthday.' He drummed his fingers on the table. 'Your turn, Alice, stop evading.'

I rolled my eyes. 'Nothing serious until med school, then a doctor, dentist and a surgeon in quick succession. I spent a while alone, then there was a dance teacher and a defrocked priest. The rest you know.' I put down my wine glass. 'How did I let the surgeon get away? He had navy blue eyes and played the piano beautifully.'

'No one has navy blue eyes.'

'He did.'

'Did he break your heart?'

I shook my head. 'It's still intact.'

He gaped at me. 'You've never been in love?'

I leant back in my chair. 'How much do you know about relationship psychology?'

'Bugger all, obviously.' He leaned closer, eyes tracing my mouth.

'Our intimacy patterns are fixed by age seven. If the blueprint's faulty, it takes work to correct it.'

'Your parents had a bad marriage?'

'With bells on.'

His fingers settled on my wrist. 'But you're different. You like mending people.'

'Patterns repeat themselves, don't they?'

'Not if you work at it.'

'Why not read the warning signs, Don? I'm not a great bet.'

'That's for me to decide. I'd settle for a night with you in my bed instead of watching you leave.'

I bit my lip. 'It's not deliberate, but you're right. Sex is the easy part.'

'How long was your last relationship?'

'Three weeks.'

'You don't scare me, Alice.' His expression had changed: more understanding than desire, his frustration mellowing.

'I feel safe with you, but it's no guarantee.'

'Maybe your pattern's changing.' He tucked a strand of hair behind my ear. 'Come and meet my boys tomorrow night. They're staying at mine.'

'I'll be at the safe house.'

His face darkened. 'You're obsessed by that kid.'

'I'm just doing my job. Everyone's let him down except his mum, and now she's gone too.'

Burns stayed silent, probably because he knew how I'd react to professional advice. At midnight we split the bill then he walked me home. He declined my offer of coffee, which surprised me. Maybe it angered him that Mikey's welfare was my top priority, or he couldn't face the solitary walk home after making love. When I closed the curtains he was still standing on the pavement, huge and immovable, gazing up at my window. His stillness seemed to prove that he'd finally understood the challenge that lay ahead.

12

At midnight the couple stand outside the lab, holding hands, the woman's head resting on the man's shoulder, at peace for once.

'I wish we could stay like this,' the man says.

'Me too, but we can't rest properly until it's done.'

The man's exhaustion resonates in his sigh when she unlocks the door and flicks on the lights. Clare Riordan is still bound to the chair, gag clamped between her teeth. The woman ignores her, turning on the radio and setting to work, swabbing the laboratory floor with bleach. When she glances over, the man is sitting on the step, head bowed. The room has an abattoir smell, fetid and dirty. Ammonia can't remove its taste from the air. The woman focuses on the song playing on the radio; a girl singing something trite about love and money. Her muscles tense when the news bulletin starts.

'Here it comes,' she murmurs, turning up the volume.

The announcer explains that more troops are being sent to the Middle East, unemployment figures falling again.

'Clare Riordan, a consultant from London's Royal Free Hospital, is still missing. This afternoon hundreds of volunteers conducted another search of Clapham Common. The police want to hear from anyone who has seen Dr Riordan since she went missing on the eleventh of October. They have described her abduction as a senseless act of violence against an innocent victim.'

'Innocent?' The woman silences the radio with a jab of her finger. 'She's hurt every blood patient in the land.'

'Anger won't get us anywhere,' the man says quietly.

'It brought us here.' She stares back at him. 'How will you cope with all the rest?'

'I'm stronger than I look.'

'That's not true. I'll finish this, then we can leave.' She turns to Riordan. 'Did you hear that, Clare? Another night in the dark. Want me to hang you from the ceiling again?'

The doctor's body writhes like a line-caught fish, a dull moan spilling through her gag.

'Give us a name. Then you can sleep in peace.'

Clare shakes her head violently, but when the pulley tightens she lets out a long whimper and the woman loosens the rag that stifles her.

'Jordan Adebayo,' she whispers, screwing her eyes shut.

The woman jerks the material back into place, then picks up a scalpel. 'Now I can finish her, can't I?'

'She may be lying; we need her alive until we've checked him out.'

'Always forward-planning, aren't you?'

She drops the blade back into the drawer with a sense of disappointment, but breaking Riordan's will has restored her good mood. She swabs the last patch of blood from the floor, humming as the water darkens to the colour of rust.

13

Saturday 18 October

Saturday began with a trip along the river. I caught a bus boat to Greenwich to see my mother, instead of driving south through the congested suburbs. It allowed me to admire the old warehouses and Hawksmoor churches lining the riverside. The air was bracing when I climbed the steep hill through Greenwich Park to Blackheath, admiring avenues of chestnut trees that had been stripped of their leaves, stark branches reaching for the sky. Tension was knotting in my stomach at the prospect of seeing my mother for the first time in two weeks. I took a detour past the Paragon, to check out Eleanor Riordan's address. The Georgian crescent was beautifully preserved; all it needed was horse-drawn carriages and women promenading in long gowns for time to slip back two centuries. I tried to imagine why someone who owned an apartment in such a stunning piece of real estate would quibble over a house in Clapham. The lawsuit seemed to be more about sibling rivalry than financial need. It struck me as unlikely that Eleanor would turn murderous over a lawsuit, but childhood jealousy could be a strong enough motive, no matter how comfortable her current life seemed.

It took my mother ages to answer the doorbell. I heard the slow drag of her feet on the stairs as she made her way down from her flat. When she finally appeared she looked immaculate, making me wonder how much time she'd needed to put on her smart grey skirt and cashmere twinset. I felt a tug of sympathy for her battling spirit. Small tasks like dressing and bathing must present major challenges now. She flinched as I kissed her cheek.

'Why not use the stairlift, Mum?'

'I prefer being on my feet. It's the only exercise I get.'

I watched her toil back to the landing. Parkinson's might have stolen her physical strength, but her stubbornness was undimmed. She looked smug as she settled into her armchair, as if the climb proved she was invincible.

'Want some tea?' I asked. 'I've brought carrot cake.'

Her tremor was pronounced as she lifted her cup, drops slopping back into the saucer. She assessed me coolly as I took a bite of cake.

'It's good to see you eating, Alice.'

'I always do. If I stopped running I'd be the size of a bus.'

'You're skin and bone, darling. Have you been overworking?'

I took a deep breath. 'I'm fine, honestly.'

'Tell me what you've been up to.'

'I've got an interesting case. Did you hear about the woman going missing on Clapham Common? I'm helping her son.'

'The poor creature.' Her eyes widened. 'You'll never cure that monster, if you find him. He's beyond help.'

'We can't ignore people like him, Mum. They still exist.'

'Leave it to some other fool.'

I shrugged. 'I'm not cut out to be a librarian like you.'

A rare look of nostalgia crossed her face. 'I still remember how the place smelled: floor polish, dust and old books. Someone should make it into a room fragrance.'

'I prefer French lavender.'

My mother spent the rest of the morning on acerbic complaints. Her assistant Elise visited daily, but remained monosyllabic, which was a source of disappointment. She seemed to expect witty repartee from her hard-pressed helper. At least Mum was still managing to attend concerts and lunches with friends, even though she had to travel everywhere by taxi.

'Can I do anything before I go?'

Her grey eyes settled on my face. 'Tell me you've found a new boyfriend.'

'I have actually. We've been together a few months.'

'What does he do?'

'He's in the police.'

She gave me a look of mock despair. 'I was hoping for a stockbroker. But you like him, do you?'

'More than I realised.'

'Then you'll make it work, darling.' Her shrewd eyes fixed on my face. 'Bad choices aren't hereditary.'

I was superstitious enough to feel spooked. Blessings from my mother were so rare that I knew she was being sincere, but how to file them away was another matter. For once she accepted my farewell embrace without pulling away.

I stood with Gurpreet in the garden of the safe house that afternoon while Mikey napped on the sofa. Fading afternoon light filtered through the copper beeches as he lit a cigarette.

'My wife thinks I quit months ago.'

'It's okay, I won't blow the whistle.' I watched him take a long drag. 'How's Mikey been?'

'Missing you, I think. It's amazing how fast you've bonded.'

'He's pining for his mother; transference was inevitable.'

He nodded. 'Still no eye contact, and the smallest noise spooks him. In an ordinary case I'd suggest Ritalin.'

'Tranquillisers would suppress his memories. He'll feel better when he shares them; I'll work with him again today.'

'Be careful.' Gurpreet turned to face me. 'One push could send him over the edge.'

'Are you like this with your own kids?'

'Like what?'

'Overprotective.'

He looked embarrassed. 'My daughter calls me the Rottweiler.'

'You're doing a brilliant job, but maybe you should take a step back.'

'Easier said than done, doc.' Gurpreet gave me a meaningful look then ground out his cigarette with the heel of his shoe.

I studied the garden again before returning indoors. Even in daylight it looked ominous. Trees cast deep shadows into every corner; shoulder-high plants had proliferated until no space was left, their leaves brushing my face as I walked back to the house.

After Gurpreet went home I tried to entice Mikey from his room, but offers of card games or ice cream fell flat.

'How about baking? We could make cookies.'

He inspected me through the crack in the door, his nod of agreement almost imperceptible. It interested me that he relaxed in the kitchen's familiar terrain, quietly weighing ingredients, then pouring them into the mixing bowl.

'You're good at this. Maybe you should cook every meal from now on.' I offered a wide smile. 'I think you're brave. You know that, don't you?'

His face brightened, then he busied himself with the biscuits. It was good to see him absorbed in cutting out elaborate shapes. Thirty minutes later we sat on the sofa to sample them with glasses of milk.

'Not bad,' I commented. 'Next time let's try chocolate chips.'

The boy didn't reply. He'd only eaten one cookie when he snuggled closer, his head resting on my shoulder, small hands clutched in his lap. I let my cheek rest on the crown of his head.

'We could watch TV, but you'll feel better if you say what's wrong.'

His silence lasted so long it seemed set in stone, but his thin voice took me by surprise. 'I left her.'

'You had no choice, Mikey. It was the right thing to do. Did you see their faces?'

He burrowed into my side so hard it felt like he was trying to climb into my ribcage. When I looked down, the muscles in his jaw were in spasm, bones locking tight.

'Okay, sweetheart. That's enough remembering for tonight.'

I lost track of how much junk TV we watched: a repeat of *Alias Smith and Jones, Supermarket Sweep* and *DIY SOS*. He didn't seem to care, so long as my arm stayed around his shoulders. I don't know why the closeness left me raw. After all, I was only following standard guidance in psychology care manuals for supporting traumatised children. Specialists stressed the value of touch to provide comfort until the child stabilised. It seemed ironic that I'd advised Gurpreet to ease back, only to find my own professional boundaries blown apart. Maybe it was just bad timing. I was wrestling with feelings for Burns, my biological clock ticking. Perhaps that explained why this child clinging to me felt like the most natural thing in the world.

It took some coaxing to get Mikey through his night-time routine. When I sat on the edge of his bed to say goodnight, he looked so exhausted his skin was translucent, but his eyes fixed on me as I touched his wrist.

'You did great today, sunshine. I'm proud of you.'

I stayed with him until he drifted into sleep.

I considered calling Burns when I got back to the lounge, but that would only have brought more confusion, so I flipped open my laptop and focused on work. Spending so much time with Mikey was turning my drive to find his mother into an obsession. I trawled for information about the sites where her blood had been left, but the locations seemed to have no uniting theme. All I had to go on was Riordan's abduction, her sister's well-documented dislike, and her lover's tendency to lie. I was still no nearer understanding how the case linked to the two previous attacks, if indeed it did. I rose to my feet and escaped on to the patio, inhaling the city's autumnal smell of traffic fumes, bonfires and decay. I took some deep breaths then went back inside, locking the door tightly.

Mikey's call woke me again at three a.m.; a racking scream that made my heart race. This time he made no effort to hold back. Tears spilled from him, the sobs deep enough to jolt his whole body.

'That's the way,' I said, rubbing his back. 'Better out than in.'

He cried himself back to sleep, but his distress left me shaken. Even though his first release of emotion had been a breakthrough, I sat at the kitchen table, staring at the solid darkness outside, struggling to pull my feelings back under control.

14

The man stands outside the door of the lab, breathing the damp air, eyes fixed on the ground. When the woman joins him he can read the anger in her face.

'We'll have to make her eat more tonight,' he says.

'Who cares if she starves? We don't owe her anything, the scales are tipping in our favour.'

'How did we get here? It's so much more than we planned.'

Her hollow stare unnerves him. 'I want them all dead, finishing with the Minister for Health, then we can release a statement. We agreed to get justice, by showing they're traitors. Clare should suffer most for breaking her promise.'

'You said we'd only kill three.'

'They committed mass murder. Why should any of them survive?'

'We need Clare alive for the next week at least.'

'Why? She's named the next victim.'

He holds her gaze, even though the conversation's a losing battle. 'Jordan Adebayo's at a conference in France; he may not talk when we catch him. You have to be patient.'

'They killed thousands, remember? It's an eye for an eye.'

Her comment hits a raw nerve. 'Biblical sayings don't convince me any more.'

'Yet you still go to Mass when you feel penitent.'

He turns away; for the first time her anger frightens him. He's longing to put his arms round her, but knows she'd brush him off. When did he lose the ability to comfort her?

Riordan is awake when they go inside, muscles in her cheeks twitching as her eyes fly open. The man watches the woman approach the chair, her voice harsh.

'We'll bring your boy here soon, if you don't give us another name.'

Clare's pale brown eyes roll back, arms thrashing against their constraints.

'Don't goad her,' the man says quietly. 'She's the one suffering now.'

'Stop protecting her.' Grim-faced, she fills a syringe with transparent liquid.

Panic rises in his chest. 'What's that?'

'Interferon. She needs some of her own medicine.'

'Where did you get it?'

'I bought it, of course.'

'That much could kill her.'

She ignores him, tapping the needle and shooting droplets of liquid into the air, then staring into her victim's eyes. 'Tell me another name, Clare, or you'll get the lot.'

The man waits for Riordan to speak, but her jaw is locked tight around her gag. The needle hovers above her face for an instant before its sharp tip plunges down.

15

I reached the station early on Sunday morning. A few journalists were loitering on the steps, hoping for scraps of information, but I skirted round them. The incident room was already a hive of activity, a dozen detectives staring at their computers, or babbling into their phones. Burns had cancelled weekend breaks and holiday leave until further notice. The evidence board was plastered with photos, Post-it notes, and a timeline showing each stage of the investigation. It looked like every detail was being chased. The plasma bags that held Riordan's blood were NHS standard issue, and could have been stolen from any medical centre in the past year. Reports had been filed on possible sightings of Riordan, witness statements, the make and model of the getaway car. The team were hunched over their desks, the air humming with frustration.

Burns was nowhere to be seen, but the evidence from the Stuart and Mendez cases had been placed in a side room, as promised. The scale of the task hit home when I scanned the box files stacked to the ceiling along the facing wall. The witness statements alone would take days to sift. I settled myself at the desk, scanning the overview report from the first case: John Mendez, a researcher at the Institute for Biomedical Science, had been stabbed in January, after an evening out with friends. The autopsy report made me wince; his death would have been quick but agonising, a knife wound to the left ventricle of his heart. I flicked forwards and found the crime scene photos. Mendez looked close to retirement age, face bleached white by the arc light, sprawled across the doorstep of his house in Chiswick. But it was the second photo that stopped me in my tracks. On the doorstep beside a pool of blood, someone had chalked a white teardrop beside a black one. I stared at the image again, trying to remember where I'd seen the marks before. It must have taken me a full minute to realise that they matched the sign pinned to the tree where Riordan had been taken. I reached for Lisa Stuart's file, riffling through the papers until I found pictures of her flat, two days after her disappearance.

'Snap.' The word was followed by a sigh of relief.

The same black and white marks had been painted on the bricks beside Stuart's front door. Definitive proof at last that the killers had left exactly the same calling card.

I rushed to the incident room to show Angie my find, but she was immersed in a phone conversation, spiky red hair standing up in tufts, as if she'd been dragging her hands through it. She turned to me when the call ended.

'What it is, Alice? You look like you've seen a ghost.'

'They're leaving a signature at every crime scene.'

'So it's a series,' she muttered, when I showed her the photos. 'We just heard that more blood's been found outside St George's Medical School. CCTV caught an unidentified male crossing the car park at three a.m.'

'They're getting bolder. St George's is even more secure than Guy's.'

The incident room was erupting at the news of another blood deposit. I hurried back to the office to gather my thoughts. When I peered out of the window, cars were moving down St Pancras Way at a snail's pace, the pedestrians making faster progress. Clare Riordan's abductors were using a symbolic language that I needed to decode fast, the haematologist's blood their chosen form of communication. The hospital packs clearly had a symbolic value, otherwise they'd be using one of the millions of plastic bottles that clogged the city's recycling bins. The locations must have a meaning too: Bishopsgate, Guy's Hospital's pathology department, and now a medical school. Facts churned through my head without forming a coherent sequence. I was acting more on impulse than judgement as I switched on my computer and searched the Internet again. It's hard to explain the prickling feeling that crossed the backs of my hands when I saw that St George's Hospital had been a pioneering centre for early blood transfusions. The breakthrough was highlighted on the webpage as if it was the organisation's biggest achievement.

It was clear I needed expert help to find the link between the three locations, but I steeled myself before calling the Home Office pathologist, Fiona Lindstrop. Her spiky brand of professionalism had appealed to me when we'd worked together before, but her temper was legendary. There was every chance she'd slam the phone down on me for disturbing her weekend.

'Of course I remember you,' she snapped. 'You were very attentive when you watched my autopsies.'

'I could use some help, Professor Lindstrop.'

'With a pathology matter?'

'I'm looking for an expert on the history of blood treatments.'

She hummed loudly at the end of the line. 'Try the Wellcome Trust Centre for the History of Medicine. The place is heaving with overpaid academics.'

'I knew you'd have the answer. Thanks for your time.' I planned to end the call fast, before her ill humour surfaced.

'Look me up tomorrow if you're visiting. I've got information on the Riordan case.'

I spent the rest of the morning sifting evidence, but found no further links between the Stuart and Mendez cases, apart from the marks left at each crime scene. At one o'clock Burns put his head round the office door, his smile so slow to arrive that it must have lain dormant for hours. He was clutching the crime scene photos in his hand.

'I've got someone hunting for the signature online. What do you think it means?'

I stared at the black and white marks again. 'They look like inverted commas. It may just be a random mark they've chosen, like a graffiti tag.'

'At least we know that a couple are attacking and killing blood specialists. It's more than we had before.'

'Is there any news about Moira Fitzgerald?'

Burns rubbed his eyes, as if he was having trouble remembering the irate nurse Riordan had sacked. 'Angie says she's got a good professional record; she and Lisa Stuart worked in different buildings at Bart's. They probably never met.'

A squad car was waiting by the back entrance, but I was still thinking of Moira Fitzgerald; her anger about her unfair dismissal had bubbled so near the surface that it would have been unwise to light a match in her small flat. But I shelved my concerns as we set off to see Clare Riordan's boss. Dr Dawn Coleman, Head of Clinical Practice at the Royal Free, had agreed to meet us at her home. Burns seemed preoccupied, even though his hand locked round mine when we shared the back seat. He gazed out of the window at the overcast sky, giving me time to consider my profile report. Patterns were beginning to form; the case held a balance between spontaneous violence and meticulous planning. I felt almost certain we were looking at two distinct personality types, idiosyncrasies emerging more clearly with each crime. One was planning the campaign, leaving their monochrome signature at each scene. The other was far wilder, with enough nerve to stab a six-foot-tall man straight through the heart. The division of roles fitted the prototype for serial-killing partnerships, which always included a leader and a follower; one member aggressively active, the other submissive. Ninety per cent of violent couples were sexual partners – only a small minority of partnership killings were carried out by friends or siblings.

The squad car pulled up outside a tall Georgian house in Belsize Park. Dr Coleman lived within walking distance of her hospital, but her home was dilapidated. Ribbons of dark green paint hung from the front door, flanked by sash windows desperate for an overhaul. The woman who answered the door was around fifty, with a curvy figure and a genuine smile. She had one of those tousled blonde haircuts that never go out of fashion; she was wearing faded jeans and a lime-green T-shirt spattered with white paint.

'Forgive the mess,' she said, beaming at us. 'Welcome to chaos.'

'It's a great place,' Burns commented. 'High ceilings and plenty of character.'

'That's what drew me, but I could be mad. We've been working flat out since we arrived two months ago.'

Coleman led us along a hallway that reeked of turpentine and fresh emulsion. Two teenage girls were covering its drab walls with pristine white paint.

'Nice work, girls,' she sang out as we passed. 'Remember, any drips mean you don't get paid.' Her kitchen was packed with stepladders, long-handled brushes, and cans of Danish oil. 'Make yourselves comfortable, if you can find room.'

'Thanks for seeing us at the weekend,' Burns said.

'We all want Clare found. How can I help?'

'Did she ever talk about feeling vulnerable at work?'

The doctor looked surprised. 'Clare doesn't discuss weaknesses. She runs marathons, works twelve-hour days even though she's a single mum and, unlike me, she never moans. Her strength is one of the reasons I appointed her.'

'Does anyone at work dislike her enough to harm her?'

'Her deputy resents her success and her perfectionism can upset people, but I can't think of anyone. Being plain spoken's not a crime, is it? That's another difference between us. I'm a wimp when it comes to confrontations.'

'Aren't we all?' Burns smiled back at her, and I sensed that she could charm anyone with the warmth of her manner.

'Someone's attacking doctors specialising in blood illnesses. Can you think why?' I asked.

Coleman looked thoughtful. 'A few of our patients are mentally ill; occasionally they blame the medical team for their condition. It doesn't happen often, thank God.'

'Did Clare treat anyone like that?'

'She never mentioned a problem. Sorry, but you'd have to check her records.'

'You make her sound invincible.'

'She's a paradox. Hard as nails at work, soft as butter at home. Her son brings out the best in her.' For the first time Coleman seemed visibly distressed, lips trembling as she spoke.

'Does Clare's work ever put her in the public eye?' I asked.

Coleman gave a slow nod. 'She was on the Tainted Blood enquiry panel in 2012. I probably shouldn't tell you; the membership's protected information, but she needed my permission.'

'What was the enquiry about?'

Her smile vanished. 'Whitehall wanted industry specialists to assess the impact of infected blood reaching the supply chain in the Eighties, and decide whether patients deserved more compensation.'

'But no one knew about her being on the panel, except you?'

'Unless she told someone.'

'Sounds like sensitive work.' Burns was already glancing at his watch. 'You've been very helpful, Dr Coleman. Call us please, if you think of anything else.'

'I will. Come back if you need anything else.'

We left her in the hallway with her daughters, giving us a parting smile as she reached for her paintbrush. The squad car drove south through the light weekend traffic. A selfish part of me wished we were heading to my flat for a lazy Sunday afternoon together, but my desire to find Mikey's mother soon banished the idea.

'I still don't get who'd target blood doctors,' Burns muttered.

'An aggrieved patient, or someone with a blood fetish. We'll need to cross-match patient records to find anyone with a record of mental illness. It would be good to find out about the Tainted Blood panel's work too.'

He gave a distracted nod, then lurched forwards in his seat. 'The vultures are gathering.'

The handful of journalists outside the station had swelled to a crowd, which didn't make sense. It was a week since Clare Riordan had gone missing, and no public announcement had been made yet about the new blood deposit. Burns instructed the driver to use the back entrance, a lightning storm of flash-bulbs flaring as we drove past.

'Looks like someone tipped them off,' Burns said. 'It has to be one of my team.'

I lost sight of him when we entered the building. He strode off to find out who could have leaked protected information, and I went back to studying the files from the previous cases.

I was still there at eight that evening, eyes strained from scanning hundreds of documents. When I stood up to collect my coat, I remembered Dawn Coleman saying that Clare was tough enough to work tirelessly and solve her own problems. I could only hope that, wherever she was being held, that tenacity was keeping her alive.

16

Monday 20 October

It's early morning when the woman watches him put on his jacket. His skin's sallow, but to her he still looks handsome; he's easily the most intelligent man she knows. If only she could freeze this moment in time, to avoid a life shadowed by his absence. Anger forces her outside, ready to seize back some of the power they've lost.

She sits beside him as he navigates the morning traffic in silence, until they pull up on a side street, near the centre of Bermondsey. She puts on a baseball cap then collects a clipboard from the back seat.

'Wish me luck,' she says.

'You'll be fine.' He touches her cheek. 'You won't need it.'

She keeps her walk steady as she climbs the stairs to the Social Services offices. The middle-aged man at reception studies her over the counter.

'Can I help?' he asks.

She offers a flirtatious grin. 'I hope so, sweetheart. I've got a delivery outside for someone called Michael Riordan, from a toy company. The docket says to ask here for the address.'

'Let me make a call for you.'

'Thanks, love. I'm on a double yellow. You wouldn't believe the tickets I get.'

Her eye contact has the desired effect. The man doesn't complain when she leans closer, watching him scribble information on his pad. She gives him another smouldering look as he drops the receiver back on to the hook.

'Leave the box with me. His nurse can give it to him.'

'That's perfect. You've saved me a journey.'

'The pleasure's all mine.' He flashes her a wink before she disappears.

The woman hurries back to the car. The attendant will soon forget the package that never arrived, remembering only the flirtation. She saw him write down a name, her excitement rising as she reaches the car. Soon the boy will be within reach.

'Any luck?' the man asks.

'The psychiatric nurse is called Gurpreet Singh. All we need now is his address.'

17

I found myself in Euston at ten a.m., just two hours after calling the Wellcome Trust Centre to locate an expert on blood, four lanes of traffic racing past me towards King's Cross. The centre was an imposing piece of neoclassicism, built from square-edged limestone. The grand interior made me wish I had more time. Signs on the wall pointed towards exhibits on the history of medicine and scientific breakthroughs. In an ideal world I could have spent hours browsing through their archive.

The academic who had agreed to see me was called Dr Emma Selby, her name vaguely familiar. When I tapped on her door she looked more like an actress than a scientist. Her hair was a wild mass of chocolate-brown curls; small, wire-framed glasses balanced on the tip of her nose. She must have been around my age, dressed in a short emerald green dress, showcasing slim legs and smart patent-leather boots. Her steady gaze suggested that self-doubt didn't feature in her emotional repertoire, a smile playing at the corners of her mouth.

'Don't you remember me, Alice?'

'Sorry, you'll have to remind me.'

'We were at medical school together. I left after the first year; the long hours didn't suit me. I jumped sideways into the history of medicine.'

'Emma, of course. How nice to see you again.' The memory returned as I looked at her more closely; she had stood out in my class of fifty trainees, more flamboyant and assertive than the rest of us. 'I managed two years, then switched to psychology. Most of my work's forensic these days.'

'You must fill me in some time over coffee. I hope you've got a complicated question, so I can neglect my research for a while.'

'It's hard going?'

'My new book's about blood-borne illnesses in Victorian days. They thought vaccines would heal the world, but even wonder drugs have limits.' She wrinkled her nose. 'How can I help?'

'I'm working on an abduction case. I need to find out if some locations in London are linked by the history of blood medicine.'

'You're in the right city, plenty of breakthroughs happened here. Which sites do you mean?'

'Bishopsgate, first of all.'

'A nobleman called Sir Thomas Gresham lived there in the seventeenth century. His house doesn't exist any more, but the Royal Society of London used it as their headquarters; one of their members was Christopher Wren. He carried out the first animal-to-animal blood transfer there in 1665 on greyhound dogs.'

'How on earth do you know all that by heart?'

She laughed. 'My PhD was on early blood treatments. I can't seem to forget a word of it.'

Evidence of her obsession was scattered across her office. Medical reference books and journals lined the shelves, wall charts listing blood disorders with dates for known cures. 'Bishopsgate was the site of the first-ever transfusion?'

Emma gave a wry smile. 'I'd have loved to be a fly on the wall, but the Royal Society barred women for another two centuries.'

'What about the path lab at Guy's?'

'James Blundell was an obstetrician there in the nineteenth century. He was the first doctor to use human blood for transfusions, but he killed as many patients as he cured. They didn't know about blood types back then; receiving the wrong kind of transfusion is a quick way to die.'

'Is there a link with St George's Medical School?'

'My memory fails me. But hang on, I'll look it up.'

She pulled down a leather-bound reference book, thumbing through pages at high speed. 'Doctor Samuel Taylor Lane carried out the first transfusion on a haemophiliac patient there in 1840. Most of them died too, from the looks of it. Blood injections were like Russian roulette until they learned about compatibility.'

'Why would those three places obsess someone?'

Her expression grew thoughtful. 'They're all cornerstones in the history of blood treatment. Someone might be curious if they'd had a transfusion.'

'Do you know much about the Tainted Blood enquiry?'

'Only that the scandal was a national tragedy, carefully hushed up,' she replied, frowning. 'No one's ever been prosecuted.'

'You think they should have been?'

'The buck stops with the government, doesn't it? They bought infected blood from abroad and patients got sick as a result.'

The phone on her desk began to ring before I could ask another question. Emma ignored it, but I could see she was eager to return to work. 'You've chosen a fascinating topic for your research.'

Her smile returned. 'It's where human life begins and ends; blood's the cause and the cure of so many illnesses.'

'If you remember any more locations that share the theme, give me a ring. Thanks for your help, Emma.'

'It was good to take a break; too much thinking about this stuff turns me into a vampire. Let's have a drink soon and catch up.'

'That sounds good.'

I only had to walk three blocks to University College Hospital to find Fiona Lindstrop's pathology department; it was in the basement beside the mortuary, for ease of access to the cadavers stored in its floor-to-ceiling fridges. The smell of formaldehyde, antiseptic and physical decay hit me as soon as I entered the corridor. Burns had arrived already, hands buried in the pockets of his coat, his scowl melting when he caught sight of me.

'Ready to enter the kingdom of death?'

I shook my head. 'Not just yet. What have you been up to?'

'Hunting for the idiot who blabbed to the press.' He nodded at the entrance to the pathology department. 'Come on, the dragon lady's waiting.'

We found Lindstrop peering at the corpse of an elderly man. His body was so emaciated it looked like he'd died of malnutrition, ribs poking through his skin. The pathologist gave Burns a mocking salute when we entered, tugging down her surgical mask. She pulled a sheet over the old man's body as if she wanted to save his blushes.

'Bothering me again, DCI Burns?'

'I couldn't stay away.'

Her eyes glinted with amusement. 'You've finally succumbed to my allure?'

'Years ago, Fiona. You know that.'

While she flirted with Burns, I wondered how long she'd spent staring death in the face. She looked around sixty, rotund with short grey curls, a flush of excitement on her cheeks, as if each new autopsy was more thrilling than the last.

She was already bustling over to a table in the corner, rolling up the sleeves of her white coat.

'I've got the toxicology reports from Riordan's blood samples.' Lindstrop slipped her plastic gloves into her pocket, then handed over two separate sets of results. 'Let's see what you remember from your med school days, Alice. This sheet's from the first deposit, the next from the most recent. See any differences?'

I scanned the reports. 'She was healthy, but now she's sick.'

'How do you know?'

'High lipid ratio, too much cortisol and markers for three different drugs.' I stared at her. 'What the hell are they doing?'

'Nothing good, I'm afraid.' Her face grew solemn. 'The lipids mean she's processing her own essential fat stores, like in anorexia cases. Cortisol's released into the bloodstream when there's prolonged stress, and someone's giving her a cocktail of the strongest drugs available.'

'That sounds lethal,' Burns muttered.

'She could last for weeks, with just enough food and water to survive,' Lindstrop said. 'The drugs are interferon and ribavirin, normally given to patients with blood-borne viruses. The heroin could just be to pacify her.'

'The blood samples show how she's being treated,' I said.

'They're as clear as a medical report.' Lindstrop's ferocity had vanished. Maybe she could tell that her usual imperious manner would have no impact. She looked almost sympathetic when we said goodbye.

Burns and I sat in a coffee bar opposite the hospital after we'd escaped from the path lab.

'Each blood sample is less than twenty-four hours old,' I said. 'They're giving her the same medicines she prescribes every day, but not telling us why. The thing I don't understand is why they changed their MO after the first two attacks. Given that Mendez was killed in minutes, the same could have happened to Lisa Stuart, even though we haven't found her body.'

'They've gone from quick attacks to torturing someone for days.'

'This kind of escalation means the violence will get worse. Serial-killing partnerships always grow more extreme. There must be a purpose for keeping Clare; maybe they're patients taking revenge for poor treatment, or she's got information they want.'

'Jesus.' Burns pushed his coffee cup to one side, face paler than before. 'She must be terrified.'

I caught a taxi back to the station with Burns, then spent the next few hours updating my profile report. Emma Selby and the pathologist had both given me food for thought. The abductors were growing clearer in my mind. It was obvious that one of them was obsessed by details and history, while the other thrived on violence. But it was too early to guess which member of the partnership held the upper hand.

I was glad to leave the station by mid-afternoon. With an overload of worry about Mikey weighing on me, it was a relief to escape into the cold air, even if the media pack had returned to block my path. I kept my head down, so keen to evade them that I almost barged into a man in a smart trench coat, blocking my escape route. I had seen him hanging around the station for days with the other journalists. He was in his early forties with well-cut blond hair, a thin, intelligent face – more like a lawyer than a journalist. Only the pale scar on his jaw undermined his air of respectability.

'Excuse me, are you Dr Quentin?' His accent was confusing, a London intonation softened by a West Country burr.

'That's me.'

'My name's Roger Fenton. Could you spare a minute?'

'You're wasting your time. I can't discuss the case, I'm afraid.'

He shook his head. 'It's the other way round; I've got some information for you.'

There was something compelling about his quiet manner. When I glanced back the other reporters were circling closer, making me desperate to escape.

'There's a café round the corner, but I don't have long.'

The walk gave me time to observe him. He was average height with well-honed bone structure, and a sombre expression, as if he was incapable of frivolity. Silence worked to his advantage. If he'd made small talk I would have suspected him of pumping me for information. It took several minutes to find a table, the café heaving with office workers enjoying late lunches.

'Why are you talking to me instead of the police?' I asked when we finally sat down.

'I read about you in the *Mail* yesterday. Someone on your team's been flouting the disclosure law.' He gave a narrow smile. 'I'm hoping you'll let me interview you when the case ends.'

His statement was a reminder that the team members Burns had suspended had comprehensively blown my cover. 'If you give me information that helps find Clare Riordan, you can have your interview, provided my name isn't used.'

He held up his hands. 'Anonymity guaranteed.'

'What have you got to say, Mr Fenton?'

'Last summer I interviewed a doctor called Lisa Stuart for a piece on the medical profession. She went missing earlier this year.'

'I know the case.'

He put down his cup. 'There are parallels with Riordan, aren't there? Both are NHS medics, and Lisa's background was in haematology.'

My experience with journalists kept me silent; I was intrigued by what he had to say, but had been caught out before. There was a chance he might be recording our discussion on his phone. Fenton's eyes held mine as he continued.

'A haematology researcher called John Mendez was killed just a few months before. It made me wonder if someone was targeting blood specialists. Have you ever heard of a campaign group called Pure?'

'I don't think so.'

'Do you remember the tainted blood scandal?'

'It's been mentioned. Infected blood was imported from abroad, wasn't it?'

He nodded calmly. 'Back in the Eighties, the government bought a clotting agent called Factor Eight from the USA. Anyone can sell their blood over there, including prisoners and sex workers, twenty-five dollars per donation. Almost five thousand haemophiliacs in the UK caught viruses from infected NHS transfusions. Hundreds more are dying from hepatitis and AIDS.'

'Why did it only affect haemophiliacs?'

'Most of them depended on Factor Eight medication. Without it many would have died.'

'But their treatment turned out to be fatal?'

'The government's never admitted responsibility. A lot of patients waited twenty years for the ex-gratia payments to arrive, and I can see why they're angry. The settlements were an insult. Pure campaigns for justice for the victims.'

'You think there's a connection?'

'Plenty of people who received tainted blood hate doctors as much as politicians. But Pure reacted badly when I contacted them.'

'How do you mean?'

'Their top man, Ian Passmore, isn't keen on negative publicity. My story mentioned that the survivors had reason to feel murderous. He threatened to sue me, then a few weeks later my flat got burgled; my computer, with all the research for the story, was stolen. I can't prove it was his doing, but it's what I suspect.'

'You think someone's targeting any doctor who specialises in blood illnesses?'

His gaze sharpened. 'It's more focused than that. Lisa let slip that she was on the panel for the Tainted Blood enquiry in 2012; I tried to find out who the other members were, but she wouldn't say. There has to be a link, doesn't there?'

My heart rate picked up as I remembered Dawn Coleman saying that Clare Riordan had been on the panel, but membership was protected information. I took another sip of coffee then studied him again. 'I read one of your pieces in *The Times*. You were a war reporter, weren't you?'

'I quit in January. A month in a hospital in Kabul was enough to make me hand in my notice.' He gave an embarrassed smile then tapped his jaw. 'The shrapnel always found me.'

'We all carry some professional scars.'

'Call me if I can help. Contrary to popular opinion, not all journalists are the scum of the earth.' He handed me his card. 'The people you're dealing with have big grievances, Dr Quentin. Take care how you approach them.'

Fenton gave me a meaningful stare then rose to his feet. I watched him cut through the packed café at a brisk pace, noticing that no one glanced in his direction. Despite looking distinguished and smartly dressed, he had a quality many journalists would envy. He could turn invisible in the middle of a crowd.

★　　★　　★

Fenton's comments stayed with me on my bus ride to Clapham Junction. My picture of the abductors was growing more complex by the minute. Now I knew that Lisa Stuart had served on the Tainted Blood panel, just like Riordan, making me wonder if John Mendez had been part of it too. The connection could be the causal link we'd been seeking; someone venting their anger on decision-makers responsible for the scandal. I had time to send a quick email to Burns about my discovery before the bus deposited me at my destination. The area had retained its village atmosphere, bookshops, florists and health-food stores lining the high street. Mikey's primary school had a mural running the length of the facing wall, rainbows and waterfalls brightening the playground as the last few children were coerced into their parents' cars. His form teacher was still in her classroom, doubled over a stack of maths books. It was clear that Mrs Richmond ran a tight ship; the desks gleamed, posters adorning every wall. She was tall and elegant, her coffee-coloured skin almost free of lines, even though the grey streaks in her hair put her in her fifties.

'I hope Mikey's coming back to us soon,' she said.

'Not yet, I'm afraid. He's too upset by what's happened.'

'It doesn't seem fair.' Her face gathered in a frown. 'That boy's had more than his share of pain.'

'Losing his father, you mean?'

She nodded. 'The speech therapist worked wonders, but Mikey struggled for a whole year.'

'Can you remember what activities helped him?'

'His mum took him running and to football club.' Her face clouded. 'He's great at anything creative too: drawing, painting, working with clay.'

'That's good advice.'

'The trouble with his aunt didn't help. Eleanor came here twice last term; the headmaster had her escorted off the premises.'

'Did she cause trouble?'

'A real commotion, shouting about wanting to see Mikey. Clare was so embarrassed.'

'Were the police called?'

'We threatened to contact them, but she hasn't been back.'

'Did Mikey speak to her?'

'Lord, no. I wouldn't let her near him in that state.' Mrs Richmond squared her shoulders, ready to beat off anyone who upset her pupils.

'Can you think of anything that sets Mikey apart from other kids?'

Her eyes glistened. 'I got them to memorise a verse from a poem, but he could recite the whole thing. He still knew it two weeks later. He remembers images, too. I showed him an illustration, and he could describe it perfectly the next day.'

'A photographic memory?'

'It's not always a blessing.' Her gaze held mine. 'He's experienced things no child should see.'

Mikey looked even smaller that afternoon, his mop of dark hair in need of a comb. I glanced at him as I hung up my coat.

'Hello, you,' I said, smiling.

He clung to me before I could take another step. Gurpreet's expression showed that he'd had a difficult shift. I leant down to observe Mikey's face, spotting the grey circles under his eyes.

'Any chance of a cup of tea, young man?'

Gurpreet handed over the case file as the boy trotted away. The last entry showed that Mikey's anxiety had shifted up a gear. He was manifesting the full range of juvenile stress symptoms: attention deficit, nail biting, poor appetite. My concern intensified; the kid must feel as though his life had spun out of control. While we sat together in the kitchen, I thought about my meeting with his teacher, but kept my comments light. Questions would send him scurrying to his room.

'Want to come to the supermarket? My car's right by the door.'

I warned the elderly uniform in the squad car outside that I would be taking the boy for a short drive. But when I returned to the safe house to collect Mikey, he hesitated in the porch, as if a leap of faith was required to cross the threshold. I put my hand on his shoulder and felt him tremble. He clung to me like a shadow as we pushed the trolley round Sainsbury's, so insubstantial that it looked as if the first strong breeze might carry him away. I let him have his pick of the chocolate bars when we reached the checkout.

'You're a brave one,' I told him. 'But I knew that already.'

It was only when we were making lasagne that evening that I attempted a question. I hoped that keeping him busy placing sheets of pasta in the baking dish might dilute his fear.

'Can I ask something about what happened?' I saw his grip tighten on the wooden spoon. 'Did you recognise the couple who took your mum?' When his eyes met mine there was a flash of acknowledgement. 'Could you draw them for me?'

His whole body froze, eyes blinking rapidly, as though he was trying to erase what he'd seen. I settled my hands on his shoulders, while he heaved for breath, remembering that he'd panicked in the same way when I mentioned his aunt and the Thorpes. Mikey's terror indicated that the people who'd attacked his mother were familiar, even if he was unable to explain. His reaction was typical of child trauma victims, shutting down communication to avoid bad memories. At this stage it could cause damage to show him photos of potential suspects. I fought my impatience. If he knew who they were, his mother might still be found alive, but pushing too hard would be dangerous. His state of mind was so fragile. One nudge in the wrong direction could produce a silence that lasted for months.

After Mikey went to bed I called Burns. His voice was gruff with tension when he greeted me.

'He may not know their names,' I said, 'but I'm certain he's seen them before.'

'Why not just ask, straight out?'

'I can't push him, if that's what you mean. He's at breaking point.'

'Don't snap, Alice. It was a simple question.'

'Have you found any more on the Tainted Blood enquiry?'

'Angie's looking into it. You sound tense, Alice. Maybe you should watch some TV and relax.'

'Whose stupid idea was it to work together anyway?'

'Not mine.'

I took a deep breath. 'We've never even been to a decent restaurant.'

Burns gave an abrupt laugh. 'Is that why you're pissed off?'

'It beats worrying about the case.'

'When this ends, I'll take you to the Ivy, my shout.'

'Famous last words.'

'We'll celebrate, big time. I promise.'

After the call ended I opened the French doors and stood on the patio, hoping to escape the overheated atmosphere, but it didn't help. The air felt clammy against my skin, like a storm could arrive at any minute.

18

It's late at night when the man scans the images on his computer screen, his body aching with fever. He takes a long gulp of whisky before turning to the woman.

'Are you sure his first name's Gurpreet?'

'Positive.' She's sitting on the settee, watching TV, monitoring how the story's being reported on the news channel. 'You should stop drinking that shit. It's making you weaker.'

'I'm enjoying every drop. There are fourteen Gurpreet Singhs on Facebook living in London.'

'Only one of them works as a psychiatric nurse in Southwark.' She stands beside him, studying the images.

'I'm not convinced we need the child,' the man says.

'Of course we do. Watching him die will hurt her more than dying herself.'

He puts down his glass. 'But her suffering won't cancel ours.'

'You're kidding. Knowing she's in pain helps me sleep at night.'

'Don't you feel any guilt?'

'Why should I? She's ruined our lives.'

'You keep changing the rules. We agreed to kill three of them, then save the minister for the finale.'

She reaches out to touch his cheek. 'It's not enough, sweetheart, for all we've suffered. Come on, you're tired. Let me use the computer.'

The man's anxiety rises as she nudges him out of the way.

They shared the same rationale at the start, but her thirst for vengeance is spiralling out of control; she's so hot-headed, her actions could lead them into the hands of the police. It no longer matters what happens to him, but she would never survive in prison. He stands behind the chair to watch the screenshot picking up blurred images from the camera in the laboratory. Riordan is lying where they left her, restraints so tight she can hardly move. She deserves to suffer, but killing the child seems a step too far. As his own end draws closer, his desire for revenge fades. When he peers at the screen again it's clear that cold and terror are weakening Riordan. They need the next name on the list before nature takes its course, in case Jordan Adebayo refuses to comply. He wants Riordan to taste the sharp flavour of betrayal again, before she meets her death.

19

Mikey's eyes widened with fear when I asked for his help that morning, but he still followed me into the lounge. We sat side by side on floor cushions, then I placed two pieces of card in front of him, explaining that anything he remembered could help find his mum. The tremor in his hands let me know that we would have to proceed with caution. If he coped with the first exercise, I might risk showing him photos of the suspects, to see if he could identify them.

'I'm going to show you some pictures. Touch the red one if you want to stop, or green to carry on. Okay? Red's no, green's yes.' When he tapped the green card with his thumb I grinned at him. 'You're a fast learner, but we'll stop if it gets hard. All right?'

He hesitated before touching the green card again, reminding me to keep my pace gentle, despite his bravery. The illustrations had been drawn by a police artist who specialised in building Photofit images. He'd done a good job of recreating the scenarios from Clapham Common. In the first sketch a slim woman in a tracksuit was running down a path dappled by shade, a young boy at her side.

'Does that look like you and your mum?' I asked. Mikey's face was strained, but he tapped the green card gingerly.

'What about this one? Is that what happened?'

The next image showed a man and woman in dark clothing, blocking the path, the boy haring away into the trees.

Mikey shook his head vehemently, his jaw clenched. 'They took you in the car as well, but you got free?' His finger skimmed the green card.

'Do you know where they were taking you?'

Suddenly his face contorted. He smashed his fist against the red card so hard it bounced into the air, and I felt a stab of guilt for returning him to the territory of his nightmares. His eyes were screwed shut when I smoothed his hair back from his forehead. For today the pictures of Moira, his aunt and the Thorpes would have to remain in my bag.

'You're doing great. Now I know they took you in the car too. If you remember things, you can draw them for me, can't you?' Tears dripped on to the thigh of his jeans as I pulled him closer.

'I won't let anything bad happen to you, Mikey. You know that, don't you?'

His cheek rested on my collarbone. The gesture proved that he'd placed his trust in me; if his mother never came home I would feel responsible for his welfare. The idea triggered a rush of tenderness and panic. Somehow the boy had tunnelled under my radar before I could protect myself.

Fewer journalists were waiting on the steps when I reached the station that morning. Burns had asked for a full psychological assessment of Sam Travers, but it was Angie who greeted me with a wan smile. I knew the pressure must be intense if her unshakeable *joie de vivre* had taken a knock.

'The boss is doing a press call,' she said. 'Talk about a pack of hyenas.'

'Did you find out who leaked about the calling cards?'

Her frown deepened. 'Two uniforms sold stories to News Unlimited. It's been a nightmare.'

'At least you've dealt with it. Is Travers being held?'

'Not yet, their car's clean and there's no evidence of Clare's DNA in their house. But we know he's been lying through his teeth. Travers made hundreds of phone calls to her from a pay-as-you-go mobile, up till a fortnight before she was taken. That's not my idea of a casual fling.' She picked up her folder and rose to her feet. 'For all we know, he's got Riordan in a lock-up somewhere.'

'My questions should open him up. I found evidence of a connection with Lisa Stuart in her crime file.'

She was already heading for the door. 'After we've interviewed him, you can talk to his wife. We think she's covering for him, and we know we're looking for a couple.'

Sam Travers seemed less relaxed than he'd been in his cool Islington flat. His eyes were shadowed, beard in need of a trim, and it looked as though it had been days since he'd eaten a square meal. A plump, middle-aged woman in an over-stretched business suit sat beside him, a briefcase balanced on her knee. It interested me that – despite his protestations of innocence – Travers had invested in a lawyer. I made a point of shaking both their hands as Angie joined me at the table.

'Thanks for coming back, Mr Travers,' I said.

'It's been a hellish few days. They won't let us go home; we've had to stay at a hotel.'

'I'm sorry you've been inconvenienced.'

The solicitor took a notepad from her briefcase. 'I'm representing Mr Travers's wife too. I'll be taking notes during their interviews.'

'Feel free,' Angie said. 'Mr Travers isn't under arrest, he's just clarifying some points for us.'

'Last time we spoke, you left out some important facts about your relationship with Clare Riordan, didn't you?' I kept my eyes on his face. 'Could you tell us a little more about how you got together?'

He shifted in his seat. 'I interviewed dozens of doctors for my documentary, but she stood out; she was so passionate about her work. I fought it at the start, but it was impossible.'

'What attracted you to her?'

'Clare knows how to draw attention. Charisma, I suppose. She can light up a room. It's not just the way she dresses and carries herself. She's unforgettable.'

'But you couldn't tell your wife you'd fallen for someone else.'

'Isabel wouldn't cope if our marriage fell apart.'

'Why's that?'

'She's sensitive. It would be too much for her.'

'You said you had an open marriage.'

'I felt ashamed.' Travers's shoulders jerked upwards. 'Clare wanted the affair kept secret, but we met whenever we could. Until she ended it two weeks ago, out of the blue.' His eyes glazed, as if the abrupt ending had left him stunned. I felt a sudden twitch of discomfort; Travers had described another similarity between Riordan and me. Not only did we share a love of running and a background in the NHS – she walked away from relationships too.

'Did she say why it was over?'

'Pressure of work, and to protect her son. She'd always made time for me, then suddenly she went cold. I thought she'd met someone else.' He gazed down at his hands. 'Maybe if I'd left Isabel at the start, this wouldn't have happened.'

When I studied him again, his suffering looked genuine. He seemed to believe that abandoning his wife could have kept Riordan safe; a simple case of symmetry: leave one woman to save another. My dislike shifted towards sympathy, even though his statements didn't ring true, as the interview continued. His yearning for Riordan sounded authentic, but even the most violent men could show regret. I'd interviewed a patient at Broadmoor who'd wept for hours over his wife's memory, then confessed to throttling her and burying her remains under their patio.

'Did you meet John Mendez and Lisa Stuart when you made your film?'

'Not that I remember. I interviewed hundreds of people.'

I glanced at my notes from the crime files. 'You interviewed Lisa at Bart's Hospital in March; she made a note in her diary. I have a copy here.'

His face tensed. 'I'd need to see a photo.'

The picture Angie passed him showed a pretty strawberry blonde in her early thirties. 'Remember her now?'

'Yes, now that I see her. Her interview missed the final cut.'

'How come?'

He shrugged. 'She didn't say anything controversial.'

'Lisa went missing, two weeks after you interviewed her, and now Clare's gone too.' I returned the photo to my folder.

The solicitor grimaced. 'Don't respond, Mr Travers. You can say "no comment".'

'I've got nothing to hide. I met that doctor once, then never saw her again. You've got to understand, I had an affair, but I've never hurt anyone.'

At the end of our meeting, Travers almost had me convinced. His body language revealed high stress levels, but his communication style was direct; there was no prevarication before answers. He'd stumbled a few times, but that was probably due to stress. Either he was a skilled actor, or his only crime had been infidelity.

My curiosity rose when his wife arrived. Isabel Travers looked younger than her husband, spiky platinum-blonde hair framing her face, her skin translucent. She was thin as a mannequin, dressed in jeans and a crisp blue blouse. Her lips were pursed, as if she was holding back a tide of insults.

'I've been waiting hours,' she said, scowling. 'You made us come here, then waste our time.' Her voice was a husky German growl, as if she'd been chain-smoking all morning.

'Forgive the delay. We need information about your husband and Clare Riordan.'

Her eyebrows rose. 'They had an affair. What more can I say?'

'Has your husband ever been violent towards you, Mrs Travers?'

'Of course not. I'd be back in Berlin.'

'How did you meet?'

'At a film workshop in Paris. He proposed three months later; you call it a whirlwind romance over here, don't you?' Under the cynicism there was a quake of emotion in her voice.

'Can you describe your husband's behaviour this past month?'

'Distracted, not quite himself.'

'Did you talk about it?'

Her eyebrows rose. 'Couples don't just merge into one. If you lose your privacy, you lose everything. I knew he'd explain eventually.'

'Have you met Clare Riordan?'

'Twice. She came to dinner, and I met her during the documentary. I found her interesting.'

'You were involved in the filming?'

'I was production manager.'

'But you never guessed about the affair?'

She gave an exaggerated shrug. 'Suspicion's pointless. I had my own life to lead.'

The interview yielded little new information. Isabel Travers's body language was so defensive, her arms remained crossed throughout the discussion, hands clutching her elbows, holding herself together. Once she'd left the room, Angie breathed out a few expletives.

'Not a happy bunny, is she?'

'Wounded pride. It's easier to be angry than humiliated. Her husband's affair cut her to the quick.'

'They could have dreamed the story up between them.' She rubbed the back of her neck. 'The boss won't be thrilled, but we can't detain them without forensic evidence.'

'Travers told a different story this time, showing us he's a plausible liar. Maybe his ego couldn't take Riordan's rejection, and Lisa Stuart may have turned him down too. But most crimes of passion are quick and brutal. The people who've hidden Clare have an obsessive interest in blood; the couple aren't a perfect fit.'

'They could have used a different car to pick her up. There's a chance they'll lead us to her, if it's them.'

'I'd like to see their health records.'

Angie blinked at me. 'Why?'

'It's possible the people holding Riordan hate the medical profession. Maybe one of them's ill.'

'I'll add it to my list. We're already looking at the records for all of Riordan's patients.' The determined set of her jaw suggested that she would complete the task as soon as she left the room. 'Do you remember Moira Fitzgerald, the senior nurse Riordan sacked?'

'Of course.' The Irish woman's animosity towards Riordan had been too potent to forget.

'She's found a new job in Dublin, starting next month. We can't find anything linking her to Clare's abduction, so she's off the suspect list.'

On one level the news pleased me. The frustrated nurse could escape from her minute flat, her anger more likely to fade in a new setting. Riordan seemed to have incited strong feelings in many of her colleagues and acquaintances, but that didn't make them guilty of harming her.

I spent the next two hours writing up assessments, aware that they could be tested to destruction in a court of law. Sam Travers had shown a tendency towards neurotic self-interest, while his wife's reaction had been classic sexual jealousy: anger mixed with defensiveness. Her rawness made her more likely to commit a crime of passion. But it didn't surprise me that the investigation team had found little to implicate them in the crime, apart from Travers's DNA in Riordan's house and car. They must have stolen afternoons together, then she'd driven him home; standard behaviour for people having an affair.

Information from the case was still spinning round my head when I visited my favourite Vietnamese takeaway that evening. Fenton's suggestion the previous day had made me rethink the nature of the crime. I'd assumed that Clare Riordan's abductors knew her personally because she had received different treatment from the previous victims, but maybe they had a bigger axe to grind. The killers might believe that medical negligence on a grand scale justified attacking doctors. That would explain why they were choosing sites where blood experiments had taken place for their calling cards: a reminder that patients had been used as reluctant guinea pigs right from the start. I wondered how the investigation team would greet the idea that Clare Riordan had been taken because of a medical scandal thirty years before.

When I pressed Burns's doorbell there was no reply, so I fished his key from my pocket, the mechanism clicking loudly in protest. So much of his personal life was on display that I felt like a voyeur. The crumpled towel slung over his cross-trainer revealed that he'd worked out that morning; a mountain of laundry was waiting to be ironed. A book about Mark Rothko lay open on the settee, and I wondered if reading about artists' lives helped him escape the tension of the case. But papers stacked on his kitchen table showed that he'd worked most of the previous evening, reports covered in his left-handed scrawl.

I dumped the takeaway bag before studying his notes. Police teams had scoured the area round Clapham Common, chasing possible sightings. The helpline had been busy too, over two hundred members of the public convinced they had seen Clare Riordan in recent days. They varied from credible stories to bizarre claims that she'd faked her own abduction and boarded the Eurostar for Paris, leaving Burns to agonise over which sightings to pursue. I pushed his papers aside and drew up a new chronology. John Mendez had been murdered on his doorstep in January, Lisa Stuart reported missing in April, Clare Riordan abducted in October. It was possible that all three victims had served on the Tainted Blood enquiry. I put down my biro and rubbed the back of my neck. If the three cases were linked, why would the killers change their modus operandi so radically? The first victim had been despatched without ceremony, as though speed was all that mattered. If she had been killed, the cover-up had been so successful that Stuart's body had never been found. This time they were indulging in elaborate staging, certain to draw the police's attention, the locations for spilling Clare Riordan's blood providing a lesson on the history of transfusion. Since talking to Emma Selby and Roger Fenton, I suspected that they weren't just baiting the police, they were mounting a protest. I would have to find out more about the Tainted Blood enquiry, to see if the journalist's hunch had been correct.

I opened my laptop and searched for the organisation Fenton had mentioned. Pure was such a common brand name that I had to trawl through listings for soap and baby milk before finding the group's website. When I finally opened the page, their logo made my jaw drop. It was the sign that had been left at each crime scene: a black droplet beside a white one. Now that I saw the two thin teardrops in context, the message was easy to read: one blood supply was dirty, the other clean. My eyes scanned the site rapidly, hunting for more facts about the organisation. They described the tainted blood scandal as an act of state-sponsored mass murder; Pure's main aim was to win fair compensation for the surviving patients and improve their quality of life. There was a chat room where sufferers could share their thoughts. Some of the messages were poignant: one woman had shared pictures from her husband's memorial service; another described the horrible side effects of anti-viral drugs. The fact that the logo had been left at each crime scene meant that I would have to disregard Roger Fenton's warning and meet Ian Passmore. I checked the organisation's contact details again before scribbling them in my notebook. I tried to call Burns to pass on the news, but had no luck. From past experience I knew he often worked around the clock while a case was at its height, but tonight I couldn't follow suit. After another hour my back was aching and I was desperate for a break.

I wandered round his chaotic flat to stretch my legs, my gaze landing on his bookshelf: a thick volume on *Flemish Art of the Seventeenth Century* sat beside a biography of Leonard Cohen and the latest John Grisham. His CDs were just as eclectic. Stravinsky concertos, hard-core American rock, and the Proclaimers' album he played to annoy me. I came to a halt in front of a framed photo of Burns with his two sons. It had been taken that summer on their camping trip to Somerset. The three of them stood in front of a tent, big-boned and dark-haired, grinning for the camera. The picture made me feel uneasy. With Mikey I knew where I stood: a temporary replacement for his mother; his conduit to the outside world.

These kids looked strong enough to fend for themselves. Meeting me might throw the whole picture off balance.

Burns's landline rang while I was still studying the photo. I hesitated before answering, then reminded myself I was entitled to be there. The female caller issued an order before I could speak.

'Liam's got flu. Get round here, can you?' She had a broad Scottish accent, her tone cold with anger.

'Don's not here, I'm afraid. Is that Julie?'

The woman's voice chilled by another degree. 'You must be the famous Alice.'

'I'm sorry to hear your son's ill.'

'Are the pair of you living together now?' She spat out the words.

'I'm just visiting.'

'Send him over. His son needs him.'

The call ended with an abrupt click. Burns and his wife had gone through a trial separation, then he'd returned for his kids' sake, only for it to break down again months later. Judging by her angry tone, Julie held me responsible, even though I'd refused to get involved until they'd separated. The raw pain in her voice made me wonder if the whole thing had been a colossal mistake. I let my thoughts settle before calling Burns again, surprised that he finally answered after two rings, voices buzzing in the background.

'Where are you?' I asked.

'Where do you think? Still at the chalk face.'

'I've found their signature. Look up Pure, it's a medical campaign group.'

'For what?'

'Patients who caught blood viruses from NHS treatments during the tainted blood scandal.'

He let out a gush of breath. 'You're a wonder, Alice. I'll get someone on it now. Are you coming in?'

'I'm at yours, with a ton of Vietnamese food.'

'Stay there, I'll be ten minutes.'

'Your son's got flu. You need to go and see him first.'

'Julie spoke to you?'

'It wasn't exactly a conversation.'

He choked out a laugh. 'I can imagine.'

'You didn't tell me she was Scottish.'

'That's the least of her worries. Look, I'll see him, then come straight back.'

'No rush. I'm going back to mine soon.'

His voice cooled. 'We're never under the same roof.'

'I miss you too, for what it's worth.'

'Tomorrow we'll have lunch. I'll arrange a meeting with Pure too. Do you want to meet the head honcho?'

'Definitely, his name's Passmore. He could unlock the case for us.'

'It's time we had some luck.' There was silence before he spoke again. 'You're in my head, Alice. I can't change it.'

'You too.'

'I'll pick you up tomorrow, sweetheart.'

I felt uncomfortable after we said goodbye. Endearments had been in short supply when I was a child, but that was no excuse; sooner or later I would have to voice my feelings. It seemed ridiculous that I'd reached my thirties without even making an attempt. I bundled my things back into my bag with a sense of frustration. The walk home through Borough took me along quiet, floodlit streets, but the cool air did me good. One of the things I loved about London was the way it kept one eye open at night, its history of apocalyptic floods, plagues and fires keeping it alert. I thought about Mikey Riordan as I reached Providence Square. With luck his night would be peaceful, with no bad dreams to spoil his sleep.

20

Wednesday 22 October

Ian Passmore's profile confronted me when I turned on my computer the next morning. One of Burns's team had sent an encrypted email overnight. He was fifty-eight years old, with just one criminal conviction for affray in 2012, and was currently working at the Courtauld Institute. He had agreed to report to the station at nine a.m. According to the report, he lived alone and didn't own a car, devoting his spare time to Pure. I felt a stab of disappointment. Given that he was single, his details were a poor match for my profile, and the group's logo appearing at the crime scenes didn't make him a direct suspect.

Burns's Audi arrived on the forecourt earlier than expected. Even from a distance it was clear he was feeling the strain, but his smile had its usual effect. It made me wish we could go back upstairs for a few hours and forget about the case.

'You're a sight for sore eyes,' he said.

'Flatterer.' I slipped into the passenger seat, planting a kiss on his cheek.

'It beats staring at a bunch of ugly, bad-tempered cops.'

It was obvious that things weren't going to plan. He'd spent hours with Angie and her team the evening before, digging for information on Pure, but his seniors at Scotland Yard held him responsible for the officers who had blabbed to the press, creating a breach of security. He growled about the reprimand they'd passed down all the way to King's Cross.

Passmore had arrived at the station before us. A tall man with a cloud of unkempt grey curls rose to his feet when we reached the interview room. He was dressed in threadbare cords and a tweed jacket, holding my gaze for a beat too long when we shook hands. His face looked pallid and careworn, as if he'd been working too hard for months.

'Thanks for agreeing to meet us,' Burns said. 'You work at the Courtauld, don't you?'

'For my sins. I'm a fundraiser,' Passmore replied in a slow, north London drawl.

'That can't be easy in this climate.'

'Even in a financial meltdown the rich stay rich, believe me.' His gaze flickered between me and Burns. 'I assume this is about Pure?'

'Partly, yes.' I took my notebook from my bag. 'Can you tell us how it began?'

'It's all on our website,' he said calmly. 'After the blood scandal we wanted justice for the victims, but the Health Department have never accepted responsibility. At least we panicked them into offering a few thousand pounds to each patient. But the most seriously ill still live on a pittance that doesn't cover their medical care. The government pays them less than the average UK wage, even though they're dying from AIDS and hepatitis C.'

'Some died before the money came, didn't they?'

'The tragedy continues, thirty years on.' His tone grew bitter. 'Factor Eight's not used any more, thank God. But people like me relied on it back then. Without it, even a small injury could have been fatal.'

'You're a haemophiliac?'

He nodded. 'My older brother was too. He got HIV from tainted blood. Retroviral drugs were crude back in the Eighties; he died at twenty-one.'

'I'm sorry.'

'Haemophilia passes from mother to son. If a woman carries the gene, there's a fifty per cent chance her sons will get it.'

'But in your case you both did?'

'The luck of the draw.'

Despite his hostility, Passmore's story spilled out easily, as though it was always at the forefront of his mind. I realised he must have been striking in his youth. Stress and exhaustion had caught up with him, but he had the chiselled features you see in adverts for whisky and aftershave – handsome men gazing into the middle distance. The fact that he lived alone made me wonder if decades of campaigning had left him isolated.

Burns leant forward in his seat. 'I won't beat around the bush, Mr Passmore. I need to find out if someone from Pure is carrying out a vendetta against medics who specialise in blood illnesses.'

He shook his head dismissively. 'That's ridiculous. We've got over a thousand members, but most are too sick to leave their homes.'

'Being given a life-threatening disease from a blood transfusion would make a lot of people want to lash out.'

'Don't you think they've seen enough suffering?'

'Anger does strange things to people. It's possible that experts from the Tainted Blood enquiry are being targeted.'

'How? I tried to get their names so we could lobby them, but the membership's an official secret.'

Passmore's stare blazed across my face, bringing the interview to a halt; long silences opened up between his statements, as if I'd insulted him personally. Burns had little more luck when he checked his alibi for the morning Riordan was taken. He claimed to have been at home with a volunteer from Pure called Michelle De Santis, contacting members who lived alone as part of their support network.

'Is Michelle your partner?' I asked.

'I told you, I live alone.'

'No need to snap, Mr Passmore,' Burns said, quietly, shunting a piece of paper across the desk. 'I want you to write down where you were on these dates, and provide names of people who can corroborate each statement. We'll take a copy of your fingerprints before you leave, and we need Pure's membership list too. Email that to me please, by five p.m. today.'

'This is ridiculous. My organisation's done nothing wrong.' He fell silent, as if the implication that anyone from Pure was capable of violence had removed his power of speech.

I was still thinking about the meeting when Burns drove me to a Greek restaurant on Birdcage Walk. The place was classier than the eateries we normally visited, with dark panelling on the walls and views across St James's Park. The waiter led us to a quiet table, beside a window.

'What's the special occasion?' I asked.

'There isn't one. It's to remind us there's life beyond the case.'

'I'm starting to forget. Did you see your son last night?'

'Liam's back at school. He had a fever, but today he's fine.'

'He sounds like a tough kid.'

'They can shrug anything off at that age.'

I studied the leafless trees outside. 'Mikey's not that robust. He'll crack if his mum isn't found soon. Even if she's dead, it's better for him to know than to carry on in limbo.'

A muscle ticked in Burns's cheek. 'We're working round the clock.'

'I guessed, from the state of your flat.'

'Maybe I should get a cleaner.'

I touched his forearm. 'It's a free world. Live like a slob if you choose.'

'You should have waited for me.'

He gripped my hand, and even though we spent the next half-hour talking about the case, he didn't release it until our orders arrived. Tania had already confirmed that Passmore was correct about the membership of the Tainted Blood panel being an official secret; Whitehall were refusing to disclose the advisors' names. Burns seemed bemused when I mentioned the symbolic locations of the calling cards again.

'You think they're teaching us about medical history?'

'Perhaps one of them's sick, which would rule out Sam and Isabel Travers. Their health records came back clean. But life's always been hard for blood patients; half of the earliest treatments were fatal.' I studied his face. 'If one of them got an infected transfusion, they might be lashing out.'

'You think they're twisted enough to kill any medic linked to tainted blood?'

'If it's a husband and wife, sickness could be stealing the person they love most. The killers' relationship's fascinating. The complexity and pace of their actions means they've got a high level of trust.'

'Could it be a brother and sister?'

'Possible but rare. Couples always condone each other's violence; it's like fanning a fire till it blazes out of control.'

'God almighty.' Burns gave a quiet groan.

'It may burn itself out, but they've accelerated since the first attack, and they're getting a kick from taunting us.' I pushed my plate aside. 'What's Sam Travers been doing since his release?'

'Staying with a friend. His marriage is over, apparently.'

'It's still possible he was involved in taking Riordan, isn't it? Have you got much on John Mendez and Lisa Stuart?'

'There's still no clear link, apart from their expertise. The NHS computer system isn't helping. Our IT guys are working on it, to see if a patient encountered all three of them.'

'Or Mendez could have been on the enquiry panel, like Clare and Lisa. We need that membership list from Whitehall urgently.' I checked my watch. 'I should get moving.'

'It's days since I saw you.' His expression darkened as we split the bill.

'What's bothering you, Don?'

His no-bullshit stare settled on my face. 'I chose the wrong time to fall for you, didn't I?'

'Are you regretting it?'

'Not yet. But I'm sick of being kept at arm's length.'

'It's not deliberate.'

'You won't even meet my kids.' The anger in his voice took me by surprise.

'I will, when the time's right.'

'The Riordan boy's got to you, hasn't he?'

'On a professional level, yes,' I said quietly. 'We'd better leave.'

When we stood outside on the pavement, Burns's closed expression showed that he was still nursing his wounds.

'This is new territory for me, Don. I've never let myself need anyone before.'

His smile slowly flickered into life. 'Everyone has to start somewhere.'

My walk to the FPU was a blur after we said goodbye. Either the case was getting to me, or the intensity of his stare.

Mike Donnelly was the first person I bumped into when I arrived. He was wearing a smart jacket, white hair shorter than before, his beard neatly trimmed.

'You're looking spruce,' I commented.

'I've got my appraisal with Christine. I'd hate to get sacked.'

'I think she'll keep you.' It was an open secret that he had been a key member of the CO's team for twenty years. The only reason Christine had chosen me to work with Mikey over Donnelly was the need for a female therapist. 'Can you help me for a minute?'

'For you, anything.'

We sat in my office, flicking through Mikey's case file. Donnelly had acted as forensic consultant on dozens of juvenile cases. I was sure he could help me form a strategy to help the child speak again. His fingers tugged at his beard as he pored over my notes.

'Talk me through your methods so far, Alice.'

'Re-enactment, prompts, guided questions, drawings, photos. Every trick in the book.'

'And you've established trust?'

'Definitely – he's in tears whenever I leave.'

'That's tough on you. Kids latch on so fast.' He studied me gravely.

'It's not me I'm worried about.'

His eyes widened. 'You should be. Cases like this can leave a mark.'

'I'll deal with that afterwards.'

'You've crossed the biggest hurdle; the kid was catatonic, but now he's reactive again.' Donnelly stacked my papers into a pile. 'You'll have to take him back to the common, guide him through the abduction again.'

'Won't that push him too far?'

'Kids are realists. He knows his mother may be dead; that's why he's suffering. This way he'll get the chance to help find her. And if there's a delayed reaction, you'll be there to support him.'

*   *   *

Gurpreet waited until Mikey was settled in the living room before sharing his update that evening. The boy had been reluctant to eat, fidgety and distracted. Childhood trauma often manifested as withdrawal and depressed mood. We both knew that the next phase would be anger, followed by slow acceptance. There was no way to comfort him, apart from offering diversion activities. Mikey seemed to relax as the evening wore on. I was still following my strategy of cooking together to help him relax. I waited until we were side by side in the kitchen before making my suggestion.

'I'd like us to go back to the common tomorrow, Mikey, so you can show me what happened. Say yes or no, I won't mind. Just nod or shake your head.'

His skin was so paper thin I could see the veins throbbing at his temple. I felt guilty for placing him under pressure, but it was unavoidable. After a minute he nodded his agreement, then clung to my side.

'It'll be fine, sweetheart.' I gave his shoulders a quick squeeze. 'We'll be together.'

I let him stay up late that evening, tension easing out of him as we watched an ancient James Bond movie.

'You'd make a good double-O seven,' I said. 'Clever and quick on your feet.'

He pulled a face before giving a rare smile, offering a glimpse of the boy he'd been before the abduction: self-mocking and bright. Seeing that past confidence made me even more determined to find his mother. I noticed the dog-eared copy of the *A–Z* lying on the floor at his feet. I'd seen him thumbing through the pages every day, but never found out why. I reached down and picked it up.

'Is there a street you're looking for, Mikey?'

His body froze, as it had done when I'd asked questions about his mum's disappearance. The boy seemed hardwired to avoid discussing his trauma, as if he knew it might cause him harm.

It was almost eleven before I was alone again. Too tense to go to bed, I flipped open my laptop and entered my Home Office password to access the Health Ministry's records. I found a record of the ministerial meeting following the Tainted Blood enquiry, the agenda flashing on to the screen. Only two senior civil servants had kept the health minister company while he signed the decision papers to deny culpability. I scrolled down to open the advisory panel's meeting notes, but an 'access denied' message appeared. When I entered the command again, the same words ran across my screen. It struck me as odd that my level two clearance couldn't break the security code. The panel's findings must be screened by a top-level protection order, just like its membership.

The claustrophobia of the house was making it hard to breathe, so I pulled open the French doors to inhale some night air. Clare Riordan had been missing eleven days, her blood spilled at locations where early transfusions had taken place. I shut my eyes and tried to visualise a couple so incensed by fate that they would turn on medical practitioners. Ian Passmore's face floated into view, followed by Isabel Travers, still outraged by her husband's infidelity. But it was possible that the people who had abducted Clare Riordan were passing as ordinary Londoners; holding down day jobs, looking after their kids. No one wanted to believe the uncomfortable truth that not all psychopaths were lonely misfits operating at the fringes of society. Sometimes they behaved just like you or me, going undetected for years.

I was about to go back inside when something caught my eye: a movement between the plants at the end of the garden, or was it the play of shadows? When I looked again, there was only a tangle of ferns and spike-leaved palms. I stood on the patio, rubbing my eyes. Exhaustion or the pressure of the case must have been getting to me. I filled my lungs with gritty London air, before stepping back inside and locking the French doors.

21

It's after midnight when the woman stands outside a garage block at the edge of the Barbican complex, dressed in jeans, gloves, a dark winter coat. She's hoping to avoid a long wait, excitement pounding inside her ribcage.

'All clear,' she says quietly.

She waits in silence as the man uses a skeleton key to open one of the garages. Once inside, she shines a torch around the space. Light arcs across the cardboard boxes lining the back wall: there's nothing to see, except a mess of oil smears on the concrete floor.

'Let's get ready.' She pushes the boxes forwards, then crouches behind them. 'We can hide here.'

Thirty minutes later a car pulls up outside. She hears a key fumbling in the lock, the engine idling. The woman's mouth feels dry as sand while she waits for the click of the driver's door. The victim has no time to fight before they pounce, the anaesthetic rendering him unconscious. She helps to lift him on to the back seat, binding his hands and feet. The woman hums quietly as the car pulls out of the estate, relaxed for the first time in weeks.

It takes all of their combined strength to lift the new victim into the dentist's chair when they reach the lab. Riordan lies on a pallet on the floor, muffled protests emerging from behind her gag. Once Adebayo's strapped down, the man retreats to a corner of the room. The woman sets to work draining blood from the new victim's arm with an extraction needle. His skin pales, but he doesn't cry out.

'Give us a name, Jordan, or I'll have to hurt you,' she whispers.

'Keep your hands off me.' His voice rises to a shout.

'Let's see how much pain you can stand.'

'I'll never tell you.'

She collects another syringe from the cabinet, determined to prove him wrong.

22

Thursday 23 October

I woke up certain that discovering who had served on the Tainted Blood panel would explain why all three doctors had been targeted. But until Whitehall could be persuaded to disclose the information, that avenue was closed. I decided to revisit Clare's workplace to see if it held any more clues, dashing out of the safe house at seven thirty, straight after Gurpreet arrived. The haematology department appeared to be empty when I arrived, smells of iodine, floor polish and hospital food lingering from the day before. I managed to persuade a janitor to unlock Riordan's office after flashing my ID card. It was obvious that Hancock's team had turned the room inside out. The contents of her filing cabinet were stacked in neat piles, computer missing from her table, every trace of her personality removed. I sat in the doctor's narrow leather chair, eyes closed, trying to enter her mind-set, but all I caught was a faint hint of jasmine, the last trace of her perfume scenting the air.

'Who were you afraid of?' I muttered to myself.

I spent the next hour riffling through her papers, reading messages she'd scribbled on her jotter and in her notebook. The office gave the impression of a woman who had split her life cleanly in two; ruthlessly ambitious, but fond enough of her son to tack half a dozen photos to her pin board so she could keep him always in sight. I flicked through Clare's desk diary and searched the books on her shelf, looking for notes she might have forgotten to throw away. It still made me uncomfortable that so many similarities had emerged between us: both driven and hardworking, keen on running, and happiest in relationships we could control. But the parallels between us could work in my favour: Riordan's son had connected with me fast. Once he trusted me completely, he might be able to describe the events he'd witnessed.

My frustration mounted as I prepared to leave, Riordan's secrets eluding me again. The dark-haired doctor I'd spoken to before was unlocking her door. Adele Novak's expression was friendly as she greeted me, but behind her welcoming smile she looked tired, her skin fine as wax paper.

'Looking for someone, Dr Quentin?' she asked.

'Call me Alice, please. I'm just trying to connect pieces of information.'

'Can I help? My clinic doesn't start till nine.'

'That would be great, thanks.'

Novak ushered me into her consulting room. I noticed more details this time; she was using the space to put her patients at ease, soft toys piled in the corner to keep youngsters occupied, a rubber plant burgeoning by her desk, colourful cushions on the chairs. She switched on her kettle, making me a cup of tea with the minimum of fuss.

'Clare's absence must be affecting you all,' I said.

'We're spreading her caseload across the department. I was here till ten last night doing ward duties, but it's more of an emotional thing. No one can relax.' She gave me an anxious glance. 'Is there any news?'

'Nothing conclusive, I'm afraid.'

'I was wondering if Clare's advisory work put her in danger. She wanted me to volunteer for a government committee, but I had no time. It's unbelievable how much she crams into every day.'

I studied her again. 'Last time we talked I thought you were being discreet. Were you holding something back, out of loyalty?'

'You're very perceptive. It seemed wrong to mention it when something so terrible had happened.'

'Can you tell me now?'

She hesitated. 'Clare knows how to manipulate men. My impression is that she charms them, then discards them.'

'How do you mean?'

'She enjoys attracting whoever she wants, then walking away.'

'People in the department?'

She nodded. 'Ed Pietersen fell at her feet. He was outraged about her getting the top job, but within days she'd talked him round.'

'You think he's attracted to her?'

'The men here either adore her or are terrified.' Her expression grew wistful, as if she was trying to imagine owning that much charisma.

'That's what you were going to tell us?'

'It seemed wrong to criticise, particularly when I owe her my job. But one of her admirers might have grown angry.' She gave an embarrassed smile. 'I'm at the opposite end of the spectrum from Clare.'

'You're not married?'

She gave a quiet laugh. 'It's not high on my agenda.'

We spent a few more minutes together and I got the sense that Novak felt guilty about drawing attention to her colleague's weakness, even though it was an element of Riordan's personality that I'd guessed for myself. The doctor seemed relieved to get it off her chest, her expression more relaxed when we said goodbye.

Once I got outside, my mobile rang. I had to cover my ear with my hand to take the call. Traffic was racing through Belsize Park, almost drowning the voice at the end of the line.

'Can you come to the Barbican, straight away?' Angie's tone sounded urgent.

'Has something happened?'

'I'm surrounded, Alice. I'll explain when you get here.'

The journey gave me time to obsess about what might be waiting five stops away. I tried not to consider the worst-case scenario, that Clare Riordan's body had been found. Angie's elfin face looked tense when I surfaced at the Barbican. She set off at a brisk trot, her speech tripping along at the same rapid pace.

'A guy called Jordan Adebayo's missing. He runs the London Blood Bank; he never made it home from his late shift. His wife found a blood pack on their step around seven a.m., another splashed over her front door. The uniforms say she's hysterical. I need you to assess her state of mind, see if she needs mental health support.'

'The blood might not be her husband's.'

'Try telling her that. She yelled abuse at me down the phone; I've asked for a family liaison officer to help calm her down.'

Gina Adebayo lived at the heart of the Barbican complex. I had plenty of time to contemplate the architecture because Angie kept lapsing into silence, as if she was rehearsing how to comfort the missing man's wife. The estate was an empire of beige concrete, a stone's throw from the Square Mile. Its three huge towers must have enjoyed stunning long-distance views across the city, but the Adebayos' apartment was in a modest low-rise block. The occupants seemed keen to inject nature into their brutalist landscape; even in autumn, trees and shrubs were flourishing on the balconies.

Someone had placed an opaque plastic sheet over the entrance to the flat, but the smears on the front door were hard to miss. Blood was congealing in long streaks across the woodwork. When no one answered the bell, we stepped through the unlocked door.

'Who is it?' A shrill female voice echoed down the hallway.

'Metropolitan Police.'

'About fucking time.' Her tone rose even higher.

Gina Adebayo was pacing beside the panoramic window in her lounge. She was medium height, slim, with short hair dyed a glowing copper, freckled skin blotchy from crying, her eyes raw. She looked fragile enough to fall apart at any moment. Angie was smart enough to keep her distance; dealing with two people was more likely to increase the woman's stress.

'My name's Alice Quentin. I'm so sorry your husband's missing.' She ignored me, turning her back to stare out of the window, but I stepped towards her. 'Would you like to sit down?'

'What difference would that make?' Her fierce gaze lit on my face. 'Who the hell are you, anyway?'

'I work for the Forensic Psychology Unit.'

Her hands clenched at her sides. 'I'm not cracking up, for God's sake. Why isn't anyone down there looking for him?'

'Dozens are, believe me. It's my job to profile the people who've taken Jordan.'

'Don't use his first name,' she snapped. 'You don't know him.'

I perched on a stool, making sure she could see me. 'Can you tell me about your husband, Gina? It would help us get a clearer picture.'

'He only got back from a conference in Paris yesterday. I told him to take the day off but he wouldn't listen.' A tear rolled down her face, splashing on to the floor, some of her tension finally releasing. 'Jordan's forty-six, passionate about his job. He never complains about the long hours.'

'How did you meet?'

'At work. I'm a team leader at the blood bank. We got married two years ago.'

A framed photo on the wall showed that the Adebayos' wedding ceremony had taken place on an exotic beach, a strip of turquoise sea sparkling in the background. Jordan was a tall, good-looking black guy, giving the camera a wide-eyed grin, as if he couldn't believe his luck.

'Do you know if your husband was on the panel for the Tainted Blood enquiry, Gina?'

She kept her gaze fixed on the square below. 'He was meant to keep it secret. Has that got something to do with him going missing?'

'We need to find out. Did he say who else was on the panel?'

'He didn't mention it.' Gina pointed at the view through her window. People were scurrying across fields of concrete, collars up against the breeze. 'I keep expecting to see him. His walk's more of a swagger; I can always spot him in a crowd.'

Angie took a step closer. 'Is it okay to ask a few more questions?'

Gina refused to meet her eye. 'If it brings him home.'

'Has your husband always worked shifts?'

'It's a requirement. We supply all the London hospitals, twenty-four seven.'

'You send out thousands of units every week?' Angie asked.

She nodded. 'Plasma and blood products. Jordan doesn't just oversee the service; he runs campaigns and advises the government.'

I looked at her again. 'Did you hear that a haematologist called Clare Riordan was abducted last week?'

She turned in my direction. 'Jordan knows her, but I can't remember where they met.'

'Can you tell us what drew your husband to his job?'

She stared at me as though I'd lost my mind. 'Do you know how many units of blood a liver-transplant patient needs?' When I shook my head she carried on. 'Fifty. Without the blood bank, thousands of people would die each week.'

I looked at her hands, twisting together as if she was wringing liquid from a piece of cloth. 'Can you think of anyone who dislikes your husband, Gina?'

'He lives for his work. Why would he have enemies?'

When the doorbell rang I left Angie with Mrs Adebayo. Millie Evans – a family liaison officer from Burns's team – stood on the doorstep, wavy chestnut hair escaping from her ponytail, her stout figure dressed in black trousers and a dark red jumper. Millie's round face opened into a smile.

'Back with us, Alice? You're a glutton for punishment.'

I explained the details as we waited for Angie to finish. Her eyes widened as she heard that Jordan Adebayo had been taken the night before, blood spattered across the doorstep for his wife to find.

'And it might be her husband's?'

'It's likely,' I said, nodding. 'She's still in shock; ring me if she gets agitated.'

'Of course. Jesus, there are some sick bastards about.'

Once she'd gone inside, I put on the sterile gloves Angie had given me, then lifted the plastic sheet. A blood pack lay on the doorstep, bigger this time and full to the brim, printed with Adebayo's name. My head swam as I looked at it. The bag must have held at least a litre. But did it mean that Clare Riordan's body had been dumped somewhere, or was she still alive, even though they'd taken a new victim? I spotted something else as I replaced the cover. Two small marks had been chalked on the doorstep – one black, one white. Pure's logo: two drops of blood side by side. I took a photo with my phone, then rocked back on my heels. Whether or not someone from the campaign was carrying out the attacks, their logo lay at the heart of the investigation. The need to investigate the group's members had just grown even more urgent.

It was eleven a.m. by the time Angie and I shared a taxi back to the station. She seemed to be digesting the information slowly, staring at my photo of the signature in silence, as if her thoughts were on overload. The panic on Gina Adebayo's face kept returning to me as we reached St Pancras Way. It was an adult version of Mikey's – disbelief, combined with full-blown rage.

Tania and Pete Hancock had already joined Burns in the meeting room. The atmosphere was grim, and it didn't take a mind-reader to sense that everyone was anxious. The series had escalated from three victims to four, the intervals shortening.

'I need all of your updates.' Burns said, scanning our faces. 'You first, Tania.'

'My lot's been looking at John Mendez and Lisa Stuart's cases. The doctors both worked at Bart's Hospital, five years apart, but it's possible they knew each other. We've been interviewing colleagues, relatives, friends. Both were well respected in their field. The big frustration is that the NHS can only give records for the past year. We're looking to see if any patients were treated by Stuart, Mendez and Riordan, but so far there are no overlaps. The Ministry for Health are still refusing to hand over details of the Tainted Blood enquiry, so we don't know if Mendez served on it too.'

Angie flicked her notebook open. 'Professor Adebayo's wife has confirmed that he was on the panel. He was abducted in his black Subaru around midnight last night. A street camera picked it up as he reached the Barbican, then leaving again about quarter past. You can see the outlines of two figures in the front seats. We think his abductors changed the plates before joining the main road. Pete's team are looking at his garage to see if they broke in. The blood at the scene hasn't been tested, but they've used a bigger plasma pack this time. His doorway's one hell of a mess.'

'Have you got a picture?' Burns said, frowning.

Angie flicked on the computer on the table and brought up an image of the blood pack, full to bursting. Beside it two small chalk marks were visible. I was still staring at the image when my turn came to speak.

'We know that three of our four victims were on the Tainted Blood enquiry. We need the membership list urgently.'

'You think they're working their way through it?' Angie's small eyes focused on me, sharp as gimlets.

'It seems likely, when all of the killers' actions are linked to blood treatments. Last night there was an unusual degree of premeditation. They extracted pints of Adebayo's blood, before returning to the Barbican to splash it across his door. It's the opposite of the normal pattern of quick, sexually motivated abductions. I still think we've got two opposing personalities working together, one weak, one strong, making up for each other's deficits, united by a sense of mission. They've upped the ante since taking Clare; they may be keeping Adebayo alive to torture him too. The pair seem to adapt their methods with each victim, but the signature never changes.'

Tania stared at me. 'Why are they using the Pure logo?'

'The group campaigns for people who received infected blood from NHS treatments back in the Eighties.' I studied the picture of the blood pack, full of dark red liquid. 'One of them could be a patient with a grievance. They're taunting us with their knowledge of medical history, and they won't just let Adebayo and Riordan go. They'll hurt them in a way that links to their theme; it's possible they're being held in a location connected to blood history. Mikey's my main concern. His visual recall's extraordinary, so I'm sure he's got buried memories about the abduction. He's agreed to go back to Clapham Common this afternoon, but the visit has to be low key.'

Burns stared at me across the table. 'Do you believe Riordan's still alive?'

'I think so, but it's unusual for a victim to be held captive so long. Either she has vital information, or they're enjoying watching her suffer. She's being treated so differently from the other victims, she may know them. They may even be reluctant to kill her.'

Everyone round the table looked tense as the meeting progressed. At the end Burns discussed the next stage: the priority was to keep pressuring Whitehall to disclose the membership of the Tainted Blood panel. The professional histories of all four victims would be checked more thoroughly for connections and claims of medical negligence. More patients would be contacted and interviewed. Pure would be investigated thoroughly too. Wherever they were, the couple in question would have been overjoyed to be causing so much debate. The efforts to find Clare Riordan were doubling, media interest spinning out of control. If one of the victims died, Burns would be hounded by every tabloid in the land.

I stayed at the station to update my profile report. The deputy commissioner arrived at lunchtime wearing a thunderous expression, as if the new abduction was Burns's fault alone. The two were still locked in his office when I fought my way through the press pack. Roger Fenton shot me a sympathetic look from the edge of the crowd, as if he didn't envy me my job. The feeling was mutual. I'd have hated the tedium of waiting for stories to break, prying into people's secrets. It took me several minutes to get past them and breathe clean air again.

*   *   *

Mikey looked frail when we set off for Clapham Common that afternoon. In the twelve days since his mum had been taken, he'd deteriorated from an athletic young boy to a pale-cheeked waif. Gurpreet sat on the back seat keeping his expression neutral, but I knew he had his doubts. My high-risk strategy could be cathartic, or it might plunge the child into a lasting silence. The new abduction had me clutching at straws. Any scrap of information might help track the victims down, even if it meant pushing Mikey faster than the care manuals suggested.

In the rear-view mirror a squad car followed at a discreet distance. I kept up a stream of chatter to put Mikey at ease. His shoulders were hunched with tension, even though the common must have looked very different from the morning when he went running with his mum. Now it was heaving with human activity: school teams playing football on the sports ground, kids chasing their dogs, new parents pushing buggies.

'Are you okay, Mikey? We could do this another day.' His eyes were terrified, but his expression was determined. Having come this far it was clear he didn't want to fail. 'We'll follow the path, then you can show us where it happened.'

He was trembling as we approached the stand of trees, passing a mound of floral tributes with messages from well-wishers. There was a scurry of activity when we arrived, two men melting into the thickets at the sight of uniforms. Drug exchanges must have been taking place there round the clock, even in broad daylight. The temperature fell by a few degrees as we entered the copse. Under normal circumstances, I would have enjoyed walking through woodland in the middle of autumn, but the place felt tainted; I couldn't forget that it was the scene of a brutal abduction. Mikey's steps faltered, like he might keel over at any minute. Gurpreet hovered closer and I crouched down, bringing my face level with the boy's.

'Was it here, Mikey?' He shook his head, pointing further down the path.

Once we got there he seemed calmer, as though his fears had been worse than the reality of seeing the place again. He pointed out where the car had been parked and the spot where the attack happened without saying a word. One of the uniforms took photographs, but the area had already been searched with a fine-tooth comb. I left Gurpreet with the uniforms and led Mikey to a bench.

'Let's catch our breath.' He let me fold my arm round his shoulders when we sat down. I waited for him to speak, but the strategy failed. After a few minutes I attempted another question.

'Do you know their names, Mikey? If you remember, you'll help us find her. You can tell me, or you can write them down.'

I pulled a notepad and biro from my pocket, but he sat motionless, eyes blinking rapidly. When his lips opened no sound emerged, exhaustion obvious as he tried to speak. I felt torn between my duty of care and the need to find his mother, but it was clear his ordeal needed to end.

'You've done brilliantly; now let's get you home.'

Reliving the trauma seemed to have drained him as we returned to the car at a slow pace. I glanced over my shoulder as we walked away and spotted a woman in a dark winter coat at the edge of the clearing, near where the flowers had been laid. Our eyes met when she lifted her face. It was Clare Riordan's sister, Eleanor, her raised collar almost obscuring her face. There was a high whimpering sound, and when I looked down Mikey was white with panic, eyes riveted to his aunt's face.

'It's okay, sweetheart. She can't hurt you.'

I tightened my grip on his shoulder, but felt him shaking as Eleanor slipped away into the trees. I alerted the uniforms immediately, telling them to find her and take her to the station. Why she would haunt the spot where her sister had been taken was a mystery, but my first concern had to be the boy's welfare.

Mikey dissolved into tears as soon as we got indoors. It was clear he needed me to stay, the anxiety locked tight inside him threatening to explode. I swapped night duties with Gurpreet and watched the psychiatric nurse's battered Volvo drive away, then I called Burns to let him know about Mikey's panic when he saw his aunt. Dusk was falling when I looked out of the window again, darkness wrapping the house as tightly as a shroud.

23

It's two a.m. when the man drags Adebayo's half-conscious body from the lab. Even though his mouth is gagged, the victim's whimpers are audible as they jostle him into the car.

'We could give him more sedation,' the woman says.

'Not yet. We have to get him inside first.'

They drive south without talking, the man's heart pounding as he concentrates on the road. The car fills with a soprano's high aria from *La Bohème* when he turns on the sound system. It eases his tension, until he hears the victim sobbing on the back seat.

He parks behind a tall building in Southwark. The site is unlit, the man's stomach tightening at the prospect of being caught. It's the outcome he fears most – for the woman, not himself.

'Let's get this over with,' he mutters.

The woman leans over, kisses his mouth. 'We're doing the right thing.'

The man is so tired when he climbs out of the car, he has to wait for his vision to clear before lifting bolt-cutters from the boot. It doesn't take long to break the lock. The place is full of ghoulish statues and pictures, obscene objects crammed into glass cabinets. So many lives were lost here, the place feels ghost ridden as he retraces his steps. Together they drag Adebayo on to the asphalt, leaving him slumped against the side of the car. It's the woman who forces him to stand. She prods his shoulder with her blade, pain making him scramble to his feet then lurch forwards, swaying unsteadily at the centre of the circular room.

'This is your last chance to tell us,' she hisses.

Adebayo shakes his head once, before the anaesthetic topples him. The man works quickly, strapping him to the operating table, ankles firmly secured. He stands back, watching the woman calmly putting on a plastic apron, then pressing another chloroform pad over Adebayo's mouth. His body bucks wildly against the restraints, then falls limp. When she turns to the man again, she holds out a scalpel on the palm of her hand.

'Want to help?'

'We agreed I'd organise it, you'd take care of the rest.'

'So I'm the executioner, the guilt's all mine?'

The man stands motionless, absorbing the accusation in her gaze. It would be cowardly to leave; his fate has reduced them to this, yet he can't bring himself to look. The first slash of her knife almost brings him to his knees.

24

A text arrived early the next day from Tania Goddard. It was a terse request to report to an address in Borough. A wave of anxiety hit me as I hailed a taxi. When I reached St Thomas Street, the crime scene was already behind cordons, the road commandeered. Sunlight glistened from the Shard's glass walls as I paid the cab driver. The building was less than a decade old, but already absorbed into the city's skyline, its jagged pinnacle piercing the clouds. Even at the worst of times, the city dazzled, old and new coexisting in harmony. The events unfolding at ground level were much less serene. CSI vans queued beside a Georgian terrace, St Thomas's Church festooned in yellow and black crime scene tape. My discomfort increased; the police only went to such lengths when a murder had been committed. I made an effort to suppress my fear that Mikey's mother had been found until the facts were established.

A young WPC instructed me to wait outside the Old Operating Theatre Museum. She wore a harassed expression as she checked people through the inner cordon. I belted my coat tight against the cold and studied the museum's façade. It was housed inside a narrow nineteenth-century church that I'd often admired when I worked at Guy's, two blocks away. It seemed odd that an operating theatre could have existed there, but a notice in the foyer explained that the church had once been part of St Thomas's Hospital. The garret had served as its apothecary, providing hundreds of tinctures and medicines. It had also been the site of London's first operating theatre: medical students, including the poet John Keats, had packed the aisles to observe groundbreaking surgery.

The WPC scribbled my name on her list then handed me a sterile suit and plastic overshoes.

'Put these on please,' she said. 'And watch the stairs, they're a tight squeeze.'

I understood what she meant when I began the dizzying climb through the atrium to the garret above. The museum was dimly lit and ill-suited to dozens of police officers and SOCOs trampling between the low rafters. Bunches of herbs hung from wooden beams, showing how the place would have looked in Georgian times. Over the centuries their scent had impregnated the walls with eucalyptus, camphor, and a faint reek of formaldehyde. Glass display cabinets held equipment from the earliest days of surgery. I stared at a row of lint-lined masks which would have been used during operations. Anaesthetics were simpler then, a teaspoon of ether sending patients into oblivion, but the technique had been hit and miss; a few drops too many meant the patient would never wake up. The obstetrics section seemed packed with instruments of torture. One case held batons as narrow as walking sticks; in the days before pain relief, mothers in labour bit on them to stifle their screams, hundreds of teeth marks imprinted on the wood.

Tania strode towards me when I straightened up, glamorous as ever, even in crime scene overalls. She would have looked elegant in a paper bag, but today her expression was blank.

'It's Jordan Adebayo,' she said. 'Someone cut the padlock off the back entrance; it looks like they brought him in from the car park.'

'That would take strength, wouldn't it?'

'Not if they frogmarched the poor sod up the steps.' Tania's Tower Hamlets accent had grown more pronounced, distress sending her back to her roots. I followed her down a narrow passageway, a flurry of SOCOs pushing past in their white suits. 'It's like Piccadilly fucking Circus in here.'

'Has Eleanor Riordan been picked up?'

'Not yet. She hasn't been home since you saw her on the common.'

Tania was so grim-faced I put my questions on hold. The passageway opened into a wood-lined amphitheatre, light falling from windows that studded the ceiling of the circular room. A skeleton hung on a wire beside the entrance, perfect teeth trapped in its jaw, grinning in welcome. He had probably stood there for centuries, teaching generations of medical students the laws of anatomy. The amphitheatre had been preserved in its original state too. Its raked seats would have allowed hundreds of trainee surgeons to spectate. So far I'd seen no sign of the body, but the room swarmed with activity. The air was sharp with unpleasant odours: meat left to fester, excrement, and the bitter tang of antiseptic. To distract myself I scanned the walls again. Someone had daubed Pure's logo on the wooden door: the familiar white and black smears, a supersized version of the marks left beside the blood packs on Gina Adebayo's doorstep.

Burns stood on the far side of the room, wearing the same clothes as yesterday, making me wonder if he'd been home at all. He was deep in conversation with Hancock, a head taller than the officers buzzing around him, as if he was the only adult in the room. His feelings were well concealed, but I knew he'd be blaming himself for the latest death. Guilt was obvious in his posture, every muscle locked in place.

'Ready?' Tania was hovering next to me.

'As I'll ever be.'

Except I wasn't, of course. I'd always preferred to witness a killer's approach first hand, but this time I was out of my depth. I'd seen plenty of crime scenes since becoming a forensic psychologist, but Jordan Adebayo bore little resemblance to the handsome man in his wedding photos. He was strapped to a wooden operating table, shirt hanging open to reveal a grossly distended torso. The colour had drained from his skin. And the reason was obvious: the pool of blood lying below his body extended for two metres.

Stale air was making my head swim. When my eyes blinked open again I forced myself to study the man's face. His throat had been cut so deeply that the pale tissue of his windpipe was exposed, jaundiced eyes protruding from their sockets. Tania's turquoise gaze was glassy when I turned round.

'Is that how he was found?'

'Covered by a surgical gown.' She nodded at a row of cotton robes, hanging from hooks on the wall. 'The curator says it's from here.'

'He died on the operating table?'

'The police surgeon said it would have taken seconds, once his jugular was cut.'

'The restraints are classic sadism, but this level of staging means they're enjoying themselves.' A fresh wave of sickness hit me as I studied the body again.

'You need fresh air.' Her hand cupped my elbow.

'I'll be okay.' I hated to admit defeat but my head was swimming. My eyes swept the scene again, then I stumbled out through the fire exit, suppressing my nausea. All I could hope was that Clare Riordan hadn't met the same fate.

When my eyes opened again the weakness was passing and Burns was leaning against the wall nearby.

'Are you all right, Alice?'

'I'll live. Has his wife been told?'

'That's where I'm heading.' His frown showed his reluctance to share the news.

'What do you know so far?'

'He was injured before they arrived. There's a blood trail on the concrete.'

'It's gathering speed. Adebayo was only kept a few days, delivered to a central London location, and killed with a theatrical flourish. They'll act again soon.' I spoke the words more for my own benefit than his. 'We have to find out who was on that panel.'

'Whitehall's still saying the information's classified by the Department of Health, but they'll have to give it to us now.' He took a step closer. 'You look ill, why don't you go home for a few hours?'

'I'm fine,' I snapped. My fears for Mikey wouldn't allow me to give up, no matter how weak I felt. 'I'll need the crime scene analysis today, and I want to be at the autopsy.'

'You're sure?'

'Positive. I'm still concerned about Eleanor Riordan; Mikey had a panic attack when he saw her on the common yesterday.'

'We're looking for her car.' He carried on studying me. 'When this is over, we're taking a serious holiday.'

I attempted a smile. 'Holidays aren't meant to be serious.'

He looked so bleak that I wanted to comfort him, but a noise rumbled behind me before I could move. A BBC press van was pulling into the car park. For once the reputable journalists had beaten the paparazzi; they must have been waiting outside the police station for the first flurry of activity. Two cameramen climbed out, followed by Roger Fenton, who cast a cool gaze across the melee of the crime scene. It made me wonder why he'd chosen a job which involved chasing ambulances; either he had a genuine belief in freedom of information, or a vicarious love of danger. Of all the journalists pursuing the story, he seemed most obsessive, but I pushed my concern aside. If Fenton was involved in any way, why would he have tipped us off about the link to tainted blood? Burns traipsed down the steps to face them with all the enthusiasm of a condemned man.

I spent that afternoon working at home, but the scene at the operating theatre kept returning whenever I slowed down. A dozen emails had arrived from colleagues at the FPU, reminding me that my day job was being neglected. Consultants were begging for funding decisions, increasing my guilt about neglecting my new role. My time with Mikey had knocked everything else aside. But, despite my best efforts, my profile report still wasn't conclusive. Only the hallmarks of two distinct personalities remained clear: one was measured and academic, the other daring and vicious enough to take huge risks. If I was correct, they were the perfect double act, compensating for each other's flaws. But I still couldn't fathom why Riordan had been kept alive so long, while Jordan Adebayo had died within hours. Leaving Pure's logo at the murder scene could be a double bluff or a telling signature. If the link was genuine, the killers were members of a group that was over a thousand strong. The final possibility was that Eleanor Riordan had a murderous axe to grind. I could understand her rage against her sister turning violent, but why would she attack other blood specialists? I needed to question her boyfriend, the novelist Luke Mann, even though he'd already been interviewed. Eleanor matched the profile for the impulsive, emotional side of the partnership. If Mann was involved, I would expect to meet a calm intellectual, capable of objectivity, even if his moral compass was broken.

I was still working when my phone rang at seven. It took me a while to realise that the woman's cultured London accent belonged to Emma Selby. I wondered whether she was calling from her office at the Wellcome Institute, its walls lined with books on the history of blood treatments.

'I hope it's okay to call out of hours,' she said.

'Of course, I was working anyway.'

'Could we meet? I've been thinking about your case.'

'That would be great.'

Emma was already at Bertorelli's when I reached Covent Garden, easily the most striking woman in the room. From a distance she still looked like the flamboyant student who'd stood out from the crowd at medical school, over a decade before. She wore a purple silk shirt with a jade necklace, hair a mass of glossy brown ringlets. A bottle of wine stood on the table beside two empty glasses. She was poring over a copy of the *British Medical Journal*, but abandoned her reading glasses when I arrived.

'Sorry to drag you across town.' She smiled apologetically.

'It's fine, especially if you're sharing that wine.'

Emma leant over to pour me a glass. 'If someone's obsessed by places linked to blood medicine, there are some more you should consider.'

She handed me a list of nine locations, written in spiky black ink. Most were hospitals or pathology labs, but she'd included the Old Operating Theatre, which made me do a double take. The discovery of Adebayo's body hadn't been announced yet.

'Why's the operating theatre significant?'

She took a sip of wine. 'Some of the first surgical transfusions happened there, but techniques were hit and miss. The theatre floor was awash with blood at the end of each day.'

'Not a great time to fall ill.' I carried on studying the list. 'This is helpful, thanks. The investigation team will check them out.'

'I needed to get it out of my system. I fret about things otherwise.'

'Me too.' I topped up her glass. 'But now you've passed it on, you can relax.'

Her smile reappeared. 'Tell me what you've been up to since med school.' There was an intense expression on her face as she listened to an abbreviated version of my transfer to psychology, and my passion for forensic work.

'The mind interested me more than the body. I'm fascinated by the reasons why people break the rules.'

'Your forensic work sounds like my research. We're both peeling back layers to reach the truth.'

Her analogy was spot on. Investigations often felt like stripping wallpaper until I hit a solid wall of fact. I ended up staying until closing time, splitting the bill with Emma, who turned out to be an interesting companion. We covered a lot of territory: family, career, relationships. She told me that she had been seeing someone for years, but they had never lived together.

'Sometimes I wonder why I care about him so much. He can be incredibly difficult.'

'Easy options are normally dull,' I said, raising my glass.

After we parted company, I felt more upbeat. It had been weeks since I'd met a friend for a drink and chatted about something other than work. She reminded me of Lola: stylish and bright, with the same restless energy. Her quick wit and intelligence made me hope that we'd meet again, but there was a layer of secrecy under her extrovert manner. Several times during the evening it had been clear that something was preying on her mind. I could tell that she'd needed to escape from herself that evening, for reasons she hadn't revealed.

25

I used the taxi ride to University College Hospital on Saturday morning to prepare myself for what lay ahead. Pedestrians were making slow progress up the Euston Road, taking leisurely strolls towards Bloomsbury and the British Museum. I would have preferred to join them instead of attending Jordan Adebayo's autopsy, but with luck it would explain how he'd died. Tania was waiting outside the mortuary at eleven a.m., her smart navy coat slung across her arm.

'Lindstrop's running late,' she said. 'Typical despot behaviour. She files a complaint if we're a minute behind, but it's fine to keep us waiting.'

'Don't expect pathologists to be rational. Anyone who chops people up for a living has to be unhinged.'

She shook her head. 'I'm dreading this.'

'At least we're in it together.'

The mortuary assistant ushered us in before she could reply. Lindstrop had reverted to type since my last visit, red-faced and belligerent, voice one decibel short of a scream.

'Morning, ladies,' she said, dragging on fresh surgical gloves. 'I see you drew the short straw for weekend duty. Let me remind you of theatre protocol: backs to the wall, no fainting, questions at the end.'

The room was full of sharp odours: ammonia, bodily fluids, and a whiff of my own fear. I watched Lindstrop circling the operating table. A microphone hung from a wire overhead, waiting for her pronouncements. Jordan Adebayo's skin had paled from brown to grey. Someone had shown enough sensitivity to close his eyes, so his wife wouldn't have to confront his terrified stare. The suffering he'd experienced in captivity showed in the deep bruises on his arms and face. Lindstrop was examining his hands, her voice dropping to a murmur.

'Someone's made a mess of you, my friend.' She flicked on the microphone and snapped back into professional mode. 'Puncture marks consistent with wide needle injections to left and right forearms, chest, neck and face; oedema and subdermal bleeding to the left wrist.'

The pathologist examined the man's skin through a looking glass.

'Blisters,' she commented. 'Your last hours were no fun at all.'

Lindstrop swabbed his skin with lint and took scrapings from his nails. Then she examined each limb, recording every mark, before turning her attention to his throat. My stomach churned as she dabbled her fingers in the wide gash. After a few seconds she turned in our direction.

'The carotid artery's been cut. It's the quickest way to kill someone; the blood loss would have been phenomenal. We can replace up to forty per cent of our body's supply, if we bleed slowly, but he would have died in two or three minutes.'

Tania groaned quietly as I tried to concentrate. Why was Riordan's blood being released over a period of days, while Adebayo had been exsanguinated in moments? I needed all my self-control to keep watching as Lindstrop performed a Y-section on the man's chest and removed his major organs one by one. Technical terms flew over my head, but she mentioned ventricular damage, clotting and arterial obstruction. The pathologist had reached the end of the procedure when she turned to us again.

'Do either of you want to see something interesting?'

'Not today, thanks,' Tania muttered.

Lindstrop smiled when I stepped forwards. 'Nerves of steel, Alice. Good for you. Do you know which organ this is?' She held out a wide metal dish.

'The liver.' I blinked at the dark red mass, surrounded by a pink foam of blood.

'But something's wrong, isn't it?'

'It's too big.'

'Quite so.' Her smile widened. 'Mine's half this size, and I've been abusing it for forty years.'

'He was poisoned?'

'In several different ways. The toxicology reports just arrived.' She peeled off her gloves and collected a printout from the table. 'There was interferon and ribavirin in his blood, like in Riordan's samples – traces of heroin, too. The wounds show that they plunged the needle at random wherever they liked.'

'Remind me what interferon's used for?'

'It slows the progress of blood-borne viruses like hepatitis.'

'Would it have enlarged his liver that much?'

She shook her head. 'It would have made him nauseous. Something else caused the organ damage; the report shows massive coagulation. He would have died quickly, even without the cut to his throat.'

'Why?' Tania asked. Now the ordeal was ending, she seemed to be recovering.

'It looks like he received an injection of the wrong blood type. Needle marks lead straight into major veins, like you'd see after a transfusion.'

'Would you need medical knowledge to do that?'

Lindstrop shook her head. 'Injections are easy; you just need to insert the needle into a vein.'

'What happens when someone's given blood that doesn't match their own?'

'The body shuts down,' Lindstrop said. 'Blood antigens reject the foreign fluid, leading to massive clotting, then heart failure. Even the skin blisters. Perhaps it's a blessing his throat was cut. It would have saved him the agony.'

Tania was speechless when we got outside, cold air failing to revive her.

'Want to get a drink?' I asked.

'God, yes. Anything to wash the taste away.'

We ended up in an Irish watering hole on the Euston Road, which was doing a roaring lunchtime trade. Tania slumped at the bar and I bought us both a double shot of Laphroaig. She knocked hers back in a single swallow.

'How does Lindstrop do that every day?' she asked.

'For the victims, I suppose. She seems passionate about it.'

Tania shook her head. 'Most of it went over my head.'

I stared down at my drink. 'The killers gave Adebayo the strongest opiate you can buy, then a blood transfusion of the wrong type, before his throat was slit.'

'Agony after the ecstasy,' she muttered.

'But did they kill Clare Riordan first, or are they experimenting on her somewhere, like an animal in a lab?'

'Do you think her sister's involved?'

'Running away doesn't make her guilty. Eleanor was at cracking point when I interviewed her; maybe the press attention got too much. They'd been camping outside her door. We need to find her, but I can't see why she'd harm the others.'

'Maybe she's been abducted, like her sister?'

I shook my head. 'She fled from the site of Clare's abduction, and none of her blood's been found. Their MO is to leave a sample as soon as a victim's taken.'

'It looks like Eleanor's boyfriend was home alone the night Adebayo was taken. Neighbours say the lights were on all evening; no one saw him go out.'

'I'd still like to speak to him.'

She gave a blank nod. 'I'll sort it.'

We spent half an hour debriefing, another shot of whisky bringing the colour back to Tania's cheeks. We were about to leave when she spoke again.

'I heard the news about you and Don,' she said. 'You know we go way back, don't you?'

'Twenty years, isn't it?'

'We joined the Met the same year.' She studied my face. 'Don't take this the wrong way, but I wouldn't build your hopes. His kids are everything to him. Julie could have him back tomorrow if she clicks her fingers.' She busied herself with buttoning her coat. 'Sorry, that was probably out of order. Booze always loosens my tongue.'

'It sounded sincere enough.'

Her face held a mix of pity and sadness. 'I spent years with a bloke who never put me first. You're too smart to do the same.'

Tania's elegant figure disappeared into the crowd. My thoughts flicked back to Burns's previous desertion. We'd started seeing each other the first time he left his wife, but he'd been drawn back because his kids were suffering, leaving me high and dry. When my phone buzzed in my pocket, his name appeared in the window, but I jabbed the off button with my thumb. The idea that he was unreliable had already taken hold.

I was in a foul mood when I got back to Shad Thames. Too many ugly images were competing for space in my head: a bag of dark red liquid lying on the ground; Jordan Adebayo's body on the mortuary slab. All I wanted was to sink into a long bath. But the door to my flat was unlocked and only two people had keys: Lola and Will. Much as I loved them both, I was in no mood for company. It irritated me that my visitors had made themselves at home, Ella Fitzgerald purring from the living room.

When I peered through the doorway, Burns was lounging on my sofa, bare feet propped on my coffee table, staring at his laptop, too immersed to hear me arrive. I was torn between wanting to hurl myself into his arms and an urge to bawl at him to leave.

'How did you get in?'

The usual stab of attraction hit me when he looked up. He was shabbier than ever in a black sweatshirt and faded jeans, five o'clock shadow turning into a beard. But none of that mattered when he lumbered to his feet, shoulders blocking the light from the window.

'Your lock was easy to pick.'

'Is that what they teach you at officer training school?'

'It pretty much opened itself. Didn't you get my calls?'

'I've been busy.'

'You went to an autopsy. I wanted to see you were okay.'

'I don't need protection, Don.'

Burns folded his arms. 'What does it take for you to accept help? Do I have to drive over you with a truck?'

'All I need is three Nurofen and some time alone.'

'Don't be ridiculous.'

'My flat, my rules.'

'I'll run you a bath, then you can tell me what's wrong.'

'I can run my own sodding bath.'

By the time I sank into the hot water, I felt embarrassed. He'd only offered me a shoulder to lean on. My anger stemmed from days of witnessing too much human damage, including

174

the post mortem. When I finally pulled the plug, the water hadn't rinsed away my cares, but it had restored some of my calm. I padded down the hall to my bedroom, thankful that Burns was nowhere in sight.

I chose black leggings and a silk shirt, unwilling to place anything harsh against my skin. Adrenalin pumped through my system again when I returned to the living room, fight or flight reflex in full swing. It happened every time a man came too close for comfort. Burns dumped his computer on the coffee table when he saw me, but I perched on the edge of an armchair at a safe distance.

'We should talk about the case, Don, seeing as you're here. Do you know the membership of the Tainted Blood panel yet?'

'The Department of Health are stonewalling. They've agreed to talk on Monday.'

'Four medics are gone and they won't hand it over?'

'The chief commissioner's hounding them, but the answer's always the same. It's classified information.' He studied me again. 'Tell me what's wrong.'

'It was a crap day, that's all.'

'So talk about it.'

I drew in a breath. 'Mikey's making slow progress. Combine that with watching Jordan Adebayo being sliced apart, and it hasn't been fun. Come to think of it, Tania pissed me off too.'

'Why?'

'She thinks you'll go back to your wife any day now.'

Burns swore loudly then crouched in front of me. 'Listen to me, Alice. She's warped by her own shitty divorce, but mine's almost done. Julie and I are acting like grown-ups for the boys' sake. We fell out of love years ago. And do you know what really pisses me off? I've spent months telling you that. Then Tania makes one snotty remark because she's bitter as fuck, and you believe her, not me.' He shook his head in disbelief. 'You're all I think about, but you never believe me.'

His direct stare had its usual effect. I owed him an apology, but couldn't find the words, so I kissed him instead. When I finally pulled back, his pupils were half an inch wide.

'God almighty. We have our first row, then you kiss the life out of me. You're a total mystery.' He brushed his thumb across my lips.

'The bath relaxed me.'

'Rubbish, you're so wired I could play a tune on you.' He pressed one of the tight muscles in my shoulder, making me grit my teeth.

'You like causing pain, don't you?'

'And pleasure.' His fingers trailed in circles across my collarbone. 'God, I love it when you do that.'

'What?'

'Shiver when I touch you.' He began exploring again, hands coasting up my back, face nuzzling the side of my neck.

'Have dinner with me tomorrow. Stay the night.'

'I can't.' He breathed out a quiet moan. 'I'll be on duty.'

'The story of our lives. Hold the thought then.'

'How could I forget?'

It was a lie, of course. He'd clear me from his mind before he reached the car park, while people with sensible professions relaxed at home with their families. At work he'd be DCI Burns again, calm and implacable, focused only on getting the job done.

I went to the safe house after he'd gone, to relieve Gurpreet until morning. His solemn expression showed that the pressure of Mikey's silence was weighing on him; he lingered for an extra half hour, discussing the strategies he'd been using to help the child open up. None of them seemed to be working; Mikey made little eye contact, taking himself off to bed earlier than usual. I spent the last few hours of my evening trawling back through witness reports on HOLMES 2. By the time midnight came, my legs were cramping from too long in front of the computer, so I forced myself to do half an hour of yoga. My muscles gradually unknotted, but my mind was still racing when I finally went to bed.

26

It's colder this morning. The man's bones ache as he huddles in his car on a quiet street in Deptford. It has taken time and effort to find Gurpreet Singh. Repeated calls to his employer brought no success, but he has finally tracked him down by the simplest method imaginable; the nurse's number is in the phonebook. Singh's address tallies with details on his Facebook and Twitter pages, stating that he lives in Southwark. Now it's six a.m. and the man is willing himself to stay awake. When Singh emerges from his front door, he must follow him to the safe house without being spotted.

He's relieved to escape from the laboratory. The woman has spent hours working on Clare Riordan with needles and knives, whispering threats in her ear. When he left an hour ago, the doctor was suspended from the ceiling again, body jerking as she fell unconscious. While he feels no shame about his actions, the enjoyment on the woman's face forced him to look away. He stares across the street at the small bungalow, its cheerful yellow façade glowing as the darkness lifts. He wonders how it must feel to lead a blameless life, no blots on your copybook. When their relationship began, the woman's passion drew them together in a common cause. It started as a crusade, but now it's spiralled out of control. Soon he must persuade her that they've taken enough victims. They should make their announcement in an anonymous letter, and end the violence. But the thought fails to reassure him. The woman seems determined to wipe out every name on the list.

He's deep in thought when the bungalow door swings open. An Indian man rushes to a beaten-up Volvo, the sight steadying the man's nerves. He has a task to complete and it's important to stand firm. He watches Singh's car slip into the morning traffic, then follows him at a measured pace.

27

Press photographers' flashbulbs snapped at me as I climbed the steps to the station on Sunday morning. Tania's hostile expression let me know that Don had already tackled her about our conversation; she was in the meeting room, beating a tattoo on her notepad with a biro. Angie offered me a subdued version of her pixie-like smile.

'The great man's been delayed,' she said.

'Is there any news?'

'We're still looking for Eleanor Riordan's car, but there's no sign.'

'I'm seeing her boyfriend later,' I said. 'I'll find out what he knows.'

Tania's eyes narrowed. 'Good luck with that. The bloke's a pisshead.'

Burns strode through the door before I could reply, excitement emanating through his pores. 'Hancock's team turned over Clare Riordan's department at the Royal Free. They found a shirt in her deputy's locker with a stain on the sleeve; the lab just sent in the results. It's Riordan's blood.'

I felt a quick surge of shock. Despite Adele Novak's suggestion that Pietersen had strong feelings for his boss, I hadn't believed the doctor was capable of harming her. His emotions seemed too rigidly controlled.

'Are you bringing him here?' Angie strained forwards in her chair, like an eager schoolgirl.

'I'm going to his house first.' He turned to me. 'You'd better come, Alice, to see how he reacts.'

The news had thrown me off course. I'd been convinced that the killers had a political axe to grind, the victims of medical negligence. But I remembered the gentle classical music playing in Pietersen's consulting room, so at odds with his tense manner.

I listened carefully while Angie reported on her team's work at the Barbican. Hundreds of home visits had built a composite picture of the killers' actions. An old man had seen a couple hanging around the garage block just before midnight from the window of his flat, but site security had arrived too late. So far Adebayo's computers and phone had revealed little apart from his affection for his wife. Their texts ranged from romantic to pornographic, as if they were still newlyweds. I wondered how Gina Adebayo was dealing with the fact that he would never return from his last night shift.

'The killers are adapting their approach as they gain confidence,' I said. 'Their style's faster and more sophisticated. The sites they're choosing are important in the history of blood treatments, and using Pure's logo tells us they're getting even for the tainted blood scandal. I think you should check all the group's members, and widen the search to everyone who received infected blood in the UK.'

'That could take a while. The NHS are slow to find information, and the patients will have scattered far and wide. The logo could be a blind alley anyway,' Burns said. 'Hancock's discovery blows everything sky-high. Pietersen's got Riordan's blood on his shirt, and it sounds like he's got anger management problems too. It's never pretty when a doctor loses the plot. Remember the Leonard Newman case? He killed fifteen patients in one year. Maybe he's getting even with colleagues who're more successful; we just need to find the links.'

'I knew there was something dodgy about him.' Angie's smug smile suggested the doctor had already been jailed.

I stepped out of the office to call Christine and let her know that I would miss our catch-up meeting at the FPU, but was distracted by noise spilling from the incident room. A dozen members of the team were thronging round Pete Hancock, who looked pleased but embarrassed, clearly enjoying his newfound hero status. I remembered his complaint about his work going unnoticed and shot him a wide smile. Whether or not his find turned out to be vital, his commitment deserved recognition.

It was eleven a.m. when Burns and I left via the back exit, photographers snapping our departure. His brisk pace made me rush to keep up, but he calmed down as we escaped the scrum of journalists.

'Fancy a week in Rome when this is over?' he said, unlocking the car.

'I'd prefer somewhere warmer.'

'Who cares, if we've got room service and a Jacuzzi?'

I was too preoccupied to quibble during the drive. Until now I'd been sure that the killers were patients with a grievance, but my judgement could have been flawed. My concern for Mikey might be blinding me to obvious clues: the use of hospital equipment and the killers' love of administering injections. My mind clicked through possibilities like it was twisting a Rubik's cube. I stared out of the window at my old stamping ground. The Maudsley Hospital's façade looked as grand as when I'd trained there thirteen years before; classic late imperial architecture, the Victorians blowing their cash on lavish building projects. Burns's Audi followed the light traffic up Denmark Hill before swinging left towards Dulwich. I'd always loved the neighbourhood, but couldn't afford to rent there as a student, settling for a rundown flat on a railway siding in Camberwell. It would require serious money to buy one of the gorgeous Regency villas near the common, covered in wedding-cake stucco.

Dr Pietersen's house turned out to be a bland Thirties semi five minutes from Dulwich village. The house was painted the same inoffensive cream as its neighbour, guaranteed to go unnoticed.

'Let me speak to his wife,' I said, as we waited in the porch.

'Okay, but I'll give him the news first.'

Mrs Pietersen was an attractive Asian woman of around fifty, with a watchful gaze, and shoulder-length black hair pinned back from her face. There was no sign of a smile when she opened the door.

'I'll get my husband,' she said. 'He's doing paperwork.'

Her absence gave me time to admire her kitchen. The glass worktops glistened as if no one had ever cooked there. Cleanliness and order ruled wherever I looked, from the scrubbed lino to the tea towels folded in an immaculate pile. When I turned round Dr Pietersen was standing by the table. He looked older than I remembered, skin sallow, as if he was sickening for something.

'Please take a seat,' he said. 'Has Clare been found?'

'I'm afraid not.' Burns sat opposite him.

'Is it okay if Imako stays?'

'We need to see you alone, please.'

'I don't keep secrets from my wife.'

'Like I said, we'll talk to you separately.'

Pietersen's wife shot us a dark look when she exited the room, clearly furious to be sent away. Burns seemed unmoved, draping his coat over the back of his chair like he planned to stay all day.

'How did you meet your wife, Dr Pietersen?'

'Why's that relevant?'

'It may not be,' Burns said. 'But you don't get on with Dr Riordan, do you? I need to understand your background.'

'Imako and I worked at a hospital in Saigon. She nursed until the kids arrived, then we came back to the UK.'

'Adapting to a different culture must have been stressful for her.'

'That was twenty years ago.' He huffed out the words. 'I think you should tell me what this is about. My office has been commandeered.'

'One of your colleagues thinks you're in love with your boss.'

His muddy eyes blinked wide. 'Clare? That's ridiculous.'

'An item's been found, linking you to her abduction.'

'That's impossible.'

'We found a shirt in your locker with her blood on the sleeve. I'm surprised you kept it. Was it a memento?'

'It's not connected to her disappearance.'

Burns folded his arms. 'You'd better explain.'

The doctor's hands clenched in his lap. 'Clare phoned me in August, begging me to go round. I found her in the kitchen bleeding heavily from a wound on her wrist. She said some-one had attacked her. Luckily her son was at a friend's house.'

'Why didn't you call the police?'

'She wouldn't hear of it. I had an emergency kit in my car, so I stitched the cut myself – that's how my shirt got stained. It was a present from Imako. I kept meaning to get it dry-cleaned.'

'Do you know how far-fetched that sounds?'

Pietersen's shoulders jerked upwards. 'She said the police would make things worse. She seemed terrified about her boy, begging me to keep it secret.'

'Someone had threatened to hurt her son?'

'Clare wouldn't say his name.'

'What did you do after stitching her wound?'

'I made her a drink then mopped the floor, so her son wouldn't see the blood. I offered to let them stay here, but she refused.'

'Why didn't you call emergency services?'

'To honour her wishes.' Pietersen's eyes closed for a moment. 'The injury seemed like classic self-harm, a deep wound to the inner wrist. It looked like she'd cut herself then regretted it. Not going to hospital meant she could pretend it had never happened.'

'No one else thought she was depressed.'

'Maybe the pressure was too much. Clare's a perfectionist; she wants to be the best mother, top of her profession, win every game.' A scowl settled on his face.

'You concealed evidence. If that's the truth, why didn't you tell us when she went missing?'

'It wasn't my place.'

'You were covering your back,' Burns snapped. 'Did you know Lisa Stuart, John Mendez and Jordan Adebayo?'

There was a long pause before Pietersen replied. 'I met Professor Adebayo a few years ago. We were both invited to a lunch in Whitehall; we'd been asked to serve on an advisory panel.'

'The Tainted Blood enquiry in 2012?'

'It looked like being a whitewash, so I turned it down. I don't know whether Adebayo agreed.'

'Did Clare tell you she was a member?'

'I had no idea.' Pietersen looked uncomfortable. 'She probably signed a non-disclosure notice.'

Burns gave a brisk nod. 'You'll be taken to the station to answer more questions, but we'll speak to your wife first.'

I scribbled notes on an evidence form while he collected the doctor's wife. Not only had Pietersen known another of the victims, all of his emotional reactions seemed blunted. My overriding impression was of an egotist more upset by professional failure than his colleague's abduction. If he was telling the truth about finding Riordan wounded, she must have exerted considerable power to buy his silence. Maybe he had been in love with her after all. It was becoming clear that Clare had made a profound impact on everyone she'd met.

Imako Pietersen seemed less composed than her husband when she perched on a stool opposite us, her hands twisting in her lap.

'Are you worried about your husband's mental state, Mrs Pietersen?' I asked.

Her eyebrows shot up. 'Why should I be?'

'He seems distracted. Have you noticed changes in him?'

'Only that his diabetes is worse. I want him to retire, but he won't hear of it.'

'A typical man, in other words?'

She scowled at me. 'Ed thinks he's indispensable.'

'Has he spoken much about Clare Riordan?'

'Often. She sounds too neurotic to run the department, but he's always been loyal. I don't see why you're asking these questions.'

'Clare's missing, Mrs Pietersen. It's our job to investigate her disappearance. Did you know that your husband asked the hospital trustees twice to demote her?'

Her voice was shrill with anger. 'A senior doctor with mental health problems is a liability. She could harm patients, couldn't she?'

There was something chilling about her rigid posture, combined with the irritation she couldn't hide. A body language expert would have found her a fascinating case study, immobile as a waxwork from start to finish, anger spilling over in her intense stare and tone of voice. When she heard that her husband would be taken to the police station, it was obvious she was barely managing to keep her temper in check.

Burns stood on the pavement afterwards, watching Pietersen being driven away. 'They're not exactly touchy-feely, are they?'

'I'm surprised you're leaving her here. She's like a bomb, waiting to explode.'

'We'll be keeping watch. There's more chance of a confession with no contact between them. If he doesn't open up, she'll be brought in next.'

'They match the profile for Riordan's abductors. He's intellectual, obsessive, highly controlled, and she's the emotional one, struggling to keep her feelings locked down. Pietersen's work could have caused a blood fetish. But his behaviour, speech patterns and eye contact suggest he was telling the truth when he described finding Riordan injured.'

'Surely Clare would have phoned a close friend if she was hurt?'

'Maybe she saw Pietersen as an old-fashioned man of his word. He might have been her best chance of keeping it quiet.'

'He could be attacking other medics out of professional jealousy. The guy had complained about feeling overlooked.'

'There's a chance it's Clare's sister, working with an accomplice. But why would she be obsessed by blood?'

Burns shook his head. 'After we talk to her boyfriend, I'll see Pietersen again.'

His gaze was so focused as he drove to Luke Mann's house in Camberwell it looked like he was navigating a tank through a minefield. The investigation had his name printed on it – success or fail, he would carry the can. Stress was evident in his tight clutch on the wheel as we pulled up outside a sprawling nineteenth-century vicarage with leaded windows and a sagging, slate-tiled roof. The building must have held rural charm before the metropolis swallowed it whole. Now it was hemmed in by grey tower blocks and rows of abandoned garages, with doors coated in graffiti.

'It's a ruin,' Burns muttered.

The doorbell chimed, but there was no sound of footsteps. After a few minutes I wandered down the side passageway to peer through the window. Luke Mann's living room was in disarray, piles of clothes draped over furniture, as if he'd packed in a hurry, decided to travel light. Burns joined me as I gazed through the window.

'There's a load of post on his doormat. Maybe he's done a runner too.'

'There could be a simple explanation. He could be out for the day, the appointment forgotten.'

He shook his head. 'Ten minutes ago I was sure it was Pietersen, now I'm wondering if Eleanor's talked her boyfriend into helping her get even.'

Burns was already punching numbers into his phone, his shoulders hunched. There was nothing I could say to comfort him. My own suspicions about aggrieved patients were fragmenting under the weight of primary evidence. Suddenly an abundance of suspects had come to light: Riordan's deputy carried her blood on his shirtsleeve and her sister's boyfriend had vanished into thin air.

28

There was no sign of Mikey that afternoon, even though he must have heard me carting bags of groceries from the boot of my car. I found him hunched on his bed, eyes glued to the iPad that Gurpreet had borrowed from his office. He hardly looked up when I said hello, his face rigid with anger.

'Want to come and play cards?' I asked.

He was on his feet before I could move, a cracking noise as the computer bounced from the wall inches above my head, fracturing the plaster. I was too shocked to react as he rushed downstairs, beating his hands on the door's toughened glass. I stood behind him, avoiding his fists. Despite his small frame, a stray punch could still have caused damage.

'You should stop now, Mikey. You'll hurt yourself.'

Gurpreet emerged from the kitchen, but I motioned for him to stay back. The boy's rage was already fading, his flailing movements weaker than before. When I touched his shoulder he pressed his face against my ribs, tears soaking the fabric of my jumper. I pulled him down beside me until we sat with our backs to the wall, Gurpreet crouching beside us.

'Today's been tough, hasn't it, Mikey?' the nurse said quietly. 'His school teacher came round; he was upset when she left.'

'That's understandable.' Seeing a familiar face would be a reminder that other people's lives were going on as normal.

'You'll feel better if we keep busy, Mikey. Why don't you help me make dinner?'

I thought he might choose to sleep off his outburst, but after five minutes he struggled to his feet. When we reached the kitchen he helped me chop vegetables for a curry. His hair stood up in tufts, eyes red from crying. It seemed heroic that he was mucking in, even though he was fraying at the seams. I wanted to hug him, but knew it was essential to let children initiate touch. I showed him how to make a dessert instead, more for the therapeutic value than any hope of him eating it. Some of the tension slipped from his face as he mixed berries with cream and meringue for the Eton mess.

'I bet Gurpreet eats most of this tomorrow,' I said.

I kept my thoughts to myself as we ate. It seemed odd that I was reluctant to meet Burns's sons, yet Mikey's trust felt like the most natural thing in the world. Sooner or later the emotional fall-out from the case would have to be analysed, but not until it was resolved. Until then my priority had to be the child's welfare. By the time I went upstairs to check on Mikey, he was in bed, eyes bleary with exhaustion.

'Feel like reading?' I asked, but he shook his head. 'You know Gurpreet and I think you're brilliant, don't you?'

He shifted his head on the pillow, ready for sleep. I dropped a kiss on his forehead, leaving the door open by a fraction, so he could see the hall light if he had a bad dream. I picked up the broken iPad on my way back downstairs. There was a crack in the casing, but it might still be repairable.

Once I was back in the lounge, I wrote up my reports from that day's interviews. Everyone inside Clare Riordan's circle seemed to be nursing complex feelings. The investigation was zoning in on Eleanor, Luke Mann and the Pietersens. I felt sure the doctor had been telling the truth about stitching her wound to save her the trauma of a hospital visit after an attack at her home. Only the pallor of his skin had made him seem ill at ease during the interview, making me wonder if the stress of Riordan's absence had worsened his health. But the fact that he knew Adebayo because of his connection to the Tainted Blood enquiry was another cause for concern. His wife's manner interested me too, even though Burns had chosen not to bring her to the station. I completed her interview report, marking high scores for denial, repressed anger and hostility. Imako Pietersen reminded me of Marie Benson, a prolific serial killer I'd interviewed during the Crossbones case. She'd had the same quality of stillness, like the sea's calm surface with riptides boiling underneath.

I was about to go to bed when my gaze caught on the iPad. It seemed to have survived intact, the motor grinding into life when I hit the start button. The image I saw made my eyes blink wider. Mikey must have used the wireless pen clipped to the device to draw a row of tightly packed houses, cars and trees scattered along the pavement, a square building that looked like a block of flats. But the feature that made my skin prickle was the dark blue car at the end of the street, passengers in the front seats too small to make out, their faces blurred. One thing was unmissable; a small figure with a mop of dark hair was hiding between two buildings. For a second I felt my pulse quicken, as if I was kneeling beside Mikey, cowering from a threat neither of us could name.

29

The woman reaches the lab at midnight. The soft rain gives her an excuse to keep her hood raised as she approaches the alleyway. When she hits the light switch, the neon brightness makes Riordan give a muffled groan, her skin chafed raw by the gag, amber eyes searching for mercy. The woman forces a straw into her mouth, making her gulp down a protein drink, aware that her victim may be needed alive for many more days. She's too exhausted to goad her as she ties the tourniquet, plunging the needle into Riordan's inner arm, ignoring her raw moan.

'Shut up,' she mutters. 'No one can hear you.'

Crimson liquid drips slowly into the bag. Maybe it's imaginary, but the fluid looks darker than before, stained by guilt. It makes the woman glad to be wearing surgical gloves, keeping her hands perfectly clean. Once the bag is full, she withdraws the needle. Riordan's eyes roll back as she falls unconscious.

'Sleep tight, Clare,' the woman whispers.

She wraps the blood pack carefully in brown paper. She doesn't care if Riordan's alive or dead as she slips back along the alleyway, then drives to a quiet west London street. She makes her deposit then glances at the building's façade with a sense of repulsion. None of the scientists who work inside are brave enough to defend their patients.

The woman feels calmer when she's back in the driving seat. She doesn't care if she has to act alone from now on; at least the man has discovered where the boy's being held. Whatever happens next, she'll keep working on Riordan until the score is settled. The sense of justice when she kills her will be personal as well as political. Riordan's voice carried more weight than any other panel member; she cast away a perfect opportunity to help the victims.

30

Monday 27 October

Mikey was hugging his copy of the London *A–Z* like a security blanket the next morning. A wave of anxiety crossed his face when he saw my print of his picture.

'This is a really good drawing,' I said. 'I'm guessing that's the car they took you in, and this is the street where you ran away?'

His nod was so small I almost missed it. 'Almost there,' he whispered. Fear had returned to the boy's face. There was no point in hurling questions at him. It looked like the first loud noise would send him scuttling back to his room.

'You've got a brilliant memory, Mikey. If you remember anything else, you can draw more pictures, can't you?'

I felt a wave of guilt when Gurpreet arrived, the child's face blanching. In an ideal world I'd have taken him with me to prove that I had no intention of disappearing from his life.

I arrived for my first appointment early, so I stopped at a café on Borough High Street to browse through a copy of the *Independent.* The front page held a picture of the stand of trees where Clare Riordan had been abducted. Members of the public had turned it into a shrine; enough cards littered the grass to fill a gift shop, hundreds of bouquets choking in cellophane, messages begging her abductors to set her free. The outpouring made me marvel at the English temperament. We repressed affection for our families, yet deified strangers. My fear of intimacy seemed to be shared by everyone in the land.

It was just after nine a.m. when Angie and I called on Lisa Stuart's mother. She had been interviewed once already, to try and establish whether her daughter had known any of the other victims, but had been too upset to comment in detail. I wanted to help Angie tease out any facts lurking in her memory, provided we could keep her calm. Mrs Stuart lived in a narrow house near Borough Market, sandwiched between a pub and a gift shop. The expression on the old woman's face when we arrived was so hopeful, she seemed to be expecting us to say that her daughter had returned safe and sound. She was a plump woman, dressed tidily in a grey skirt and matching twinset, white hair framing her face. She inspected us closely through glasses with thin gold frames.

'Have you got news?' Her hand settled on Angie's arm as we stood in the hall.

'I'm afraid not, Mrs Stuart. Why don't we all sit down for a minute?'

It was obvious that her home was her pride and joy. Every surface in her living room glittered with polish, tasteful dark wood furniture, nothing out of place. A cluster of framed photos of Lisa hung on the wall; junior school portraits through to a picture of her looking stunning in an evening dress, strawberry blonde curls swept back from her face. Mrs Stuart watched us avidly, fingers tapping the arm of her chair.

'This is about those other doctors going missing, isn't it?'

Angie nodded. 'It may be linked to Lisa's disappearance.'

She studied us so closely it felt like she was measuring each blink. 'You think she's been killed, don't you?'

'I'm afraid that's possible, but we don't have proof,' Angie said. 'Two other doctors have been taken in the past fortnight; one of them has been found dead.'

She let out a gasp. 'It's not knowing that's hardest. I lost my husband three years ago, and that was terrible, but at least he got a proper funeral. With Lisa there isn't even a gravestone.'

'That must be hard.'

'I put my life on hold at the start, waiting for news. Now I make myself see friends each week. My other daughter Jenny's been brilliant.'

'Do you remember much about the weeks before Lisa went missing?' I asked.

Mrs Stuart peered at me over her glasses. 'Not really. She came by as usual that Sunday; we cooked lunch together.'

'Did she mention the work she was doing as an advisor on a panel?'

'That was something hush-hush. I can't remember what it was about.'

'Had anything unusual happened to her?'

'She got these letters, but didn't think it was anything important. She brought one round to show me. I showed it to the police at the time.'

'Could we see it?'

She reached into her bureau drawer and handed me an envelope. Lisa's name and address were typed on a printed label, when I opened it there was a grey postcard with Pure's logo drawn at the centre.

'Could we keep this for now, Mrs Stuart?'

'Of course, dear. But it's just a few scribbles; it doesn't give you much to go on, does it?'

I smiled at her. 'It could help a great deal. We'll come back if there's any more news.'

Her eyes were flooding with tears. 'I'm so glad you came. At least I know Lisa hasn't been forgotten.'

I felt choked when we walked away. Angie fell silent for once as we trudged down the road. The woman had spent eight months waiting; there would be no closure until she could give her daughter a formal burial. The postcard brought a new dimension to the case; in addition to organising and researching each crime, one of the killers was communicating with the victims they singled out. It was likely that the others had received the same cryptic message through the post.

The atmosphere had changed when we reached St Pancras Way just after ten. More journalists were massing on the steps, faces alert after days of gloom. Clearly they'd heard that an arrest was imminent. Burns greeted me in the incident room, face drawn as he broke into a smile.

'Heavy night?' I asked.

'A late one, that's for sure. We kept Pietersen in a holding cell and arrested him on suspicion this morning, but we need more time. Another pint of blood was left outside the Institute for Biomedical Science in Kensington last night.'

'So that rules Pietersen out?'

'But not his wife. The surveillance guys lost her car when she went out last night. I'm about to arrest her. We've got a warrant for a full house search; Hancock's there now.'

I felt a twitch of sympathy. Imako Pietersen's immaculate home would be comprehensively turned over, even if she was innocent, crime scene officers ransacking every cupboard. For someone so house proud, it would be the ultimate punishment. I showed Burns the card that had been sent to Lisa Stuart, and heard him take a sharp breath.

'The link to Pure keeps getting stronger.'

'Have you got the membership list from Ian Passmore?'

'He's given us eight hundred names, but there are more. We're chasing it up.'

I nodded in reply. 'What's the news on Luke Mann and Clare's sister?'

'Tania's handling it,' Burns said. 'Pietersen's our top priority. I've been at the Health Ministry, grilling them about the advisors on the Tainted Blood enquiry, but they're not budging.'

'Can I observe your interview with Imako?'

'Feel free,' he replied. 'I've made an appointment for you and Tania to see Ian Passmore later.'

Burns's body language was upbeat despite long days and blind alleys. He seemed to believe victory was near, but I felt less certain as we approached the interview room. I wondered how the leading light of Pure would react to another interview, but there was no time to speculate. Imako Pietersen was already being escorted through the door, a thunderous expression on her face. By contrast her solicitor was cheerful and avuncular, his paunch straining the buttons of his shirt, working hard to compensate for his client's gloom. Her eyes looked cold enough to freeze any surface within ten metres. She snapped out her first request before Burns had finished reading her rights.

'I want to see my husband.'

'That's not possible, I'm afraid,' he replied.

'If he gets sick, you'll be to blame.'

'Crimes have to be investigated, Mrs Pietersen. Your husband knows several of the victims, including his boss.'

'My husband heals people. Why would he hurt anyone?'

Burns gazed at her steadily. 'We asked for your whereabouts on the morning of Clare Riordan's abduction. No one can verify that you were at home; maybe you and your husband went to Clapham Common, picking up a car along the way.'

'Ed went to work and I did housework. Is that so hard to believe?' Imako's voice was rising to a shout.

'What did you do last night?'

'I visited friends in Kensington; I didn't want to be alone. Neither of my kids live in London.'

'You were told to stay at home. I'll need the time you left home and your friends' contact details.'

She scribbled words on the paper Burns pushed across the table. The impression she gave was of rigid self-control, too many emotions trapped inside her skin. Her unquestioning loyalty to her husband was a feature of most violent partnerships. Serial killers shared a sense of exclusion, pitting themselves against all-comers like Bonnie and Clyde. Maybe both of the Pietersens had felt overlooked. She had been a housewife in a foreign culture for two decades, and her husband's CV showed him switching jobs regularly, never progressing past the rank of deputy. It was easy to imagine them railing against the world's injustices over dinner. The only time Imako's softer side revealed itself was when she spoke of personal matters.

'How long has your husband been ill?' I asked.

'Years.' Her voice faltered. 'From stress and overwork. He doesn't take care of himself.'

Burns leant closer, his arms resting on the table. 'Mrs Pietersen, I'm afraid your husband's been charged with abducting Clare Riordan. I'm arresting you as his accessory.'

'I don't believe it. You can't keep us here.'

Her solicitor made a hushing sound. 'On what grounds?'

'Primary evidence links Dr Pietersen to Clare Riordan's abduction. We know the abductor works with a female accomplice, and Mrs Pietersen has no confirmed alibi. She'll be taken to a holding cell then questioned again later.'

Imako gave us an outraged stare. 'You'll regret this. I could sue you.'

'Is there anything else you'd like to say?'

'We've done nothing wrong.' Her voice was a shrill protest. 'Plenty of people must hate Clare Riordan. She's the type to smile at you, then sleep with your husband.'

'You think they were having an affair?' Burns asked.

'Of course not, but I bet she tried.' Her voice cooled, as if she'd retreated behind a layer of ice.

Burns gave a low whistle after she'd been led away. 'She's not crazy about Riordan, is she?'

Imako Pietersen's outburst fascinated me. When her control had finally ruptured, her true feelings were exposed; Clare Riordan had been a threat. Perhaps her cold fish husband had been drawn to her vibrancy, even though she'd stolen his dream job.

Burns strode away to update his detectives, but I peered out of the window at the red buses hurtling down St Pancras Way, like blood cells borne along the city's arteries. The Pietersens' intense feelings towards Clare Riordan could have mutated into violence, but why would they harm Adebayo and the previous victims? Professional jealousy seemed too weak a motive for so much bloodshed, and why would they appropriate Pure's logo? Burns seemed convinced that he'd found his culprits, but too many pieces of the puzzle were missing.

Tania collected me at two o'clock. It was clear she was in no mood for small talk. She looked as stylish as ever, in a dark blue suit that must have cost a fortune, but her expression was weary. She donned a pair of sunglasses before we faced the press. The attempt at anonymity didn't work, journalists shouting questions until she raised her hand.

'The briefing's at three o'clock, guys. Move aside, please.' Her strident East End voice parted the crowd like the Red Sea.

'Impressive,' I commented as we reached my car.

'Why take shit from that lot? They'd walk over your dying body for a story.'

'Roger Fenton seems like an exception.' I caught sight of him as we drove away, patiently leaning against the railings, waiting for his scoop.

'The tabloid sleazebags are the worst.' Her fingertips drummed on the wheel. 'Passmore's been causing us grief. It says on Pure's website they've got over a thousand members, but he hasn't told us all the names. If he doesn't give us the rest today, he'll be arrested for withholding evidence.'

'Where does he live?'

'Cherry Garden Pier.'

The area was familiar terrain, only a stone's throw from my flat. Tania used the journey to discuss details. I got the sense that she was speaking more for her own benefit than mine, testing different angles and laying her doubts to rest. By the time we'd woven east through the city, I understood how hard Burns had been leaning on Pietersen since he'd been arrested, making him repeat his story, trying to fracture his alibis for the times of the abductions, and expose his wife's involvement. No doubt Imako's statement would be tested to destruction. So far there had been little progress on finding Clare's sister or her elusive boyfriend. Eleanor's car had vanished, and she hadn't been seen at work. Mann had left his property in the early hours of the morning carrying only a backpack. Neighbours had seen bailiffs outside his property, and thought that he'd been evading debt collectors. I was still trying to compare Clare's sister and Imako Pietersen as potential culprits when the car reached Shad Thames.

Ian Passmore's Victorian house was sandwiched between converted warehouses, so near the river it must have been worth a fortune. A tall woman with a sweep of long black hair greeted us. It was hard to guess her age, but she could have been anywhere between forty and fifty, strikingly beautiful, with an oval face and smooth olive skin. If I'd had to guess her origins, I'd have said Native American. Her unflinching stance suggested that she'd be a tough opponent in an argument. Slim trousers and a fitted top accentuated her athletic build. A slow smile of welcome lit up her face.

'Are you looking for me?'

'We've got a meeting with Ian Passmore.'

She stepped back to admit us. 'I'll take you to him. I'm Michelle De Santis, a volunteer with Pure.'

I returned her smile. 'My name's Alice, and this is Tania.'

'It's been a busy morning. We're doing a mail-out today.'

'Do you often help out?'

'Whenever I can.' She stopped to push open a door. 'Two ladies for you, Ian.'

I took a sharp intake of breath when we stepped into his living room. Folders and loose papers covered every piece of furniture, manila files lining the walls, dates scrawled on their spines. Passmore sat at the table, looking like his temper could flare at any minute; his wild grey hair couldn't have been combed in days, elegant clothes dishevelled. He snapped out a terse greeting but his brusqueness softened when he spoke to his assistant.

'Do you mind waiting in the kitchen, Michelle? This won't take long.' Passmore didn't turn to us again until she had retreated.

Tania perched on the arm of a chair loaded with box files. 'Mr Passmore, I still need contact details for the rest of Pure's members.'

'I told you, they're not all online. I keep paper records of every family here.'

'Print off your full circulation list for me now, please.'

Passmore scowled. 'Contacting them would be an invasion of privacy. Several of them are dying.'

'You've withheld the names of your sickest members?' Tania asked.

'Being interrogated now would be the final straw.'

While he defended his position against Tania's questions, my eyes scanned his living room. Whatever money he earned as a fundraiser wasn't being spent on home improvements. The carpet was threadbare, curtains fraying, his mantelpiece the only clear surface. It held two framed photographs: one showed two teenaged boys standing on top of a mountain, wearing jubilant smiles. The other was a graduation photo of a young man in a gown and mortarboard, colours so badly faded that the image looked ghostly. Passmore glowered at us while his printer spat out the remaining names.

I gestured at the photographs. 'Is that you and your brother on Ben Nevis, Mr Passmore?'

He gave an abrupt nod. 'We climbed it decades ago.'

'And that's his graduation photo?'

'His name was Grant. He died the year after it was taken.'

'I'm sorry,' I said quietly.

'Are you?' he snapped. 'Then why not take your manhunt elsewhere?'

Tania looked up from her notebook. 'Pure's logo is connected with some violent crimes, Mr Passmore. We have to investigate why.'

'Your killer's got a sick sense of humour. Thousands of people must know our symbol.'

I nodded at the stacked envelopes to defuse the tension. 'It looks like we disturbed your work.'

'We post out bulletins each month.'

'I'm sure your members are grateful.' I studied him again. 'Last time we spoke, you said you'd tried to find out the membership of the Tainted Blood panel. Can you explain why?'

'It was their job to decide if compensation should be increased. We wanted to petition them, but they refused to tell us. In the end the government refused to act.' Passmore looked so incensed, I could almost see the anger pulsing through his skin.

'We may need to contact you again,' Tania said. 'It's possible someone from Pure has taken matters into their own hands.'

'That's utter nonsense.'

Passmore was still complaining as we left. At the end of the corridor, I caught sight of Michelle De Santis, half concealed in the kitchen doorway, as if she couldn't decide whether to join the argument or remain in hiding.

'What do you think?' Tania asked as we walked away.

'He's got a quick temper, but that doesn't make him homicidal. He's an intellectual in a public position, spearheading a campaign group. It would be madness to leave his charity's symbol at the crime scenes, and he seems fully rational. I'd like to know about his volunteers, though.'

She shook her head dismissively. 'We've already checked them out. They've all got alibis for the attacks, but it sounds like Pure's members have got reason to be angry. My team'll go through the last names with a fine-tooth comb.'

'Can you send me an encrypted copy?'

She gave a distracted nod. I'd worked with Tania often enough to tell that she suspected Passmore. He came over as a lonely obsessive, his life dominated by a compulsion to protect those who had suffered his brother's fate.

'He ticks every box,' she said. 'But does he hate the medical profession enough to murder people?'

'Pietersen's not a safe bet?'

She shook her head. 'All we've got is the blood on his shirt, and there's no sign of him or his wife cracking.'

'Ian Passmore fits the pattern for a serial killer: stressed, disaffected, hostile. But he's smart enough to know that individual doctors aren't to blame for infected blood hitting the supply chain. It could just be a raging case of unresolved grief. If one of your siblings had died from an NHS treatment, wouldn't you be angry?'

'Anyone would. My team will run more searches on him today.'

By now we were standing on the river walk, a clipper heading west at high speed, destined for Westminster. 'Have you got half an hour?'

'Why?'

'My flat's nearby. We could have coffee.'

Tania came to a standstill. 'I'd love one, but I should get back.'

'Take a breather then. Let's watch the river for a few minutes.'

We leant against the railing as the water oozed by, pewter grey, two shades darker than the sky.

'You're not a typical shrink, Alice.'

'How do you mean?'

She gave a tense smile. 'Most are arrogant wankers who love the sound of their own voices.'

'A few are decent human beings.'

'Not in my experience.' Tania stared across the river towards Limehouse. 'Burns gave me hell after we spoke. He called me a cynical cow and told me to back off.'

'That was harsh.'

'He was right.' She kept her eyes fixed on the opposite bank. 'Did he tell you about him and me?'

I tried not to flinch. 'Not in so many words.'

'We had a fling at training school, then he met Julie and we ended up mates.'

'I guessed as much.'

She turned to face me. 'I'm sorry you caught me on a bad day. The autopsy followed by neat alcohol turned me into a prize bitch.'

'How come you know all about my love life, but I don't have a clue about yours?'

'There isn't one. Steve's put me off men for life.' Her bleeper buzzed loudly, expression hardening as she pulled it from her bag. 'No rest for the wicked.'

Tania left in a hurry, a blur of slender limbs trotting across the pavement to her car. For the second time she'd left me flailing. It didn't require much intuition to know that she still had feelings for Burns, even though he'd kept their fling quiet. It had been there in her tone of voice as well as her body language. I waited until she'd gone before heading for my flat at a rapid march. My system was so overcharged, I needed to release some adrenalin before I blew a fuse.

31

Tuesday 28 October

Lola made me breakfast the next morning. It was a habit we'd adopted since nights out had become a rarity. We were more likely to eat croissants together at eight a.m. than drink late-night tequila.

'God, I miss booze,' Lola sighed. 'I can't wait till Neve's on solids, so we can go clubbing.'

'Your inner wild child's alive and kicking?'

'Hell, yeah. When Mum took Neve to the park yesterday, I put on Rudimental and danced myself sick.'

'That's my girl.'

The image seemed incongruous. While telling me about her need to party she was breast-feeding my goddaughter. Neve seemed blissfully unaware of her mother's conflict of interests, lying in the crook of her arm, so full of milk she looked ready to pass out.

'You and Don are coming to Neal's birthday do tomorrow, aren't you?'

'Thanks for the reminder. The case has addled my brain.'

She narrowed her eyes. 'Don't let me down.'

'I wouldn't dare.'

'Have you told him how you feel?'

'God, you're like a cracked record.'

She sighed loudly. 'Bring him tomorrow, the poor guy needs moral support.'

'There's more to worry about than my love life.'

'Such as?'

'The boy I'm working with has got under my skin. The other day I found myself googling adoption procedures in case his mother isn't found.'

Lola gaped at me. 'You won't meet your boyfriend's sons, yet you've fallen for a kid you've known a few weeks.'

'I'm all he's got.'

'Burns is turning you soft.'

'You could be right. I found out he had a fling with a colleague and it's stuck in my head, even though it ended years ago.'

'You're jealous, Al.' She gave a whoop of laughter. 'That must be a first.'

I changed the subject, unwilling to admit she was right. The tension that had been churning in my gut since Tania made her revelation was still there on my walk back to the car, but my phone rang before my bad mood could worsen. The tense whisper at the end of the line belonged to Denise Thorpe, Clare Riordan's closest friend.

'Could you come over, Dr Quentin? I need your help.' Her voice was tight with anxiety.

I arranged to call by later that morning. It didn't take long to reach Wandsworth, but I sat in a café for an hour checking Gurpreet's case notes, measuring Mikey's progress. His night terrors were as bad as ever, but he was becoming more inter-active. I felt certain he was close to speaking again, although another crisis could shatter his progress. Mikey was still at the forefront of my mind when I reached Denise Thorpe's house. My sympathy rose when I saw that her eyes shone with repressed tears. She was wearing her usual drab assortment of clothes, so anonymous she almost blended into the pale walls of her kitchen.

'I wanted to see you while Simon's out.' Her words ground to a halt, as if she'd lost her thread.

'You've remembered something?'

'My husband would call me disloyal. The thing is, Clare's marriage was on the rocks before her husband died. She had affairs, before and after his death. Normally she met the men at conferences or through work.'

'Do you know their names?'

She shook her head. 'She's casual about it. But one of them could have got angry, couldn't he? I can't get it out of my mind.'

The statement echoed Dr Novak's description of Riordan's behaviour so directly that my concern grew. 'You're doing the right thing telling me. The team will try and track down men who attended the same conferences.'

'She acts like it's a joke, but I'd hate being treated that way.'

'It sounds as if Clare was chasing happiness, but your life seems much calmer.'

'Things aren't always as easy as they look.' Her eyes glistened. 'Can I see Mikey soon?'

'Not yet, I'm afraid.'

'Why not?' Her tone suddenly sharpened. 'It's cruel that he's so alone.'

She burst into a sudden storm of tears, hands covering her eyes. I sat in silence until she was composed enough to accept a tissue. Over the years I'd seen hundreds of people weep during therapy sessions: young men fighting their emotions, old women releasing a lifetime of sorrows. Denise Thorpe's outburst was loud and dramatic, racking sobs that made her shoulders heave. But by the time we said goodbye, her outrage had resurfaced.

'Why can't you tell us where Mikey's being kept?' she snapped.

'It's a security issue, Denise.'

'But we've known him since he was born. We've got a right to see him.'

'I promise to contact you as soon as you can visit.'

Her frown hardened. 'It's negligent to treat a child this way.'

Denise's eyes remained cold with disapproval when I said goodbye, as if I was the source of Mikey's unhappiness. Her husband's car was pulling up outside as I headed for mine. The confrontation had been so unsettling that I was keen to get away, but he headed straight towards me. Thorpe looked smarter than before in a well-cut suit, his smile widening as he shook my hand. It made me wonder whether he was an effective psychotherapist. To listen to patients fully, his ego would need to accept second place.

'I seem destined to miss your visits, Dr Quentin.'

'Your wife's upset today, I'm afraid.'

'This business with Clare has affected her terribly.'

'What about you?' I noticed how drawn he looked when I studied him more closely.

'It's Denise I'm worried about. If Clare doesn't come home, it'll put her back to square one.'

'How do you mean?'

'She's been battling depression for months. Looking after her mum hasn't helped, but this has come at the worst possible time.'

Simon Thorpe looked weary as he turned away, as though he was dreading going inside to comfort his wife.

I called Angie from my car en route to the FPU, to let her know that Clare Riordan might have had multiple short affairs with professional acquaintances before her fling with Sam Travers. But it was Denise Thorpe's state of mind that had triggered my concern. It could be due to anxiety or depression, but she seemed more vulnerable than before. During my visit she had lapsed from rationalism into fierce criticism, then resentment. Her desire to see Mikey struck me as unnaturally strong. There was no evidence to implicate her in Clare Riordan's abduction, yet I could imagine her going on the attack. The investigation team would be unwilling to look more closely at the Thorpes even though their alibis were weak for the Stuart and Mendez attacks, because there was nothing to implicate them. The couple claimed to have been at home together on both evenings, their neighbours stating that they were a quiet couple who rarely socialised. There was proof that they had visited Denise's mother at her care home early on the morning of Clare's abduction, both of their names printed in the visitors' book.

I spent that afternoon at the FPU, riding a wave of guilt, despite doing my best to catch up with voicemail and the notes cramming my in-tray. If the case didn't get resolved soon, I would fall hopelessly behind.

I was still frazzled when I keyed in the security code at the safe house that evening, but Mikey's greeting lifted my mood. The boy smelled of lemon soap and childhood when he hugged me, as though he'd been outside in the fresh air instead of stuck indoors. Our evening followed its usual routine. We went to the supermarket, played cards then cooked together. I allowed silences to open up, but no words emerged. He hummed loudly to himself as he stirred the chicken casserole simmering in its pan.

'Lots of people have been asking about you,' I said. 'Your mum's friends Denise and Simon want to visit soon.'

Mikey's reaction was intense. His face blanched but I caught him before he could fall, half carrying him to one of the kitchen chairs.

'Take a breath, sweetheart. That's it, nice and deep.'

I couldn't tell whether his reaction meant that he was desperate to see them, or afraid. It had been so extreme he'd almost passed out, his state probably worsened by lack of food. It seemed as though any mention of life before his mother's abduction could throw him into a state of panic. I had been considering showing him pictures of Pietersen and Ian Passmore, to see if he recognised them, but he seemed too fragile to cope with any more challenges. Gurpreet had told me that his appetite failed whenever I left. It was hugely frustrating that every time I pressed for information, Mikey shut down. I still had the sense that the boy held the key to the whole investigation, if I could only open him up. I waited until he'd gone to bed before calling Burns.

'You could hear a pin drop in the incident room,' he said. 'The Pietersens are in their cells and all's quiet on the western front.'

'I just mentioned the Thorpes to Mikey and he almost blacked out.'

'He must be missing people he knows. The Pietersens look good for it.'

'You haven't found the getaway vehicle yet.'

'Cars are easy to hide.' He sounded nonchalant.

'I'd still like a background check on the Thorpes.'

He groaned quietly. 'I told you, we've got nothing linking them to the abductions; the nurses at her mum's care home say they both visit her three or four times a week, morning and evening, since she had her stroke. It's Eleanor Riordan we should be worrying about. There's still no sign of her, but her boyfriend's back home. He was visiting his dad in hospital.'

'Good, I need to assess him.'

'Come with me tomorrow.'

'Don't forget it's Neal's birthday do in the evening.'

'I may not make it.'

'Don't get Lola angry. It's a terrifying sight.'

He gave a quiet laugh. 'I can imagine. A red-haired tornado, spitting out flames.'

'My brother wants to see you too. It's years since you met.'

'I'll do my best.' His voice fell to a murmur. 'Got to go. Love you, bye.'

I stared at my phone after the call ended. Love you, bye. For Burns it really seemed to be that simple: a big man with a big heart. He'd loved his wife and now he loved me – maybe Tania and all of his old flames had received pieces of his affection, too – yet I'd never felt more at sea. I wasn't convinced that the words existed in my vocabulary. I held my phone to my ear and repeated the phrase into a blizzard of white noise.

'Love you, bye.'

The words sounded dry and unconvincing before they had even passed my lips.

32

At three a.m. the city slips by in silence. The woman is alone in the car, but she doesn't have far to travel. Two blood packs lie in a holdall on the back seat as she drives through Southwark, aware that she must complete the next stage alone. If the man was here, he would fill the car with music, but she prefers silence. From now on, it will be her responsibility to carry the burden.

Her first port of call is a quiet neighbourhood in Shad Thames. This is where the shrink lives, blonde and self-righteous, certain that she knows best. She's the worst kind of apologist: bright enough to sympathise, but too weak to take sides.

She parks on Providence Square and enters the apartment block through the fire exit. In moments she reaches the third floor. Back pressed to the wall, she approaches the security camera, covering the lens with duct tape. There's no sound as she hurls the pack against the door. The impact makes a dull thud as it hits the wood, blood arcing across the lintel. Dark red liquid oozes across the tiles as she runs back down the stairs.

The woman's next destination is higher risk. She threads west through Borough to the Elephant and Castle, crossing the ugly shopping centre bordering the roundabout. It's not easy to avoid street cameras when she conceals the car between office blocks on Ontario Street. She puts on a blue apron like the ones worn by cleaners in the compound, then takes a bucket and mop from the boot. She adjusts her walk by a fraction, shoulders down, long fringe shading her face. By the time she's crossed the street, she's gained ten years, ready to start her second job of the day.

The security guards are deep in conversation when she arrives at the entrance. 'You're late tonight, love,' one of them comments.

'I got myself some overtime.' She shoots him a grin. 'Lucky old me.'

'Come on then, let's be having you.'

He presses the button to raise the barrier without a second look. She hurries across the quadrangle as if she knows exactly where she's going. Night cleaners are two a penny, an invisible workforce scouring the city while the executives dream. She can taste the evil on the air. The decision was rubber-stamped here: ministers agreeing a policy that failed so many, after lifetimes of suffering. She hides in the shadows. No one sees her empty half of the blood through a letterbox, leaving the rest on a wide set of steps.

She exits by a different gate. This time the guard is busy on his phone; releasing the gate when he spots her mop and overalls. The woman is miles away before the alarm goes up, sirens screaming from the compound's walls.

33

The smell hit me first – that butcher's-shop stench of meat decaying. I'd jogged up the steps to my flat, intending to collect a fresh set of clothes, but now I was frozen on the landing, choking back nausea as I studied the mess on my doorstep. The Pure symbol had been chalked beside a blood pack imprinted with Clare Riordan's name. The pulse of anger that hit me was strong enough to make me grit my teeth. Once I'd gathered my senses I grabbed my phone. Angie was a safer bet than Burns, who was bound to have a knee-jerk reaction.

Fifteen minutes later I saw her arriving from the landing window. Angie looked pale in the early morning light, grim-faced as she emerged from her car, Pete Hancock in tow. Reality hit home when two more squad cars appeared. Someone had walked into my apartment block while I slept at the safe house and spattered blood across my doorway. My mind chased back to the start of the investigation, trying to pinpoint who would target me, thoughts travelling too fast to make sense.

'Causing trouble again, Alice?' Hancock was already kitted out in his white overalls as he climbed the steps. 'You did the right thing staying outside. Are you okay waiting here till we finish?' His thick brows lowered a centimetre above small dark eyes, but today there was a flash of sympathy. Hancock's attitude had definitely softened since our chat in the café.

'I'll survive, Pete.'

'We'll talk when this is done.' His assistant was already securing tape across the stairwell, turning my home into a crime scene.

My legs felt like water as the drama unfolded. Angie was still downstairs organising her team, two uniforms stationed by the gates to the car park. I tried making myself useful by knocking on my neighbour's door, to find out if she'd heard anything, but there was no reply. My eyes were drawn to the horse chestnut tree at the centre of the square. It had finally shed its leaves, crooked branches poking fingers at the sky. I hugged my arms tighter around my body, feeling like a strong wind had stripped me to the bone. I was still standing by the window when Angie appeared beside me.

'Cup of tea?' she asked.

'Do I look that bad?'

'Just a bit shocked. Are you up to talking?' She touched my shoulder. 'Come on, Pete says we can go inside, if we wear overshoes.'

The tables had already turned. I'd used the same gentle tone on Gina Adebayo a week ago when her husband's blood had been left outside her Barbican flat, but this time I was the victim. Hancock and two junior SOCOs were still working in silence, dusting the doorframe and taking photographs of the darkening pool of blood. Even with overshoes it turned my stomach to step over it and unlock my door; there were a few red marks on my floorboards that I was desperate to scrub away. Angie's expression changed as she scribbled my statements in her notebook, a frown bisecting her forehead.

'It can't be the Pietersens,' I said. 'They're still in custody.'

Angie nodded. 'Their house came up clean, so we're letting them go; they're off the suspect list. You know how this works, Alice. I need you to name all the people linked to the case who might know where you live.'

'I'll do it now. Can you take another look at Denise and Simon Thorpe? They seem obsessed by Clare.'

'The boss already asked me. I'll go back over their transcripts.'

'Did the list of advisors come through yet from Whitehall?'

'They're still refusing. Apparently the health minister was sent death threats before the enquiry began, so their names were classified. The civil servants are terrified about the press getting hold of the connection to the murders. The MoD's putting security in place for the other panel members.'

'They haven't done a great job so far.'

Burns's footsteps announced him before he arrived, thundering across the landing. I heard him barking instructions at Hancock, then he loomed in the kitchen doorway, face chalk white against the black fabric of his coat.

'Give us a minute, can you?' he told Angie, without shifting his gaze from my face. The kitchen door clicked shut as his hand gripped my arm. 'You scared the living shit out of me.'

'Why?'

'I thought you'd been hurt.'

'It's okay, I'm alive and kicking.'

'Have you packed your bags?'

'Sorry?'

His eyebrows rose. 'They know where you live, Alice. You can't stay here.'

My mouth suddenly went dry. 'If I've been followed, they'll know about the safe house too.'

'We've doubled the level of patrol, but they probably don't even want the kid, it's medics they're targeting.' Burns sat at the kitchen table. 'You'd better pack enough stuff for a few weeks.'

'I can stay here, if the place is guarded.'

'Whoever did this tortured Jordan Adebayo, then cut his throat. You don't want to be around if they come back, do you?' His voice had slowed, as if he was explaining something obvious to a five year old.

'Don't patronise me, Don.'

'Behave like a grown-up, then. Blood was left at Skipton House too, where the health ministry's civil servants are based. Get your stuff, then we're leaving.'

I exited the room to avoid a full-scale war. Knowing he had a point made me even more incensed. The stubborn part of me hated being driven from my home, but common sense confirmed that it was better to be safe than sorry. I stuffed clothes, shoes and underwear into a holdall, then grabbed my makeup bag. My foul mood deepened when I found Burns hunched in the same position, tapping out a phone message.

'I should call Will,' I said.

'Why?'

'He'll let me stay on the boat.'

He didn't even look up. 'You're coming to mine. The security's set up.'

I forced myself to count to ten. There was no point in haranguing him, even though I was ready to blow a gasket. The next half-hour passed in a blur of activity that left me even more frustrated. Burns and Angie were organising briefings, getting the blood pack couriered to the forensics lab, uniforms guarding the cordon. By the time we left, Hancock had my door key in his pocket and the place was no longer mine.

'Let me carry those.' Burns reached for my bags when the lift arrived.

'I can manage.'

He sighed loudly. 'Jesus, you're hard to help.'

We drove through Borough without speaking, the radio on his dashboard bleating out a headache of messages. The turn of events meant that I would have to conquer my fear of intimacy in double-quick time. Burns's flat had just two bedrooms, one the size of a shoebox, filled by his sons' twin beds. The only place to sleep would be his king-size bed. When we stood in the hallway, the air felt cold. He stared down at me, hands buried in the pockets of his coat.

'Whatever it is, get it off your chest, Alice.'

'I don't want you making decisions for me.'

'Is that what this is about?'

'You never negotiate. You just take over.'

It irritated me hugely that the attraction was still there, even though I felt like punching him; it was yet another thing I couldn't control. Desperate to do something practical, I carted my holdall to his bedroom and began to unpack. Tears came unannounced, spilling on to the clothes I'd piled on the bed.

'Get a fucking grip,' I muttered to myself.

Burns appeared before I could wipe my eyes. It always surprised me that someone so large could move soundlessly. His arms closed round me before I could push him away. To his credit he didn't flinch, as if holding a woman while she sobbed was something he did every day. After a few minutes I was calm enough to listen when he spoke again.

'Put your stuff anywhere you like. The guard'll be here till I get back.'

His thumb rubbed across my cheek, wiping it dry, then he was gone, leaving me to adjust. It occurred to me that I hadn't even thanked him for letting me stay.

I helped myself to a bowl of cornflakes and waited for the shock to subside. The rush of sugar helped stop my hands shaking, my mind steadying too. I flipped open my laptop to compile a list of suspects. It was depressingly clear that anyone with enough motivation could have found my address; the article in the *Mail* had exposed my role at the FPU. They could have waited outside head office and followed me home from St James's Park; I'd been so preoccupied that I wouldn't have noticed someone trailing me to the Underground. I still felt certain that the killers had an intellectual interest in blood transfusion. Some of the people I'd interviewed had close links to Clare Riordan. But why would they target other blood specialists, unless they had a bigger point to prove about the Tainted Blood enquiry? Despite the ministry's refusal to reveal the members, the killers could somehow have tracked down the names and be working their way through the list. And the sites chosen for the blood deposits were no longer just places with historic relevance to blood medicine; now they included personal targets too. Gina Adebayo's husband had been taken, and I was helping to chase the killers down; blood had been thrown over both our doorsteps. But that took me no closer to finding the culprits. Ed and Imako Pietersen couldn't have deposited the blood because they'd been in police custody, their names removed from the suspect list. Sam and Isabel Travers might have done it, even though their relationship had broken down. They could have personal reasons for hating the NHS doctors they'd interviewed, Sam's failed affair with Clare Riordan triggering a rush of violence. Denise and Simon Thorpe both had medical backgrounds, but Burns was adamant that their alibis stacked up. And then there was Eleanor Riordan, running from the furore ever since I'd spotted her at the scene of her sister's abduction. The last on my list was Ian Passmore, whose righteous anger had become his modus operandi. I scanned the names again. Whoever was carrying out the crimes was calm enough to stroll past security into the Health Ministry's compound, while their partner was capable of unparalleled violence.

I kept working until everyone I'd met since the start of the case was included on my list, then sent an encrypted email to

Angie. Too edgy to relax, I ran another search into Pure and found a *Times* article from 2012: PROTESTERS REJECT TAINTED BLOOD FINDINGS. The first thing that caught my eye was a picture of Ian Passmore being dragged along Downing Street by two policemen. His expression was calm but defiant, as though his crusade could last for ever. It had seemed too obvious that his campaign logo had been left at the crime scenes, but maybe he had uncovered the names of the government's advisors, his grief for his brother turning into violence. The article gave a measured account of the government's decision. A panel of experts had been consulted, but the health minister had denied guilt for allowing infected blood into the country, refusing to increase the victims' compensation. The story explained the situation coolly, but left no doubt that the patients deserved justice. When I scanned the report, the journalist's name jumped at me: Roger Fenton. I felt another pulse of concern. The journalist had shown a fascination with the case from the start, hanging around the station, quizzing me for information, and arriving first at the scene when Jordan Adebayo's body was found. But he was only doing his job as an investigative journalist, and it sounded like his injury had put him out of action at the time of the initial attack in January. I scribbled a reminder to contact him again. My mind still baulked at the idea that I was in personal danger, even though I'd seen the evidence lying in a dark red pool outside my door.

By four o'clock I was exhausted enough to flake out on Burns's sofa. I read a paragraph of his book on Jackson Pollack, then fell asleep. It was dark when I woke up, streetlight spilling through the windows. Lola had sent a terse message reminding me that Neal's birthday party would start at nine. I forced myself on to my feet; even in a crisis her temper was best avoided. It blew through her like a whirlwind, uprooting everything in its path.

Burns arrived while I was zipping myself into a dark red dress that looked demure from the front, but low enough at the back to expose most of my vertebrae. He stood in the hallway while I put on silver hooped earrings, with a stunned expression on his face.

'This is how you face a death threat? Dress up and hit the town?'

I studied him over my shoulder. 'It beats moping indoors.'

'Don't you believe in staying safe?'

'You're coming too. I'll have a personal bodyguard.'

'Can't we stay here?' He skimmed his index finger down my back. 'You look amazing.'

It crossed my mind to call and make an excuse, but the repercussions would have been endless. It took all my powers of persuasion to drag him into the taxi.

'Is there any news?' I asked, as his hand closed over mine.

'The blood at your flat's definitely Riordan's. The exit doors in your block weren't even locked.' Burns shot me a look of disgust, as if the security lapse was my fault alone.

Lola's flat was crammed with actors determined to enjoy themselves, which suited me fine. For a few hours I needed to forget that my home had been targeted. By eleven p.m. the party was in full swing, the room so packed that I lost sight of Burns. I chatted to a stunning Portuguese dancer, who made her living in the chorus line of a West End musical. A minute later I caught sight of Don on the other side of the room, absorbing Lola's chatter. From a distance he was a mass of contradictions: expensive jeans and cheap shoes; hard as nails but capable of tenderness. Someone tapped me on the shoulder while I observed him. When I swung round, my brother stood there, a bottle of beer gripped in his hand. I felt a quick stab of worry. Alcohol mixed badly with his psychoactive drugs – I scanned the room for Nina but couldn't see her anywhere. There was no point in telling Will what had happened earlier; he lived with enough fears of his own. He looked edgier than I'd seen him in months. The strain showed in the tense set of his shoulders.

'Let's get this done,' he said. 'Where's the new boyfriend?'

I smiled. 'You don't need to interview him. You met him years ago, remember?'

'Come on, let's see if he's made of the right stuff.'

Lola was still at Don's side when we crossed the packed room, cooing in his ear, no doubt spilling all my secrets. Burns squared his shoulders when I brought Will over, like he was preparing to be inspected. The two men were polar opposites: my brother slim and fine boned, Burns towering over him.

'My sister's quite a handful. You're a brave man.'

'Tell me about it,' Burns replied, laughing.

Will's expression suddenly turned sombre. 'But you love her, right? She matters to you?'

Burns looked startled. 'More than anyone.'

'Good answer. You passed the test, my friend. We'll talk another time.'

My brother's face relaxed before he stepped back into the crowd. I lost sight of him immediately, a surge of dancers and music closing round him like a raging sea.

34

'You'll be here months at this rate, Clare.' The woman breathes into her face.

'Leave me alone.' Her words are a dry whisper.

'Remember, you've only got yourself to blame.'

The needle pierces Riordan's shoulder, her arms jerking sharply as she submits to the pain. The doctor looks ready to give up, cheeks dark with fever, but the woman feels no pity, crooning softly while she injects more interferon.

'Did you know they experimented on patients here? The medics didn't care how many died, just like you.'

The woman watches Riordan's eyes roll back, body jolting against the restraints as she pulls the needle from her arm.

'You'll finish her if you carry on like that,' the man says.

'Why do you care?' she snaps, his sympathy grating on her nerves.

'We need her alive, to tell us another name.'

'I want her to see the others die.'

When she looks down again, Riordan has lost her beauty, head shaven, her cheeks hollow. Only the flutter of her eyelids proves she's still alive.

'I'll deliver it this time.' The woman holds the pack to her chest, the liquid warm against her skin.

It's a relief to leave the man behind. Despite her love for him, it angers her that he's losing his resolve, illness diluting his courage. She drives north from the laboratory as drinkers spill from brightly lit bars, then it's a ten-minute wait outside the museum before the coast's clear. She picks her way across the car park, chalks the black and white marks on the step, then hurls the plastic pack. She turns away as it explodes, unwilling to see the wasted blood splashing to the ground.

35

Lola seemed reluctant to let us go. Every time we edged towards the door, she pressed another drink into our hands. I didn't have the heart to say what had happened, knowing it would sour the party's mood. By now alcohol had numbed the shock of standing in my hallway, knowing I'd been targeted.

'Stay till midnight, can you?' she whispered. 'We've got an announcement.'

'Burns is edgy. We need to leave.'

Lola's cat-like eyes snapped open. 'You're going to tell him how you feel?'

'Anything's possible.'

'On that condition, I'll let you go.'

'Tell me the news first.'

Her smile widened. 'We're getting married. I'll need help choosing a dress.'

I gave her a tight hug. Across the room, her boyfriend Neal was living up to his nickname of 'Greek God', blond with classic good looks, every inch a mythological hero. It didn't seem to matter that he was twelve years younger than Lola; he looked like a man who'd landed on his feet, his copper-haired daughter asleep on his shoulder while he chatted to friends. I blew him a kiss as Burns appeared with my coat. It was tempting to stay – while strangers danced around me, my worries fell silent. There was no sign of Will when we finally made our getaway.

Burns seemed glad to escape, dragging me downstairs. When we reached the pavement he stared at me so intently he seemed to be trying to memorise my features.

'Can't wait to get you home,' he murmured.

I smiled in reply but felt a lick of panic. When we got back to his flat, we'd share the same bed for the first time. Sex had never been a problem, but waking up together would be a different matter. 'It won't be long. Our chauffeur's arrived.'

A squad car had pulled up a hundred metres away. We were getting into the back seat when Burns's phone buzzed. His expression blanked, personal feelings evaporating.

'What's happened?'

'A blood pack's been found in Euston,' he said.

'I'll come with you.'

The car raced through the night-time streets and I felt a pulse of surprise as we reached the Wellcome Institute. Days ago I'd spoken to my flamboyant ex-colleague there, but the place hadn't featured on Emma Selby's list of locations.

When we reached the back of the building, it was clear the killer had acted recently; fresh blood glistened on the building's pale stone. The security guard stood with one of the first responders. He was in his sixties, balding, expression perplexed, as if his discovery had addled his brain.

'I got the licence number,' he said. 'If I'd run faster I'd have caught her red-handed.'

'You think it was a woman?' Burns asked.

'Seems like it on the CCTV.'

'I'll take a look.'

I stayed in the car park with two uniforms guarding the doorway. One of the killers had been there minutes before, and I wanted to breathe the same air. Behind the cordon the Pure symbol was clearly visible, black and white teardrops scrawled on the limestone step, urgency visible in each chalk mark. Their audacity was growing. They had visited three sites in twenty-four hours, desperate to make their point.

'Why are you so angry?' I muttered to myself.

Long arcs of blood spattered the museum's doors. The substance carried its own messages; it would give an update on Riordan's health, and the conditions she was suffering, revealing how recently it had been drawn. The locations and style of delivery were part of the conversation, but their meaning eluded me. Only the strength of their rage was clear. The blood pack had been hurled at the door with the force of a grenade.

Burns was scowling as he walked back across the car park. 'Any luck?'

'The camera only got her from behind. I'm not even convinced it's a woman; all you can see is someone with a slim build in a hooded coat. I bet the car's licence plates aren't registered either.'

'We should check on Ian Passmore.'

Burns stared at me. 'The Pure symbol doesn't make him guilty. He's already complaining about harassment.'

'Find out where he is, at least. Not many people carry that much anger.'

Tiredness showed in his face. 'I'll take you home, then go to the station.'

'It's gaining pace, Don. They're bound to slip up soon.'

'Christ, let's hope so.'

Burns insisted on walking me up to his flat. The uniform sitting outside on a folding chair jumped to attention when we arrived, as if we were visiting royalty. I hated the feeling of being passed between guards like a china doll, but there was no alternative. Once I got inside, I was too wired to go to bed, so I checked my emails on Burns's computer. Tania had sent through a complete list of Pure's members, past and present. I spent a fruitless half-hour scanning for alibis and connections to the victims. The details added by her team made grim reading; a quarter of the names had the word 'deceased' printed beside them, removed from Ian Passmore's circulation list. I was about to log off when my eyes caught on a familiar surname: Fenton. When I clicked on it, the first name was Roger, his home address had a Southwark postcode, and he'd been a member since 2012. All my suspicions about the journalist resurfaced. It could be that he had joined for research purposes, but surely he would have told me when he first mentioned Pure? I stabbed the computer's off button with my thumb with a sense of frustration. I was starting to suspect people with a legitimate interest in the case, and the fact that my fate was tied to Clare Riordan's was inescapable. I needed to turn over every stone to find her, so Mikey could return home, and I would get my liberty back.

36

Thursday 30 October

The face beside mine on the pillow next morning revealed a history of conflict. Burns had broken his nose in a school rugby match, then his jaw ten years ago during a house arrest, leaving him with a lopsided smile. The effect was still oddly beautiful, like a statue that had stood outside for decades, altered by hard weather. I crept out of bed without waking him. Traffic droned on Southwark Bridge Road as I switched on his cross-trainer. I would have preferred a quick sprint along the river path, but that was off limits until the killers were found, police protection a necessary evil. After stepping off the machine I sent Roger Fenton a text, requesting a meeting. At eight thirty he rang back, his urbane voice wishing me good morning.

'Could I pick your brains about something?' I asked.

'How can I help?'

'Face to face, if possible. Let's try a café, like last time.' I knew he might be recording our conversation, ready to sell my words to the highest bidder. 'I'm afraid I can't share information in return.'

'I know, but I'm still hoping for that interview when the case ends. Where do you live?'

'Southwark.'

'Let's meet at Elliot's, one o'clock.'

It interested me that Fenton would drop everything at such short notice; in my experience journalists were rarely so biddable. Burns appeared in the doorway as I put down the phone, wearing nothing but a pair of boxer shorts and an ominous expression.

'You can't just disappear, Alice.'

'I'm an early riser.'

'Come back to bed, for Christ's sake.'

'Aren't we seeing Luke Mann?'

'We're off duty till eleven.' His hand closed round my wrist, pulling me along the corridor.

'I've been exercising, I need a shower.'

'I don't care.' My shoulders thumped against the wall when he leant down to kiss me.

Desire mixed with panic, threatening to cancel each other out. Maybe it was delayed shock at seeing blood spattered across my door that caused his sudden intensity, but the pace felt reckless. The bed-board clattered against the wall, his gaze locked on to mine. He didn't even blink when he came, too focused on watching me lose control at exactly the same time. Afterwards he collapsed on the pillows beside me, his expression satisfied.

'Lola's right.' He dropped a kiss on my shoulder.

'About what?'

'You're crazy about me. I saw it just now, plain as day.'

'God, you're smug.'

It would have been the ideal time to admit defeat, but the words never arrived. My silence didn't dent Burns's good mood. Despite only getting three hours' sleep, he hummed contentedly as he headed for the bathroom. There was a mismatch between my irritation and the glow lingering on my skin. It was still there when I joined him in the shower before he could drain all the hot water.

Luke Mann was waiting for us in his dilapidated porch when we arrived. My father's alcoholism had taught me to recognise a drinker instantly: the telltale tremor was in his hand when he shook mine, a sour tang of booze on his breath. I made an effort to curb my instinctive dislike. The man was suffering enough without anyone casting judgements. He was around my age, with an eager-to-please expression and a fragile, almost feminine face, dark hair a little too long. Mann looked every inch the troubled writer, as if the world battered too heavily on his senses.

'Sorry I missed you last time. Please come in.'

His voice was gentle, with a cultured Home Counties accent. But it was the interior of his house that caught my attention. The hallway held more reading material than I could have absorbed in a lifetime, niches stuffed with novels and volumes of poetry. A small wooden cross hung above his kitchen door, as though religion trailed him into every room.

'I'm sorry to hear your father's ill, Mr Mann,' I said.

'He's recovering, thank God, but I had to drop everything and drive to Norwich.' He stood by his old-fashioned cooker looking apologetic, then motioned for us to sit down.

'We'd be grateful for some information about your girl-friend,' Burns said.

'I've been so worried. Ellie's not answering my calls.'

'How did you two meet?'

Mann looked embarrassed. 'Speed dating, five years ago. I couldn't believe my luck. Of course I was more successful then; one of my books had been nominated for a prize.'

He was trying hard to seem in control, but I felt sure he'd been knocking back vodka since he woke up. A stack of unopened envelopes lay on his counter, red stamps identifying them as county court judgements. Mann's neighbours must have been right about his debts.

'Have you heard from Eleanor recently?'

He shook his head anxiously. 'I've been calling round the clock. She hasn't been herself since her sister went missing.'

'How do you mean?'

'Ellie's a bit obsessed by Clare – an inferiority complex, I suppose.'

'Why do you say that?'

Mann blinked at me. 'Their parents made her feel second best, and there's the baby thing too.'

'Sorry?'

His gaze dropped. 'She's had three miscarriages, the most recent in July. The doctors told her another pregnancy would be dangerous, but she won't hear about adopting. Losing contact with Mikey hurt her more than the lawsuit. She's gone off by herself before; for a week last time, without telling me. She said she needed to let off steam.'

'Can you tell us where she went?'

'A guest house in Brighton. I called, but they haven't seen her.' His voice was raw with anxiety.

'It sounds like you've both had a tough time,' I replied.

'It's worse for Eleanor.' His eyes glazed. 'Nothing prepares you.'

'Has she had support from her doctors?'

'Not enough. That's part of why she's so angry.'

Mann's exhausted tone revealed that Eleanor's rage had been all-consuming. So many factors fuelling it: losing her childhood home, her babies, and access to her nephew. Burns continued his questions, patiently noting down Mann's alibis for the dates of the attacks.

'You seem to spend a lot of time alone, Mr Mann,' he commented. 'Do you and Eleanor plan to live together?'

'We're getting married this summer. That's why I've been here, doing it up, but it may have to be sold.'

'Any particular reason?'

'Financial necessity, I'm afraid. Eleanor's legal fees have cost us a fortune.'

Burns nodded. 'Do you own a car, Mr Mann?'

'Not any more. I hire them if I need one.'

'Where from?'

He hesitated for a moment. 'National Cars, on Camberwell Road.'

'Thanks for your time,' Burns said. 'Contact us when you hear from Eleanor, please.'

'You don't think she's been taken, do you?' Mann's panicked gaze darted across our faces.

'There's no proof of that. Clare's abductors have left an evidence trail around the city, proving that they're holding her, so this is very different,' Burns said. 'We'll do everything in our power to find Eleanor.'

Mann was still standing on his doorstep looking crestfallen when I slid into the back seat of the squad car.

'The bloke's still high from last night,' Burns commented.

'Or he had a Bloody Mary for breakfast. He's a functioning alcoholic, but he knows what he's doing. He could be shielding Eleanor somewhere.'

'We've tapped his mobile. He's right about calling her number nonstop.'

'The guy's smart. He probably knows his phone's hot.'

'We'll keep an eye on him, but he was at the hospital with his dad when the last blood pack was left.'

Burns was still preoccupied when we reached Borough Market, eyes glassy, as though a showreel of suspects was running through his head. He gave me a distracted kiss then folded himself back into the car, speeding away before I could say goodbye.

The market was heaving with well-dressed shoppers picking through stalls loaded with kumquats, mangoes and limes, selling for exorbitant prices. Elliot's Café was small and stylish, the window full of artisan bread and cakes. A waft of cinnamon and hot milk hit me when I opened the door. Roger

Fenton was dressed casually, in jeans and a dark blue wind-cheater, browsing through the *Guardian* when I arrived.

'Do you write for them?'

'Rarely.' His face relaxed into a smile. 'Just checking out the competition.'

'Thanks for coming. Let me buy you lunch.'

He shook his head. 'Tea's fine. I had a late night with some colleagues.'

Fenton looked under the weather, cheekbones more hollow than before, but his expression hadn't changed. He seemed alert to every movement, sharp gaze assessing me as I gave the waiter our order.

'You didn't tell me you were a member of Pure.'

I saw him flinch. 'Anyone can join. It's for supporters as well as sufferers.'

'It seems odd, especially as you think the leader had your flat burgled.'

He held my gaze. 'I joined before that, on the Internet, to access their bulletins. I wanted to know more about the Tainted Blood enquiry. Ian Passmore organised the protest in 2012. I think it was a last-ditch effort to make the government accept responsibility.'

'Who else was involved?'

'A guy called Gary Lennard was very bitter about catching HIV as a child; he was the youngest victim in the UK. I don't know if he's still alive.'

'I'll track him down.' I took a sip of my Americano. 'It surprises me that you're still following the Riordan case so closely. Hanging around outside police stations isn't some-thing I associate with serious journalism.'

'This is the perfect story. Someone's attacking the medical profession for an ethical failure.' His eyes glittered with excitement.

'But they're hurting foot soldiers, not power holders.'

'I don't agree. The victims are influential in the medical world.'

'When you were doing your research, did you find out about anyone on the Tainted Blood panel?'

He held my gaze. 'Would a name guarantee me that in-depth interview?'

'You have my word of honour.'

'I saw an email when I interviewed Lisa Stuart, from someone called Emma Selby.'

The name pulled me up short. 'You were snooping through her papers?'

'It was lying on her desk in plain sight. The subject line was "Tainted Blood", so I guessed she was on the panel.'

I was struggling to process the idea. 'You stole information from an interviewee.'

Fenton leant forwards in his seat. 'Journalists really aren't your favourite species, are they?'

'How do you mean?'

'If you find the bastards who're hurting these people, you won't care where the facts came from, and I can feel smug about helping put them away.' The conviction in his tone raised my curiosity.

'Do you mind me asking why you quit being a war reporter?'

'Too many of my colleagues died.' He hesitated for a moment. 'My spell in hospital was the deciding factor.'

Something in his eyes had shut down, making me wonder how many fatalities he'd witnessed. It was clear he had nothing more to say, so I thanked him again and paid the bill. I scanned the crowd as I wove between the market stalls, but he was nowhere to be seen. Fenton still had the ability to vanish like a puff of smoke.

The journalist's comment gave me food for thought as a new squad car delivered me to the safe house, but my suspicions were growing. He had told me about Pure days before I realised that their logo was scrawled at every scene, and seemed to have a vested interest in how the story unfolded. I reassured myself that there was no reason why a reputable journalist would begin a murder spree, yet his interest in the case seemed unnaturally keen. Burns would probably think I was crazy, but I made a mental note to get him checked out. I called the station before entering the safe house to let them know that Emma Selby might have been on the Tainted Blood panel. If Fenton was correct, she would need immediate protection, before she met the same fate as the other victims.

Gurpreet passed me his case notes hurriedly, which wasn't his usual style. Normally he lingered over our catch-up meetings, concern for Mikey making him reluctant to leave.

'My daughter's birthday party starts in half an hour,' he said. 'My wife'll kill me if I'm late.'

I touched his arm. 'Enjoy it. I'll see you tomorrow.'

Mikey kept trying to speak that afternoon, his jaw straining although no sound emerged. The patients I'd worked with often described muteness as a physical constraint, like choking or being gagged. He only seemed to relax when we cooked together. We were finishing our meal when a loud explosion sounded outside, his spoon clattering to the table, expression terrified.

'It's just fireworks, Mikey; it's bonfire night soon. Want to take a look?'

The boy's bravery showed itself again when he followed me into the garden, even though he was trembling. We stood together as another rocket showered the horizon in silver and

238

gold. When I looked at his face, something had changed. For once Mikey's expression was like any other child's, rapt and optimistic as he watched the skyline glitter. The sight of his enjoyment made me relax for the first time in weeks, even though the explosions overhead were loud as gunshots.

37

The woman's tension rises when they travel to Bermondsey on a night bus. Nothing disturbs their journey except a flurry of late traffic, taxis carrying revellers home from an evening on the tiles. They walk along side roads, then hide behind a building at the end of the cul-de-sac. Trees cluster protectively around the safe house, but the police car outside it is empty.

'No security,' she whispers. 'We could take him now.'

'The guard'll be back any minute.'

'Sooner or later we'll have to risk it.'

'The house is overlooked from two sides,' the man replies.

'Let's do it now,' she insists. 'The back way's safest.'

'You could blow the whole thing.'

She shrugs his hand away when he reaches out to her. 'We'll never get him at this rate.'

'At least we've seen the place. We can come back another night.'

She argues with him in whispers as the lights in the safe house flick out, one by one. Her anger rises again as a solitary policeman returns to the squad car, a takeaway bag in his hand. No one sees them leave; two shadows fading into the dark.

38

Friday 31 October

Burns's Audi pulled up outside the safe house next morning, instead of a squad car. His eyes were shielded by sunglasses so opaque that his expression was unreadable.

'Shouldn't you be at work?' I asked.

'Give me a break. It's my first day off since this started. I got Angie to check out Roger Fenton last night, by the way. Everything he said stacks up; his flat was burgled in 2012, other than that his record's clean as a whistle. He spent most of January in a military hospital in Afghanistan.'

'He's too interested, Don. Something's not right.'

Burns rolled his eyes. 'It's his job to obsess about stories. Come on, we're taking a road trip.'

'I promised I'd visit my mum.'

'That's where we're going. You can't travel alone, remember?'

'You're protecting me from the mean streets of Blackheath?'

A muscle ticked in his jaw. 'Rules are rules, Alice.'

'If you come along you'll have to wait in a coffee shop.'

He stared at me. 'She doesn't know I exist, does she?'

'Of course she does.'

'Then we should get acquainted.'

My heart rate quickened. 'She's frail, Don, and she hates surprises.'

'It's just a flying visit. I've already got her a present.'

The bouquet lying on his back seat must have cost serious money – gardenias, roses and hyacinths. Showy, romantic blossoms designed to melt the hardest of hearts, but they failed to shift my resentment. My relationship with my mother was so fragile I hadn't introduced her to any of my boyfriends for years. Burns must have sensed my tension, his silence lingering until we reached Elephant and Castle.

'You never talk about your childhood, Alice.'

I shrugged. 'There's not much to say. My parents' marriage broke down, but they stayed together anyway. Dad drank, she rolled with the punches.'

'Did you get hit too?'

'I was good at hiding.' I studied his profile. 'What about you? I don't know much except you grew up north of Edinburgh.'

His kept his eyes on the road ahead. 'It was a mining village, the industry dying on its feet. Dad joined the army, then worked as a bin man, but it wasn't much of a vocation; he'd have preferred to be a farmer. Mum looked after me and my sisters. She died of breast cancer at thirty-four.'

'How old were you?'

'Twelve.'

'That's a tough age to lose someone.'

He rolled his shoulders. 'The girls took it worse. They were five and seven.'

Suddenly my irritation dropped away. Burns had been a year older than Mikey when he lost his mother; I could picture him comforting his sisters when he was barely mature enough to look after himself.

'You bastard,' I muttered.

'Why?'

'For hitting the sympathy button. Now I can't even hate you for manoeuvring me.'

He shot me a grin. 'She's got to meet me sooner or later.'

'Don't blame me when she eats you alive.'

By the time we reached Wemyss Road my stomach was in knots. The expression on Mum's face was a picture when she finally answered the door. Normally her emotions were hidden behind a veneer of cashmere and pearls, but the sight of Burns, large and thuggish in his leather jacket, had stunned her into silence. She wavered on the threshold as if she was considering pressing her panic button, Parkinson's tremor making her voice quake when she finally said hello. The meeting could have gone either way. Mum always made snap judgements about people, but Burns was wise enough to offer his bouquet in double-quick time.

'These are for you, Mrs Quentin.' He gazed down at her. 'Now I can see where Alice gets her looks.'

I waited for her to snarl at his insincerity, but her expression softened.

'It's a pleasure to meet you at last. Tell me your full name.'

'Donal McIntyre Burns.'

'That's a fine Scottish title. And an Edinburgh accent, if I'm not mistaken?'

He beamed at her. 'Impressive, you've got a good ear.'

My shock persisted while I retreated to make coffee. When I came back, Burns and my mother were on first-name terms and my irritation was rising to the boil. He was listening to a lengthy account of her visit to the Rembrandt show at Tate Britain with a look of rapt interest. She quizzed him about his time at art school, and seemed fascinated by his decision to join the police instead. Somehow he'd neutralised the tension that always hung in the air. His phone hummed quietly in his jacket pocket in the hall, but nothing in Burns's manner indicated that he was leading a nationwide manhunt.

When we left at midday, Mum looked well for the first time in months. She gave me her usual cursory goodbye, but

243

offered Burns a tender kiss on both cheeks. His smugness lingered as we got back into his car, making me feel like punching him.

'God, you're slick,' I snapped.

'The old girl's lonely, that's all. I promised to take her to the Rothko exhibition next month. Can you drive back?'

For the second time in as many days, he'd rendered me speechless, setting up a lunch date with my mother like it was the most natural thing in the world. Already he was hunkered in the passenger seat, checking his phone messages.

Once my anger had faded, the journey helped clear my mind. The car slipped north through easy midday traffic, while I added items to my mental to-do list. Angie was tracking down Gary Lennard for me. If he had been arrested during the tainted blood protests, his record would be lurking somewhere in the police national computer's vast memory banks.

The elderly uniform standing sentry outside Burns's flat looked ready to fall asleep. I doubted strongly that he would be able to overwhelm two violent murderers if challenged, but manpower must have been in short supply. I got a sense of how Burns spent his days off when the door closed behind us. He hurled his shoes into the corner, then reached for the remote control.

'Arsenal played Bayern Munich last night. Mind if I watch the highlights?'

'It's your flat, Don. You get the casting vote.'

Knowing that Mikey was stuck in the gloomy safe house made it hard to relax, even though I'd been working nonstop for two weeks. I opened my laptop to find a series of messages from Angie. She had already located Gary Lennard. Other than Ian Passmore he had been the only member of Pure to be arrested at the Downing Street protest in 2012, his mugshot showing a bespectacled man of around forty giving the camera an irate stare. I scanned the rest of the information she'd sent, including a recent photo. In the years since his arrest in 2012, he'd lost weight and abandoned his thick-framed glasses, his expression mellowing. He was an architect, running a practice in Deptford. Angie had arranged for us to visit his home the following morning. I switched off my computer then glanced over at Burns. The football commentator's drone had rendered him unconscious, his face pillowed on his hands. Either the stress of meeting my mother or lack of sleep had felled him like an Easter Island statue. He didn't wake up until the evening, when I made penne arrabiata using his last scrap of Parmesan. Rest and a large glass of wine seemed to revive him; his eyes were suddenly alert when I asked how Emma Selby had taken the news that she would need round-the-clock protection until the killers were found.

'She wasn't on the panel. Apparently Lisa Stuart contacted her for background information about the history of the tainted blood scandal.'

The information sent an odd sensation of panic across the back of my neck. 'She could still be vulnerable if she knew any of the panel members.'

Burns shrugged. 'I've had no luck getting Whitehall to hand over their names.'

'Why are they holding out?'

'Fear of a media inferno. The MoD say they're keeping watch on the other members' security. They thought Mendez died in a violent mugging, and Stuart's a "mis per". But now a third one's been killed, they're in meltdown. The health minister's been sent to Sweden on an official jaunt.'

'While his advisors are hung out to dry.'

Burns's jaw clenched. 'I'll get the list, don't worry.'

I knew from experience he would be as good as his word. Before long the civil servants would grow tired of his efforts to beat down their door.

39

The squad car delivered me to my first port of call by ten a.m. the next day. Gary Lennard's home stood on the outskirts of New Cross, with London plane trees guarding either end of the road, tall and immovable. The area might have been less affluent than Clare Riordan's, but Lennard's Edwardian home was equally large and imposing. I spotted Angie close by, locking her car. The DS wore her usual look of fierce determination, as if her entire professional future rested on our next meeting.

'I've done more searches,' she said, as we approached the house. 'He's never been in trouble, apart from his public order offence in 2012.'

'He's got more reason to be bitter about the tainted blood scandal than most. He spent months in hospital as a kid, and only he and Passmore were singled out at the protest.'

The slim brunette who answered Lennard's door bell made me do a double take. It was Dr Novak from the Royal Free, giving us a cautious smile of welcome. Without her white coat she looked younger and more fragile, dressed simply in black trousers and a pale blue top that emphasised the darkness of her eyes.

'Come on in, Gary's expecting you.'

'I didn't know you made house calls, Adele,' I replied.

'It's rare, but travelling to the clinic's beyond him now.'

I understood the situation when I saw Mr Lennard for the first time. The photo on his website must have been taken

246

before his illness took hold. He was hunched in a chair in his conservatory, pale skin stretched across gaunt cheekbones, pepper-and-salt hair thinning. Clear plastic tubes were feeding oxygen into his nostrils via a canister on a trolley at his feet, while soothing classical music spilled from his sound system. Lennard's thin face opened into a smile, restoring his handsomeness for a second when we introduced ourselves.

'Thanks for getting the door, Adele.' His voice croaked, as if each word took effort.

The doctor touched his shoulder then picked up her bag. 'Call us if you need anything, Gary. I'll drop by next week.' Her concern seemed more genuine than the breezy style most medics adopt, making me wonder if she carried her professional concerns home each evening.

'I'll show you out.' Lennard struggled out of his chair.

'There's no need.'

'Please, it's the least I can do.'

We waited in his conservatory while Dr Novak took her leave. The room was dominated by a wall full of CDs, but it was the garden that drew my attention. Exotic ferns like the ones at the safe house circled his patio, but these were perfectly controlled. There was a pond filled with water lilies, decking surrounded by cherry trees that would have looked stunning in bloom.

'You've got a beautiful view,' Angie commented when Lennard returned.

He pushed the oxygen canister back under his chair, his breathing laboured. 'It's a Zen garden – guaranteed peace for the soul.' He gave an ironic smile. 'What can I help you with?'

'We're trying to find out about Pure's campaign since the tainted blood scandal,' I said.

'You've read about my exploits? I don't see myself as a victim these days, but once information's on the net, it's impossible to undo.' He gazed out of the window, at the bamboo plants lining his back wall. 'Where should I start?'

'The beginning, please.'

'I don't have much breath, I'm afraid.'

'That's okay, take your time.'

'I was the youngest person in the UK to receive infected blood from a Factor Eight transfusion in '86. I'd fallen from a tree and cracked my skull. When I came round, they'd injected me with hepatitis C and HIV. Not a great birthday present for a twelve year old.'

'I'm sorry.' Mental arithmetic told me the man could only be in his early forties, but he looked decades older.

'My father blew his savings on lawyers, but got nowhere, of course.'

'Why's that?'

'No one accepted liability. There were five thousand patients in this country alone; full compensation would have cost the government millions.' His voice was unnaturally calm.

'Yet you don't seem bitter.'

'Believe me, I was. The Health Department stalled for twenty years, hoping we'd die before they had to pay a penny. I was seen as a medical miracle, something in my bloodstream helped me fight the virus, but I was still furious. All I could imagine was a future of drugs and hospitals. Qualifying as an architect was the turning point; seeing buildings grow revived me.'

'Why were you arrested?' Angie asked.

'It's a long story.' His sunken eyes sparked with anger. 'The government made tiny ex-gratia payments to avoid getting sued. Guess how much they paid me?'

'I can't imagine,' she replied.

'Twenty thousand pounds. That's why I went on the march. You can't put a value on the chance of a future, but it's got to

248

be worth more.' A faint tinge of outrage echoed in his voice. 'A policeman asked me to step aside, so I yelled some ridiculous insult. They fined me two hundred pounds; exactly one per cent of my compensation.'

'But your feelings changed?' I asked.

'Not about the unfairness; my annual pay-out is less than the minimum wage. I just see it differently now.'

'How do you mean?'

He nodded at the window, then directed his gaze at Angie. 'Some people would say gardens look barren in autumn, but you imagined mine in the summer, didn't you?'

'The fruit trees will be in bloom,' she said, nodding.

'A bit of insight turns bleakness into something promising, doesn't it?'

'But that takes discipline,' I said.

'Not when you've got double pneumonia. For me every day's a gift, and I've got people like Adele looking after me. Anger would only spoil the time I have left.'

I could see he was tiring. We sat in silence, watching the breeze rearrange dark red leaves on the gravel.

'One last thing, Gary. How well do you know Ian Passmore?'

'I haven't seen him all year, but I respect him. He gives all his spare time to supporting us.'

'He never switches off?'

Lennard shook his head. 'I doubt it; Ian's a man with a cause.'

'Some people think missionary zeal can be dangerous.'

'They don't understand altruism, do they?' Gary's face darkened.

I wanted to ask more questions, but his voice was fading. We left him to watch the play of shadows in his garden. Through an open door in the hallway, I saw that one of the rooms held a metal-framed bed and a nebuliser. Angie stood beside me as we peered at the medical paraphernalia, the sight filling me with discomfort. Gary Lennard was clearly preparing to die at home, yet he emanated calm. The idea that he could be involved in the attacks seemed ridiculous; the man appeared far too sick to harm anyone.

Angie was behind me when I stepped on to the porch. A tall woman with a swathe of poker-straight black hair collided with me, shopping bag spilling at her feet. She looked startled when she pushed back her fringe to inspect me, then gasped out a laugh. It was the woman who had been helping Ian Passmore at Cherry Garden Pier, Michelle De Santis.

'You gave me the fright of my life.'

'We were just visiting Gary.' I turned to Angie. 'This is Michelle, she's a volunteer with Pure.'

'Sorry to scare you.' Angie smiled widely, then stooped down to help collect the scattered groceries, packing cereal, bread and oranges back into Michelle's bag. 'Gary seems amazingly calm,' she commented.

'That's his style, he never moans.' When De Santis straightened up again she was taller than I'd realised, her lovely olive-skinned features more strained than before. She glanced at both of us before speaking again. 'I don't suppose you've got time for a cup of tea?'

Angie nodded. 'Love one, if you don't mind.'

She led us back indoors to the kitchen. I stayed on my feet, noticing a rack full of medicines on one of the counters, as if tablets were Lennard's main food source.

Michelle saw me looking at the drugs while we waited for the kettle to boil. 'He's getting by on fresh air. It's just willpower that keeps him going.'

'Have you known Gary long?' I asked.

She blinked at me. 'Fifteen years. I'm his ex-wife. I come by most days to help.'

'He's lucky. Not every divorced couple stays so close.'

'It was his choice to separate. He'd rather be left with his garden and his music, but he needs help with everything now.'

'It's amazing you still find time to work for Pure,' Angie commented.

'The victims are in the same boat as Gary; we're their life-line. I fit it in around my job as a physio.'

'That must take organising,' I observed.

'I'm part-time, but I could use more hours in the day.' The rawness in her voice revealed that she was at cracking point; one badly chosen word could open the floodgates.

'Can we help you with anything, Michelle?'

She swung round to face me. 'You're a psychologist, aren't you? Can you give me the name of a counsellor?'

'For Gary?'

'He's made peace with it,' she said, shaking her head. 'I'll need support when he goes.'

'Of course.' I pulled out my notepad and copied my friend Tejo's number from my phone. 'Doctor Chadha specialises in grief counselling; she's one of the kindest people I know.'

'The whole thing's so bloody wrong.' Her face tipped forwards, but she swabbed her eyes hurriedly, as if tears were a sign of defeat.

I saw a new side to Angie during the visit. The woman's vulnerability had brought out a patience she rarely exercised. She sat quietly, while Michelle explained the challenges of juggling her work with caring for Gary. The meeting reminded me that hundreds of families were in the same situation, and some would be less accepting. Any one of them might have decided to take revenge.

My first action when I reached the FPU mid-morning was to plough through my backlog of emails. Working on a Saturday wasn't my idea of fun, but it was my only chance of dealing with the work that had piled up on my desk. I assumed that I was alone in the building, but Christine called to summon me to her office at midday.

'Why are you here?' she asked. 'I only come in on Saturdays because the place is quiet.'

'I'm falling behind. The case is eating my time.'

'Want to update me?'

'I need today to catch up. There's a ton of work on my desk.'

'Leave it for now, I want to hear how you are.'

Her clear-eyed stare focused on my face as I described Mikey's reticence and the drawings he used to explain his experience. When I told her the Home Office was still refusing to reveal the names of the health minister's advisors, she looked incredulous.

'Why's the information safeguarded?'

'The minister received death threats, so they put a protection order on the panel's identity. We know for certain three of the victims were on it, but we need the other names.'

'Isn't anyone prodding the Home Office?'

'They're not playing ball.'

'I'll make some calls, see what I can do.' She scribbled a note on her pad. 'How are you coping with all this?'

Christine listened more attentively than before. Until then she'd seemed uneasy with emotions, even though she was an expert on human communication. She stayed silent while I talked about being exiled from my flat and my fear of over-involvement with Mikey, our relationship becoming emotional rather than therapeutic.

'It's inevitable in these cases,' she replied. 'But when it's over, you need a holiday.'

'It's hard to relax while Riordan's missing. Her son's more traumatised than any child I've treated before.'

'Maybe you should step down.'

I stared at her. 'Don't be ridiculous.'

'I was wrong to give you such a big case after the last one. You're under too much stress.'

'You've been assessing me?' I forced myself to smile. 'The curse of working for a body language expert.'

'This level of exposure is high-risk, Alice.'

'The kid's had enough people desert him. You can't remove me.'

She gave me a considering look. 'I'll get the information from the Health Department, but I may still replace you. We'll review it next week.'

I backed out of the room before she could change her mind. She had a point about my stress symptoms: low appetite, nightmares, disturbed sleep. But, despite the personal risks, I couldn't abandon Mikey while the search for his mother continued.

I stayed at the FPU that afternoon, ploughing through a backlog of paperwork, but no news arrived from Christine. Even her seniority must be failing to win the battle for protected information. The frustration made me even more certain that someone affected by the tainted blood case was taking revenge. I let my eyes wander down the printout of patients infected during the crisis, hundreds already dead. Gary Lennard appeared on the third page, still hanging on by a thread, but so far Tania's team hadn't found anyone with a criminal record or links to the victims. I rose to my feet and studied the clouds scudding across the sky, shrubs in the gardens opposite reduced to a handful of twigs. When I glanced round my office again, the room looked equally lack-lustre. The carpet must have clung to the floorboards for decades, mahogany desk in need of polish, and the chair that always gave me backache.

Burns called at four o'clock. 'What makes me think this is the lull before the storm?'

'Your innate Scottish gloom?'

He broadened his accent. 'I'm a wee ray of fucking sunshine compared to a Glaswegian.'

'Even Christine can't get the advisors' names.'

'I hope she has more luck than me. Better go, I've got a press briefing. Love you, bye.'

Something twitched inside me when the phone slipped back on to its cradle. I'd survived two consecutive nights at Burns's flat, more than I'd managed with any other man. With luck my tension would gradually ease, but right now his affectionate goodbyes still sounded like a foreign language.

Something was wrong when I reached the safe house. There was no sign of Mikey in the living room, Gurpreet's quiet voice echoing from the kitchen.

'You can't do that, Mikey. We have to keep you safe.'

The child's body was taut as a tripwire, fists balled at his sides. When he ran past me his face was a hard white mask. His footsteps pounded on the stairs, bedroom door slamming loud enough to loosen the hinges.

'We've entered the angry phase?'

'With bells on.' Gurpreet dropped on to a chair. 'Today's been a disaster.'

'How come?'

'Mikey found a copy of the *Mail* in the health visitor's bag. There was a story about his mum, and the murder at the Old Operating Theatre.'

My first reaction was pure anger: if I'd been there, I would have monitored everything the boy touched. But it was too late to cast blame. Mikey had seen the tabloid version of his mum's disappearance, and he knew how Jordan Adebayo had been killed.

'How did he react?'

'He escaped through the French doors. I had to stop him scaling the wall.'

Gurpreet's face was ashen while I processed the facts. The newspaper story had driven a child fearful of the outdoors to make an escape bid. I tapped on Mikey's door once we were alone in the house. He was sitting on his bed, poring over the pages of the *A–Z* he carried from room to room. He slapped the book shut, arms locking around his knees. When I sat beside him he made no attempt to move.

'Papers make things up, Mikey. Believe me, hundreds of people are looking for your mum.'

His gaze stayed fixed on the bedspread. For the first time in days he remained closeted in his room while I cooked dinner. I was furious with myself for leaving him alone, and with the health visitor for cancelling all of his progress in a single day. But my real outrage was reserved for the killers. What kind of people would steal a mother from her child, then splash her blood across London's streets? Psychosis could have left them devoid of sympathy, or they were proving a point. The picture wouldn't come into focus, no matter how often I turned it over in my mind.

Mikey refused to eat at dinner time. The TV blared from the living room but he stood by the French doors, hands pressed against the glass, just as he had at the start. I tried speaking to him, but he looked through me like I didn't exist. When I checked on him that night he was lying in bed, the *A–Z* clutched against his chest. Maybe the map book reassured him. All of London's streets were drawn on its pages, one of them marking the location where his mother was being held. I double-checked every door and window, less worried about anyone breaking in than Mikey trying to escape. The newspaper story seemed to have convinced him that the best option was to track his mother down all by himself.

40

The man huddles inside his thick coat. Electric light blazes from the high tower of the hospital as they loiter in the car park. He knows the registration number of the car they're seeking, and the moment when the doctor will finish her shift, but a dull sense of panic is rising in his throat. Events are unravelling, like a carousel spinning out of control.

'We don't have to do this.'

The woman's eyes glitter in the half-light. 'You should want it more than anyone.'

'Hurting them won't cure me.'

Her stare is furious. 'It's justice we need. I'll do it myself, if you're too scared.'

He watches her in silence. Her fury is more destructive than ever, obliterating everything in its path. That passion used to excite him, but now it leaves him exhausted, draining the last remnants of his strength.

Soon after midnight, the doctor heads towards them; average height, blonde hair pinned back from a face that looks designed for laughter. But she's not smiling tonight; she trots across the tarmac without turning in their direction.

'Dr Coleman?' The man steps into her path. 'Clare Riordan gave us your name.'

The woman smashes a cudgel across the doctor's neck before she can reply, her body crumpling to the ground. It takes moments to remove the keys from her pocket, then load her inert form into the boot of her car. He's shaking as the woman drives away, hands jittering in his lap. The woman turns to him at the first traffic lights.

'Now we just need the child,' she says.

'Then we have to stop.'

She doesn't reply, turning the radio on instead, filling the gulf between them with a barrage of sound.

41

Sunday 2 November

Midnight blue walls pressed in on me when I woke. I groped on the bedside table for my phone, but no email had arrived yet from Christine, Whitehall clearly still unwilling to comply. Mikey was in his room, staring down at the garden, his small face gaunter than before. The wind had dropped overnight, not a branch stirring, as if the trees were coated in resin.

'Want to go for a drive?' I asked.

He gave a rapid nod, then hurried away to dress. When he returned he was holding his drawing of the street where he'd escaped and the London *A–Z*. I didn't have the heart to explain that his mother could be anywhere, adrift in a city with over eight million inhabitants. He opened the dog-eared book, poring over each page.

'Are you looking for where you were found?'

It took moments to locate Walworth Road, at the centre of a dense tangle of streets due south from London Bridge. Mikey's finger chased across the paper like he was deciphering Braille. He tapped the page insistently, but the police guard was less enthusiastic. The uniform was in his early twenties, face shiny with ambition, convinced that his sole mission was to keep us under house arrest. I had to call Tania for permission, and even then he insisted I drove slowly so he could follow.

Mikey sat in the passenger seat, alert and watchful as we threaded through the light Sunday traffic. By the time we reached Walworth, the city's affluence had faded; deluxe estates were replaced by precincts and treeless squares, packed between tower blocks. In this territory the car reigned supreme, belching out lead for the residents to inhale. I kept my voice low and reassuring, but it was anyone's guess how much Mikey heard. When I pulled up at a set of lights there was no warning before he leaned over to release the child lock, then launched himself outside.

Even my fastest sprint was no match for a fit eleven year old, my breathing ragged as the gap between us closed. The kid moved like a whippet, weaving through crowds of shoppers laden with bags from Walworth Market. His head was twisting from left to right as he ran. Luckily he came to a halt at Westmoreland Road. When I finally reached him he was busy comparing his drawing with the buildings ahead. His photographic memory had been put to good use: the square office block and postbox stood at the end of the street, chains of terraces running down to Portland Street. I could even see the spot where he'd hidden, in a narrow passageway between dilapidated houses.

'Is this where you got free, Mikey?'

'Not far now.' His voice was raw as nails on a blackboard. 'Almost there.'

It was the first time in days that I'd heard him repeat his mantra. 'Did you hear them say that, in the car?'

He didn't reply, already moving again. The squad car crawled along the kerb as I jogged after him, hazard lights flashing. The boy seemed to be scanning every driveway for signs of his mother, frustration obvious in his rapid movements. I got the sense that he would have lifted every manhole cover if he'd had the strength. His memories of the abduction seemed to be surfacing, but it was difficult to help when he had no way to explain his search. After an hour Mikey's exhaustion was obvious. We'd paced through the network of streets around Walworth Road, barely pausing for breath.

'We can come back another day,' I said.

He shook his head violently at first, but soon had to admit defeat. When I finally coaxed him back to the car I jabbed the child lock with my thumb before fastening my seatbelt, determined to stay on guard so he couldn't pull the same trick again. My heart was still hammering with the knowledge that I'd almost lost him. Mikey stared out of the window while I called Angie to request more street searches, almost certain that the words he'd been repeating had been used by his abductors. When I glanced at the phone again, Christine's encrypted email had finally arrived; I forwarded it to Burns, then concentrated on getting Mikey back to the safe house.

The boy was so tired by his adventure that he let me fuss over him, accepting the temporary comfort of hot chocolate and a DVD. It was impossible to guess what he was thinking as characters from the last Harry Potter film raced across the screen, but I took advantage of his inertia to check the list from Whitehall. My eyes widened as I studied the ten names. The killers were working their way through the advisory panel, one by one: John Mendez, Lisa Stuart, Jordan Adebayo and Clare Riordan. The other six were medics with a blood specialism. The only familiar name belonged to Dawn Coleman, Riordan's boss from the Royal Free.

'Have you seen it?' I asked when Burns picked up his phone.

'We're setting up protection; the MoD's stepping back.' Traffic thundered in the background.

'Where are you?'

'Outside the Royal Free. Dawn Coleman's been missing since last night.'

I cursed silently, remembering the consultant's warm manner when we visited her dilapidated house. Her name appeared on the list straight after Jordan Adebayo's. 'They took her from work?'

'She never got home after her night shift.'

Burns's voice was flatlining, guilt and frustration echoing in each sentence. His next few hours would be a tough ride; the press would be sure to use the latest abduction to criticise his investigation. I told him about Mikey showing me the street where he'd escaped, and how desperate he seemed to retrace his mother's journey.

'Where's the health minister?' I asked. 'If they're taking his advisors, he's in danger too.'

'Still in Stockholm, surrounded by bodyguards.'

I could tell his sole concern was for Dawn Coleman. His voice sounded even bleaker when he said goodbye.

I felt too jittery to return to Burns's flat when Gurpreet took over at midday. Even the striking landscapes in his living room were a reminder that my apartment with its bare white walls was out of bounds. The sight of my police escort waiting to follow me felt unsettling. Clare Riordan came into my mind as I slipped into the driving seat; I'd never believed in hunches, but instinct told me she was still alive. The killers seemed to be saving her for their big finale, or maybe they were enjoying watching her suffer. The only person I'd interviewed who seemed angry enough to attack those responsible for the government's failings was Ian Passmore, but Burns's team was convinced by his alibis.

I called Emma Selby more in hope than expectation. It seemed presumptuous to ring her on a Sunday, but her voice was welcoming when she invited me round. I drove to Pimlico on autopilot. Her flat was in a mansion block on a leafy street, five minutes' walk from the Thames. I felt another rush of guilt when she opened the door. It looked as if I'd prevented her from going out for lunch; she wore a fuchsia-pink knee-length dress, dark curls pulled into a chignon, effortlessly stylish.

'Good to see you, Alice. This is a surprise.'

'I hate to bother you like this.'

'Don't worry, I wasn't going anywhere.'

'But you're all dressed up.'

She winced. 'It's a habit of mine. Making an effort always lifts my mood.'

Her living room was elegant too. She seemed to be well travelled; beautiful Japanese figures on her mantelpiece, walls painted a glowing terracotta, hand-woven Indian rugs on the floor. Her fascination with medical history showed in the books on her shelves: histories of medical developments; anatomy; essays on the history of blood treatment.

'How's the case going?' she asked, handing me a cup of coffee.

'It's grinding along. You heard about the blood thrown at the door of the Wellcome Institute?'

She wrinkled her nose. 'The stain's still there. The red oxide pigment in blood's almost indelible.'

'Trust you to know that.' I let out a laugh. 'Why do you think it was targeted?'

'I'm not entirely sure.'

I studied her again. 'You know Lisa Stuart, don't you?'

Her gaze remained steady. 'Only via email. She contacted me for information about the origin of the tainted blood scandal. I didn't have much to give, but I sent her links to some journal articles. I was shocked to hear she'd gone missing.'

'Were you asked to join the enquiry?'

'No, thank heavens. Sitting in a room with a bunch of senior medics touting for OBEs isn't my idea of fun. They used our meeting room back in 2012; I wanted it for my research students but the bigwigs poached it.'

I gave a slow nod. The news explained why the killers had targeted her workplace. 'Did you meet them?'

'I never even saw them. They only visited three or four times.'

'Would many people have known their names?'

'Senior admin and security staff, probably. I was curious, but the membership was kept quiet.' Her gaze was a fraction out of focus, like she was struggling to concentrate.

'Are you okay, Emma?'

'Sorry, I'm a bit out of sorts. Things have been messy here.'

'With your partner?'

Her smile crumbled. 'We keep arguing. I think he wants me to be someone else.'

We spoke for a while longer. Emma described a relationship that seemed to cause more pain than pleasure; she and her partner were chalk and cheese, unable to agree about their future, even though they'd been together so long. It struck me as unusual that such a glamorous woman was tearing herself apart over a man.

'We should have another drink soon.'

'You must be great at your job, Alice. I always end up offloading my woes.' She dabbed at her mascara.

'Feel free. Next time we'll sink another bottle of wine.'

'Can we make it next weekend?' Her smile rallied. 'I promise to be better company.'

'I'll look forward to it.'

She cut a lonely figure when I glanced back, isolated in her large doorway, barely managing a smile. When I returned to my car I fired off a quick message to Burns, asking him to check the security staff and receptionists at the Wellcome

264

Institute. They were among the tiny number of people who knew the identity of the Tainted Blood panel.

I spent the evening kicking my heels at Burns's flat. I considered making dinner, but there was no sign of him by eight thirty, so I opted for a cheese sandwich, marooned on his vast settee. An hour later I was bored enough to clean his kitchen. There was something therapeutic about scrubbing surfaces and polishing taps until the chrome showed my reflection. At ten thirty I grew tired of domesticity and phoned for a progress report on Dawn Coleman, but there was no news. Burns sounded so low when he described the team's frantic efforts to track down her car that I changed the topic.

'I must be losing it,' I said. 'I've been cleaning your flat.'

'Another good reason for us to cohabit.'

I laughed at him. 'After a three-night trial period?'

'You could rent out your flat.'

'You're not even divorced.'

'That's irrelevant. Guess how long I've wanted you there?'

'A few months?'

'Since you walked into my office four years ago. This hot little blonde with a big vocabulary.'

'The long words did it for you?'

'It was the whole package.'

'Stop rushing, Don.'

'Why fight it? Your mum loves me already.'

There was a low grumble of laughter before he hung up.

42

The woman feels exhausted when they finally cross the small car park behind the laboratory at two a.m. The pair work fast, lifting the doctor's lifeless form into the boot without making eye contact, neither commenting on the marble pallor of her face, or the iciness of her skin. She regrets the mistake which caused the doctor's death – extracting too much blood stopped her heart. It angers her deeply that she failed to tell them another name. They must rely on Riordan again, but she's growing weaker every day. The woman pulls down the lid of the boot, then there's a loud click of metal as something falls from her pocket on to the tarmac. A gun lies at her feet, tarnished silver, small and compact.

'Jesus,' the man hisses.

'It's to protect us, that's all.'

'Where did you get it?'

She gives him a scornful gaze. 'From a man in a pub.'

'A plain-clothes cop, probably.'

'Of course not.' The patronising answer makes her grit her teeth.

'Get rid of it, for God's sake.'

'There's no way I'm going to prison.' She shoves the weapon back into her pocket, then turns away.

Her anger rises as she twists the key in the ignition. She loves night driving, but tonight the journey brings no peace, the car edging through the suburbs.

'It's too much,' the man says. 'We said we'd only hurt the decision-makers.'

She shakes her head. 'Clare's not talking, so we need the child. We've got no choice.'

The woman's eyes focus on the road, refusing to acknowledge the judgement written on his face. She accepts the morality of what they've done. A whole generation has suffered and died; someone must take responsibility. Gradually her tension reduces as she steers a twisting line north, surrounded by lost souls. The city's casualties have risen to the night's surface: hookers on the London Road, vagrants huddled in a bus shelter, a young girl crying on a park bench.

It's impossible to avoid the street cameras on Borough High Street, so she raises her hood to shadow her face. After three more blocks they reach O'Meara Street. Satisfied that no one's watching, she leaves the car unlocked before they escape into the maze of buildings.

43

Monday 3 November

It was two a.m. when something woke me. Burns must have returned while I slept, but now he was stumbling around, dragging on his clothes in the dark. He swore quietly to himself when I switched on the light.

'Clare Riordan's been found?' I asked.

'It's a female, unidentified, five minutes from here.'

I launched myself out of bed on a wave of panic, grabbing enough warm clothes to ward off the autumn cold. Burns was busy listening to the announcements spilling from his radio as we drove the half mile to O'Meara Street. It turned out to be narrow and unremarkable, full of office blocks and Victorian houses that had seen better days, lit by the streetlights' orange glow. The crime scene bore an uncanny resemblance to the Old Operating Theatre: a church with a stained-glass window above the door and two thin bell towers. A railway bridge hugged its roofline so closely that the windowpanes must have rattled whenever a train rolled past. The sign outside announced that it was the Roman Catholic Church of the Precious Blood and the parish priest was Father Brendan O'Casey.

I steadied my nerves while Burns jogged towards the crime scene. If the body belonged to Clare Riordan, my next job would be to inform Mikey that his mother would never come home. I waited by the outer cordon while the uniform scribbled my name on her list. The WPC gave me a sterile suit and

268

overshoes, then led me down a narrow passageway once my ID had been checked.

'Who found her?' I asked.

'Father O'Casey; you'll find him in the church.'

Arc lights had already been set up in the car park, SOCOs crawling across the tarmac on hands and knees, eyes riveted to the ground. Tania and Angie walked towards me, the two women's greetings revealing their different personalities: Angie gave a double-handed wave, while Tania barely managed a nod.

'The body's in situ,' Angie said. 'I hope you're feeling strong.'

'It's that bad?'

'The priest fainted before the ambulance arrived.'

'Where's Burns gone?' I asked.

'To the station. The press have got wind of it; he's keeping them away.' She turned to face me. 'Ready to see her?'

I grimaced. 'No time like the present.'

The BMW was parked on the far side of the car park, beside swathes of plastic sheeting that covered the asphalt like red carpet. Plenty of people had stood there already: the police surgeon, pathologist and photographer had finished their work already. But Hancock would be here for the rest of the night, bagging litter and poring over the car's interior, praying for DNA. He gave me a nod as he rose to his feet.

'How are you bearing up?'

'I'll live, Pete. When this is over, you owe me a strong black coffee.'

'Too much caffeine addles your brain.' He pressed a torch into my hand. 'You'll need this for a proper look.'

Pete's appearance showed the pressure he was under, white brows lowering in a deep frown, his skin sallow. TV shows did forensic scientists no favours by pretending they could conjure answers from even the most barren crime scenes.

I came to a halt once I had a direct view into the car's boot, my vision blurring. There was something surreal about the way Dawn Coleman had been folded like a piece of origami, dozens of test tubes strewn across her body. She lay on her side, knees curled to her chest, swaddled in black fabric. The collar of her blouse was so filthy it was impossible to guess its original colour. Her face was as pale as candle wax, lips such a dark blue they looked as if they'd been tattooed, her blonde hair matted with blood. I thought of her two teenage daughters coating her hallway in fresh white paint, concealing every blemish.

When I forced myself to look again, torchlight revealed the level of staging. The test tubes were the sort used in medical labs, each one containing a splash of bright red liquid. The Pure logo was drawn in chalk on the raised lid of the boot. Something shifted inside my stomach when I saw that her bound hands were raised like she was offering a last prayer. There was no way of guessing what kind of treatment she'd suffered, or where she'd been kept for forty-eight hours, but the need to know burned at the pit of my stomach. Years ago I'd spent time locked in captivity but, unlike Dawn Coleman, I'd had the good fortune to escape.

'How long before the body goes to the mortuary?'

'By morning.' Hancock's eyes scanned the ground again. 'She needs identifying.'

I made my way inside the church, partly to clear my head, but also to locate the priest. Father Brendan was kneeling at the altar, which held a row of candles glowing brightly in the dark. His Irish brogue was audible from twenty paces, even though he was reciting a Latin mass. I perched on one of the pews to steady my nerve. Churches always had a calming effect on me, even though mysticism left me cold. Even at Sunday school I'd been unable to imagine anything beyond what I could touch and taste and hold. A confessional box stood in the corner of the nave, the air heavy with incense and dust. The priest's words echoed from the vaulted ceiling. In the flickering light I could see that he was tall, grey curls springing from his skull in all directions. I expected him to be in his fifties, but when he eventually turned round, his face was boyish; he couldn't have been much older than me. He collected one of the candles from the altar as I approached, hands trembling as he studied my ID card.

'Could I ask a few questions, Father?'

'Of course. This is such a tragic thing.' His face clouded.

'Were you saying a mass just now?'

'A requiem. I'd have done it sooner, but shock got to me.'

'That's not surprising; you've had a dreadful experience.'

'I visit the sick and dying all the time, but that's different.' His voice lapsed into silence.

'How did you find her?'

'I saw the car when I drove home from a prayer meeting, late last night,' he said, frowning. 'No one in their right mind would leave a BMW here overnight. Its doors were unlocked.'

'Had anything unusual happened before that?'

He looked thoughtful. 'It may not be relevant.'

'Tell me anyway.'

'Yesterday afternoon a man came to confession; he said he'd done terrible things. I could hear the pain in his voice.'

'Did you see his face?'

'The confessional grille blurs people's features, for anonymity. He'd gone by the time I looked for him.'

'Can you remember what he said?'

'Not in exact words, just how despairing he sounded.'

'Would you recognise his voice, if you heard a recording?'

He rubbed his hand across his jaw. 'I doubt it, I'm afraid. After a while one voice blends into another.'

I nodded. 'One thing before I go, Father. Can you explain your church's name?'

'The precious blood refers to Christ's sacrifice. He gave his life for us, didn't he?' His parting gaze was stern, as if I'd failed my first catechism.

My eyes struggled to adjust when I stepped from the candlelit church into the harsh glare of arc lamps. Even though it was the middle of the night, people were milling by the side of the road. Gawkers always fascinated me. This lot varied in age from a couple of young men who looked the worse for wear, clearly on the way home from the pub, and an old man who should have known better. Roger Fenton was the only journalist in sight, which made me wonder who had tipped him off when Burns had been fighting to keep them away. The intensity of his gaze gave me another twitch of discomfort, despite the team's certainty that he had no connection with the crimes. He had passed me key information, and been first at Jordan Adebayo's crime scene too. If he was one of the abductors, his job allowed him to follow the investigation's every move; but why would a reporter suddenly turn killer? I blinked my eyes shut for a moment, aware that my closeness to the case might be clouding my judgement.

When Tania and Angie walked towards me, I decided to speak my mind.

'Could one of you check Roger Fenton's alibis again? The guy's an expert on the Tainted Blood enquiry.'

Tania raised her eyebrows. 'The only link is that he joined Pure in 2012, but you said he did that for research purposes.'

'Humour me, please. Look at him again.'

'I'll see what I can do.'

She and Angie exchanged a look of disbelief, as if the request proved I was cracking under the strain. I stayed silent on the way to the station, perched in the back of Tania's car, redrawing my image of the killers. Whoever had murdered Dawn Coleman had a strong sense of symbolism; their enjoyment of high drama had been part of Jordan Adebayo's murder too, but this time the site was religious instead of historic. Maybe their biggest thrill came from imagining witnesses' faces as they peered into the boot of the car.

Burns was holding court back at the station. His expression had changed, panic replaced by stoicism, but his team looked exhausted. The incident room smelled of heat and entrapment, dozens of people locked indoors for days without respite. I watched him organising the crowd, more by body language than instruction. The heft of his shoulders ensured that any request was granted instantly, but his confidence seemed to falter when he spotted me, like I'd caught him play-acting. Once the briefing began, his swagger returned. He gazed around the room steadily, as though he was awarding points to the best listeners.

'The case has taken a new direction. Now we have proof that the killers are politically motivated; they're killing government advisors on the Tainted Blood enquiry. There are ten names on the list; Dawn Coleman's the fifth to be taken. Lisa Stuart's still missing, and they're holding Clare Riordan. We have to make sure that the remaining five get round-the-clock protection until the killers are found. Let's run through what we know so far. Alice, do you want to start?'

When I rose to my feet, the team watched with varying degrees of scepticism. 'I still think we may be looking for a couple who know Clare Riordan, professionally or personally. It's rare for a hostage to be held this long; the killers may blame her most for denying the patients compensation, or they're using her to gain information. We're looking for a couple with reason to harm all five victims. The suspects include Sam Travers, Clare's lover, still bitter about her rejection. His work as a film-maker put him in touch with dozens of medics, including Lisa Stuart. Most urgently of all we need to find Eleanor Riordan. She's disappeared from home before without telling her boyfriend, but there's an outside chance she could be working with a man with a blood fixation. It's unlikely that she's been taken, because the killers always leave a sample of a new victim's blood within twenty-four hours. Any of the tainted blood victims could be seeking justice for the illnesses they've received, so you need to take each one of the names on Pure's membership list seriously.

'The killers chose a religious site this time because they're on a moral crusade, convinced that right's on their side. We also know that they're obsessed by the history of blood medicine. I think it's likely that Riordan's being held at a location linked to their theme, so it's worth checking abandoned hospitals and health clinics. Location analysis suggests that the killers are based in south London, targeting victims inside a two-mile radius of Walworth. Clare Riordan's son escaped from the killers there; he seems certain that's where his mother's being held. More street searches in the area would be a good place to start.'

Burns gave me a quick nod of thanks, but I didn't get the chance to say goodbye. When I paused by the doorway he was motionless in the centre of the room, people whirling around him, like a ship's mast in a storm. It must have consumed all of his energy to project so much calm while Clare Riordan was still being held, vulnerable to the same fate as Dawn Coleman.

274

44

My stomach carried on doing slow somersaults at the memory of Dawn Coleman's murder scene as the morning passed. I was still feeling queasy at lunchtime, but at least my profile report had a new dimension: the killers' fascination with blood extended beyond medical history to religious symbolism. It was worth looking at anyone in Pure with religious convictions; it seemed too coincidental that Father O'Casey had heard such a tortured confession just before Dawn's body was found. As the afternoon ticked past, my anger grew harder to control. The choice of location underlined how sick the killers were: they had shown no remorse about depriving children of their parents, yet they still believed they had right on their side.

The ageing copper guarding the safe house that afternoon gave me a baleful stare, as though I was guilty of keeping him from his dinner. Most of the Met's spare manpower had been diverted to investigate Dawn Coleman's murder, and protect the five remaining members of the advisory panel. Gurpreet's smile looked strained when I found him in the kitchen.

'Mikey's gone even deeper into his shell,' he said.

'That's not your fault, you've been great with him.'

He seemed so upset that I gave him a brief hug goodbye. I was grateful for the unconditional kindness he'd shown Mikey since the start of his ordeal.

The boy was kneeling on the floor in his room, using the art materials I'd brought him days before. He was building an elaborate structure from folded pieces of card, his stare a little too focused, as if he was running a fever.

'You look busy, sunshine.'

'Almost there,' he muttered.

His hands flew as he worked on the model. It looked like a miniature fortress, with square walls and turrets.

'I like your castle,' I said. 'Dinner's in half an hour.'

He was too busy sticking down corners to respond. The evening followed the same pattern as before. We sat in front of the TV, his head on my shoulder. He seemed glad to accept the comfort of a mother substitute, but my feelings were more complex. The people I loved could be counted on the fingers of one hand, and I'd never had a child depend on me before. Behaviourists say that parental love stems from biological programming, but my feelings for Mikey had nothing to do with genetics. He'd breached my emotional defences and it was too late to shut them down. I let my hand coast across his temple, smoothing his hair back from his forehead.

'Time for bed, Mikey.'

He was close to sleep when I checked on him again. His sky-blue gaze fixed on me as he pointed at his cardboard fortress, windows and brickwork picked out in black ink. It looked so impregnable that anyone entering the huge doors would never escape.

'Not far now,' he said firmly.

'Get some sleep, sweetheart.' I kissed his forehead, then left him alone.

Back downstairs I toiled on my computer, entering the coordinates of the Church of the Precious Blood. New location analysis software was part of the Home Office's latest profiling programme, helping to link sites in a crime series.

The killers seemed to be using different systems for the calling cards and murder locations. The blood samples were scattered across a wide radius, but the killing sites were much more focused. The Old Operating Theatre and the Church of the Precious Blood were a stone's throw from each other, connected by a jagged red line. The software indicated that the killers were based at the heart of south London, not far from where Mikey had escaped from his abductors' car. My thoughts spun across suspects who lived inside the zone: the Pietersens, Gary Lennard, the Thorpes, Luke Mann. The names were another source of frustration. Dr Pietersen had been cleared, Lennard seemed too sick to harm anyone, and the Thorpes had a solid alibi for the morning Riordan was taken. Mann had a clean record and no identified motive for a string of blood-related attacks.

I was still puzzling at eleven o'clock when I called Burns. There was a quiet hiss of traffic when he picked up.

'Where are you?' I asked.

'The church on O'Meara Street. Pete's lot are back for the final check.'

'Did they find anything?'

'A syringe in the car. It's gone to the lab for DNA testing.'

'That's a good start.'

'What are you up to?'

'Looking at maps. I'm sure Riordan's being held near where Mikey was found in Walworth. Maybe he heard or saw something that's leading him back there.'

Burns gave a loud sigh. 'We've been through there like a dose of salts.'

'Everything they do is symbolic. I'm almost certain the building they're using will be linked to haematology or blood sacrifice.'

'We've just found out that some of Pure's members were

treated by Clare Riordan. They probably never realised she signed their rights away.'

'Someone did. Is there anyone we know?'

'Gary Lennard was a patient of hers years ago.'

'He never mentioned it.'

'We're checking his alibis.'

'He's dying, Don. The guy can hardly stand up.'

I pictured Lennard at his elegant house in Deptford, struggling to breathe as he surveyed his oriental garden, with his ex-wife nursing him. Surely he was too sick to harm anyone now? But how would he react if he knew that one of his own doctors had signed a mandate denying him full compensation?

Burns gave a muffled curse, followed by loud footsteps.

'Are you okay?'

'It's pissing down here, I had to run to the car.'

Outside the French windows, a flurry of rain pelted the glass. 'Do you ever wonder how life'll be when this is over?'

'We'll be sunning ourselves in Morocco.'

'Don't make idle promises.'

'I've found the perfect hotel.'

I let out a laugh. 'Get some sleep before you keel over.'

The rain had stopped when I rang off, the grubby walls of the living room collapsing in on me. I followed my night-time tradition and stepped outside, breathing the city's smell of diesel and damp air, listening to the mosquito buzz of a plane landing at City airport. But when my eyes opened again, panic flooded my system. This time there was no room for doubt; a hooded figure stood at the end of the garden, motionless between the trees. It was too dark to be sure, but the slim frame convinced me it was a woman. I hit the panic button as I rammed the door shut behind me, fumbling with the key. Were all the bedroom windows locked? I ran upstairs and peered into Mikey's room. His thin form lay curled under the duvet, my pulse steadying again.

The taciturn policeman was in the kitchen when I got back downstairs.

'Something wrong?' His tone suggested that I'd raised the alarm just to annoy him.

'Someone was in the back garden just now.'

His eyebrows rose. 'You'd better show me.'

I pointed through to the French windows, feeling a twinge of embarrassment. The back wall was at least eight feet high; an intruder would have to be pretty limber to hurl themselves over.

'We should call the station.'

'The garden's empty now.' He studied my face. 'You look exhausted, love. Maybe you're imagining things.'

I counted to ten before responding. Something about being blonde and child-sized made it easy for people to doubt me. I grabbed my phone and called Burns's number on speed dial. 'We've had an intruder, Don. The building's secure, but I need more guards. Forensics should check outside.'

The officer threw me an angry scowl. 'You'll look pretty stupid if you're wrong.'

'Why don't you wait outside? New officers are coming to replace you.'

My hands were shaking. The combination of seeing the shadowy figure and having my judgement questioned had kick-started an adrenalin rush. Hancock listened in silence when he arrived, then searched the garden with one of his juniors, torch beams strafing the back wall. Pete's face was grave when they returned. They'd found scuff marks on the bricks and damaged plants where someone had landed on the undergrowth. I felt grateful that he'd come himself, instead of sending a team member, after toiling at Dawn Coleman's murder site all day.

'Thank God,' I said. 'I was beginning to think I'd seen a ghost.'

Pete shook his head. 'Ghosts don't leave dirty great boot-prints on wet ground. You might as well put the kettle on; I'm staying till the guards arrive.'

45

The woman's body aches, legs bruised from hauling herself over the wall. Anger and frustration make her head pound as she hides in the shadows. From here she can keep track of the police cars arriving and leaving, grim-faced men thrashing through the shrubs. It angers her that she came so close. She'd been hiding between the trees when the shrink raised her stupid, doll-like face to the sky. If she'd waited nearer the house, she could have overpowered her and taken the child. It would have been easy to force him over the wall then drag him back to the car.

When the boy appears at an upstairs window, she feels a shot of pure hatred for his mother. Another police car pulls up on the alleyway behind the house and she steals a last look at the child. The distance is too wide to read his expression, but she can see his hands splayed on the glass, like he's trying to claw his way out.

'Any day now,' she promises, then backs away.

46

I caught a whiff of gunpowder when I crossed the Thames the next morning. Two huge barges were slowly drifting west, laden with fireworks for the following night's display. Guy Fawkes Day had almost arrived without me noticing time slipping by. There was an incendiary atmosphere in the incident room when I arrived, too. The roar of conversation from detectives gathered round the coffee machine told me there must have been a development. Angie bustled over as I took off my coat, her face animated.

'Where've you been, Alice? I left three messages.'

'My phone was on silent, sorry.'

'We found Eleanor Riordan. She's confessed to killing her sister.'

My briefcase slipped from my hand. 'She admitted to it?'

'One of the sergeants heard the whole story in the car when she was picked up. The boss wants her assessed in half an hour. You can read this in the meantime; it's Roger Fenton's background file.'

She passed me a slim manila wallet before returning to her colleagues. The journalist's youth had been affluent but unremarkable: born in Surrey in 1978, he'd attended a minor public school, then read law at Edinburgh University. Just one conviction on his record for cannabis possession in his twenties, which had incurred a fine and community service. Maybe casual drug use was the reason he'd abandoned law and opted for journalism, working as an intern on *The Times* before gaining a staff job. He'd spent years jetting between war zones: Iraq, Syria, Afghanistan. The next page was a medical report. Fenton had been caught in a bomb blast in Kabul, returning to the UK by the time of the attack on John Mendez at the end of January. The journalist had sustained a ruptured spleen, his operation requiring a full blood transfusion. I flipped the folder shut again, trying to steady my nerves. There must be millions of people who'd gone through similar experiences without becoming obsessed by blood, yet Fenton's life history left me wondering if there was something I'd overlooked.

Eleanor Riordan's arrival seemed to have changed the team's mood from despair to relief; everyone was in party spirits. Burns was standing by his desk when I found him in his office, phone pressed to his ear as he motioned for me to sit. I could tell he was urging Scotland Yard to suppress news of the arrest. After the conversation ended, he settled both hands on my shoulders, the height difference between us making me wish I was a foot taller, so we could see eye to eye.

'You had another drama last night, didn't you?'

'I survived,' I said. 'But PC Plod didn't help.'

Burns looked embarrassed. 'He's been warned, and the kid's being moved today. We can't take any chances.'

'How did you find Eleanor Riordan?'

'One of the sightings from *Crimewatch* came up trumps. She's been lying low in a B&B in Richmond, using a false name.'

'Has she got a solicitor?'

'He's been here an hour. Let's see what she's got to say.'

Riordan was waiting in an interview room, where morning light spilled on to grey lino and a scratched Formica table. The space wasn't ideal for sharing secrets: chilly, with a smoked-glass observation window sunk into the wall. Half a dozen people would be crammed into the monitoring room next door, watching our every move. Eleanor Riordan looked calmer than before, her hair swept into a neat ponytail. She wore jeans, knee-length boots and a charcoal grey jumper; smart but comfortable clothes, ideal for a weekend away. Her makeup was flawless too, mascara and pale lip gloss, deliberately low key. Riordan's solicitor was much less well groomed; a balding, middle-aged man who looked out of his comfort zone, sweat glistening on his upper lip.

'Good to see you again, Eleanor,' I said.

'I bet.' Her expression soured. 'You can relax now, can't you?'

'That depends on your story.'

'I killed my sister. There's nothing else to say.'

'Talk me through what happened, please, from the start.'

She folded her arms. 'She was out running with Mikey in the clearing where you saw me. I drove to some woodland and dumped her there.'

'How did you kill her?'

'I put a pillow over her face on the back seat of my car.'

'What did you do with the pillow?'

Her mouth flapped open then closed again. 'I threw it away.'

'Did Luke help you?'

She blinked rapidly. 'Of course not. He's not involved.'

'Where did you leave her body exactly?'

'Epping Forest. We went there as kids for picnics.' Her composure was cracking, a panicked look in her eyes.

'Luke's been worried about you, Eleanor. Why didn't you answer his calls?'

'I couldn't.' She pressed her hand to the side of her face. 'It's been hard to think straight.'

'Have you seen the news?'

She shook her head. 'There was no TV in my room.'

284

'Your story will be checked very carefully. Are you sure the details are correct?'

'Why would I lie?'

'Tell me about John Mendez, Lisa Stuart, Jordan Adebayo and Dawn Coleman.'

'It was my sister I hurt. No one else.' She fell silent, her face contorting. I understood now why she'd dressed so smartly: she wanted to look in control as the last shreds of her sanity slipped away. Her voice was little more than a whisper when she spoke again. 'I went for her with a knife; I couldn't stop myself.'

'We found Clare's blood on her kitchen floor, but she was attacked back in August. You haven't seen her since, have you?'

When she spoke again her tone was as high and singsong as a lullaby. 'I feel better when I walk on the common. We used to play hide-and-seek there, before things turned bad. Mum taught us the names of all the trees: alder, blackthorn, elder.'

'Life's been tough lately, hasn't it? We heard about your pregnancies.'

'Luke never could keep a secret,' she said, scowling.

'What kind of medication are you on, Eleanor? Fluoxetine, sertraline?'

'I'm not ill,' she snapped.

'Postnatal depression's a serious condition. You need to see a counsellor.'

Her eyes glistened. 'I hurt my sister. You have to believe me; we attacked each other for years.'

'Your claims will be investigated, but if they're false you'll need to spend time in hospital. A Home Office psychiatrist will see you tomorrow.'

Maybe she realised she was inches from being sectioned, because she burst into a storm of tears. Her solicitor's hand hovered above her shoulder, like it was unethical to offer comfort.

'That won't please the bigwigs,' Burns muttered when we got back to his office. 'They're desperate for a conviction.'

'At least we know why Riordan's blood was on her kitchen floor. Depending on how long Eleanor's recent pregnancy lasted, it could be post-partum psychosis, which increases violent tendencies. Or the grief of so much loss could have destabilised her. The sisters had been at loggerheads for years. Clare had everything Eleanor wanted: their parents' love, the house, a child. The court case had taken all her money.'

Burns frowned. 'She might still be one of the killers.'

'The psychology doesn't make sense. She's got no reason to harm any of the other victims; she didn't even recognise their names. A fit of temper made Eleanor stab her sister, and now the guilt's hit home. It's interesting that Clare protected her identity when Pietersen came to the rescue; perhaps there's more residual loyalty between them than you'd expect.'

'You think Clare going missing was one loss too many?'

'She seems obsessed by it. The psychiatrist can assess her again tomorrow, but if I'm right she'll need counselling and medication.'

When I looked at Burns again, he was on his feet, the crown of his head level with the light fitment. It was tempting to walk into his arms for a quick shot of comfort, but Angie burst in before I could move a muscle.

'Riordan's solicitor's bleating about mental suffering, boss. He wants her bailed.'

Burns's work persona snapped back in an instant. 'Tell him to get real. If she's lied, she'll be put on a psychiatric ward, or we'll sue her for wasting our time.'

47

The man spends the afternoon alone at home. When he peers from the front window there's no sign of her, and she's not answering her phone. It terrifies him that she may have been caught. He levers himself from the chair, the stab of pain in his right side strong enough to take his breath away. But there's a last promise he has to fulfil, and he can't let her down. He drags himself along the hallway to collect his keys.

It takes half an hour to drive to Bermondsey; he leaves his car parked at the end of the cul-de-sac. Classical music drifts from the radio, a Chopin étude for piano, one of his favourites. While the music plays he can almost imagine himself young again, with nothing to forgive. He does his best to stay awake, but the melody lulls him. When his eyes snap open again dusk has fallen and it's almost too late. An unmarked police car is pulling away and he catches a glimpse of the boy's dark hair. He keeps the vehicle in sight as they cross Tower Bridge, but by Shadwell it's vanished. Traffic clogs the road ahead; the dark blue car is swallowed by a sea of metal. It surfaces again at the next lights and he parks by Shadwell Pier; through his binoculars he sees the child being led away, clutching a duffel bag.

Another flare of pain burns across his torso as he slips the binoculars back into their case. Now he knows where the boy is being kept; a flat this time, close to the river. It crosses his mind to keep the information to himself so the child can stay safe, but he can't let the woman down. He takes out his phone and calls her again.

48

There was still no sign of Burns when I woke after a fitful night, but it was clear that he'd been home – yesterday's shirt was heaped on a chair. I was getting a picture of why his marriage had failed: with two small boys to look after, his wife must have viewed his work ethic as constant desertion. I pushed the thought to the back of my head and focused on Mikey; my first impulse was to check on him. The house in Bermondsey might have been drab and comfortless, but moving to another location was bound to disturb him. In a world without certainties, he needed as much security as possible. I called Gurpreet as soon as I'd showered.

'We're off to the supermarket,' he said. 'See you in an hour.'

The conversation felt surreal. We were sharing responsibility for a child whose mother was being tortured, yet calmly chatting about going shopping. I used the extra time to smarten my appearance, relieved that there was no one hogging the bathroom while I straightened my hair and applied makeup. When I'd put on slim black trousers, a cashmere sweater, low-heeled suede boots and my favourite Liberty's coat, I felt presentable for once. A text from Lola arrived as I was about to leave. It was a reminder that I'd promised to help her shop for a wedding dress later that week; there would be champagne and canapés for the bridal party while she tried on endless outfits. I sent a quick reply promising to be there, then set off down the stairs.

My new driver blinked at me when I reached the car park in the basement. The officer was in his mid-twenties, Middle Eastern with black hair and classic good looks. He opened the passenger door with an old-fashioned flourish. My vanity expanded when I caught him checking me out while I fastened my seatbelt. So far he'd been too tongue-tied to say hello.

'What's your name?' I asked.

'Hussein. I'm your driver for the day.'

'I guessed you might be. Shadwell first, please, Hussein.'

He gave me his life story while traffic stalled on Southwark Bridge Road. His parents were from Damascus; he'd finished a social policy master's degree in London, but opted for the Met instead of social work. His long-term relationship had just ended because his girlfriend hadn't wanted to get married. He studied me thoughtfully, as though I might cure his romantic problems.

'What about you?' he asked.

'I've been a psychologist for years. It's the only job I ever really wanted.'

'Single?'

I glanced at him. 'Don't push your luck.'

'We could have dinner some time.'

'Nice offer, but I'm seeing your chief officer.'

'DCI Burns?' His shoulders stiffened. 'Sorry, I didn't know.'

'It's okay, he won't fire you.'

By the time we swung right down Wapping High Street, Hussein had switched to friendship mode, lamenting the smallness of his rented flat and telling me about his desire for promotion. When he pulled up behind an apartment block near Shadwell Basin I was about to say goodbye, but he insisted on escorting me inside. I'd been so spooked by the previous night's intruder that it felt good to have company. Hussein seemed in his element as we crossed the tarmac, keeping up a steady stream of chatter.

The apartment block was far more upmarket than the safe house. A concierge in a smart navy uniform was guarding a set of lifts with mirrored doors. Despite my fear of confined spaces, I forced myself inside, watching the numbers tick by until we reached the tenth floor. The flat resembled a new hotel, with minimal furnishing, bare floorboards and mirrors to maximise the light. Silence echoed from its walls instead of the usual throb of the TV. I explored the place while waiting for Mikey and Gurpreet. The outlook was the apartment's best feature, floor-to-ceiling windows giving a panoramic view across the Thames. The river looked dark as gun metal, bus boats scratching its surface like etching needles on a steel plate.

'Any danger of a cup of tea?' Hussein hovered in the doorway.

'I'd love one, thanks.'

He muttered a quiet insult before retreating to the kitchen. I was still admiring the wraparound balcony when my phone hummed in my pocket. Tania's voice was too garbled to make out her words.

'Slow down, I can't hear you.'

'The boy's been taken,' she said. 'We just found out.'

My thoughts ground to a standstill. 'How?'

'From the car. Our guys were following but it happened in moments. Singh's being treated for a broken jaw.' She blew out a long breath. 'There's nothing you can do, Alice. Sit tight till Burns calls.'

The line fell silent and my thoughts scrambled, even though calmness would be my only chance of helping to find Mikey. Tania's advice slipped from my mind; it would be impossible to wait quietly when someone I loved was in danger.

49

The woman waits for a convoy of squad cars to chase east, sirens blaring. Then she drives in the opposite direction, a serene smile on her face. The man studies her again. She's still beautiful, even though she's lost her humanity.

'Thank God,' she murmurs. 'I thought we'd never get away.'

'You realise this is where it ends for me, don't you?'

'I'm not surprised. You've been squeamish about it from day one.'

'He's an eleven-year-old boy.'

'And our biggest weapon. He'll make her tell us more names.'

The man grits his teeth. 'We had a point to prove. But you don't even remember it, do you?'

'You're so self-righteous.'

'I'm too tired for this.'

Suddenly her face softens, her hand on his arm. 'I know, sweetheart, but it's nearly over. Just meet me in the lab tonight like we agreed.'

The man looks away. It's painful to glimpse the tenderness her rage is destroying, the light fading as the city speeds past. He doesn't want to consider what lies ahead. If she makes him stay in the room when she hurts the boy, he'll be forced to cover his eyes.

50

Hussein had enough sense to leave me alone, his flirtatious manner gone in an instant. The facts didn't add up. I kept picturing Mikey struggling in the back of a stranger's car as it speeded away. It was difficult to focus on what to do next. I had always believed that he knew where his mother was being held, hidden on one of the narrow Walworth streets we'd already explored.

Mikey's new room was at the end of the corridor, large and airy, with pale blue walls. The sight of his abandoned clothes made my stomach convulse; a hooded top slung across the chair, as though he might return at any minute. I scanned the room for anything that could help. There were few personal items, apart from his Xbox and phone, pens and pencils, and the square cardboard fortress he'd been building. The drawings in his sketchbook gave no new information, apart from reminding me that his memory was extraordinary. Each picture recreated Clapham Common with obsessive clarity. I found his drawing of Portland Street, where he'd escaped three weeks before, but it offered no new information.

It felt like I was clutching at straws when I searched my bag for Emma Selby's sheet of addresses, eyes racing across the list of buildings relevant to blood history, her notes scribbled in spiky black handwriting. The only one with a Walworth postcode was a World War Two depot that had stored seventy thousand gallons of blood during the Blitz. The locations on the list had already been checked by Angie's team, but I couldn't just twiddle my thumbs, waiting for the phone to ring.

'There's somewhere I need to visit.'

Hussein raised his head. 'Aren't you meant to stay here?'

'Change of plan.'

Luckily he was too green to argue. A fleet of police cars raced towards Wapping as we got back into the car, the Met focusing on the spot where Mikey had been taken before the evidence went cold. But my approach would be different. It didn't matter where he'd been abducted, I had to discover where he was being held. The killers believed that Skipton House in Elephant and Castle was where their cause had been lost, because the health minister had signed papers there after the enquiry, denying full compensation. It made sense that they would torture their victims near the site of the biggest injustice. I did my best not to let my mind settle on Mikey as the car edged through traffic. If I dwelled on what he was suffering, my nerve would evaporate.

The blood depot lay at the heart of Walworth. It was a large 1930s building with striking Art Deco features, arched windows and ornate plasterwork, but its days as a warehouse had ended decades ago. The place had been divided into flats, rows of doorbells beside the glass entrance. A wave of disappointment hit me when I realised that the killers couldn't be using the place as their headquarters, even though its history would have attracted them. The depot might have kept the city's heart beating during the war, but it wouldn't serve as a hiding place now. Floodlights lined the car park's boundary, any suspicious behaviour visible from the higher floors. Hussein tagged me as I circled the building, but a glance through the windows of an outhouse revealed nothing more incriminating than a lawn mower, cans of paint and a set of ladders.

'Shouldn't we go back?' he asked.

'Not till I finish searching.'

Luckily he agreed without complaint, even though his expression was baffled as we continued south down Walworth Road. I asked him to pull up when we reached Burgess Park. My eyes were scanning the tennis courts and boating pond when the sky ignited. So many fireworks burst on the horizon, it looked like the sky was on fire. Even though I had always loved bonfire night, the display failed to lighten my mood. The only thing that could brighten my day would be to find Mikey unharmed.

'We've come too far,' I muttered. 'Take me back to Westmoreland Road.'

I wanted to return to the spot where Mikey had escaped from the killers' car three weeks before. It terrified me that the boy had evaded death once already. I stared at the lights flaring on the horizon as we drove, aware that the boy would need more than luck to escape a second time.

Hussein navigated the narrow streets of Walworth, and when we drew close to Portland Street, Mikey's catchphrase repeated in my mind: 'Almost there, not far now.' I felt certain he'd heard the abductors saying the words. I stared at his drawing again, focusing on the figure hiding between ramshackle buildings, surrounded by garages and parked cars. What if Mikey hadn't been running away at all, but following the car to find his mother? An odd pressure built in my chest, like a dam waiting to burst.

'Let's walk from here.'

The young PC gave a half-hearted nod. 'What are we looking for?'

'I'll know when I see it.' I brought up a street map on my phone. 'We need to search all the roads off Portland Street for old buildings and churches.'

'Want me to bring a torch?'

'That would help.'

Hussein sighed as we set off, fireworks still exploding over our heads every few minutes, lighting our way then leaving us in darkness again. The young officer must have been longing to be back in Wapping, part of a huge team solving a crime. Instead he was traipsing through the suburbs on a wild-goose chase, taking orders from a woman who was fraying at the seams. Luckily he was too polite to voice his doubts, running his torch beam across the pavement, like the answer to Mikey's disappearance lay trapped between paving stones. I called Burns as we reached a crossroads, but was patched through to his answering service.

'Where now?' Hussein asked.

I studied my map. 'North first, I want to cover a half-mile radius from here.'

'That'll take hours.' A peevish tone had entered his voice.

I turned to face him. 'A child's in danger, Hussein. He's escaped from a car near here once already. It's possible they've brought him back. You want him found, don't you?'

My urgent tone seemed to prick his conscience. He gave a rapid nod, increasing his pace as we set off again. Our tour revealed an area of London that lacked money, but had plenty of pride. A small, well-kept primary school stood opposite narrow houses built cheek by jowl. Our search was yielding little except evidence of gentrification, skips full of old-fashioned baths and abandoned kitchen units.

'What about down there?' Hussein asked, pointing to a dark alleyway.

'It's worth a look.'

The ground was rough underfoot, leaves rotting on the cobbles, wrappers from fireworks, a stink of decaying food. Something fluttered in the shadows at our feet.

'What's that?' Hussein's voice was edged with panic.

'Rats, probably.'

His breathing was ragged as we retraced our steps. I didn't have the heart to point out that we were outnumbered; the city contained far more vermin than human beings. The search was starting to feel like a bad dream, but it beat waiting at the station, chewing my fingernails to the bone.

We headed north up Brandon Street. There was little to see, apart from a sign outside a Seventh Day Adventist church claiming that God loves the faithful. I would gladly have offered a prayer to keep Mikey safe, even if it felt like a shot in the dark. We passed a sign for community art studios and a new building development without slowing down. Somewhere in this teeming city, a young boy was being held captive. To stop myself falling apart, I had to believe that he was still alive.

51

The laboratory is colder than before. The man huddles on a stool, failing to keep warm; his fever's worse today, ice water chasing through his veins. The child lies hog-tied on the tiled floor, a hood over his face. His mother is too weak to stir, only her eyes fully alive. They burned like lasers when the boy's inert body was dragged through the door. Her shoulders jerk as she coughs against her gag. The woman told him not to give her water, but small acts of cruelty only make him feel worse. He picks up the bottle and releases the gag. Riordan's almost too weak to swallow, liquid splashing across her cheek.

'Let him go, please.' She chokes out the words.

'It's too late, Clare.'

Her voice is a low growl. 'You evil bastard.'

The man jerks the gag back into place. Her eyes are darker now, dull brown instead of amber, tarnished by everything she's seen.

He settles on the stool again, scanning the room. The porcelain sink has stood in the corner since Victorian times. A hundred years ago, gaslight would have fallen on test tubes and specimen jars, the pallid faces of human guinea pigs. He shuts his eyes and imagines the sufferers, too weak to fight for their lives.

The room is prepared for the last punishment, drip line suspended from a metal stand. Mother and son will lie side by side, her blood flowing into his arm. If their blood types are incompatible, the child will die in agony. First his lungs will fail, then his heart. The man rubs his hand across his face. He understands now that their campaign will achieve nothing. Even though doctors like Clare Riordan caused his illness, he lacks the strength to witness more suffering. The sky outside the frosted windows is absurdly celebratory, pulsing with red, silver and gold. Only his loyalty keeps him there, waiting for the woman to return.

52

Rain fell as we scoured the neighbourhood. Hussein was still following me doggedly, even though he was soaked to the skin. My hopes faded as I scanned the recreation ground at the end of Alvey Street. Inside the park's neat privet hedges, three homeless men were huddled under a tree, passing a bottle to keep warm. Lights burned in the houses nearby, families keeping warm in front of the TV, instead of braving the rain to watch the Guy Fawkes display. Mikey was galaxies away from such ordinary pleasures, and it struck me again that he might already be dead, the killers grabbing the prize they'd been chasing from day one. The most devastating fact was that there was nothing I could do.

Burns finally called back at nine p.m., voices grumbling in the background. 'Where the hell are you?'

'Walworth, doing a street search.'

'You should be here.' He let out an exasperated sigh. 'The commissioner needs briefing.'

'Give me one more hour.'

His tone sharpened. 'Are you listening? You're wanted at the station, pronto.'

'Tough. Only Christine gives me orders.'

Hussein smirked as I hit the mute button, the snappy exchange certain to fuel fresh gossip. My phone vibrated in my pocket again: Burns would be leaving an irate message, but I didn't care. Stopping my search would feel negligent, even if I was proved wrong. We had half a dozen more streets to check before I could call it quits. The rain had slowed to a steady drizzle, pavements slick with litter and fallen leaves.

'Let's take a look at that church,' I said.

The Baptist chapel ahead had seen better days. The oak door was so dented it looked like someone had tried to kick it down, each blow more forceful than the last. Hussein disappeared to check the grounds and I peered through the window at orderly rows of pews, a simple altar and pulpit. I was still standing there when a shout went up. The sound made me break into a jog, torchlight leading me to where Hussein lay sprawled on the asphalt.

'Don't try to move. What happened?'

'I slipped, banged my head.' His voice was groggy, a shallow gash on his forehead.

'You'll live.' His injury reminded me that the chase might be pointless, my urge to find Mikey producing nothing except a headache for my new colleague. 'Can you walk to the car?'

'Of course.' He swayed drunkenly, then steadied himself.

When we reached Portland Street I paused by a streetlamp to study the map again. We'd checked all the streets linking with Walworth Road, but found nowhere suitable for a hiding place. Maybe I'd been wrong all along. The killers were holding him in a lock-up or a cellar, the location unconnected to the theme of blood. I had just helped Hussein into the car when my eyes caught on a passageway we'd missed. He rolled down the window when I tapped the glass.

'There's one more alley to check.'

Hussein gave a quiet groan as he lurched from the car. We passed a sign advertising artists' studios, but it was hard to imagine people tapping into their creativity at the end of a dank alley. I was about to turn back when something loomed out of the darkness. An old man stood directly ahead, clutching a broom. He must have been seventy at least, thin and slightly stooped in his waterproof coat, his gaze as inquisitive as a child's. I did my best to return his smile.

'You gave me a fright,' he said.

'Sorry. We're looking for old buildings in the area.'

'At this time of night?'

'It's a long story. We work for the police,' I said, flashing my ID card.

His eyebrows rose. 'Most went in the slum clearances, but the place where I work's Victorian.' He pointed at the end of alley. 'It's down there.'

'Can we take a look?'

The old man gave a nod of agreement, his pronounced limp slowing our progress across ground that reeked of urine and spilled beer. His name turned out to be Stanley Moorfield – a Walworth native, born and bred.

'It's listed, so no developer wants it. They'd need a fortune to do it up.'

'And you keep an eye on the building?'

'Each morning and last thing at night. I clean up and do repairs.'

The old man hit a light switch and a square two-storey building appeared in front of us. Its name was carved into the stone lintel above the door: The Health Laboratories. The place looked solid as a Gothic fortress, towers at each of its four corners. An odd chill travelled across the back of my neck. It was just like the structure Mikey had built from cardboard and glue, but how could he have seen it?

'What was it used for?'

'Experiments, I think, testing vaccines for the government.'

A faint light shone from the back of the building. 'Is anyone using it now?'

'Just one bloke since the heating broke down. He rents a double unit at the back. I can't remember his name; he and his wife are photographers.'

'Have you spoken to them?'

'They're not the friendly type. He's put a lock on the door so I can't go in and sweep up.'

Hussein was starting to look bored. 'Shouldn't we get back?'

I shook my head firmly. 'Not till we've seen inside.'

The old man seemed pleased. 'I'll show you the entrance hall, if you like.'

'Do the windows open, Stanley?'

'Not any more. The ones at the back are barred; we had a break-in last year.'

'Do you know much about the couple who're renting?'

'Nothing, except they often work late.'

There were broken tiles on the floor of the entrance hall and wood panels splintering from the walls. But it was the smell that raised the hairs on the back of my neck. It was like the Old Operating Theatre, a faint reek of antiseptic combined with the bitterness of chloroform.

'Call the Armed Response Unit,' I told Hussein quietly as Stanley walked ahead.

'What?'

'Just do it,' I hissed. 'Then block the fire exits outside. Make sure no one escapes.'

The old man hadn't heard our exchange. Hussein was already heading away, muttering into his radio. At the end of the corridor, light seeped from below a locked door. There were no other sounds apart from the old man's murmur as he played tour guide.

'Go home now, Stanley. The police will arrive soon; there's going to be a lot of noise.'

'The owners won't like it if I don't clean up.'

'Don't worry, I'll take the blame.'

Luckily he didn't argue, limping back down the dark alley, sheltered under his umbrella. I waited for the armed unit with mixed feelings. I could be about to disturb a photographer at work, or to find Mikey. Thank God the windows were sealed. If the killers were closeted inside, their only exit would be via the front door.

My call to Angie got no reply; she was probably at the commissioner's briefing with the rest of the team. But two anonymous grey vans had already arrived. The sergeant's vicious crew cut would have suited a marine, his calm, grey-eyed stare at odds with the weapons strapped across his chest. He listened to my explanation, then issued a string of curt orders before escorting me and Hussein outside.

'Stay in your vehicle,' he said. 'Don't move till we give the all clear.'

Hussein wouldn't stop babbling. Concussion or an over-load of excitement seemed to be getting to him. My muscles felt like they'd been pulled taut. Cascades of silver and gold were still showering the horizon. If I was wrong, ten highly skilled officers would have wasted their time, and the blame would fall on me. When I scanned the street again an ambulance was arriving, reminding me that a third of armed call-outs ended in bloodshed. A second later there was a loud blast, then a stutter of gunfire, followed by a deafening silence. My hands clutched into fists. Instinct told me to run into the building, but armed officers would only haul me out again.

Things happened fast after that. One of the men in bullet-proof gear told us that victims had been found. I didn't stop to ask whether they were dead or alive before dashing down the corridor behind the paramedics. The door at the end of the corridor had burst from its hinges. The woman strapped to a chair had to be Clare Riordan, bruises littering her neck, wrists chafed raw by leather cuffs. Her face was so bone white that I thought she was dead, until her eyes blinked open. One of the ambulance crew was already leaning down to untie her restraints. Relief surged through me when I saw Mikey lying on the floor. I was determined not to cry as I undid his gag. When the cotton fell away, his raw howl echoed from the walls, so loud and heart-rending it sounded as if he was releasing all the pent-up fear he'd bottled for weeks.

'You're safe now, sweetheart.'

He clung to me as his mother was stretchered away. It was only after they were both in the ambulance that I noticed my surroundings again. Maybe it was shock that made the air taste bitter, each mouthful loaded with chemicals. An elaborate system of ropes and pulleys dangled from the ceiling, ties and buckles to hold the victims in place. A table by the wall carried transfusion bags, syringes and phials of unidentified fluids. I pulled on sterile gloves and opened the fridge in the corner. Two blood packs full of red liquid lay on a shelf, neatly printed with Riordan's name. My stomach tightened with nausea as I scanned the white walls and scrubbed tiles. The place was as clean and orderly as a dentist's surgery, yet it had been a torture chamber. Suddenly my head swum with the reality that Mikey might never have been found.

All I could do was sit on the concrete step outside with my head between my knees, waiting for the dizziness to clear. When I straightened up again, Hussein stood in front of me, a euphoric look on his face, as if he'd already been promoted.

'They're holding the bloke in the van. Do you want to see him?'

'Who is it?'

'He's not talking. No ID on him either.'

I stood up too quickly, the ground shifting below my feet, but curiosity dragged me back towards the van. Gary Lennard came to mind first; few people had suffered more because of tainted blood. Maybe he'd exaggerated his illness to throw us off track? My head felt woozy again, shock and exhaustion catching up with me as I struggled to put one foot in front of the other.

53

The woman's panic rises as she reaches Portland Street. Three squad cars sit at the mouth of the alley, blue lights flashing as she drives past, her hands shaking on the wheel. She parks two blocks away and walks back slowly, hiding between buildings; he may still be in the laboratory, facing a barrage of questions. Anger floods her system. Her main regret is not killing the boy when she had the chance. Drizzle mists her face as she stands there watching.

When she lowers herself back into the driver's seat, her power has vanished. The idea of returning home to wait for the knock on her door is horrifying, but there's no point in running, with no one to help her escape. She takes the gun from her pocket and places its cold muzzle against her lips, tastes the steel with her tongue, but her finger refuses to pull the trigger. The gun falls back into her lap as she stares blank-eyed through the window.

54

Tania arrived while I was preparing myself to look inside the van. For a second I thought she might hug me, but she converted the gesture into a pat on my arm.

'Maybe shrinks have a purpose after all.'

'High praise, Tania. I don't know who he is yet.'

'Are you up to seeing him?'

'Just about. Let's do it.'

My legs still felt unsteady as we approached the vehicle, its doors firmly closed. When one of the officers unlocked it, a man was hunched inside the metal cage, handcuffs round his wrists. Shock hit me when his gaunt face came into view. Simon Thorpe's skin was paler than before against the dense black of his hair; he looked exhausted, dark grey circles under his eyes.

'Where's your wife, Simon?' I asked.

No answer arrived; his face was expressionless. I watched in disbelief as he turned his face away. The man who had killed four medics and spent weeks torturing another was a qualified psychotherapist, and one of Clare Riordan's closest friends.

Tania answered a string of calls on her radio as we drove to the station. It sounded like Burns was suppressing the news that Riordan had been found until Denise Thorpe was arrested. I gazed out of the car window at the night-time streets, too numb to feel anything but relief.

Someone placed a cup of coffee in my hands in the incident room and my curiosity revived. There was no sign of Burns in the hubbub, my head full of unanswered questions. Why would the Thorpes set out to harm a child they had both professed to love? I still couldn't see a motive, apart from the fact that they were both frustrated medics. Maybe they had felt locked out of their chosen profession, united by bitter resentment. But that didn't explain the elaborate staging, their fascination with the history of blood treatments, or the fact that nurses at Denise's mother's care home had seen them both at the time of Clare's abduction. I was finishing the dregs of my coffee when Angie appeared. Her greeting was the opposite of Tania's restraint. She threw her arms round my neck, bellowing congratulations. The station was erupting with the news that the case was closed, jubilant faces looming at me. The atmosphere was so giddy, it felt as if lead weights had been lifted from the roof. Angie led me to Burns's door, then gave me a gentle shove before anyone else could shake my hand. I forgot my rules about distance at work and walked straight into his arms. I could have stayed there hours, but he eased back, his lopsided smile widening.

'You'll give me another heart attack at this rate,' he said.

'That's not my plan.'

'The tabloids all want a piece of you. Our phone lines are crashing.'

'Tell them to get lost.'

'That's my girl.' Burns gave a shaky laugh. 'A car's waiting for us outside.'

'I need to assess Thorpe first.'

'Not till tomorrow. His wife's cool as a cucumber, which is surprising given what she's done.'

I stared up at him. 'Let me interview her now.'

'Switch off, Alice. No solicitor's going to work at midnight, even for a case like this.'

I listened as he explained that Clare was in intensive care, high fever and a cocktail of drugs placing her in danger. Mikey had been taken back to the flat in Shadwell to rest. I thought about him as we left Burns's office; his ordeal had been terrifying, from being dragged into Thorpe's car again, to seeing his mother at death's door. I fought my urge to rush to the apartment to check on him. With luck he'd be asleep, and I could see him in the morning. The last face I saw as we headed for the exit belonged to Denise Thorpe, being taken to the holding cells, face blank with shock. Maybe she had believed they could hurt people indefinitely, shielded by middle-class respectability. There was something chilling about her anonymous appearance, which would allow her to walk down any street unnoticed. I ignored the flashbulbs as we trotted down the steps, unable to wipe her from my mind.

Back at the flat I was still jittering with pent-up adrenalin. Burns stood in the kitchen, facing me.

'Need a drink?'

'Apple juice please.' The cloying taste of the laboratory's atmosphere was still in my mouth, sour with chemicals.

'How in God's name did you find him, Alice?' Burns pressed the glass into my hand.

'Listening skills, logic, and mapping software.'

'You took one hell of a risk.' His shoulders tensed. 'And you were wrong about the line of command. While you're my consultant, I'm in charge. I could fire you for insubordination.'

'Are you too macho to apologise?'

He shook his head. 'Tell me what happened.'

'Mikey's clues matched my location analysis. He knew his mum was somewhere in Walworth, and I thought the killers

309

were so obsessed by blood history that they'd choose a symbolic building. I was wide of the mark; I thought it would be another old church after the previous two sites.'

'Angie's lot checked out the history of the Health Laboratories. It's pretty dark; the MoD used them to test nerve agents on soldiers in the Thirties. Fifteen men died of blood poisoning, but they kept it hushed up for decades.'

'How would the Thorpes know?'

He shrugged. 'From local history websites, like us, probably.'

'It's their motive I don't get. Serial killers normally fall into three categories: sexual predators, psychopaths or sadists. Simon and Denise were getting even for a past injustice, but the reason's not clear. One of them could be seriously ill.'

'Just be glad they're off the streets.' Burns hooked his arm round my shoulders, then held out his phone. 'Take a look at this.'

A large building appeared on the screen, stone bleached pale by intense sunlight. Each room was more sumptuous than the last; the roof terrace had a turquoise swimming pool, surrounded by sun loungers and parasols. 'It looks amazing.'

'It's a five-star hotel in Tangiers. We can fly there on Friday for a week if I hit send.'

I reached out and tapped the button for him, to end the debate.

We talked nineteen to the dozen, debating theories about the Thorpes' case. At four in the morning I passed out against his shoulder, still fully dressed.

55

Thursday 6 November

A psychiatric nurse called Paula Ryman was with Mikey when I reached Shadwell the next morning. She was a colleague of Gurpreet's, a slender fifty year old with grey hair cut in a short, no-nonsense style. She looked concerned when I asked how Gurpreet was recovering from the attack.

'He's on the mend at home, thank God. Apparently he tried to fight them off.'

I smiled at her. 'That doesn't surprise me.'

'I had one hell of a job getting Mikey to sleep,' she said. 'The news about his mum isn't good. They're keeping her in the ICU.'

Sleep was what Mikey needed most, but I couldn't resist tiptoeing into his room. His thin face looked peaceful, no visible damage, even though his mother was fighting for her life. I crouched down to study the cardboard model at the foot of his bed. It was an accurate replica of the Health Laboratories, right down to the tiles around the central door, every detail correct. He must have tagged the killers to the place where his mother was held, but the drug he'd received had affected his memory, making it impossible to find his way back after he went looking for help. His mantra – 'almost there, not far now' – finally made sense. He'd been able to picture where his mother was all along, but lacked the power to explain.

Anger overtook me during the taxi ride to the station. It was an emotion I normally ignored in professional contexts, unwilling to let that quick surge of bitterness harden my mind. Most of it was directed at Denise Thorpe for lying through her teeth as she coolly demanded access to Mikey. I indulged a quick fantasy of strapping her to her own torture chair, before pushing it aside. The only way to bring the Thorpes to justice would be to ignore personal feelings and concentrate on evidence.

The incident room was running on a skeleton staff, just a handful of detectives hunkered over their computers filing late reports. Without the constant jangle of bleepers and phones, the place felt ghostly.

'Peaceful, isn't it?' Angie appeared at my side.

'It's like the *Mary Celeste*.'

'The boss is at Scotland Yard. He wants Thorpe interviewed first, then his wife.'

Simon Thorpe's lawyer arrived early to meet his client. He was dressed in a sharp suit, ridiculously young and bright eyed, clearly aware that such a notorious trial would guarantee his place in legal history. Thorpe looked the worse for wear when he was brought from the holding cells, wrists straining against his handcuffs. The circles under his eyes were almost as black as his hair, making me doubt that he'd slept at all. There was no trace of his old charisma. He looked thinner than before, his skin jaundiced.

'Ready to talk, Mr Thorpe?' Angie asked. He didn't reply, his stare chilly as a blast of cold air. 'Say "no comment", please, or your case will be tried on evidence alone. Do you understand?'

After a while her constant questioning seemed to take effect. His hands wouldn't keep still, a line of sweat thickening on his upper lip. Maybe he'd been hoping that silence would bring a measure of control. I flicked through his file as Angie chipped away at his defences. He had been born in Santa Monica, trained in London as a medic, then he'd worked in France for several years before abandoning his medical career for psychotherapy.

'You worked fast the day you took Clare,' Angie said. 'A nurse saw your wife with her mother around nine o'clock, but you must have arrived later. I'm guessing Denise walked there alone. Did you leave Clare at the laboratory then go straight to the care home?'

Thorpe refused to answer, but his health record had caught my attention.

'I see that you're a haemophiliac, Mr Thorpe.' I glanced at the page again. 'Did you receive tainted blood in France? Is that what turned you against the medical profession?'

For the first time his expression faltered, as if I'd pinched a raw nerve, his silence forcing me to carry on.

'Now that your hepatitis C has progressed to cirrhosis, it's surprising you're getting by on mild painkillers. Most patients would be using morphine. I can see why your medical history has made you angry.'

His American drawl sounded harder than before when he finally spoke. 'My feelings aren't relevant. The UK treated its victims worst; the government lied and destroyed evidence. Everyone on the health panel was rewarded afterwards, with promotions and opportunities. Lisa Stuart admitted it.'

'Where did you put her body?'

He looked contemptuous. 'Regent's Canal by Acton's Lock.'

'You threw her in?'

'She fell.'

'I'll bet she did,' Angie muttered. Her face was angry, but I felt relieved. Police divers would plunge into the canal's black water until Lisa Stuart's remains were found; her mother would be able to hold the funeral at last.

'How did you get her name?' I asked. 'The panel's membership was protected information.'

His eyes glinted. 'Lisa was a client of mine, suffering from anxiety. She blamed the stress of working on the panel, but she accepted a promotion on the back of it.'

'She told you that in a therapy session?'

'That's how it began. She gave us Mendez's name straight away, and he was even more of a coward. He bleated out Clare's name in thirty seconds.'

'You didn't know she was on the panel, even though she was a close friend?'

'That was the worst thing. She knew how I'd suffered, but kept it secret. She did nothing to help.'

'But she gave you Jordan Adebayo's name?'

'And Dawn Coleman's. The guy from the blood bank wouldn't say a word.'

I felt a surge of respect for Adebayo. Despite his terrible death, he'd died a hero. It had taken weeks of torture to make Riordan reveal two names. If she lived, she would have to carry the consequences of naming her colleagues, but I doubted I would have shown as much courage.

'Using the Pure logo was misleading. You must have realised it put Ian Passmore under suspicion.'

'The symbol represents all the victims. We planned to announce our reasons at the end.'

'Why did you and Denise target the panel members?'

'They could have reversed the damage. If the government had apologised and compensated the victims fairly, every country in the world would have followed suit.'

Thorpe's lips sealed themselves in a thin line, but his gesture was different from Mikey's silence. While the boy had been desperate to shout the truth, Thorpe wanted to conceal his secrets. He refused to say another word before being taken back to his cell.

We had little time to compare notes before Thorpe's wife arrived, accompanied by her lawyer. He was elderly, dressed in an ill-fitting tweed jacket, but his gaze was focused as a laser. Denise seemed even more detached than before, barely acknowledging us, her cloud of mouse-brown hair obscuring her face.

Angie offered a narrow smile. 'Mrs Thorpe, you and your husband have been arrested on suspicion of multiple murders, plus the abduction and torture of Clare Riordan and her son. This is your chance to explain what happened.'

She looked confused. 'I keep telling you, I had nothing to do with it. Neither did Simon. We've been married twenty years. I'd know if he'd done anything wrong.'

'How does your husband's illness affect him?'

'The pain's worse at night. When it's bad he goes for a drive; he finds it calming.'

'He goes out alone at night?'

'I went too at the start, but he prefers to be alone.'

Angie huffed out a laugh. 'That's convenient, isn't it? Your husband kills people while you sleep peacefully at home. Except we know he had an accomplice.'

Denise's gaze met mine. 'You believe me, don't you? It's not in Simon's nature to be violent.'

'Are you taking any medication at the moment, Denise?' I asked. Her reactions seemed unnaturally slow, combined with her unfocused gaze.

'Just lorazepam to help me sleep.'

'One or two milligrams?'

'Two, most nights.'

'And anti-depressants?'

She shook her head. 'Not any more; they made me feel worse.'

'How long have you been feeling low?'

'All year. Things haven't been right between me and Simon; I've been so worried since he stopped going for his check-ups.' Her voice tailed away.

If she was telling the truth, she was taking one of the strongest tranquillisers on the market. One dose would be enough to knock out most adults for twelve hours straight. I let Angie complete the rest of the interview while I took notes. I had been certain all along that the killers would be diametric opposites: one coolly organised, the other wildly emotional. But Denise Thorpe seemed too fearful to do anyone serious harm, even though her husband could have planned the attacks. Her anxiety came over in the strain in her voice. The more I listened, the greater my concern. The woman's behaviour seemed fuelled by genuine panic.

'Search our house,' she insisted. 'You won't find anything.'

'Your husband was caught in the act, Mrs Thorpe. He's not denying it.'

Her lower lip trembled. 'You're lying. I know you are.'

Denise held her line right to the end. After she'd been led away, Angie released a string of expletives.

'God, she's slippery. It'll take hours to nail her down.'

'Have you got much circumstantial evidence?'

Angie's face clouded. 'By tomorrow we'll have plenty. Pete's lot are at their house in Wandsworth now.'

She vanished before I could voice my doubts, but I logged them on my assessment form. Denise Thorpe's speech patterns, eye contact and body language suggested she was telling the truth. The idea that she was innocent refused to leave my mind.

56

The woman's rage burns brighter than ever. She stands motionless, arms straight at her sides, gathering her courage. There must be a way to fight back, even from this point of weakness; if she concentrates, she'll find it. It sickens her that Riordan has been rescued. She should have acted faster, but with luck the drugs injected into her veins will finish her soon. That still leaves the child free, even though his mother condemned hundreds to a painful death. There's no such thing as an innocent bystander, like the shrink with her cold green stare. Her kind are a hundred times worse than the rest.

Beyond the locked door, the world continues its business. Voices drift through the wall, and someone wheels a trolley down the echoing corridor, the sounds increasing her isolation. Simon needs her more than ever, even though they've been forced apart. She must find a solution without his calm logic to guide her. There has to be a way to finish what they started.

57

The idea that Denise Thorpe was innocent dogged me for the rest of the morning, despite everyone else believing the killers were behind bars. On an objective level she ticked all the boxes: medical background, unstable, dominated by her husband's powerful personality. Yet something in my head couldn't accept it. A text arrived from Lola while I was mulling it over, reminding me to meet her in Knightsbridge that afternoon. I considered cancelling, but the bridal shop was already booked. I slipped my phone back into my pocket and set off for Wandsworth, hoping the visit would silence my doubts.

Pete Hancock was in the hallway of the Thorpes' house, combing a jacket that was hanging in the hallway with a brush small enough to apply mascara. I grinned at him as I zipped up the sterile suit.

'Your wife must love you, Pete. I bet you're great at cleaning.'

He shook his head firmly. 'Not if I can help it.'

'What are you doing?'

'Collecting fibres from Denise Thorpe's clothes. If I can match them with ones at the lab, it'll prove she was there.'

'Can I look upstairs?'

'Why? The boss says it's open and shut.'

'Certainty's an overrated virtue, isn't it?'

'Go on then.' He gave a loud sigh. 'Make sure you don't touch anything.'

The forensics team had started on the top floor, leaving dust trails on windows and doorframes. At first sight it looked like a typical family home. The Thorpes' daughter had left evidence of a teenage fascination with One Direction, the posters in her bedroom hopelessly out of date. I wondered how she was coping. The police were shielding her while she stayed with friends in York, but journalists would soon be baying at her door.

The bathroom revealed little apart from the Thorpes' reliance on medication. I peered at the packets of painkillers and tranquillisers stacked in the cabinet. With so many drugs in their systems, it was a wonder they'd been able to function, let alone plan a murder campaign. The master bedroom was a jumble of knick-knacks and mismatched furniture, a Lloyd Loom chair in need of paint, shelves full of crystal ornaments. A leather-bound diary lay on the chest of drawers, wrapped in an evidence bag. I paused for a moment before picking it up; if the diary belonged to Denise it could contain evidence to prove her innocence, which the police might overlook. Only the spare room revealed a masculine presence: a man's towelling dressing gown lay across the bed, the latest Robert Harris novel on the windowsill. I needed to understand if marital differences had forced the Thorpes apart, or if Simon had elected to sleep alone so he could escape at night without alerting his wife.

His office had been used for consultations with private patients, different in style from his wife's clutter. The furniture was tasteful and modern, subdued still lifes on the wall, the coffee table topped by a box of Kleenex. It horrified me that his clients had poured out their woes in this room, while he'd been completing his murderous campaign. Simon and Denise Thorpe had divided the house in two; his space clinically organised, while hers was chaotic. Maybe I'd been wrong about Denise Thorpe's innocence. The place seemed to prove my original theory that the killers would be chalk and cheese.

Hancock appeared as I peeled off my Tyvek suit. I brandished the black leather book at him, still wrapped in its transparent bag.

'Can I borrow this till tomorrow morning?'

He looked dubious. 'It's logged in the evidence file. You'll get me sacked if you lose it.'

I tucked it into my bag. 'I won't let you down. You're a star, Pete.'

He looked shocked then gratified when I planted a kiss on his cheek, proving that he was capable of human emotions after all.

I had no chance to study the diary that afternoon. My promise to Lola had to be honoured, so I met her outside an upmarket bridal shop, a stone's throw from Harrods, her mother footing the bill. She looked as gorgeous as ever – mile-long legs showcased in tight jeans; emerald green blouse accentuating her long auburn curls.

'It's the heroine of the hour,' she said, hugging me.

'Sorry?'

'You're a reclusive genius, according to the news. They had a picture of you in shades looking like a petite version of Michelle Williams.'

'Just what I need,' I muttered. 'Burns said he'd keep them off my back.'

'There's no such thing as bad publicity, Al.'

'There is in my line of work.'

Neve gazed up at us from her pram, swaddled in blankets. My irritation faded when I inhaled her smell of peaches, talcum powder and brand-new skin, her face puckering into a grin as I scooped her up.

'Jesus, you're broody,' Lola said. 'Come on, they're waiting for us.'

The Tremaine family had arranged a bridal extravaganza, taking over the whole boutique. I sat with Lola's mum and two of her aunties, cooing as she tried on dress after dress, assistants plying us with Prosecco and canapés. After a while, the outfits blurred into a mile of white chiffon awash with lace. I tried to stay focused but my thoughts kept slipping back to the diary. Eventually Lola emerged from the changing room in a pencil-slim gown that reminded me of Hollywood in the Jazz Age, ivory silk heightening the glow of her skin.

'What do you think?' she purred.

'Gorgeous,' I confirmed.

At that stage I tried to escape, but more paraphernalia kept arriving: shoes, gloves, a veil. She even made me help select her garter and underwear for the honeymoon.

I was exhausted by retail decisions, but Lola was in high spirits. She gave me a grateful hug then let me hail a taxi. I checked my email during the ride to Burns's flat. Christine's message offered her usual low-key praise, followed by a terse instruction to take immediate leave, even though queries from the FPU were clogging my inbox.

For the first time in days there was no guard outside the front door. Now that the danger had passed I could return to my apartment, where no object ever strayed out of place. I started to gather my belongings, but couldn't ignore my urge to check the diary.

It was disappointing to discover that it belonged to Simon, not Denise. At first sight its contents were just a log of appointments. I wondered why the therapist had stopped attending his health clinic twelve months before. He seemed to have lost all faith in medical treatment, taking matters into his own hands. His handwriting was small and tightly controlled, confirming his status as the rational member of the double act, but Denise still seemed an unlikely partner. She was hardly a wild maverick, capable of slitting a man's throat without qualms. I thumbed through the pages again, but appointments with his clients were recorded by initials instead of names. The tone of the entries was world-weary: almost every week he'd written the comment 'another meeting' under one of the dates. What nameless friend had he been seeing, and for what purpose? Something about the diary filled me with unease, but I couldn't pinpoint why.

My phone rang as I was dropping it back into the evidence bag. A voice whispered at the end of the line.

'Who's this?'

'Emma Selby. Sorry to bother you, Alice.' It sounded like she was trying not to cry, her breathing uneven.

'Are you okay?'

'Could I come round? I need some advice.'

Burns appeared in the doorway, studying me as he removed his coat.

'Emma, I'm afraid that's not possible. Could we meet another night?' My guilt increased as she stifled a sob.

'Of course. I feel terrible for calling you in this state.'

'Is it your boyfriend?

'He finished it over the phone. The bastard didn't even have the guts to tell me to my face.' She sounded so desolate that I considered jumping in my car, but knew I was in the wrong frame of mind to play counsellor.

'I promise to ring tomorrow. Don't be alone though, will you? Get a friend to come round.'

It struck me as odd that she'd phoned me instead of a close friend or relative; maybe she was less socially adept than she seemed, with few people to rely on. Burns reappeared before I could give the matter more thought. He'd abandoned his suit in favour of jeans, a faded blue shirt and ancient trainers, but the relaxed clothes hadn't diluted his scowl.

'Something wrong?' I asked.

'A couple of things, yeah.'

'Go on, then, I'm not a mind-reader.'

'You can't wait to leave, can you? Your stuff's already packed.'

'I've got my own place to look after, remember?'

'How could I forget? You spend all your time there.'

'You're in an ugly mood.'

He scrubbed his hand across his face. 'Is this how you end all your relationships? Goodbye and thanks for the memories?'

'Don't be ridiculous. You know how I feel.'

'So spit it out, for fuck's sake.'

'If it was that easy I'd have said it by now.'

'I won't sue you if you change your mind.' His mood changed as he watched me trying to summon the words, anger changing to amusement. 'Aren't shrinks meant to be emotionally sorted?'

'No way. Freud was a basket case.'

We set our differences aside to order a takeaway. It frustrated me that my feelings were still buried too deeply to access, but at least we were heading in the same direction.

'We ordered too much,' I said. His table groaned with cartons of chow mein, Peking duck and egg-fried rice.

'Enough for an army.' Burns pushed his plate away. 'Angie and I kept pushing today but got nowhere. Thorpe collapsed in his cell; the police medic wants him in hospital, and his wife's still denying everything.'

'We're missing something obvious.'

'It must be them. Thorpe's contacts say he's isolated, rarely leaves home.'

'Apart from all those long night-time drives. And he's not a loner; he sees dozens of clients each week.'

'You think it's a patient?'

'That's possible. There's someone else I'm worried about: Emma Selby from the Wellcome Institute. I know she's been checked out already, but she knows more about blood than anyone in London.'

Burns shrugged. 'We'll take another look. But it has to be Denise Thorpe, doesn't it? How could she not notice her husband was a serial killer?'

'Selective blindness; we only see what we want to see.'

I didn't go home that evening. If we'd parted company, both of us would have brooded about the future. Instead we shared a bath then went to bed early, the sex between us slow and thoughtful, like we had all the time in the world. For once he let me take charge, pushing him back against the pillows, my hands on his shoulders as he lost control. Streetlight filtered through the curtains afterwards. The case was still nagging at me. Denise Thorpe had shown no sign of cracking after long bouts of questions, convincing me that my suspicions were correct; such profound shock would have been hard to fake. I closed my eyes and listened to the silence. The city was resting for once, no traffic stirring on Southwark Bridge Road. I felt certain a woman was out there somewhere, wide awake like me, planning her next attack.

58

Friday 7 November

I'd been working for hours by the time Burns joined me for breakfast, pages from my profile report scattered across his kitchen table.

'You never quit, do you?'

'I'm certain Denise Thorpe's innocent, Don.'

He took a swig from my coffee mug. 'What makes you so sure?'

'It could be any of her husband's female clients. You should be checking the case notes on his computer.'

He cast me a long-suffering look. 'People don't always confess, Alice. Maybe he forced her to help; she feels guilty about the effect on her daughter. In her shoes I'd play innocent too.'

'Why not look at other suspects?'

'Like who?' His eyes narrowed. 'We've covered every avenue.'

'Thorpe might know someone affected by the tainted blood scandal.'

Burns's face was deadpan as he put on his coat; there was no way to guess whether he would follow my suggestion. 'What are you up to today?'

'Visiting the hospital with Mikey at midday.'

'I'll meet you there. When Riordan comes round, we'll check her story.'

He made a swift exit, leaving me convinced that I was the only person questioning Denise Thorpe's involvement.

I travelled to the Royal Free at ten o'clock, hoping that revisiting Clare Riordan's haunts a final time might reveal the identity of the second killer, but aware that I might be clutching at straws. The hospital still looked like a grand architectural mistake, a drab hunk of concrete wreathed in traffic fumes. Patients were queuing in the haematology department as I waited for the receptionist to unlock Riordan's office. I saw one of them disappear through Dr Novak's half-open door as Brenda Madison turned to me. She looked even more flamboyant than the first time we'd met: lacquered nails long as talons, hair a startling traffic-light red. She smiled widely as she reported how thrilled everyone was that Clare had been found, then offered me a cup of tea.

'I'll be back in two ticks. Make yourself at home.'

Riordan's consulting room was still in disarray; the same Post-it notes stuck on her jotter, reminding her to book holiday flights, a pair of running shoes hidden in a drawer. The overall picture was of someone who raced through life without looking back. Maybe she had travelled forwards so heedlessly she didn't notice all the people she'd trodden on, including her best friend. I carried on sifting Riordan's papers, hoping for a missed clue about the woman who'd abducted her. It still seemed hard to believe that she was clinging to life in the ICU three floors above. A sound disturbed me as I finished thumbing through the list. The receptionist stood there looking apologetic, offering me a cup of tea.

'Sorry it took ages. The phone wouldn't stop ringing.'

I smiled at her. 'Can I ask a few questions, Brenda? You must see everything on the front desk.'

She nodded thoughtfully. 'I've been here donkeys' years. Not much gets past me.'

'Do patients ever complain?'

'Not often; it's the carers who sometimes lose the plot.'

326

'Women as well as men?'

'A few months ago this lady made a real scene. Michelle De Santis – she was shouting about not getting enough help. She'd been caring for someone at home, doing all his injections. The poor thing must be in an even worse state now.'

'Why?'

She blinked rapidly. 'Her bloke died last night. Apparently she was with him at the end.'

'That's sad.' I felt a rush of sympathy, remembering Gary Lennard staring out at his Oriental garden, dreaming of summer.

'Dr Novak visited him every week after the complaint.' Her face softened. 'Most of the others wouldn't bother. Maybe it's because she went through it herself.'

'How do you mean?'

'She told me her dad died of a blood virus. Maybe that's why she's so kind to her patients.'

The receptionist's comments stayed with me after she left. I thought about Gary Lennard, his ex-wife's terror of losing him, and Adele Novak's determination to offer him first-rate care. Tania's response was frosty when I called to suggest that De Santis should be monitored. Michelle had reason to hate the people responsible for her ex-husband's illness, and Gary had been one of Clare's patients in the past, but Tania's long silence made it clear that she considered the case closed.

Adele Novak's door was open when I left Clare's office. She was on her feet, listening intently to a patient, white coat buttoned to her throat. The doctor lifted her head when she saw me, gaze sharpening, as though she had something urgent to say. But Mikey was due to arrive in reception any minute, so I raised my hand in recognition before hurrying away.

Angie had sent a text warning me that Clare Riordan's condition was no better, and it struck me that it would be the cruellest irony if she died without being properly reunited with her son. Mikey's jubilant smile revealed his certainty his mum would recover, a bunch of yellow roses clutched in his hands as the psychiatric nurse left him with me. My concern increased as we crossed the hospital campus. I had an odd sensation that we were being watched, though there was no one nearby apart from a gaggle of nurses laughing at each other's jokes. I gazed at the windows of the tower, but sunlight reflected too brightly from the glass to tell whether someone was looking down at us.

My anxiety doubled when we reached intensive care. The high-dependency suite was empty, a gurney standing in the corridor outside. I mustered a smile for Mikey when we stopped by the nursing station.

'Wait here, sunshine. I'll be two minutes.'

The nurse gave me a blank look when she heard Clare Riordan's name, hurrying away to fetch a doctor. My heart was beating a nervous tattoo when the medic finally appeared: a middle-aged Indian woman, long hair woven into a plait. She studied me through thick horn-rimmed glasses before her face relaxed into a smile.

'Clare's a bit stronger today. She's not fully conscious, but her fever's down; you'll find her in the recovery suite. We'll talk again after your visit.'

I thanked her before turning away. A transfer to recovery didn't put Riordan out of the woods, but it increased her odds. If she could survive without intensive nursing she stood a better chance. Mikey was where I'd left him, hugging his flowers as one of the nurses tried to coax him into talking. His mother was sleeping peacefully, but her appearance was worse than I remembered. She was skin and bone, a stubble of grey hair covering her scalp, deep bruises littering her face. It was hard to believe this was the woman I'd spent the last three weeks obsessing over; full of complexities, her strong personality affecting everyone she knew. Puncture marks from wide needle injections were still visible on her shoulders and arms, but that didn't stop Mikey from making a beeline for her. A stab of jealousy arrived out of nowhere when he reached for her hand, then whispered a string of words only she could hear. It was an intimacy I couldn't hope to understand. Seeing his mother again had opened the floodgates for Mikey. He was so focused on her sleeping face that a bomb could have detonated nearby without catching his attention. It finally dawned on me that if his mother survived, he would forget about me, and in time I would forget him too. We'd only bonded so quickly because of the danger we'd faced. But that didn't explain the sense of loss that hit me when I thought about losing him. It was sharp as a body blow, forcing me to step outside to catch my breath.

The medic I'd spoken to before was waiting in the corridor. She had that aura of unnatural calm that comes from hauling patients back from the brink every day. She explained that Riordan was being treated with anti-viral drugs and antibiotics to increase her chances. The doctor had moved on to the next room by the time Burns and Pete Hancock appeared.

'How is she?' Don asked.

'Better, but not fully conscious.' I turned to Pete. 'You can buy me that coffee at last.'

'Why do you drink that filth?' Hancock rolled his eyes. 'I might. If you give me the diary.'

'Much good it did me.'

Burns's phone rang loudly as I fished it from my bag. 'It'll be the *Mail*, Alice. You're front-page news.'

'God help me. I should get back to Mikey.'

'We'll get you a coffee from somewhere.'

'What's wrong with a nice glass of water?' Pete muttered.

I watched them stroll towards a drinks machine, arguing about their choice of beverage. When I turned back, Adele Novak had appeared at the other end of the corridor. For a second I wondered if she had a question about the case, although she was more likely to be seeking reassurance that her boss was recovering. I walked towards her, but the look she gave me was impatient.

'I need to see Clare.'

'She's not conscious yet. You might want to come back later.'

Her gaze was trance-like. 'Are you trying to stop me?'

'Is something wrong, Adele?'

'Get out of my way.'

When her hand dropped to her pocket, the scene spun into slow motion. In a split second I understood her passionate work ethic, her father affected by tainted blood, all those house calls to the dying. I screamed for help, then heard Burns's heavy footsteps thundering down the corridor.

'Get down!' I shouted the words at the top of my voice.

There was a blur of movement, then Adele's eyes held mine, charcoal dark, completely focused. I didn't feel any pain, even though the gun's blast echoed from the walls, blood pooling at my feet. Nurses scattered from view, then I saw Novak's hand jerk upwards as another shot rang out. A bloodstain marked her white coat, more bullets ploughing into the ceiling. When I looked back, Hancock was leaning against Clare's door, eyes losing focus as his legs buckled. Burns had shunted Novak against the wall, her gun clattering to the floor. I knelt beside Pete to use my jacket as a pressure pad on his chest wound, but it was a losing battle. Blood soaked through the fabric, welling between my fingers.

'You stopped her, Pete. Pretty brave, for a scientist.' The terror on his face was slowly turning into acceptance. 'Don't you dare. Come on, talk to me.'

The red circle spilling from his body kept on expanding. I was so focused on keeping him alive that the shouting and footsteps fell silent; all I could hear was the hiss of his breathing.

'My wife,' he murmured. 'Lizzie.'

'She's coming. You'll be okay, Pete.'

Someone pulled me away. Two doctors were jamming a line into his arm, an oxygen mask over his face. Then he was on a gurney, wheels racing into the distance. My vision blurred then cleared again. I made the mistake of glancing at the blood on my hands, and the ground rocked up to greet me. I didn't lose consciousness completely, aware of Burns's voice rasping out a string of swearwords. When I came round, someone had put me in the recovery position, my cheek cold against the lino; Don's face loomed over me, his grip on my shoulder tight enough to hurt. I insisted on getting to my feet, head still spinning, desperate to check on Mikey. But when I peered through the observation window, he was in the same position as before, still clutching his mother's hand. I wondered why he was smiling, until I saw that his voice had worked its magic. Clare had finally woken up, her eyes trained on his face as if she couldn't bear to look away.

59

The doctors wanted me to rest in a treatment room in case of concussion, but I had to see Adele Novak. I leant against the wall of the lift, feeling worse as the floors ticked by.

'And you call me macho,' Burns muttered.

'I fainted, that's all. I'm perfectly fine.'

'So why are you shaking?'

The image of Hancock lying at my feet was lodged in my head. He'd been rushed to theatre to have a bullet removed from his collapsed lung.

'I need to know why,' I insisted. 'Then I can rest.'

Novak was in an isolation room, guarded by a couple of uniforms. She was handcuffed to the metal bedframe, bandages taped to her wounded shoulder. The manic glint had left her eyes, her short hair and thin frame making her look as vulnerable as a child. Pain throbbed at the base of my skull as I sat down, but that didn't matter. I wondered how long her defences would hold out. Silence is always the most powerful trick in a psychologist's book; used to good effect, it can crack even the hardest nut.

She kept her eyes on the window when she finally spoke. 'I did it for the victims.'

'Of tainted blood?'

'Many of them are already dead.' Her voice was a low monotone.

'You father was a victim, wasn't he? You must have been young when you lost him.'

'Ten years old. He was a haemophiliac, like all the rest. My mother fell apart after he died.'

'I'm sorry.'

A burst of hatred crossed her face. 'Your kind are the worst. You apologise, but do nothing.'

'Why did you become a doctor?'

'To help the victims, of course. No one else cares.'

'But you killed people, Adele.'

'Just the ones who deserved to die. People with blood illnesses have been experimented on all their lives; the scales are balanced now.' She seemed calm again, satisfied by her actions.

'How did you meet Simon?'

'I went to him for counselling. The grief never goes away.' She shut her eyes.

'That's how you found out he'd received infected blood too?'

She kept her gaze fixed to the wall. 'Only a liver transplant could save him now.'

'You fell in love?'

'He's too gentle. He lost faith in the end.' Tears welled in her eyes. 'I wanted them all. We should have taken the health minister too.'

'Do you feel any regret?'

There was no hesitation before she shook her head. 'Simon helped me plan each stage, but he didn't hurt any of them. It took me days to force the names out of Riordan.'

Her expression was chilling: pride mixed with elation. She would have tortured her victims all over again, given the chance. The shrink in me was fascinated to find out the exact factors that had made her ill, but Burns brought the interview to a close then escorted me from the room. He bullied me into getting a CAT scan, which revealed nothing more than a soft tissue swelling above my left temple.

We were leaving the hospital when the news came about Hancock. Burns's expression changed as he listened to the phone message.

'He's out of theatre,' he said. 'The operation went well.'

'Want to see him?'

'Tomorrow. His family's with him now.'

We didn't say much on the drive back to his flat, mute with tiredness and relief. I was still piecing together the reasons for so much human damage. Adele Novak's affair with Simon Thorpe had begun a chain reaction a year ago, but I wanted to know why violence had ignited between them like a struck match. I had suspected so many innocent bystanders; people like Roger Fenton and Emma Selby, who had only been offering me help. I made a mental note to call Emma as I'd promised, and give Fenton his in-depth interview. One more piece of the puzzle clicked into place. 'Another' in Thorpe's diary must have been shorthand for A. Novak, the first letters of her name buried in the word, in case his wife happened to look inside. The car eased through traffic on Southwark Bridge Road, autumn leaves turning to paste in the gutter. It would be a relief to get back to the FPU and give my job the attention it deserved. I pulled out my phone to call Christine, listened to the relief in her voice when she heard that the case was solved.

I felt a pang of homesickness for my clean white rooms when we got back to Burns's flat, but maybe it would always be like that: the loner in me fighting the part that longed for his company.

'She won't even go to jail,' he said. 'She'll end up at Broadmoor.'

'Not necessarily – she may be perfectly sane. Adele thinks the murders were justified revenge. Falling for someone in the same position as her father triggered all that childhood grief.

I'll assess her tomorrow, then write my recommendation for the court.'

Don raised his hands. 'Right now I don't care how sick she is. I want her banged up permanently.'

'That's a balanced view, DCI Burns.'

'Maybe I should quit my job. We could run a pub instead.'

'You'd be bored senseless.'

'Not at all. I'd choose a quiet inn, close to the sea.'

I looked at him steadily. 'I love you, by the way.'

His eyes blinked wider. 'Run that by me again?'

'You heard.'

'At long last. How do you feel?'

'Shocked, but relieved.'

The smile on his face expanded by another centimetre. When I returned with two glasses of Merlot, he raised a toast. 'To Morocco. If Pete's okay, we're going there before another case hits my desk.'

I kissed him, then headed for the shower. My outfit would have to be thrown away, dark brown blood staining my trousers and the cuffs of my cotton shirt. I scoured myself clean until my skin felt polished. Once I was dressed in fresh jeans and a silk jumper I felt human again. Burns was asleep on his outsized sofa, phone buzzing on the coffee table. I covered it with a cushion to silence the noise. He'd drained his glass of wine, but mine was untouched. The sight of it suddenly made me feel nauseous. It reminded me of the garnet-coloured blood pooling on the floor that afternoon, far too much of the precious substance spilled in the last few weeks. I watched it swirl down the plughole in the kitchen sink, then drank a glass of water slowly, feeling my stomach settle.

Burns was still out for the count. I slipped off his shoes then studied him again, heavy and immovable as a carthorse. Even in sleep, the set of his jaw made him look incapable of backing down, but for once I was too tired to worry about the future. I settled myself beside him, my back cradled against his chest. My last thought was for Mikey, sprinting away to find his mother, the tie between us loosening until he became a speck in the distance. When I fell asleep, no bad dreams disturbed me, my mind wiped clean.

THE TAINTED BLOOD SCANDAL

In the late 1970s, a revolutionary new medicine was developed to treat haemophilia. Made from human blood, Factor Eight seemed like a miracle product, and pharmaceutical companies raced to mass-produce it. They bought donor blood from anyone in the USA prepared to sell it, including habitual drug users and prisoners with infectious diseases such as HIV and hepatitis. The methods used to acquire blood were exposed in Kelly Duda's powerful film, *Factor 8: The Arkansas Prison Blood Scandal*. Contaminated Factor Eight was shipped around the world and given to haemophiliacs, thousands of whom became fatally ill.

Over 4,800 British haemophiliacs were infected with hepatitis C through tainted blood products administered by the NHS. More than 1,200 of this group were also infected with the HIV virus. Since the early 1980s, more than 800 people have died from AIDS, and hundreds more from hepatitis C.

In 1991, under threat of court action for allowing contaminated blood products into the country, the British Government made small ex-gratia payments to the survivors through the Skipton and Macfarlane Trusts on condition that they signed an undertaking never to take further legal action. By this time, many victims had already died of their illnesses. No fault has ever been admitted by either the government or the pharmaceutical companies who supplied the contaminated blood products. In 2009, the government published its response to

Lord Archer's report into the scandal. After a long and bitter battle, the sickest patients now receive annual compensation, far below the national average wage, even though the majority are too ill to work.

The victims' story is an intensely personal one for me. My husband was given hepatitis C in the early 1980s, and lived with the illness for twenty-five years before undertaking a gruelling six-month course of interferon and ribavirin. It took twenty years for his small compensation to arrive, yet he was one of the lucky ones, finally regaining his health.

I have taken a few small liberties with history to simplify my story. There was no panel of medics and specialists advising the minister for health on compensation, and the campaign group Pure does not exist.

Kate Rhodes, 2016

ACKNOWLEDGEMENTS

I would like to thank my agent Teresa Chris for being such a good friend and excellent shopping companion. My editor Ruth Tross always manages to see far below the surface of my stories, with an unerring eye for accuracy and structure. I remain a huge fan of Nick Sayers, who took me to a lovely pub in Harrogate last year simply to cheer me up, and continues to be the kindest man in publishing. Rebecca Mundy manages to be clever, funny and ridiculously glamorous, all at the same time; thanks for being such a great advocate. Many thanks are also due to Dave Pescod, Miranda Landgraf, Penny Hancock, Sophie Hannah, Killer Women, and the 134 club for their readings and sound advice. Thank you to the staff of the Wellcome Institute for excellent information about the history of blood transfusion. I am also indebted to the staff of the Old Operating Theatre for allowing me to make a night time visit via the fire exit, to check out the terrain by torchlight. This book could not have been written without the help I received from the Haemophilia Society, who gave me clear and detailed information about the tainted blood scandal. Thanks as ever to DC Laura Shaw for her excellent guidance on police matters. DS Dan Miller, I salute you, and after so many phone calls, definitely owe you a pint. Grateful thanks too to Twitter pals Julie Boon, Claire Brown, Peggy Breckin for making my day on a regular basis. Emma Selby, thanks so much for allowing yourself to appear in my book.

Note: Some of the locations in this book are real, but many are imaginary. Apologies for changing some of London's geography and street names; my motive is always to tell the best possible story.

Discover more books in the Alice Quentin series

RIVER OF SOULS

Jude Shelley, the daughter of a prominent cabinet minister, was assaulted and left for dead in the river Thames. Her attacker was never caught. A year later, forensic psychologist Alice Quentin is asked to re-examine the case.

Then another body is found: an elderly priest, washed up at Westminster Pier. An ancient glass bead is tied to his wrist.

Alice is certain that the Shelleys are hiding something – and that there will be more victims unless she can persuade them to share what they know.

The Thames has always been a site of violent sacrifice. And Alice is about to learn that some people still believe in its power . . .

Out now in print and ebook

MULHOLLAND
BOOKS
HODDER

CROSSBONES YARD

Crossbones Yard was a burial ground once. Now it's waste-land, tucked away in the back streets of Borough beneath the shadow of the Shard. The perfect place to leave a body . . .

Alice Quentin finds the murder victim lying there – the woman's hand outstretched, as if begging for her help. A psychologist who sometimes works with the Metropolitan police, Alice is no stranger to sick minds. But this case is worse than anything she's seen before, and the killer is determined to make it personal.

Out now in print and ebook

MULHOLLAND BOOKS

HODDER